Ask Me Again

A Novel of Faith in Colorado

Jenny Berlin

Anglocentria, Inc.
Aurora, Colorado

For information, address:
Anglocentria, Inc.
P.O. Box 460458
Aurora, CO 80046-0458

ISBN 978-0-9835042-8-3

Acknowledgements

I owe many thanks to my Beta Readers for their candid and constructive feedback. Ladies, your comments were more helpful than you'll ever know. Thank you!

And to my sisters, who are always supportive and always willing to read about romance.

To have a lovely garden,
Start with a lovely soul.
*—Mrs. Plowright's 1908 Guide
for the Genteel Lady Gardener*

September
Denver, Colorado

Mother! I'm home!"

From the far reaches of her expansive back yard, Minda McAllister could hear her daughter's voice echoing through the house.

Mother.

Tracy didn't usually call her "mother" unless she was with a new acquaintance and desperately trying to appear older than her seventeen years. Minda pushed at the wide brim of the gardening hat she wore, squinted up at the early evening sun, and vaguely wondered who her daughter had brought home.

"Mother? Where *are* you?"

"I'm out here! In the garden!"

Minda plunged the hand trowel into the ground, then carefully levered a weed, roots and all, from her bed of purple asters. She let loose a sigh of satisfaction, content to revel in small victories.

She heard the old kitchen screen door creak open and slap shut. In the next moment, Tracy bounded down the steps and crossed the lawn to stand over her.

"Mom, what are you doing?" Tracy's voice was heavy with censure, as if the sight of her mother on her knees, toiling in the dirt, was something she hadn't seen countless times before.

"Pulling weeds. I haven't tended this garden in weeks and now I'm paying for it." Minda pushed back the wide brim of her gardening hat and looked up, past her daughter's immaculate skirt, past her pristine blouse, and up to her modestly-but-perfectly-made-up face. "I could use some help."

"Are you kidding? I can't pull weeds now." Her tone left little doubt that she questioned her mother's sanity. "There's someone I want you to meet. He's in the kitchen waiting. Are you coming?"

He. That explained the "mother" bit. Since Minda knew all of Tracy's friends from church and school, she wondered who the boy might be. A new student at school? A new neighbor on the block?

She attacked another weed and said mildly, "I'd like to meet him, honey. Why don't you ask him to come on out here?"

"Mo-o-o-m!" Tracy's groan stretched the simple word into multiple syllables. "I'm not going to bring him out *here* to meet you! Not in the back yard!"

"There's nothing wrong with our back yard, Tracy. It's a lovely and serene place that's the envy of our neighborhood. And if I remember correctly, you've hosted plenty of parties for your friends and church groups on this very spot. Why shouldn't I meet your friend here in the back yard?"

"Couldn't you just come inside?" Tracy pleaded.

Minda rocked back on her heels and looked up at her daughter. The expression on Tracy's face surprised her. Anxiety, happiness, strain—that unique mix of emotions could mean only one thing.

"Tracy, honey, did you bring a . . . a *special* boy home to meet me?"

Tracy stiffened. "He's not a *boy*."

"But he's someone important? Someone you want to make a good impression on?"

"Yeah, well . . . sorta."

Minda didn't know whether to laugh or cry. Tracy had brought boys home before but they'd always been more of the friendship variety. Tracy dated—A girl as pretty as Tracy was bound to attract boys her own age—but she had yet to show any particular interest in any one boy.

Until now.

Minda's spirits lifted as she conjured an image of the special young man. He'd be a little taller than Tracy, with nice eyes and an attractive smile. He'd be a bit gangly, too, like a lot of teenaged boys, but Minda would be able to see the potential for grace in his movements. And, of course, he'd share Tracy's Christian beliefs and together they'd walk in faith, allowing the Lord to guide their relationship.

Minda found herself smiling. She had been almost the same age when she'd become engaged to Tracy's father. She had never regretted marrying Dale McAllister at such a young age, but marrying straight out of high school and having a baby right away—though much loved and wanted— were decisions Minda wouldn't recommend to anyone, especially Tracy. And when Dale had died, leaving Minda to raise their daughter alone . . .

Deliberately, Minda blocked those thoughts. She hadn't

even met Tracy's young man, yet her over-fertile imagination was already running rampant to the point of planning their wedding.

She squinted up at Tracy and said, reasonably, "I understand you want to make a good impression, honey, and I suppose I could come into the house and meet the young man you've brought home. But unless your guest wants to wait an hour while I shower and change and do my make-up and hair, he'll have to take me as I am right now. I know I don't look my best, but here—working in the gardens, taking care of this house—this is the real me. And isn't that who you want your guest to meet?"

Tracy didn't look convinced, but she after a moment she said, a little sullenly, "I guess so."

She retreated to the house and Minda turned her attention back to the garden. Again she heard the screen door creak open and slap shut; but this time she heard two sets of footsteps descend the back steps and shuffle across the grass.

Minda suppressed an urge to jump to her feet. Tracy was always telling her that she wasn't like other mothers. Other mothers, according to Tracy, didn't impose strict curfews. They didn't force their children to exist on meager allowances or report which friends they were seeing and when. Other mothers were *cool*.

She wasn't sure how cool she was going to be about Tracy's young man. Certainly, Tracy would want her to be nonchalant, as if bringing a boy home to meet her were an everyday affair.

But it wasn't an everyday affair. It was a singular, important event or Tracy wouldn't be so nervous and jumpy, so insistent that everything be right.

Minda smiled softly. She was witnessing her daughter's first serious crush; no small milestone in a young woman's life. She had a feeling she was really going to really like this boy.

Minda continued to dig away at the soft soil, plying her trowel in a way she hoped Tracy would approve as having just the right amount of coolness.

Two pairs of shoes appeared within the limited view afforded by the broad brim of Minda's hat. She recognized Tracy's sandals. Next to them, the toes of a sizable pair of expensive Italian leather loafers peaked from beneath the cuffed hems of perfectly-creased wool pant legs.

Tracy cleared her throat and said, in her best imitation of a cultured adult, "Mother, there's someone here I'd like you to meet. Mother, this . . . this is Mark Cartier!"

Minda found that a masculine hand was being extended toward her. She dropped the trowel and knew instantly that the strong fingers that gripped hers didn't belong to a boy in high school. This hand held hers firmly and purposefully.

Her gaze traveled up along a tanned forearm, dusted with dark hair. Her gaze traveled higher, past broad shoulders, past a full, tanned neck above a loosened starched collar and tie, up to his face.

This was no high school student.

This was a man.

A man with strong, lean features and the faint shadow of a beard on his face. A man with little laugh lines exploding from the corners of his brilliant blue eyes. Those blue eyes widened for the briefest of moments when they first made contact with hers.

So, she thought, he was just as surprised by her as she was by him. Good. Because Minda was really surprised.

She'd been expecting a teenager. A young man near Tracy's age, but . . . *this*? The man had to be in his late twenties; he might even be thirty. So what in the world was he doing with her daughter?

His pull on her hand was easy and strong, as if setting bemused women on their feet was a task he performed countless times each day.

For a moment she stood practically toe to toe with Mark Cartier, her surprised gaze fixed on his handsome face, her hand in his, as half a dozen disjointed thoughts careened like bumper cars around her brain.

Up close, her initial impression of him didn't change much. He was definitely thirty-ish. He was also definitely good-looking in a polished sort of way that made her think he was used to women fainting dead-away at his feet.

There had to be some mistake.

Minda's eyes flew to Tracy's face. Her daughter was smiling nervously, her expression aglow and shy and anxious all at the same time.

There was no mistake. Minda's heart sank a little.

With her free hand she swept the hat from her head and tried to pull herself together. "It's nice to meet you . . ." His name deserted her. "I'm sorry."

"*Mark*, mother," Tracy hissed. "I told you, his name is Mark Cartier."

"I beg your pardon."

He was still holding her rather grubby hand in his. He didn't seem to mind, though. He flashed a self-possessed smile as he looked her right in the eye. "It's a pleasure, Mrs. McAllister. I've been looking forward to meeting you."

Mrs. McAllister? Who was he trying to kid? He wasn't *that* much younger than she and Minda was thirty-six.

She pulled her hand from his and said, coolly, "If you call me Mrs. McAllister, I probably won't answer. I'd rather you just called me Minda."

"I will. And I hope you'll call me Mark."

If he'd been a seventeen-year-old boy like he was supposed to be, there would have been no question what she would have called him. "Oh, I was planning to," she said, as the shy, gangly teenage boy of her imaginings faded forever away.

He smiled and slipped his hands into the pockets of his trousers. "You have a very lovely home here." His blue eyes scanned the big back yard, from the arbored corner at one end to the tree-hung swing at the other. "Altogether I'd say you have an acre or so of valuable, rich land. I wouldn't have expected to find such a place so close to downtown Denver. It's almost like an oasis of your very own right in the middle of the city."

Minda didn't know whether to be annoyed or pleased. He was standing there so casually, talking about acreage and land as if he were just one of the folks, dressed in overalls with a long shaft of wheat dangling from his perfectly-straight, incredibly-white teeth.

On the other hand, he'd said the very thing that could usually make Minda swell with pride. Her home *was* her oasis. This house and its surrounding land, along with the old commercial building downtown that housed her business, had been in her husband's family for generations. They had come to her when Dale died and meant all the more because they represented all she had left of the things he loved most.

But she wasn't going to tell that to Mark Cartier, nor was she going to stand there and exchange small talk with a man who owed her some big explanations.

She looked from Tracy to Mark and asked deliberately, "Why don't you tell me how you two met?"

"We met at school today." He flashed a gleaming smile.

Minda's heart dropped a little lower. Schoolgirl crushes on

handsome young teachers could be the most devastating kind. "I see. What subjects do you teach?"

"Oh, I'm not a teacher."

"A student?" She sounded more sarcastic than she intended, but she had a feeling Mark Cartier was being deliberately uncooperative, making her drag every little bit of information out of him.

Tracy intervened. "Mother, Mark spoke at our school today. It's career week and he was a guest speaker."

Minda plopped her gardening hat back on her head and bent down to pick up her abandoned trowel. "Is that so? Do you regularly make speeches to auditoriums full of teenagers?"

"I don't make it a habit."

"Any particular pearls of wisdom you passed on to them today?"

"Just . . . stay in school." He didn't react to the sharp tone of her questions. "I think a good education is the key to success in life."

She stared at him for a moment. Maybe looking into his eyes would give her a window into his thoughts and help her make sense of the situation.

It didn't help. He simply looked back at her with a calm expression and that too-perfect smile that she was sure was meant to quell any further questions.

But Minda had plenty of questions, and she was beginning to think she wasn't going to like the answers.

She held her palm up in a surrendering gesture. "I think you have me at a disadvantage, Mark. Please make yourself at home while I wash some of my garden off my hands." She looked at Tracy, who was smiling adoringly at the man as if he'd just promised her the moon. "Tracy, would you help me for a minute, please?"

She started for the house without waiting for a reply. She didn't want to hear that man's voice again or look up once more into his self-satisfied smile. In less than five minutes time she'd had her fill of Mark Cartier.

Inside, she went upstairs to her bedroom and it's big, master bath. In its original state, when the house had first been built in the 1920s, the bathroom had been a tiny tiled room no larger than a closet. But years ago, when Minda and her husband had updated the house for late-twentieth-century living, they had converted an adjacent sitting room to a bathroom. Now its large proportions and relatively modern fixtures, combined with a few scented candles and a good supply of bubble-bath, gave Minda one of few opportunities to pamper herself when she felt the need.

She felt the need now. But she hadn't the time. Her seventeen-year-old daughter and her incredibly unsuitable, would-be boyfriend were downstairs behaving for all the world as if nothing were wrong.

Minda hadn't the faintest idea what to do about it.

She knew some fast thinking and ardent prayer were called for. She bowed her head as she turned on the taps at the sink, but a light knock at the door interrupted her.

"Can I come in?" Tracy asked. Without waiting for an answer, she sat inelegantly down on the edge of the tub. Her expression was glowing. "Isn't he great?"

Minda struggled for a moment over how she should reply and offered up a silent prayer for guidance. She pumped a dollop of liquid soap onto her palm. "Oh, he's something, I'd say."

"And he's so handsome. Everybody thought so and practically every girl in the whole school stayed after the assembly to try to talk to him about his speech." Tracy's words came out in a rush. "And whenever one of us would, like, ask him a question, he would, like, ask us our names and stuff. And when I told him my name, he, like, seriously *stared* at me. I was so nervous! And then I asked my question and he said it was the best question any high school student had ever asked him! He said it revealed a good deal of maturity on my part," she added, proudly.

"What was it?"

Tracy frowned. "What was *what?*"

"What was the question you asked him?"

"Mo-o-o-o-m! Who cares what I asked him? I hardly remember myself and, besides, it doesn't matter."

Minda reached for the towel and dried her hands in a slow, deliberate way. "I guess you're right." She hesitated for only a second, then decided to dive right in. "To tell you the truth, honey, I'm a little surprised. To be honest, I think Mark Cartier is—"

"Gosh, me, too! You know what? When he first talked to me, I could hardly pay attention to what he said, you know what I mean? I've never met anybody like him before. He's so good looking and he dresses so perfect and he's like somebody out of the movies or something."

One look into her daughter's face made Minda doubt whether the time was right for a heart-to-heart discussion. Tracy was too full of emotion to see sense; too spellbound by the man waiting downstairs to understand all the reasons he shouldn't be sitting in their living-room in the first place. Minda judged that any conversation they had now would only set Tracy's defenses up and end disastrously.

They'd already had more than their fair share of conflicts during the last year, which their pastor had diagnosed as little more than garden-variety teenage rebellion. But those conflicts had been painful to Minda and she sometimes wondered how much more strained her relationship with her daughter might be if not for Pastor Walker's intervention and counsel.

Minda took a deep breath, determined to wait for God to help her show Tracy the choice she was making was the wrong choice.

She reached down and gently brushed Tracy's hair back from her face. And for the first time in a long time, Tracy allowed her to do it.

"You're right, honey. Men like Mark Cartier don't come our way very often. I guess it's easy enough to be dazzled by a handsome face that looks like it's attached to a big bank account."

Tracy flashed her a sour look. "I'm not *dazzled*, Mom. He happens to be, like, the most perfect guy I ever met."

Minda declined to remind Tracy that her knowledge and experience with guys was limited. "I happen to think you're pretty perfect, yourself."

A reluctant smile tugged at Tracy's lips. "Thanks, Mom. So, do you think I look all right? I mean, do I look pretty? You know, like someone Mark will think is pretty?"

Minda felt a door open in the conversation. "Tracy, honey, the man you're with should like you for who you are, not who you pretend to be."

She made a face. "I know. But I don't want to be just plain, old Tracy McAllister—at least, not when I'm with Mark. It's hard to explain. He's just special. Like, you know, when girls say they've met The One? You know what I mean, Mom? Like when you met Daddy and you just knew you were going to marry him. You know?"

"No, Tracy, it's not like when I met Daddy." Minda felt a danger alarm go off in her head. "Your father was ten and I was eight years old when we met. We had a lifetime to get to know each other and learn what love was about. We didn't just fall in love one afternoon after school—" She stopped short as she realized her voice had carried a tinge of sarcasm. She took a deep breath and said in a voice she hoped was much calmer, "I'm sorry, honey, but it's not the same. You know nothing about this man . . . And I do mean *man*."

"You make it sound like there's something wrong with him," Tracy said, defensively.

"That's because there *is* something wrong. He's too old. You're too young."

"I'm not too young. I'll be eighteen in two weeks."

"But right now you're seventeen. You're too young and the man downstairs is not suitable for you to think of in a romantic way."

"In two weeks it won't matter *what* you think!" Tracy's voice rose a little. "In two weeks I can do whatever I want. In two weeks, I'll be eighteen and *I'll* be the one deciding who's suitable!"

"Tracy, you can't really be interested in that man. What on earth could the two of you possibly have in common?"

In a flash Tracy's arms were folded across her chest. "You mean: what could he possibly see in *me*."

"Honey, that's not what I said."

"No, but it's what you meant. You don't think a handsome and hot guy could ever possibly be interested in me. You refuse to see that I've grown up!"

"Yes, you've grown, but you'll never catch up to *him*. The man downstairs is ten years older than you are, Tracy."

Tracy's brown eyes, that had glared so hotly at Minda only a moment ago, softened a little.

Minda knew that look and her breath caught a little in her throat. "He's *more* than ten years older, isn't he?"

Tracy looked away but a faint tinge of pink stained her cheeks.

Minda sat down on the edge of the tub beside her daughter and clasped one of her hands. "Just how old is he, Tracy?"

Tracy shrugged her shoulders and tried to pull her hand away but Minda wouldn't let go.

"I think he's, like ... thirty-two," she mumbled, still unwilling to make eye-contact.

After a long moment Minda asked gently, "Honey, do you see that this is a problem?"

"No! You know, Mom, you just don't know him, *that's* the problem."

"And you *do* know him?" Minda challenged. "Okay, then tell me about him." Minda waited expectantly, but Tracy didn't speak. Instead, her chin jutted out to a militant angle as she glared back at her mother.

Minda wasn't deterred. "Is he a Christian, Tracy? Does he go to church? What's his favorite color? What does he like to eat for dinner? Does he have any brothers or sisters?"

Tracy pursed her lips into a straight line.

"The fact is, honey, you really don't know anything about him. So here's my idea: Let's learn about Mark Cartier together."

The look on Tracy's face wavered between hope and distrust. "You aren't going to interrogate him or something, are you?"

"No, I thought I'd ask him to stay for dinner. He can eat pot roast and tell us about himself. What do you think?"

Tracy studied the pattern on the tile floor for a moment. "I *think* it sounds like a good idea, but there must be a catch somewhere."

Minda shook her head. "No catch. No trap. No hidden strings. We'll just have a nice dinner and we'll both get a chance to know our guest better. Maybe I'll find out I was wrong and he's really a great guy who's suitable for my daughter."

"Oh, yeah, right. You're really hoping I'll find out *I* was wrong and I won't like him after all."

"Anything can happen," Minda said, with a slight shrug of her shoulders.

"Not that. Mark's an awesome guy. You'll see. You'll change your mind about *him*."

For the hundredth time in less than thirty minutes, Minda wondered how things could have progressed so far in a single afternoon. Tracy had only met the man a few hours ago, yet she was clearly deep in the throes of a heart-felt crush. Minda truly questioned whether Mark Cartier felt the same moon-eyed, isn't-life-wonderful kind of first love that Tracy was feeling. It didn't make sense that a man as polished and good-looking as Mark Cartier couldn't find half a dozen women his own age to date.

So why on earth was he interested in her daughter?

Minda wasn't going to tease herself over the answer. She made up her mind. She was going to find out what his intentions were and have him out of Tracy's life by the end of the evening.

Tonight would be Mark Cartier's first—and last—meal at the McAllister house.

M ark Cartier drew another deep breath, enjoying the savory smells coming from the kitchen. With a few well-placed compliments and a little bit of his own brand of charm, he was certain he could get Minda McAllister to invite him to dinner. It had been a long time since he'd had a home-cooked meal and this one smelled particularly delicious. Pot roast, if he trusted his memory, and he'd bet it tasted as good as it smelled.

The aroma of dinner cooking added to the overall hominess of the McAllister place—a home that had initially surprised him when he'd first followed Tracy through the front door. From the outside, he thought it was nothing more than a big, old barn of a house. A yellow clapboard beast.

Once inside, the businessman in him had immediately cataloged its contents with a practiced eye, from the warm tones of the wood mouldings around the windows and doors, to the gently over-stuffed furniture and faded, but still valuable area carpets that were scattered over the hard-wood floors. He figured the place had to be about a hundred years old, yet there was nothing musty or out-dated about it, as he had expected. It was a warm, charming place that was welcoming, yet elegant. A home that was surprisingly serene amid the bustle of downtown Denver.

There were few houses left in the surrounding area. Most of the old homes had been torn down years before, replaced by office buildings, trendy towers of open-space lofts, and multi-level parking structures. Minda McAllister was one of the few property owners who declined to sell out in the name of progress, but Mark had a feeling he could change her mind about that.

Without thinking, from habit born of practice, he had been sizing up Minda McAllister since the moment he had first caught a glimpse of her. She was, to a certain extent, the enemy. She had what he wanted and he was smart enough to remember that.

Yet she had surprised him, too. He had come to think of the Widow McAllister as just another adversary to be vanquished, another obstacle to be overcome in his quest for success in his career. He hadn't expected her to be so pretty. He certainly hadn't expected that the sight of her—working her garden with tell-tale signs of dirt clinging to her hands and a light breeze gently ruffling her shoulder-length brown hair—could be so attractive.

But those thoughts, he knew, were dangerous. They diverted him from his purpose and distracted him from his goal. Determinedly, he blocked them from his mind, replacing them with a more sensible variety.

He'd spotted a large, old roll-top desk in a shadowed alcove at one end of the living-room. It was an enormous piece of furniture that rivaled the size of the upright piano on the other side of the room, and it looked twice as old.

Alert to any warning sound that Minda and her daughter

were coming down the stairs, Mark approached the desk. He saw papers and bank statements neatly stacked on the desktop beside a Bible-study lesson plan. One by one, Mark pulled at the heavy wooden desk drawers. To his relief, they didn't squeak or scrape when he opened them.

He shuffled quickly through the drawers' contents and found nothing to cause surprise: an over-due property tax notice, a clutch of unpaid bills, some church tithe receipts. In another drawer he discovered a collection of probably every single report card Tracy ever brought home from school.

In the wide pencil drawer he found several unopened pieces of mail, including a large envelope imprinted with the familiar return address of his employer: Goble, Haines and Wyman.

His boss, Robert Haines, would have a heart attack if he knew his last best offer had been tossed, unopened, into a desk drawer. Robert Haines would never be able to understand that a woman could be so disinterested in a multi-million dollar offer to buy her property. Mark was having a bit of trouble understanding it himself. If it was some sort of ploy on her part, Mark would get to the bottom of it.

He quickly stuffed the envelope back into the drawer at the sound of footsteps descending the stairs. By the time Tracy and Minda reached the bottom step, Mark was casually sitting on the living-room sofa. He looked up at them and smiled.

Minda smiled politely back. "Mark, I'm about to put the finishing touches on dinner. I hope you'll stay and join us."

"I appreciate the invitation," he said, smoothly, "but I don't want to impose."

"In that case, maybe you'd feel better about staying if you worked for your supper. *You* can set the dinner table."

He actually smiled then. Not that plastic, movie-star smile that was meant to charm her into doing his will, but a genuine smile that lit his blue eyes and transformed his expression.

Slowly, Mark left the sofa and rose to his feet. He stood almost toe-to-toe with her, his size towering over her petite frame.

She didn't back up and she didn't flinch. She looked him full in the eyes for a moment that seemed to last a lifetime.

The light in his eyes intensified. "In that case, I'd love to stay."

Minda sat back in her dining-room chair and surveyed the remains of their meal. Mark had done justice to the pot roast. Under other circumstances, she might have found that gratifying. Tonight, however, she didn't want Mark to get too comfortable in her home or think that any future dinner invitations were in the offing.

So far, their dinner conversation had centered around Tracy and school, books and movies. But Minda had promised her daughter they would learn about Mark Cartier together and that was a promise she intended to keep.

"What do you do for a living, Mark?" she asked.

"I dabble a little in real estate."

"Here in Denver?"

"I don't live in Denver."

She waited expectantly for more details, but he concentrated instead on chasing a few wayward peas around his plate with his fork.

She was starting to suspect Mark didn't like talking about himself, and she had to wonder why. Was he a real estate agent or a secret agent? For pity's sake, what on earth could the man have to hide?

"So you're visiting Denver. Visiting from where?" she persisted.

"New York."

Tracy's eyes widened. "New York City? Is that where you live? Wow, it must be great to live there."

"I've lived there many years. And, yes, it can be a very exciting city."

"I'd love to go there someday. Do you seriously *love* it there?"

"I guess I do," he said, after a moment's thought.

Minda thought she saw a small chink open in his protective armor. "What do you love about New York, Mark?"

"The tall buildings. The crowds of people. The fast pace."

"I bet you live in a penthouse," Tracy suggested.

He smiled. "Not a penthouse. But I do have a condo with a view of the river. I really don't spend much time there, to tell you the truth."

"That sounds so awesome," Tracy gushed. "What does your condo look like?"

"I guess you could say it's contemporary. Everything's new and pretty streamlined. Of course, it's not as welcoming a place as your home is, but it meets my needs."

Minda thought she detected a pattern: Every time the topic of conversation veered toward Mark, he deflected the focus back. And he was doing a good job of it, too.

"You truly have a lovely home, Minda," he continued. "And I would imagine that between this house and the land it sits on, you own some of the most desirable real estate in Denver."

That was the second time Minda recalled him making a comment about her home and its value. She frowned as she realized she might have stumbled upon the reason behind his interest in Tracy. Did he think Tracy was some kind of heiress?

"I really don't know how desirable this property is, Mark, because I'd *never* sell it."

He nodded, as if he agreed with her. "Aside from this house, do you own any other property?"

"I own a commercial building downtown, about a mile from here. On the street level I have a Christian bookstore," she said.

He nodded again and seemed interested. "Good location?"

"The best. It's right off the 16th Street Mall. Do you know where that is?"

"I think I do. The Mall is a pedestrian-only street, isn't it?"

"That's right. Lots of foot traffic means lots of shoppers looking in the windows. And lots of shoppers means lots of customers."

"Business must be good."

She couldn't honestly claim that her business was wildly successful when it wasn't, but she wasn't willing to give him the details of her profit and loss statement. "I can't complain."

"All the buildings in that neighborhood have several stories, don't they? If your bookstore is on the first level, what businesses occupy the remaining floors?"

"No businesses, just apartments."

"Are they all rented?"

"One-hundred percent occupancy."

"I'm impressed."

She smiled. "Don't be. The building is old and maintaining it is a challenge. The apartments are small but I try to make them comfortable for my tenants. I'm sure they're not the kind of apartments that can compare with the ones you find in New York."

Tracy drew her admiring gaze from Mark's face long enough to flash her mother a smile. "New York does sound pretty exciting, doesn't it, Mom? I'd seriously *love* to go there. Denver is so small and old-fashioned."

Minda didn't think New York could be all that exciting if one of its residents didn't even want to talk about it, but she doubted Tracy would agree with her reasoning.

"Maybe we'll go there someday, honey."

Tracy barely heard her. Her attention was reserved only for Mark. She watched as Mark drank the last of the iced tea from his glass. Eagerly, she reached for the pitcher on the table to refill his glass, only to realize the pitcher was empty.

"Oh, gosh, I better get some more tea. I'll only be a minute, Mark." Tracy disappeared into the kitchen before Mark even had a chance to stop her.

He turned to Minda, a little bemused. "Is she always so eager to please?"

"Not always. But she's a little excited tonight, I think. This is a different kind of evening for her than she's ever had before."

"It's different for me, too," he said, and meant it. He was genuinely surprised to realize he was actually enjoying a quiet evening of dinner and conversation. If anyone had told him a week ago that he would have dinner with a distrustful widow and her gushy teenage daughter and like it, he would have said they were crazy. But the truth of the matter was something of a revelation to him: He liked Minda McAllister's house. He liked being there. And if he wasn't careful, he could end up liking her.

So far, the feeling was not mutual. She had a definite wariness in her expression whenever she looked at him and for the life of him, he couldn't figure out why. He'd already determined she didn't know who he was or the real reason he had insinuated himself into her home. She couldn't know or she would have kicked him to the curb hours ago. Yet there was something about him she distrusted; something she just wasn't warming up to.

He intended to change that. He didn't mind if she put up a little bit of a fight along the way as long as he got what he wanted in the end.

But it was hard to charm a woman if she refused to even look at him. Her gaze was fixed on some point outside the dining-room window. Her expression was a little pensive.

He saw a small smudge of garden dirt next to her ear that she had missed when she washed up before dinner and he had to fight an urge to reach out and gently brush it away. That would have made her jump and he didn't want to alarm her. He wanted her to trust him. He needed her to trust him, if he was to succeed. He had to find a way to disarm her. His instincts told him she would respond to gentleness.

To recall her attention, he said her name softly.

"Minda."

Her eyes met his, an expression of mild inquiry on her face, and immediately—magically—he forgot what he was going to say.

For the first time, she looked at him without suspicion or wariness. Her eyes were the most extraordinary variety of hazel, with distinct flecks of fiery green and soft yellow circling each iris. Her eyes were full of warmth and sparkle and life. She gazed back at him, her expression open and expectant as she waited for him to finish the sentence he had begun.

"More iced tea, Mark?" Tracy was at his side again, the pitcher poised and ready at the rim of his glass.

"Thanks, Tracy." He felt his good sense return, along with

his purpose for being there. He marshaled his senses and made a mental note to avoid looking into Minda McAllister's hazel eyes in the future.

"So, Minda, you said your building has apartments? How many apartments—"

"Will you be visiting Denver very long, Mark?" Minda asked, cutting him off.

"I'm not sure yet what my plans are." One of his cardinal rules in life was, *Never Commit.*

"If you'll be in Denver for the weekend, Tracy and I would love to have you join us for church services on Sunday."

Mark's smile froze slightly in place.

Minda saw the change and felt a small amount of satisfaction. In fact, she felt a lot of satisfaction in knowing she had jolted him a little. She'd ask God's forgiveness for it later, but right now she decided to push the smile off Mark's face altogether. "You *do* go to church, don't you?"

Mark took a long drink of iced tea and when he set his glass back on the table, that practiced smile of charm had returned to his lips.

He looked Minda straight in the eye. "I'd love to go to church with you on Sunday."

She blinked first. The heat of a blush slowly crept up her neck and added patches of color to her cheeks.

"What church do you and Tracy attend?"

"We're members at Eternal Joy Christian Church. It's just a few blocks north of here."

He nodded. "The big Gothic church with the bell tower on the corner."

"That's right. For someone who's just visiting Denver, you certainly seem to know a lot about it."

It was his job to know about Denver and its buildings. Just as it was his job to know about Minda McAllister and the value of her house and how big a mortgage she carried. It was also his job to know that her bookstore barely turned a profit and the building that housed it cost more to maintain than she could ever make off rents from the tenants she allowed to live in her apartments.

When Mark Cartier took on an assignment, he did his homework, he identified his obstacles, and he exploited the weaknesses of his opposition.

Minda McAllister was his opposition; and her hazel eyes and wary watchfulness were most certainly obstacles. But he had to admit she was the most attractive obstacle he'd come up against in a long time.

He reached into his trouser pocket and withdrew an old pocket watch that chimed melodically when he opened it.

"It's getting late," he said. "I should be going."

He stood and returned the watch to his pocket, then held out his hand to Minda. "Thank you, Minda, for a very pleasant evening and a wonderful dinner. I enjoyed it very much."

"It was my pleasure, Mark." She immediately pulled her hand from his grasp and moved toward the front door as Mark and Tracy followed.

"Don't forget church on Sunday," Tracy said, anxious to make sure he didn't forget his promise. "We usually go to the eleven o'clock service."

"At Eternal Joy Christian Church," he recited. "I'll be there."

Tracy watched him walk to his car and drive away before she closed the door and flashed her mother a triumphant smile. "See, Mom? You were wrong about Mark."

"I didn't see anything of the sort." Minda scooped up the dessert plates from the table and headed for the kitchen.

Tracy followed her. "How can you say that? He's amazing.

He's perfect! He's even going to church with us on Sunday. He promised!"

"Yes, he promised. But the real proof of the pudding will be if he actually shows up!"

3

Every Sunday morning, almost without fail, Minda and Tracy walked the three-block distance from home to church. It was their time to prepare together for worship, to make their minds ready to receive the word of God, and to push the distractions of the past week and coming days from their thoughts.

There were many Sundays in Minda's life when it was hard to keep the distractions at bay. The problems of unpaid bills, disruptive tenants, and a somewhat rebellious teenager often seemed overwhelming. But there was something about that walk in the quiet of a Sunday morning that helped settle the tumult of her mind.

But this Sunday was different.

On this Sunday, her thoughts were filled with Mark Cartier and the promise he'd made to meet them at church. She found herself praying—*begging* was a better word—that God would keep Mark away.

Minda hadn't heard from him or seen him since he left the house on Friday and she was pretty certain Tracy hadn't heard from him either. Instead of spending Saturday with her friends as usual, Tracy had hung around the house, jumping whenever the phone rang and listening for the sound of a car pulling up at the curb.

But this morning her demeanor was completely different. Tracy almost skipped the three blocks to church. Her expression was glowing, her anxiety was almost palpable, and she couldn't keep herself from talking about Mark.

"We don't have any special plans today, do we? I was thinking, maybe we can invite Mark to have supper with us after church."

"Sure, honey." Minda's pleadings with God increased several levels of intensity.

Tracy brightened. "Can we use the good dishes?"

"No."

"Can we eat by candlelight?"

"No."

"Can we tell Mark that I made the dinner?"

"You can tell him you helped. That means you'll have to make the salad."

Tracy flashed a happy smile and Minda felt her own anxiety increase.

For the last several months Tracy had been going through a moody, sullen teenager phase. It seemed that no matter what Minda said, Tracy could be counted on to take the opposing view. They were clashing frequently over the most basic issues; and to Minda's way of thinking, if a disagreement over the appropriate amount of eye-liner could bring on an explosion of hurtful words, then their disagreement over Mark Cartier was certain to end in something close to a nuclear meltdown.

Again she prayed that Mark wouldn't show up at church. If God answered her prayer, it would be easy to push home to

Tracy that Mark wasn't trustworthy; that Tracy shouldn't waste another millisecond of thought on the man. Then their lives would go back to normal. Then Tracy's biggest concern would be what outfit to wear to school and they could both look back on his brief appearance in their lives as nothing more than a bad memory.

Eternal Joy Christian Church sat on the corner of two residential streets. The large sanctuary had been built in the middle of the nineteenth century, financed by the wealth of the silver barons who resided in the neighborhood at the time. Since then, the neighborhood had changed drastically. The silver barons' homes disappeared, their lands parceled off, but the church remained.

As they approached the beautiful old sanctuary, Minda saw a small group of Tracy's friends gathered on the sidewalk, while other members of the congregation climbed the steps toward the open, welcoming doors of the sanctuary.

Her eyes scanned the area. There was no sign of Mark Cartier.

She let out a soft sigh of relief and looked at Tracy.

Tracy's excited chatter ended mid-sentence as she stopped on the street corner across from the church. She frowned, her expression a mixture of hurt and disbelief.

Minda pressed her lips together to hold back the words of comfort she wanted to offer. She knew Tray would reject them. She hated to see her daughter like this. She resented having to watch the roller-coaster of emotions Tracy was experiencing over a man that she should never have met in the first place.

With a mother's instinct to protect her child, Minda wished she could see Mark Cartier one more time, just to inflict a few choice punishments on him for hurting Tracy.

"Come on, honey. We don't want to be late."

They crossed the street and approached the group of teenagers, all friends of Tracy's who regularly sat with her during the service. One of the young men, whose sheer size proclaimed him to be a football player, brightened visibly when he saw them.

"Hello, Mrs. McAllister. Hi, Tracy."

Minda smiled encouragingly at him. She had suspected for some time that Josh Stuart was a little smitten with Tracy and she couldn't think of a better person to help her daughter forget all about Mark Cartier.

"Good morning, Josh. Good morning, everyone."

She put her hand on Tracy's shoulder and murmured, "I know you're disappointed, but these are your true friends. Why don't you sit with them this morning, like you usually do?"

She could feel Tracy's body stiffen beneath her touch. Tracy stared straight ahead and her lips clamped together into an angry line of defiance.

Minda stood it gladly, secure in the knowledge that God had answered her prayers by keeping Mark far away from Tracy and Eternal Joy Christian Church.

She said, brightly, "I'm going in now, but I'll see you all in Fellowship Hall after the service."

She took a step back, and as she turned away, she immediately collided with an immovable force. She looked up and saw that the one man she had hoped never to see again had been standing right behind her.

"Mark!" Tracy gasped with sudden delight. "I'm so glad you came!"

"I promised I would, and I always keep my promises." He looked at Minda, still smiling, but with a challenging light in his eyes. "Shall we go in?"

"Yes, let's!" Tracy smiled up at him in a way that caught

Josh's attention.

"Wait a sec, Tracy. You mean you're not going to sit with us? We've been waiting for you. We sit together every Sunday."

Tracy's chin rose. She said, in her best grown-up voice, "I'm sorry, Josh, I won't be sitting with you today. I made other plans." She turned away from her friends and looked up at Mark with a soft expression. "Shall we go in, Mark?"

"Sure." He looked quickly over at Minda.

She stared back at him with a stony expression. She'd been so close to getting rid of him. She'd been so sure he wouldn't show up. But there he was, big as life, and the only person who seemed genuinely happy to see him was Tracy.

As Mark and Tracy walked toward the steps of the church, Josh drove his hands into the pockets of his khaki slacks. "What's with the Queen of Sheba act?" he muttered.

Minda reached over and touched his shoulder, consolingly. "Mr. Cartier is a family friend and Tracy is trying to be a good hostess this morning."

"So, is she gonna sit with us or not?"

"Not today, Josh. But we'll catch up with you in Fellowship Hall after the service, okay?"

Minda hurried up the steps to where Tracy and Mark were waiting for her. She went into the sanctuary first, leading them past the weathered brass plaque inscribed with the year 1864 and through the heavy oak doors that stood open to welcoming worshippers.

She hadn't gone very far down the center aisle of the sanctuary when she realized their entrance was garnering a good amount of attention. She was uncomfortably aware that her fellow worshippers were watching and whispering as they made their way toward the pew where Minda usually sat. She wasn't used to being the subject of such scrutiny and it unnerved her enough to make her completely miss the chance to make sure she sat between Tracy and Mark. Instead she was the first to dart into the pew, leaving Tracy to follow and earn the small prize of sitting beside Mark.

Minda realized her mistake too late; but with a little reflection, she decided it might not prove to be a bad idea if Tracy were to learn for herself that Mark was wholly unschooled in the subject of worship services. Perhaps then Tracy would understand that a relationship with a man who didn't share her faith was out of the question. Perhaps then Tracy would see reason.

The church organ sounded and the congregation stood for the first hymn. From the corner of her eye, Minda watched Mark. She braced herself, waiting to catch a glimpse of the tell-tale signs of a non-believer fumbling with the hymnal, expecting to hear him grope for the right notes of an unfamiliar song.

Softly and tenderly Jesus is calling . . .

Mark's rich baritone joined with the congregation in a strong and confident tone.

Calling for you and for me . . .

And he wasn't looking at the hymnal. Instead, it was Tracy who was clutching the music book like a lifeline and timidly singing along as if she had never before set foot inside a place of worship.

See, on the portals He's waiting and watching . . .

Minda frowned, not quite able to believe what was happening. All she needed now was to hear him harmonize and she'd probably fall right over.

Watching for you and for me.

So Mark wasn't a stranger to going to church, after all, Minda realized. Singing hymns didn't seem to stump him and she soon discovered that he had a pretty good grasp of knowing when to stand and sit with the congregation.

The final note of the hymn sounded and the congregation sat down under the paternal eye of Pastor Walker. Pastor gave his welcoming remarks and invited the congregation to open their Bibles for the scripture reading.

Once again, Mark surprised Minda by joining in the congregational response, speaking the words of scripture without a glance toward the Bible Tracy was self-consciously offering to share with him.

Minda frowned. Had she completely misjudged Mark? Or was he simply some kind of chameleon who easily adapted to any given situation? He didn't strike her as a man of faith but he was certainly exhibiting the behavior of someone who attended church often.

Nothing about the man made sense to her. He certainly had money and he was handsome enough to be able to get a date with a real, honest-to-goodness supermodel, yet he was following her teen-aged daughter around. The conservative charcoal suit he was wearing probably cost more than Minda made in an entire month, yet he'd been anxious to share a simple meal of pot roast at her dining table. Just who was this guy, anyway?

The question distracted her attention from the service so much that she scarcely heard Pastor Walker's sermon.

At the end of the service, Pastor Walker smiled upon the congregation as a father would smile upon a favored child.

"I'm glad you came to worship with us this morning," he said. "We're all brothers and sisters in the Lord and it's good to see our family has grown a little on this beautiful Sunday morning. We're the better for each of you who chose to worship with us today. If you're new to Eternal Joy Christian Church, I hope you'll stay after the service and give us an opportunity to meet you and let you know how much we want you to worship with us again."

He extended his hand invitingly toward an elderly gentleman who was seated in the first pew. "Coach! Come on up here and tell all these good people how the reunion is coming along."

Coach obediently joined Pastor Walker at the front of the church. Coach Morgan's hair was white and his face was lined, but he was still a healthy, robust specimen of a man who kept his eighty-something-year-old body in peak physical condition. He crossed his muscular arms over his barrel chest. In a booming voice that was more at home on a football field than in a house of worship, he said, "Arrangements for the Train Riders Reunion are pretty well wrapped up. The reunion will be held next door in Fellowship Hall in just two short months and we're anticipating a good turnout. There are a lot of train riders and families of train riders coming from around the region— not just from Colorado, but Kansas and New Mexico and Wyoming, too. The turnout will be more than any of us dreamed it would be."

"I think it's become apparent to all of us," said Pastor Walker, "that this reunion of Orphan Train Riders is a special ministry that our church—and especially our brother, Coach—is uniquely qualified to provide. When we first began planning this event, we did so with the thought that it would be a meaningful way of showing our love for Coach. But, as it sometimes happens, our small ministry to one beloved brother in faith has blossomed into a much larger ministry that will touch the hearts and the souls of many people we have yet to meet. The Lord has truly guided our path on this project and we're excited to see His handiwork."

Coach nodded vigorously. "Today, after the service, we'll have special donation buckets in the foyer just for funding the reunion. And we could really use a couple more volunteers to help with the registration table on the day of the reunion. In fact, if any of you would like to volunteer your time—even just for an hour or two—I'm sure we can find the right job for you to do."

Pastor Walker placed a fatherly hand on Coach's shoulder. "We all know the reunion is a project that is dear to Coach's heart. If you'd like to help make this reunion a success, talk to Coach or to Minda McAllister or any of the reunion organizers."

Coach nodded. "That's right. If we all work together as a team, we can take this to reunion all the way to the finish line."

"And if you can't be one of the volunteers at the reunion, I hope you'll all take a few moments before you leave today to speak with Coach and express your love and support," Pastor said, encouragingly. "Now, join me in prayer, won't you?"

Pastor Walker ended the church service as he did every Sunday morning: by encouraging his flock to greet at least three people before they left the sanctuary. To Minda's surprise, almost half the congregation decided that Minda, Tracy and Mark were the three people Pastor had in mind.

She introduced Mark to one person after another in a wave of well-wishers whose names she was sure he couldn't possibly remember.

Slowly, they made their way from the pew to the foyer, where Pastor was stationed at the sanctuary doors, greeting each congregant as they stepped out into the bright sunshine of a fall afternoon.

Again Minda performed the necessary introductions, and added, "Mark is a friend of our family."

"Welcome, Mark." Pastor warmly shook Mark's hand. "I'm glad to have you join us in worship this morning."

They moved on, following other worshipers in a steady stream across the paved patio toward Fellowship Hall. Inside, large coffee urns, punch bowls, and trays of cookies were arranged on long tables against one wall. The sliding-glass doors were fully opened so people could easily move between the Hall and the patio as they greeted each other, talked in groups, laughed and shared.

From habit, Minda led the way toward the glass doors.

"Wait."

She looked back. Mark was standing still, his expensive leather shoes rooted to the pavement. His gaze was fixed on the people milling about Fellowship Hall.

"I think I'll leave."

His demeanor had changed so suddenly, Minda felt curious and cautious at the same time. She slowly walked back to where he was standing.

"Mark? Is something wrong?"

"No."

He still wasn't meeting her eyes. She couldn't guess why he was suddenly so hesitant to join the others in Fellowship Hall. He certainly wasn't the shy type. A few minutes ago he had been holding court with congregants in the sanctuary, smiling, shaking hands and making small talk with ease. But for some reason she couldn't guess, he didn't want to mingle with them in Fellowship Hall.

"Why don't we stay out here on the patio?" she suggested. "It's such a beautiful, warm day. Why spend it inside?"

"Listen, I don't want to keep you," he said. "Why don't I just—"

"Oh, don't go now!" Tracy exclaimed. "You haven't had a chance to meet my friends."

He hesitated. "I guess I can stay, but only for a couple minutes."

"Oh, good," Tracy said, relieved. "I mean, there's no reason why you have to rush off, is there? Why don't I get us some juice? Or would you rather have coffee, Mark?"

"Juice is fine, Tracy. Thanks."

She flashed him a glowing smile and headed toward Fellowship Hall.

"Hi, Minda!" Minda's sister-in-law and best friend Ellen Dailey joined them, pulling her husband Jim behind her. "So, are you going to introduce us?"

Before Minda could react, Ellen reached out and gripped Mark's hand in a hearty shake. "Hi, I'm Ellen Dailey and this is my husband Jim. I'm Minda's sister-in-law. Formerly, that is. She was married to my brother but we're still friends and I work for Minda at the bookstore. But I expect you know all that. My husband Jim is the music director here at church."

When Ellen paused for breath, Mark said, politely, "It's very nice to meet you both."

"Have you met Coach yet?" Ellen intercepted Coach Morgan on his way toward Fellowship Hall. As Ellen introduced Coach to Mark, Tracy returned with three cups of juice and several of her friends, including Josh Stuart. Within minutes a sizeable group of people surrounded Mark, each eager to make his acquaintance, each eager to gain his attention even for a moment or two.

As Mark made small talk with the people around him, Ellen looped her fingers around Minda's arm and pulled her a little away from the group.

"Yowza, where'd you find *him*?" she demanded, in an awed tone.

"I didn't find him," Minda replied, frowning. "He found me. Actually, he found Tracy. It's a long story and I don't think this is the time to go into it."

"You can tell me all about it tomorrow at work," said Ellen, determined to get the details. "He's almost too gorgeous to be true. What's he do for a living, anyway?"

Minda frowned. "To tell you the truth, I don't know."

"He's good looking enough to be a model. I bet he's rich, too. That suit of his didn't come off the rack."

"Don't be silly. He's not a model."

"A lawyer?"

Frowning, Minda glanced over to where Mark was tolerantly conversing with the people around him, each one gazing admiringly up at him, each eager to capture and hold his attention. Whatever had been troubling him was gone now. He was smiling that smile of his that was precisely designed to charm and he was having great success. Pastor Walker, Jim Dailey, Coach—they were all hanging on his every word, taking turns welcoming him, encouraging him to return for the evening service.

He was, she decided, pretty amazing to watch as he patiently answered their questions, completely at his ease in a circle of admiring strangers. The afternoon sun brought out the shine in his dark hair and for the first time, Minda admitted how perfect he was. From his face to his hair to his physique, he was faultless.

Lawyer, schmoyer, she thought. Mark Cartier's money didn't come from practicing law.

So where did his money come from? Minda realized she had never asked him about the speech he gave at Tracy's high school on career day. She had never got a straight answer from him about how he made his living and why his occupation would have made a flock of high school girls swoon over him, as Tracy had described.

"I don't think he's an attorney. He said something about

real estate."

"Yeah? Well, I'm going to go talk to him some more and see what I can find out." Ellen made a bee-line back to Mark's side.

Minda pursed her lips together and wondered what would happen if the smiling people gathered around Mark knew his true intentions. They wouldn't be so welcoming if they knew that behind the dazzling smile and firm handshake was a wolf in sheep's clothing. What if she marched right up to them and told them that the smooth-talking thirty-two-year-old man was bent on dating her teen-aged daughter? Or what if she went into the church office and picked up the microphone to the public-address system and pushed that little red button and . . .

"Minda?" Pastor Walker's voice brought her to her senses. He was standing beside her, looking at her with a curious expression on his face.

"Sorry. I was daydreaming."

"So I could tell. I asked what you thought of my sermon this morning."

His sermon? The sermon she hadn't paid attention to because Mark Cartier had hi-jacked her thoughts all morning?

"Well, Pastor, I thought it was . . . very insightful."

"I'm glad to hear you say so because I got the impression you were a little preoccupied during the service." He leaned closer and said, confidentially, "You'd be surprised what I can see when I'm standing up on that elevated pulpit."

She decided there was no use denying it. "Maybe I was a little distracted."

He nodded. "Your friend, Mark, seemed very attentive, though. And I see he's turning out to be a popular fellow with our congregants. He seems like a very nice man."

Up until that moment Minda always thought Pastor Walker had a talent for sizing a person up with unerring accuracy within moments of making their acquaintance. Now she wasn't so certain.

"I agree he *seems* like a nice man, but to tell you the truth, Mark is—" She stopped herself before she betrayed too much of her fears. "Maybe now is not the time to discuss this, Pastor. But I would like to make an appointment to see you this week. I'm hoping I can get some more of your excellent advice about raising teenagers."

He gave her a soft look of sympathy. "I'm not always certain that my office is the best place to talk about kids. I've got a better idea. I'll be home all day tomorrow and I wouldn't mind some company, if you'd like to drop by."

She shook her head. "I couldn't intrude, Pastor. Monday is your only real day off during the week."

"And what could be more restful than having a nice conversation with a good friend?" he asked with a gentle smile. "Besides, I plan to work in my garden tomorrow and I'd value your advice. Please come by."

"Okay. I'll see you tomorrow afternoon. And thank you."

Pastor Walker moved away to greet other members of his flock and Minda's attention shifted back to Mark. Whatever had been bothering Mark before was gone now. His confident smile was back on his lips and his seemed very much at his ease. Tracy was at his side, beaming proudly as he talked with Coach Morgan, Josh Stuart and quite a number of ladies of varying ages—people Minda once considered her friends but now recognized as traitors, every one.

He was doing all the right things: laughing at their jokes, making eye contact when they spoke, nodding politely at their insights on Pastor's sermon. But when Minda approached the group, his attention shifted to her.

And stayed.

She ignored him and flashed her best Sunday-morning smile at everyone else. "Good morning."

Coach Morgan said, "I was just about to tell your friend, Mark, about the baseball game." His sharp gaze rolled appraisingly over Mark's broad shoulders and athletic build. "You look like you'd make a pretty good outfielder."

"Short-stop," said Mark, unruffled by Coach's scrutiny.

Coach's eyes lit up a little. "I could use a short-stop on the church team."

Laughing, Mark shook his head. "Wait a minute! It's been a long time since I—"

"Don't worry, all the players are a little rusty. You're going to tell me you haven't played since high school."

"College."

The light in Coach's eyes increased a couple of watts.

"So you've got some experience! Good to know."

Tracy looked up at Mark, her expression a mixture of pride and admiration. "You play baseball? I didn't know that about you!"

"It was a long time ago." Mark said, dismissively. "Coach, I'd love to play, but, you see, I'm not sure when I'll be leaving town."

"There's no long-term commitment here. The game's in less than two weeks and I'm going to try to squeeze a couple of practices in before-hand. The game's just a friendly match against one of our neighboring churches to help raise money for the reunion. And I could really use a good short-stop."

Tracy touched his arm. "Please say you'll play. I love watching baseball."

"*What*?" Josh exclaimed, incredulously. "Since when do you love baseball?"

"Since always," she retorted. "There are other sports besides football, you know."

"And if you can name two, I'll eat my church bulletin," Josh muttered.

"Come to our team practice, Mark," Coach said. "We're practicing Thursday night at the high school."

"I'll have to check my calendar . . ."

"Seven o'clock on Thursday. At the high school down the street."

Mark hesitated. It wasn't often that he succumbed to the force of another man's personality, but he was certainly feeling the effects of Coach's single-mindedness. He already regretted even admitting he knew how to play, but baseball had been a love of his since he'd learned to play the game in a dirt field with a gaggle of ragged boys his age. He'd continued to play in high school and college, where his natural talent had earned him a reputation as a star athlete. Baseball had given him his first taste of *being somebody.*

He knew he was only going to be in town for a few days— just long enough to get what he wanted out of Minda—so he was tempted not to get involved. But Minda was looking at him with that wary, watchful look in her eyes and he got the distinct feeling his answer was important to her. If agreeing to show up for a baseball practice was going to get Minda to sell her building to Goble, Haines and Wyman, who was he to argue?

"Okay, I'll see what I can do," he said.

Coach nodded, satisfied. "Then I'll see you Thursday."

Mark laughed and shook his head. Later, as he walked with Minda and Tracy toward the lot where his rental car was parked, he asked, "Is Mr. Morgan always so persistent?"

"Call him 'Coach.' Everyone does," said Minda. "And yes, his personality is pretty forceful. It comes from a lifetime of riding herd over energetic teenaged boys."

"Speaking of teenagers, Josh seems like a pretty focused young man, too."

"Josh is just a boy," Tracy said, with a touch of scorn. "All he cares about is sports and hanging out. He doesn't have any ambition or real purpose in his life."

"I don't think that's such a bad thing," Mark said, reasonably. "There's plenty of time to grow up and deal with responsibility and life's challenges. There's something to be said for just enjoying being a teenager."

"Oh, I agree," Tracy said, quickly. "I just meant that he's not very mature. Women mature much faster than boys, you know."

"So I've heard."

"Take me, for instance. I'm only seventeen, but I'm much more adult in my thinking than most people my age. I guess that's why I'm more comfortable being with people who are my intellectual peers than I am with people who are the same physical age I am."

"That makes sense." Mark glanced at Minda, hoping to read something in her expression that would help him understand Tracy's point.

"As a matter of fact," Tracy continued, "in just a couple weeks I'm going to celebrate a birthday. My *eighteenth* birthday," she added, meaningfully. "When's your birthday, Mark?"

"Exactly two months after yours. I was born on the same day of the month you were, but in December."

Tracy's eyes lit. "Oh, my gosh, that is so-o-o-o amazing! We almost have the same birthday! Mom, did you hear that? Mark's birthday is the same day as mine!"

"Which means that for two months he'll be *fifteen* years older than you instead of sixteen," Minda said, pointedly.

They stopped near Mark's car. He opened the front passenger door and looked at her expectantly.

Spending more time with Mark was the last thing Minda wanted to do. Her instinct was to wrap her protective arms around her daughter and run—not walk—back to their house and erase every memory of Mark Cartier from Tracy's mind.

Mark saw her hesitate. "I know. It's only three blocks to your house but I have a question for you and if I ask it while I'm driving and you're walking, it'll be a little tough for me to hear your answer."

"Can't you ask your question now?"

"I talk best when I'm driving."

She didn't believe him. He was trying to charm her and she was determined not to give him that satisfaction. She wracked her brain to conjure up a reason to refuse but Tracy decided the matter for her.

Tracy's gaze was locked on Mark's face and her smile stretched from ear to ear as she marched up to the car. He stepped forward to open the back door for her. Then he turned his blue eyes toward Minda.

"Won't you join us?"

Reluctantly, Minda slipped into the front passenger seat of the car.

Mark started the engine. He glanced over at Minda's stony profile as he maneuvered the car out of the parking lot. "What's the reunion everyone was talking about this morning?"

"It's a reunion of orphan train riders." She threw him a resentful look. "Is *that* the question you wanted to ask?"

"Train riders? Sounds like a band."

Her expression softened. "*Orphan* train riders. And you're not even close."

"So, what's it about?"

"During the Great Depression there were parents in big eastern cities like New York and Chicago who couldn't afford to feed their families. Their children and orphaned children were put on trains going west. The trains stopped in different cities where the children were adopted by families who could support them. That's what happened to Coach."

Mark stared at her. "*What*? I've never heard of such a thing! What kind of parents would do that?"

"Parents who wanted better lives for their children than

they could provide. Watch where you're going."

He turned his attention back to the road. "But to give them up? They put their children on a train never knowing the next time they'd see them?"

"There was no next time. The majority of the children never saw their biological families again."

"And Coach Morgan was one of those kids?"

"Coach and his sisters. He was the youngest of four children. But he was lucky; he was adopted by the Morgan family here in Denver."

"They must have been good people to take in four children and give them a home."

Minda shook her head. "You don't understand. They only took Coach. He never saw his older sisters again. Over the years he's searched for them and tried to find out anything he could about what happened to them, but he's never had any luck. He's hoping the reunion will help. Maybe one of the train riders who attend the reunion will remember one of his sisters and provide the missing piece of information that will lead Coach to one or all of them."

Mark was quiet for a moment, wrestling with the unaccustomed emotional response he felt for Coach's story. "I hope he's successful. I hope he finds what he's looking for."

"I do, too. Coach is a good man with a big heart who truly cares about kids. He's been a good friend and mentor to every child he's ever met. Maybe a lot of it stems from his own background and experience. Actually, the reunion was his idea, as a way to recognize the parents who had to give up their children for a better life, and for the families that took them in and loved them as their own."

"That's a very powerful story. Does Coach ever talk about his experience? About how it felt to be a kid on one of those trains?"

"Not in those terms. Coach isn't the kind of person who dwells on sadness or life's hard knocks. But I know how much time he's spent over the years searching for his sisters. I think he really wants to feel that connection that you can only feel with someone who shares your bloodline and history."

"I have to say, that's one of the saddest stories I've ever heard."

"Don't let Coach hear you say that because he'd immediately tell you he's had a good life. He's always upbeat and always positive about his life and his faith. He's been married for many years and raised two kids of his own, and every kid who's come in contact with him at church and at the high school is devoted to him. The problem is that he's in his eighties now. He knows he's running out of time and, because his sisters were older, he realizes that he may be too late. I don't think he's willing to give up, though. Not yet."

Mark stopped the car at the curb in front of Minda's house. He quickly got out and went to Minda's side of the car to open the door for her.

As they walked toward the front steps of the house, Tracy said, "I'm glad you went to church with us this morning, Mark."

"I'm glad you invited me," he answered, politely.

"We have Bible study on Tuesday evening in my Sunday School room and Wednesday is choir practice. I was thinking maybe you'd like to join our choir."

He couldn't think of anything he'd be less likely to do; but he smiled politely and said, "Thanks, Tracy. I'll give that some thought."

"Would you like to stay and have Sunday supper with us?"

"As much as I would like to, I'm afraid I can't."

"Oh," Tracy said, clearly disappointed. "Well, if you can't stay, you can at least take a piece of cake with you. You like chocolate cake, don't you? Wait just a sec and I'll wrap up a piece for you." Tracy disappeared into the house.

Mark shook his head slightly, a little bemused by Tracy's eagerness to please him, but glad for the chance to speak to Minda alone for a few minutes.

"Mark, there's something I'd like to talk to you about," Minda said. "But I can't talk now."

One of his dark eyebrows went up. "Is there something in particular you want to discuss?"

"Yes, there is and it's private. Just between the two of us."

"Sure." His voice was even as he mentally flipped through a catalog of topics she might want to talk to him about, none of which seemed to him to fall under the category of *Private*. "Why don't I stop by later—"

"No, not here," she interrupted. "I don't want Tracy around. It would be better if we met somewhere else. Or maybe we could just talk on the phone."

For a moment the only sound was the slight rustle of fall leaves skitting along the sidewalk on a soft breeze. Mark could hardly believe his good luck: Minda wanted to talk with him, away from other people and away from the annoyance of her ever-present teen-aged daughter. Before he'd had a chance to ask her to meet him privately, she'd asked it of him.

"All right," he said, keeping his voice even. "I'll call you to pick a time and place."

The front door opened. Tracy reappeared with a large slice of chocolate cake covered in plastic and nestled on a plate from Minda's best set of china.

"Here you go, Mark. I hope you like it."

He took the plate from her. "Thanks. It looks delicious and

I'm sure I'll enjoy it. But I'm afraid I've got to get going."

Mark walked back to his car. He paused before he got in and looked back at Minda and Tracy as they stood on the wide front porch. "I'll call you."

Minda immediately wished he hadn't said that. She wished he had just left well enough alone. His words had an instant impact on Tracy, who looked like a child who had just been promised free reign in a candy store. Suddenly Minda wasn't at all certain which of them he'd been talking to. And when she realized she'd never given Mark her phone number, she could only assume he'd been talking to Tracy.

She felt her jaw tighten as she followed her daughter into the house. Every instinct had told her not to trust Mark Cartier, but she'd allowed her guard to drop anyway. A verse from Psalms leapt to mind: *His talk is smooth as butter, yet war is in his heart; his words are more soothing than oil, yet they are drawn swords.*

If Mark Cartier thought he could placate her with smooth talk and a Hollywood-calibre smile, he had another thing coming. She pressed her lips together with determination and offered up a silent prayer: *Please God, keep him away from my daughter and make him call me. We have to get this thing settled once and for all. He has to call.*

———

Mark put the car in gear and drove down the tree-lined residential street, leaving Minda, her daughter and his morning at church behind. It had been a long time since he'd last been inside a sanctuary. He had to congratulate himself on handling the whole experience as well as he did. In fact, it wasn't half as bad as he thought it would be. He didn't embarrass himself by saying *Amen* at the wrong time or sing a hymn in a different key than the rest of the congregation. It all came back to him, as if he'd done it only yesterday.

Surprisingly, he'd rather enjoyed singing those old hymns. Their lyrics and melodies felt as familiar and comfortable to him as a favorite pair of slippers. He'd felt good singing them and for a few minutes he even forgot the reason he'd gone to church in the first place. But as soon as the service had ended, he remembered himself and all the reasons he stopped attending church so many years before. He was only there because of Minda, because she'd dared him to go to church with her.

True, she hadn't actually invited him to church with those exact words, but he'd seen that glint in her eye. She'd been so sure of herself, so certain he'd decline her invitation. Even now, he could almost laugh just thinking of the look on her face when he agreed to meet her at the church. Her hazel eyes widened and her lips parted in surprise. Her expression had been so priceless, so . . . adorable.

He smiled as he picked up his cell phone from the car's center console and touched the voice dial icon.

"Call Paul."

Moments later he heard his older brother's voice on the speaker.

"Mark? Hey, bro, where are you?"

"In my car, heading your direction."

"You're in Denver? Why didn't you tell me you were coming to town?"

"I didn't know it myself until just before I showed up at the airport. I don't want to take up your entire afternoon, but I thought I'd at least drop by and say hello."

"Sure, I'd like that. It'll be nice to remind myself what you look like."

Mark felt a small pang of guilt over the amount of time that had passed since he'd last seen his brother. It was a pang he quickly suppressed. "Is that a crack about how long it's been since we last saw each other?"

"Yeah, it is," Paul said, in his usual, straight-forward style. "Come on over to the house and we'll have some lunch."

"Good. I'm starving."

About twenty minutes later Mark rang the doorbell at his brother's house. Paul Cartier opened the door and greeted him with a wide smile. He clapped his arm around Mark's shoulders and drew him inside.

"Let's go in the kitchen. Sara and the kids are still at church, but I found some stuff to make sandwiches. Want a soda?"

"Do you have any iced tea?" Mark couldn't help thinking of the perfectly-sweetened tea Minda had served at dinner.

Paul's eyebrows went up. "You're getting picky. No, I don't have iced tea and making some is a little beyond my abilities in the kitchen. I can slice meat and open jars. Those are my specialties."

"Soda is fine." Mark slipped his coat off and draped it over the back of one of the chairs at the kitchen table.

Paul eyed him critically as he pulled some plates out of an upper cabinet. "Nice suit. What are you dressed up for?"

"Church."

The plates clattered against the countertop and Paul stared at him. "*You* went to church?"

"Very funny. Yes, I went to church this morning."

"I didn't think you did that anymore."

"You know I don't. At least, I don't for my own purposes. Today I went for business reasons."

Paul set two cans of soda on the kitchen table. "Are you buying a church now?"

"No, I'm buying a commercial building but the owner of the property goes to church."

"Ah, I see. So, how was it?"

"Just like riding a bike. It all came back to me. I knew when to stand and when to sit, when to sing and when to keep my mouth shut."

Paul grinned at him. "You idiot. So you're in town to buy some more real estate, huh? Which building are you buying this time?"

"The McAllister Building."

"I wish you luck. There have been plenty of offers made on that building over the years. I should know. Harmony House made one of them."

"Your charity was going to buy a piece of prime commercial real estate in downtown Denver? Wasn't that a little ambitious?"

"Where do you think the people are that Harmony House serves?" Paul asked, as he dealt slices of bread onto a cutting board and began to layer them with cheese and carved turkey. "Most of those people are in the downtown area. And by the way, Harmony House isn't *my* charity. It's an organization that I founded and you contribute to very generously."

"It's a good write-off," Mark said, dismissively.

"Yeah, right. Do you ever take a break from your heartless businessman act?"

"What makes you think it's an act?"

"I'm an optimist, although I have to admit you sounded pretty cut-throat in that magazine article."

"You read the article? What did you think?" Mark hoped his questions hadn't sounded too eager. It had been eight months since a national business news magazine had published a feature story on him. He thought the article had accurately portrayed his business style and successes, and it had certainly been a boon to his career. When the edition first hit the newsstands, Mark had texted the news to his brother but Paul had never texted back. He never sent Mark his congratulations; never told Mark he was proud of him; never even said whether he'd read the article.

When he didn't hear back from his brother, Mark had been a little surprised, then angry, then hurt. Who needed Paul's approval? Mark sure didn't. After all, he was Mark Cartier, the boy wonder of commercial real estate investing. He was the star employee at Goble, Haines and Wyman and Robert Haines was grooming him for partner, although partner wasn't going to be enough for Mark. He had even bigger plans for himself.

"I think," Paul said, "it made you sound like America's next great real estate tycoon. Sara bought eight copies of the magazine. She wants you to autograph them."

Mark took a drink of soda while he watched his brother's expression. Paul had never been good at hiding his emotions and Mark could tell he was holding back. "And?" he prompted.

"And . . . some of your real estate deals have been pretty ruthless, too, if even half of what that article said was true. *Was* it true?"

"You'll have to be more specific."

"Okay, then. *Specifically* . . . the article didn't come right out and say it, but it implied that you bribed officials at a small town city hall in order to close a deal. That particular city hall condemned an entire neighborhood and evicted the residents from their homes so you could buy the land and turn it into a commercial property. Is it true? Did you do that?"

"If I say *yes*, am I going to get a sermon?"

Paul turned away from cutting the sandwiches to stare at him, the knife still in his hand. "You mean to tell me, you evicted people from their homes for a *mall?*"

"It was a shopping and dining promenade. Besides, those residents were handsomely paid to find new places to live. They were never cheated out of any money and most were paid far more than their homes would ever be worth on the open market."

"The article didn't say that."

"The article didn't say a lot of things. It never once mentioned my blue eyes or the fact that I live out of suitcases for eleven months out of every year. Listen, Paul, I work hard for every rung I climb on the ladder. The truth is, some deals require warfare-like tactics to be successful. I won't apologize for achieving my goals."

Paul turned back to cutting the sandwiches. "Just tell me you can sleep at night. Tell me your conscience is clear."

"I sleep like a baby."

"In hotel beds?"

"Sure. I'm in hotel beds more than I'm in my own bed in New York. I'm hoping, though, that this trip will be a quick one. It shouldn't take long for me to convince Mrs. McAllister to sell."

"So why are you interested in that old building?"

"I'm not. I'm interested in the land it sits on."

"Gonna buy it and tear it down, huh? Don't let the Widow McAllister hear you say that or she'll never sell."

Mark's interest quickened. "Have you met her before? What do you know about her?"

"Almost nothing. I never got the chance to meet her in person."

"But based on your experience in trying to negotiate a deal with her, did she give you any hints about what it *will* take to get her to sell?"

"She shut down negotiations before they ever got off the

ground. To tell you the truth, I think the old woman's just fiercely attached to that building."

A spark of amusement lit Mark's blue eyes. "*Old* woman?"

"She must be. I hear she's a little bit of a firecracker, too. She might even be a little senile by now, which would explain why she hangs on to that building. It's too bad, too, because the McAllister Building would be perfect for Harmony House. That building has apartments on all the upper floors. Do you know how many families Harmony House could help with that many apartments?"

"No, and I really hope you're not about to tell me."

"I promise not to bore you with the details, as long as you promise to keep writing those monthly contribution checks." Paul hesitated a moment, then said, earnestly, "But if you do decide someday that you want to hear the details, I can tell you about the families—"

"Thanks, I'll let you know."

Paul turned away and concentrated on piling the sandwiches onto a plate as an uncomfortable silence stretched between them.

"Sorry," Mark said. "I didn't mean to sound abrupt. But I'm not like you, you know. I'm not the type to follow in Mom and Dad's footsteps. I never felt the calling to join the family business and spread the Gospel."

"No, you're not like me. I was the brother who joined the family business because I believed it was what God wanted me to do with my life. You, on the other hand, are the brother God chose to bless with everything necessary to be successful in life: talent, charm, and good looks. You just chose a different measurement of success."

Paul set the plate of sandwiches and a big bag of chips on the table and sat down facing Mark. He flipped open his can of soda and raised it in a mock toast. "Here's to success with the Widow McAllister." He took a drink of his soda and picked up a sandwich. "So how do you plan to convince her to sell that building? Are you going to throw a lot of money at her or just rely on your incredible charm?"

"Why not a combination of both?" Mark asked.

"I hear she's pretty demanding."

"She hasn't come up against me yet. I don't think it's going to take too much effort to get her to sign on the dotted line. I'll take her to dinner once or twice and show up at her church one more time. I figure I'll have this deal wrapped up by the end of the week."

"Good luck, Slick. And no matter how it turns out— whether you end up buying the building or not—I hope someday I'll get the chance to meet the Widow McAllister. I want to congratulate her on accomplishing the one thing no one else has been able to do in over fifteen years."

Mark frowned. "What's that?"

"Getting *you* to go to church again."

5

He didn't call.

Minda found small comfort in the fact that she hadn't spent her entire Monday morning sitting around waiting for the phone to ring. She was a busy person. She had things to do and tasks to accomplish. Still, she was conscious of almost every minute that ticked by without a phone call from Mark Cartier.

In the middle of the afternoon she left the bookstore and went back to the house. She wanted to be there when Tracy got home from school. She wanted to see for herself if Mark was with her. She wanted to see if she could tell whether Mark and Tracy had been in touch with each other.

The thought of Mark pursuing her daughter angered her. She was also angry that he hadn't kept his word and called like he said he would. She should never have believed him. She should never have trusted him to keep his promise when every instinct had told her not to.

She was in the kitchen when Tracy got home. Tracy barreled through the front door as if she'd been shot out of a cannon.

"Did anybody call for me?"

Minda emerged from the kitchen with a roll of paper towels. "No calls, honey. How was school?" She stuffed the paper towels into a duffel bag that was lying open on the dining-room table beside a pile of other items she intended to take to work.

Tracy dumped her backpack on the floor beside the table. "It was okay. Did you check the voice mails?"

"Yes. No messages."

Tracy threw herself down onto one of the dining chairs. "Mom, I really need a cell phone."

"We've already talked about that."

"I'm the only seventeen-year-old on the entire *planet* who doesn't have a cell phone."

"I doubt that."

"All my friends have one."

"Your school doesn't allow students to have cell phones turned on during class. If you can't use your phone for the majority of the day, what's the point of having one?"

"I can use it during lunch and after school and on weekends."

"Using it between classes will distract you. After school and on weekends you have a house phone." Minda pointed toward the kitchen where a cordless phone handset sat on the countertop by the fridge for as long as Minda could remember. "Beside, I just don't have the money for another cell phone. It's all I can do to afford the one I have for work."

Tracy opened her mouth to respond, but quickly closed it again.

"Is there something else you want to talk about?"

Tracy's chin went up, as if she were preparing for a confrontation. "If he *did* call, would you tell me?"

Funny, Minda thought, *that we both know who "he" is without having to say his name.* "I'd tell you the truth. I'd tell you if he called. I wouldn't lie to you, Tracy." She packed the other items into the duffel bag. "Now it's my turn to ask a question. If he did call, would you tell *me*?"

Tracy's nose wrinkled. "You know, Mom, it's not like I want to keep secrets and stuff, but you make it hard for me to talk to you when I know you don't like him. You don't even try to hide it."

"That's not true. I don't dislike Mark. But I do dislike his judgment. He's not an appropriate person for you to think of in a romantic way. He's too old for you, and he has no business being around you. That's what I dislike. And if he does call you, I want to know about it."

"Well, he didn't. He didn't call. Are you happy now?"

"No, because I don't like seeing you disappointed."

Tracy looked down at the gleaming hardwood floor. Her whole body seemed to deflate. "He probably didn't call because he knows you hate him."

"I can't hate anyone who likes my pot roast as much as he did." She watched for a reaction but Tracy didn't smile or even lift her head. Minda didn't have to be a mind-reader to understand Tracy's disappointment. She didn't like to see her daughter hurt, especially by a man who had no business influencing her teen-aged emotions in the first place. "I have to get back to work. Why don't you come with me?"

"No, I'll stay here. I've really got a lot of homework so I probably should start on it right away."

And stay close to the phone in case it rings, Minda thought. "You can do your homework in my office," she suggested. "And after you're done, you can visit Miss Whimple and Brady and deliver their invitations to your birthday party. That would be a nice touch instead of mailing them."

"Okay, but can I do it later this week? I'm really not in the mood this afternoon. And I really have a lot of homework."

"Sure. Later," Minda said, brightly, even though her heart ached for Tracy. "I guess I'll head back to work. Call me if you need me. I'll be home late tonight because I have some work to do on one of the apartments, but I should be back by the time you get home from Bible study." She waited for a response.

Tracy frowned slightly as she stared off into space.

"There's leftover pot roast in the fridge. You can warm it up for dinner before you go to Bible study. Honey, did you hear me?"

"Yeah."

Minda picked up the duffel bag. "See you tonight."

―――――

Minda tried to keep busy at the bookstore that afternoon, all the while rehearsing in her mind the carefully-worded speech she intended to deliver to Mark. If he wasn't going to call her, she was certainly going to track him down. She wasn't quite sure how to do that, since she had no idea how to get in touch with him. Oh, he was sneaky, she thought, grimly. A sneaky man who broke promises and smiled too much.

Ellen Dailey disrupted her mental rehearsals several times. She peppered Minda with questions in between waiting on customers and stocking shelves. Finally, during a quiet moment when there were only a few customers in the store, she cornered Minda near a display table that bore a placard announcing "New Releases." Minda was pulling older books from the table and loading them on a cart so she could wheel them into the back room.

"Are you going to tell me about Mark or not?" Ellen demanded. "Quit stalling and spill."

"There's not much to tell. He spoke at Tracy's school on career day last Friday. Tracy met him during a question-and-answer session afterward and brought him home to meet me."

Ellen stared at her a moment. "That's it? You met that gorgeous hunk of man through your teenage daughter?"

"That's it. He stayed for dinner and I invited him to church."

"You did good," said Ellen, approvingly. "I'll bet he calls you today."

"I'm really hoping he does. In fact, I'm counting on it."

Ellen nodded with confidence. "He will. I saw how he looked at you and he's definitely interested. He'll call."

Minda looked at her, debating the wisdom of confiding in Ellen. She'd been Minda's best friend since childhood, and when Minda had married Ellen's brother, Dale, their bond had grown as sisters. She decided to take the plunge and said quickly, "Tracy has a crush on him."

Ellen took in a big whoosh of air. "No! Wow, that does complicate things, doesn't it?"

"A little. Actually, it complicates things a lot. I'm going to talk to Pastor Walker about it this afternoon."

"Are you going to keep dating him?"

"*Dating* him? Me? No!" Minda said, shocked. "I told you, Tracy has a crush on him. Mark is interested in Tracy."

"*What?*"

"You heard me. He wants to date Tracy."

Ellen frowned. "Are you nuts? I saw how Mark looked at you yesterday. I also noticed how he looked at Tracy. He treated her more like a little sister than a date."

Minda shook her head. "You don't understand. He

followed her home. He met Tracy at her high school and came home with her."

"That's a pretty progressive high school," Ellen muttered. "Maybe it's time you thought about home schooling."

"That's not funny. Tracy told me all about how they met. How he singled her out and was attracted to her as soon as he saw her. She's been eating and sleeping and walking and talking nothing but Mark Cartier ever since."

Ellen shook her head slightly. "I guess I was wrong about yesterday. I mean, I saw the two of you together and my instincts were practically screaming that it was you that Mark was . . ." She stopped, and shook her head again.

"Ellen, what am I going to do? If I forbid Tracy to see him, she might run away like she did last time. I couldn't bear to go through that again. I couldn't stand another year like last year."

"Hey, don't start thinking the worst yet," Ellen said, as she stretched a comforting arm around Minda's shoulders. "I know Tracy has put you through a lot, but she's a good girl. She's just going through that normal, teenage rebellion stuff."

"Dating a man twice her age is not normal teenage rebellion."

Ellen's eyes widened. "They're *dating*?"

"No, not yet. At least, I don't think so."

"Well, has she gone out with him or not?"

"No. Maybe. I mean, she could be with him right now, sneaking off to see him while I'm at work." The thought frightened her. "Ellen, what am I going to *do*?"

"For starters, you're going to rein in your imagination. I don't believe for a second that Tracy's sneaking around behind your back. Don't you know your own daughter better than that?"

"The problem is that I don't know what *he's* capable of. He acts like all he has to do is crook his little finger and everyone does exactly what he wants them to do. I mean, have you seen the way he smiles?"

"Yeah, his smile is dreamy."

"His smile is fake."

"We must not be talking about the same guy."

Minda frowned. "Why are you defending him?" she demanded, exasperated. "Why are you taking his side?"

"I didn't know it was a war."

"Of course it is. This Mark Cartier guy wants to date my teenage daughter," she said, slowly enunciating every word for emphasis.

"So you keep saying."

"Why else would he keep following her around?"

"I don't know. But I do know you shouldn't jump to conclusions. Have you talked to Mark yet to hear what he has to say for himself?"

"Not yet, but I made it very clear that I wanted to talk to him about Tracy in private. He said he'd call me but so far he hasn't. If he happens to call here at the store and you answer, be sure you don't let him hang up." Minda added the last of the books to the cart and started pushing it toward the back of the store.

Ellen smiled. "Oh, I'll keep him on the phone, all right. His voice is dreamy."

"His voice is fake," Minda said over her shoulder as she disappeared into the stock room.

By the time Minda left the store to keep her appointment with Pastor Walking, she was convinced that Mark's promises were just as insincere as his smile.

Why hadn't he called? And why was he deliberately trying to avoid her?

Maybe he had divined what she wanted to talk to him about. Maybe he wanted to delay their confrontation as long as possible. The thought only served to reinforce what every instinct told her: She had to get Mark Cartier out of her daughter's life as soon as possible.

When she arrived at the church manse, Pastor Walker was in the front yard, delicately raking fall leaves from his flower beds.

"Hello, Pastor."

He looked up and smiled. "Minda, I'm glad to see you."

"Can I help you do that, Pastor?"

"Oh, no. As a matter of fact, I'm using your visit as an excuse to take a break." He drew off his gardening gloves. "I do my best with my flower beds but I know they can never compete with yours. I often wish I had your green thumb, Minda. You've made a beautiful home for yourself and Tracy."

Minda followed Pastor to the front porch where a pitcher of cold lemonade and a tray of glasses were set out on the table. He motioned for her to take a seat on a comfortably-cushioned bench while he claimed his usual place on an old cedar rocker.

"So, Minda, tell me how you and Tracy are getting along," he invited as he poured out a glass of lemonade for her.

"To be totally honest, it's a little touch-and-go right now. Tracy keeps reminding me that she'll be eighteen in less than two weeks and then she can do whatever she wants."

Pastor laughed softly. "Teenager talk. You may not think so, but Tracy values your good opinion. She cares what you think. And she'll still care what you think in two weeks when she turns eighteen. Two weeks from now or twenty years from now, Tracy will always want your approval and will always try to please you."

"That's not what *she* says," Minda countered with a laugh that was more strained than light.

"So, what exactly does Tracy want to do when she turns eighteen?"

Minda took a deep, steadying breath. "Tracy has met a . . . a *man*. She's developed a crush on him and I think she's prepared to defy me in order to be with him."

Pastor Walker smiled kindly at her. "It's normal for one teenager to develop a hard and desperate crush on another. When kids reach their teens—"

"He's not a teenager," Minda interrupted. "That's the problem, Pastor. Tracy has a crush on Mark Cartier, the man you met yesterday at church."

He sat a little straighter in his chair. "Oh! Yes, I see. I imagine that does complicate things."

"There's more," Minda said, in a worried voice. "Mark doesn't want to talk to me about it. I practically begged him to call me today so I could talk to him but he hasn't. I feel like I've given him every opportunity to tell me he's romantically interested in Tracy and he won't even admit it."

Her words caught Pastor's attention and his eyes snapped to hers. "Interested in Tracy? Is *that* what you think?"

She nodded, unable to meet his gaze, fearful that if she saw any sign of sympathy in his expression she might burst into tears.

"I don't know what to do," she said. Her words came out in a tumble. "He's wrong for her. The whole idea is wrong. There's no reason a man in his thirties could possibly have for wanting to date a teenager. But if I forbid her to see him, I'm afraid she'll defy me and see him anyway. You know how difficult a time I had with Tracy last year. I don't want her to run away again. I don't want her to hate me again. I don't want . . ." Her voice failed as a wave of emotion welled up in her throat. From the corner of her eye she saw Pastor's hand come up to thoughtfully rub at his chin.

It took her a moment to get command of her emotions, but at last she said, "And the worst part is, that man seems to be—" She searched for the right word. "—*encouraging* her. The way Tracy explained it to me, Mark *wanted* her to invite him home to meet me. He *wanted* to stay for dinner. He was even eager to go to church with us yesterday. He does nothing to discourage Tracy or to make himself seem less attractive to her." She shook her head. "I just don't understand what he wants with her."

A long silence stretched between them. At last Pastor Walker said, "I have to admit you've surprised me, Minda. Tell me, what are the signs you've seen that tell you Mark is interested in Tracy?"

"Aside from the fact that he's suddenly insinuated himself into our home and lives?"

He smiled. "Yes, aside from that. Does he hold her hand? Or smile at her in a certain way?"

"Just because I haven't seen—I mean, no, he hasn't done those things. Not in front of me, anyway."

"Then how do you know he's romantically interested in Tracy?"

"Pastor Walker, what other reason would a thirty-two-year-old man have for going home with a teenaged girl? Besides, Tracy can do nothing but talk about him."

"That only proves Tracy has a crush on Mark. It doesn't prove Mark feels the same way about Tracy."

She frowned. "Then why did he show up at our house?"

"I don't know but there are a couple ways to find out. You can simply ask him or you can let him keep showing up and see what happens."

"No-o-o-o-o thanks!" Minda held up her hands in a

defensive motion. "Letting Tracy see more of Mark would be like waving a red cape at a bull. I don't want her to ever see him again. Besides, I'm not even sure Mark Cartier is his real name. I mean, *Mark Cartier*! The name sounds so fake. So romance hero!"

Pastor laughed softly. "But Minda, Cartier isn't that uncommon a last name. Just ask any number of ladies who wear diamonds. And I seem to recall reading about a man named Cartier who runs an organization here in town . . . it was a charity of some sort." His voice trailed away as he thoughtfully rubbed his chin again.

"But the man you read about wasn't *Mark* Cartier, was it?" she asked, just to be sure.

"No, but my point is that his name isn't necessarily a made-up name and it isn't that uncommon."

"Okay, you've convinced me that Mark Cartier's name may be real, but that doesn't mean I like him or trust him more than I did five minutes ago."

"What is it about him you distrust so much?"

"Other than what I've already mentioned?"

He nodded.

"Well, there's that smile of his. It's too bright, too perfect. It's as if he knows his smile will open doors and get him anything he wants."

"If you say so."

"I know I just sounded petty and judgmental and I'm sorry. But I'm truly worried about this man."

Pastor looked at her kindly. "Do you want my advice, Minda?"

"Of course!"

"Don't do anything."

"But, Pastor, Tracy is my daughter and she's too young to realize how foolish she's being."

"But it isn't foolish to her. If everything you've told me is true, Tracy is experiencing her first serious crush. Of course, it's an unsuitable crush, but she doesn't know it. Not yet. But she will."

"When?"

"Maybe tomorrow or maybe next week. It's hard to say. But I can say with assurance that Tracy's a lovely young woman with a good head on her shoulders, thanks to the fine job you've done raising her. She won't abandon her faith—or you—for a man."

"How can you be so sure?"

"Has she suggested not going to church on Sunday? Or skipping Bible study or choir practice?"

"No, I guess she hasn't."

"And she won't. Give her a chance to come around and work this out for herself. You don't have to give her a long chance—just a chance."

Minda looked doubtful. "What if he asks her on a date? What if they're meeting and hiding it from me?"

"Well, that's a different story. If that ever happens, you should take immediate action. But right now, I don't see that happening, do you?"

"No."

"My advice is to be watchful but let Tracy come to her senses on her own. In the meantime, will you trust me to talk to Tracy about this? She might open up to me again."

"Would you, please? You were so helpful last year when we were going through that terrible time. If Tracy won't communicate with me, I want Tracy to be able to confide in someone she trusts and I know she trusts you."

"Then give me a chance to talk to her. I think she'll open up to me again, just like she did before."

"Pastor, if you'll do that, I will be so grateful to you!"

"Consider it done. Tomorrow night after Bible study, I'll make a point of speaking with her."

Minda immediately felt a good deal of pent-up tension leave her body. "Thank you, Pastor."

"Shall we ask the Lord to watch over Tracy and to give us the wisdom to guide her through this situation?"

She nodded. She bowed her head and listened with an open heart as Pastor Walker prayed in his deep, soothing voice.

When they both said "Amen," he looked at her and smiled. "And now, Minda, it's your turn to give *me* some advice. I've got some cyclamen bulbs to plant in my garden, and I'm not certain where they should go. Any ideas?"

From Mark Cartier's perspective, strategy was everything. You had to have a plan in life. You had to know your competition and stay one step ahead of everyone else every moment of every day. That's what separated the winners from the losers, and Mark Cartier was no loser.

His strategy with Minda was simple: Let her stew a little. He knew she wanted to talk to him about something, and he was smart enough to know that she hadn't yet figured out why he had suddenly appeared in her life. What she wanted to talk about he couldn't guess, but he hoped by keeping his distance, she'd be a little more eager to see him.

As it turned out, there was just one problem: he was the one who was anxious to see *her*.

That wasn't part of his strategy. He was the one who was supposed to charm and coerce Minda into doing his will. Instead, he found himself wondering what it would feel like if she were to look at him just once without any trace of the mistrust he always saw in the depths of her hazel eyes.

Determinedly, he pushed that thought from his mind and

concentrated instead on formulating his next step. The sooner he started his campaign against Minda, the sooner he could accomplish his purpose and head back to New York where he belonged.

He remembered Tracy telling him that on Tuesday evening she had Bible study. Check.

With Tracy at Bible study, he could see Minda without her daughter interrupting them.

He also knew what time Minda's bookstore closed. Check.

He'd show up just before closing time and invite her to open up to him, to talk about whatever it was that was on her mind. Maybe he'd get the chance to show her what a great guy he was and get her to trust him a little.

Ten minutes before closing time, Mark stood outside Minda's bookstore in lower downtown Denver.

The McAllister Building wasn't actually located on the 16th Street Mall, but on a side street that still had plenty of foot traffic. More importantly, the McAllister Building was located in Denver's most desirable area. By day the area bustled with shoppers and trendy businesses. By night the area transformed into the city's hottest neighborhood of clubs and entertainment venues. To Mark's thinking, it was nothing short of a sacrilege that a hulking, out-dated eyesore like the McAllister Building should be allowed to take up a prime portion of Denver real estate for the meager profit margin it generated.

For several minutes he stood outside on the street, surveying the old, Federal-style building with its brick and marble façade that dated back to the turn of the 20th century. Marble surrounded the large, glass-paned windows of the first-floor bookstore and trimmed the sashes of the windows on the building's upper floors. He quickly categorized the building as nothing more than an antiquated white elephant, a blight on the city's landscape that deserved to be razed. Certainly the old building was not worth clinging to with any of the passion that Minda McAllister wasted on it.

Out of habit, his fingers checked to ensure the perfect Windsor knot of his necktie was centered, and the lapels of his expensive suit coat were laying flat. Then he crossed the street and pushed through the glass door of Minda's bookstore. An old-fashioned bell jingled above the doorframe. There were a few customers inside browsing the shelves. A woman behind the counter, who looked vaguely familiar to him, was ringing up a customer's purchase.

Mark wandered through the aisles of books, assessing the assets and liabilities of the place in a way that was second nature to him. He recognized that Minda's was no ordinary, out-of-the-box bookstore. It had high ceilings lit by abalone-shell light pendants that looked like they were original to the building. Tall windows on the front and side walls stretched almost from floor to ceiling, letting in plenty of natural light. The bookshelves were tall, too, and made of quality woods, then stained and polished to bring out the natural beauty of the wood grain that hinted they had been lovingly erected by a skilled carpenter decades before. Overstuffed reading chairs dotted many of the wide aisles, inviting customers to linger over their selections.

There was something homey about the place, yet elegant— the very same adjectives he recalled applying to Minda's home a few nights before.

"Hi, there! It's nice to see you again." The woman behind the counter interrupted his reverie.

Her voice was familiar enough to jar his memory loose a bit. "Hi. It's nice to see you again, too. We met at church, didn't we?"

Her eyes lit up. "That's right! My name's Ellen. Ellen

Dailey. I don't blame you for not remembering me. You met so many people all at once on Sunday, I bet our names are just a blur. I'm Minda's sister-in-law and my husband is the youth pastor and choir director." She cocked her head to one side. "Can I help you find something?"

"As a matter of fact, you can. I'm looking for Mrs. McAllister."

"Minda? She's upstairs."

"The store has a second floor?"

"No, I meant upstairs in the apartments. Go back out to the sidewalk and go in the first door you see on your left. That's the lobby and you can take the elevator up to the third floor. You'll find her in apartment 304."

"Thanks, Ellen." He flashed his best smile at her and started moving toward the door.

"You're welcome!" Ellen called after him. "I hope to see you again. Maybe at church. Maybe sooner!"

Mark gave her a final wave as he exited out onto the sidewalk. He followed her directions and went through the next door he came to. Immediately he felt as if he had stepped through a time warp and into the lobby of a 1930s hotel. The lobby was a large space with comfortably upholstered chairs and tables set in groupings throughout the room. Several elderly people were engaged in reading the newspaper, playing chess, and chatting amiably in small groups.

The place was certainly in need of some updating, but with its over-stuffed chairs and warm, dark wood tables, he could see Minda's hand in the comfortable, yet tasteful décor.

Mark's brows came together in disapproval. The whole place was something out of another era. It was certainly clean and serviceable and even a little homey; but it had none of the vibrancy or activity the lobby of a modern building would have.

The ancient elevator looked like it had been installed in the 1930s. It had an art-deco motif etched into the highly polished wood-paneled doors. An old-fashioned dial above the elevator door indicated the car was on the seventh floor.

Mark pushed the call button and waited expectantly. The dial commenced a slow, laggardly swing to the left—a sure indication that the elevator car was making an inch-by-inch descent toward the lobby.

He almost groaned. He could reach retirement age before the elevator made it to the lobby level. Making a muted sound of disgust, he opted instead for the stairwell, taking the steps two at a time.

He reached the third-floor landing, pulled open the door, and stepped into the hallway.

He had been expecting the upper floors to sport a utilitarian atmosphere, with bare walls and serviceable carpet on the floor. Instead, the hallway was actually very pleasant and brightly lit, with tastefully framed prints adorning the walls. Fresh flower arrangements in glass vases stood atop console tables tucked in niches that dotted the length of the hallway.

There was an overall feeling of hominess about the place and that, he knew, was a sign of trouble. It was indicator of how attached Minda was to the building. It was a sign that she thought of it as more than just a business and income stream. It was going to take a lot more effort than he had planned to get her to part with the property.

"Hello!"

The unexpected voice took Mark by surprise. He looked up and down the length of the hallway and saw no one at first. Then he realized that a boy's head was sticking out of one of the apartment doors. The boy was wearing a baseball cap that cast a shadow over his face, making it difficult for Mark to tell his age, but from the sound of his voice, the boy seemed pretty young.

"Hi," Mark replied, dismissively.

"Looking for any apartment in particular?"

Mark studied the numbers on the nearest doors and realized that apartment number 304 was at the other end of the hall, just past the door where the boy in the baseball cap was standing guard.

"Yes, but I think I can find it, thanks." He didn't exactly growl at the kid, but his tone didn't invite conversation.

The boy didn't flinch. "You're not thinking of living here, are you?"

Mark made a big show of looking at some of the books neatly stacked beside the flower arrangement on one of the hall tables, hoping the kid would stick his head back into his own apartment and close the door.

"No, I'm not going to live here."

The boy's blue eyes traveled appreciatively over Mark's charcoal grey suit, snow-white shirt and perfectly-knotted necktie. "I knew it. You're not the type."

Mark looked up. "Yeah? What types of people *do* live here, if you don't mind my asking?"

"Elderly people. People like my mom and me. People who can't afford to live anywhere else. Not famous people like you."

One of Mark's eyebrows went up. "What makes you think I'm famous?"

"Aren't you? You must be, 'cause you look really familiar to me even though I know we've never met before."

Mark was certain there was something wrong with the kid's logic but he wasn't in the mood to debate the point. "No, we've never met before and I have no intention of living here." Without trying, he added a contemptuous emphasis to the word *here* that he hadn't intended.

The boy nodded, as if he judged Mark's implied insult to be fair. "I'm not surprised. While this building is in a prime location that's close to both the Capital Hill district and the Denver commerce center, the address doesn't have the caché other buildings in the neighborhood have. The McAllister Building is a bit of a white elephant, commercially speaking, although the value of the land itself and its potential for development are substantial."

Mark stared at him a moment. The kid sounded like a real-estate listing. "How would a little kid like you know about commercial viability and land values?

The boy smiled. "I'm not as young as I look. And I read a lot. I've got the time."

When Mark was a boy, he was reading any comic book he could get his hands on, but this kid must be devouring business journals and financial publications.

"Wouldn't you rather spend your time reading something fun? Like a sports page or a video game magazine?"

As he spoke, Mark walked down the hall toward the boy and as he stood over him, he registered a small shock.

The boy had no eyebrows. No eyelashes. No hair peaking from beneath the ball cap. His complexion was pale, almost ashen, and there were dark circles around his eyes.

From a distance, Mark had judged him to be about ten or eleven years old but now, up close, he saw something in the boy's eyes—a knowing kind of worldliness that could only come from hard experience—that made him think the boy was older than he looked.

"I'm not that into sports," said the boy, "and I don't have a video game system."

"So how old are you, anyway?" Mark asked, carefully

maintaining a casual tone.

"Fourteen. You married?"

"No. Are you?"

"Heh. Good one. My name's Brady."

Mark stuck his hand out and clasped Brady's thin, small hand in a perfunctory shake.

"I'm Mark. And I'm actually on my way to see somebody, so if you'll excuse me?"

"Oh, sure. But if you want to talk again, I'm usually home," said Brady, cheerfully.

"Thanks. I'll keep that in mind. See you around."

Mark thrust his hands into his trouser pockets and set off down the hall. After a few steps, he succumbed to the impulse to look back over his shoulder to see if Brady was watching him.

He wasn't. And as Mark continued on his way, he heard the door to Brady's apartment softly close.

At the end of the hall, the door to apartment 304 was open. Mark stepped across the threshold to find the furniture pushed into the middle of the room and draped in canvas covers.

A short guy on a ladder was running a paint-spattering roller against the upper regions of the far wall.

The heavy canvas drop cloth muted the sound of Mark's shoes against the floor as he crossed the room to where the painter toiled away, clad in a painter's hat and coveralls that were easily three sizes too big.

Mark rapped on the wooden ladder with his knuckles. "Hey, guy, I'm looking for Mrs. McAllister. Any idea where I can find her?"

Startled, the painter on the ladder turned quickly and sent the rickety old ladder swaying.

"Hey, watch yourself!" Mark grabbed at the ladder just in

time to keep the ladder, the painter, and the paint tray from toppling to the floor.

"For pity sake, Mark, you almost scared me to death!"

Mark blinked and, for a split second, wondered if he was hallucinating. Beneath the painter's hat, Minda McAllister's lovely face peered down at him.

"*Minda?*"

She looked down at his confused expression and laughed. "Don't look so surprised. Don't women in New York ever paint?"

"Sure," he said, with a slight shake of his head. "Landscapes and watercolor flowers on canvas."

"Hmmm." She gave him a skeptical look. "Welcome to the real world, Mr. Cartier."

Assured that the ladder and its occupant were in no imminent danger, he let go and took a step back so he could survey the room. It wasn't overly large, but the ceilings were high and there were plenty of windows and doors, each surrounded by freshly painted, elaborate trim work. The walls were dingy and contrasted sharply against the fresh paint Minda was applying. On one wall he noticed a small section had been painted from floor to waist-level height in a hideous shade of green.

Painting the room was a big job … too big for a petite woman who stood barely to his shoulder in her Sunday high heels.

"You're not going to be able to reach up to where the walls meet the ceiling," he said, pessimistically. "Not with that creaky old ladder."

She looked down at him, unconcerned. "I'll figure something out."

"Can't you hire someone to do this?"

"No. The landlord's too cheap." She smiled down at him

before she turned back to her task.

He watched her a moment as she rolled the paint onto the wall around the window, content to enjoy the sight of her small frame clad in coveralls atop a ladder, working her head off.

From the moment he met her he'd thought she was pretty; and despite the fact she obviously considered him a highly suspicious character, he kind of enjoyed being with her. She seemed so determined.

"You were supposed to call," said Minda without missing a stroke of her roller. Her voice was even, without any trace of emotion to tell him whether she was disappointed or glad that she hadn't heard from him since Sunday.

"In person is better." His frown deepened. "Listen, why don't you wait to do this until tomorrow? I can make some calls and arrange for ladders—A small scaffold would be better—and I'll help you hire a couple of guys who do this sort of thing for a living."

Minda set the paint roller on the paint tray with deliberate care before she looked down at him. "I appreciate your concern, but I meant what I said before about the landlord being cheap. But the reason she's—*I'm* cheap is that there's no budget for professional painters. It's really no big deal, Mark. I do this kind of thing around here all the time. It's my building and these are my tenants and it's up to me to make certain they have comfortable and safe homes."

Mark could hardly trust he had heard her right. A landlord who felt responsible for her tenants? It was no wonder Minda McAllister was barely keeping her financial head above water. Good grief, did the woman believe in leprechauns, too?

"Why do you have to paint this apartment in the first place?" he asked. "Are your tenants so demanding?"

"The one who lives in this apartment is. She's an elderly lady named Adelaide Whimple and she's been bothering me to paint this place for months. See that spot over there?" She picked up her paint roller again and waived it in the general direction of the far side of the room, sending several drops of paint splaying dangerously close to Mark.

"You mean that patch of green color on the wall?"

"That's the one. When I told Miss Whimple a couple weeks ago I wasn't planning to paint her apartment, she decided to paint it herself."

"Why'd she pick such a horrible color?" His straight nose wrinkled with distaste.

"She didn't exactly pick that color, it just came out that way. You see, she didn't have any money for paint, so she went up and down the alleys in the neighborhood, rummaging through trash cans, finding different cans of paint. Some had small amounts of paint left in them and others had a bit more, but when you mix them together," she made a funny little stirring motion with her hand, "you get a lot of paint."

"Yeah, but that color!"

"She swears it didn't look that bad when she mixed it in the can. She tried to tell me the color looks so horrible because there's something wrong with the walls."

A lop-sided half-smile softened Mark's features. "She sounds like a real character."

"You haven't guessed the half of it. But the bottom line is, I don't blame her for wanting to live in a freshly-painted apartment. So, I moved her for tonight into a vacant unit down the hall while I get this room painted. I'm not leaving until it's finished."

He was quiet for a moment, comfortably standing with his hands in his pockets, surveying the room, silently judging, measuring, planning.

"If that's your bottom line," he said, at last, "I'll help."

Minda's hazel eyes widened. "*You?*"

"Why not? Don't you think I'm capable?"

"Not in those clothes." She eyed the expensive fabric of his suit as it molded over his broad shoulders and fell in razor-sharp creases down the front of his trousers. "You look more like the foreman type. Why don't you just sit over there and give orders while I do the real work?"

Her words sounded very much like a challenge. Mark Cartier never backed down from a challenge. He shrugged out of his suit jacket and hooked it over the doorknob.

She frowned. "What are you doing?"

He loosened his tie and collar and pulled his shirttails from the waistband of his trousers. "I'm getting into my painting outfit. Admittedly, it won't be as charming as yours but I always score effort higher than style, don't you?"

"You'll ruin your clothes," she said, discouragingly.

He finished undoing the line of buttons down the front of his shirt and pulled the fabric aside to reveal a white tee shirt beneath. "Then I'll take them off."

"You'll *what?*"

He popped his cufflinks into the shirt pocket and draped that over the doorknob, too, then he turned to survey the room. "What do you want me to do? Cut in or roll? I should warn you, I'm pretty good around trim but I'm a wizard with a roller."

She shook her head. "Mark, there's really no need for you to help."

"No? Then let me see you reach the top of that wall at the ceiling line." He saw her hesitate and knew he had made his point. He picked up a paint brush and held his other hand out to her meaningfully. "Face it. You need someone with some height on your crew. I'll handle the high parts and you can handle the low. Deal?"

Minda stared down at the hand Mark held out to her. After some thought, she put her hand in his and his warm fingers closed over hers.

"Deal."

Mark didn't let got of her hand until he had gently drawn her down off the ladder.

"It's been a long time since I've done this," he said, as he climbed up a couple of ladder rungs and dipped his brush into the paint tray, "but I'm sure it'll all come back to me. Try to keep up, okay?"

He flashed that dazzling smile of his and this time—for the first time—Minda didn't respond with a look of wary resentment. He took that as a promising sign and decided not to push her. He stretched up to brush a straight line of paint along the ceiling line as if he did that sort of thing on a daily basis. After a few minutes, he realized he hadn't heard the sound of the paint roller slapping against the paint tray. Carefully, so he wouldn't overturn the rickety old ladder, he turned his head and caught her staring at him.

"Are you going to paint or not?" he demanded, looking down at her.

The challenge in his voice brought her to her senses. Minda's face reddened as she picked up the roller and deliberately moved to the other side of the room.

"I *am* painting. And you missed a spot."

He laughed softly and turned back toward the wall.

They worked quietly for a few minutes, before he said, casually, "I met one of your neighbors."

She looked up. "Which one?"

"The kid down the hall."

"Brady?"

"He cornered me when I got off the elevator."

"He was probably watching for his mother. She sometimes sneaks away from her job to run home and check on him. Did he talk your ear off?"

"He seemed to be headed in that direction but I didn't give him much of a chance." He was quiet for a moment then asked, "He's sick, isn't he?"

"Yes, he is," she said, cautiously, "but I'll leave it to Brady or his mother to give you the particulars."

"He seems like a smart kid. Why isn't he in school?"

"Some days he can't go to school. Some days he has a hard time just walking from his bed to the sofa."

Mark stopped painting and looked down at her. "Then why isn't he in a hospital?"

"He does go to the hospital regularly for treatments. That's why he and his mother are living here. The children's hospital is close by and the rent here is affordable for them. Brady's mother waitresses at a little restaurant down the street. It was the only job she could find that would let her take time off to take Brady to his medical appointments or let her be with him when he couldn't be left alone. She does her best but they're barely making it on what she earns."

There was something in the way Minda suddenly drew her eyes away to concentrate on her painting that made him suspicious.

"So *you* help them out."

"Sometimes. Everybody needs help once in a while."

"And to you, helping is letting Brady's mother slide a little on the rent."

When she didn't reply, he decided to press her. "How often? Every couple of months?"

When she didn't even look up, he knew the answer. "*Every* month?"

"You've met Brady and now you know what his situation is," she said, sounding defensive. "What would you do, if you were me?"

"For starters, I would never let anybody think its okay not to pay you."

"Sometimes they can't pay."

"Doesn't matter. What people pay for, they value."

"Do you truly believe that?"

"When people get something for free, they take it for granted."

"Brady and his mother are not living here for free."

"But they're not paying full rent, either. Don't you ever worry about your bottom line?"

"I worry more about what will happen to Brady and his mother. One day, Brady's name is going to come up on the list and he'll have only hours to get on a plane and travel to the medical center that will do his surgery and hopefully save his life. What will they do then? In a strange city Brady's mother may not be able to afford an apartment or hotel room near the hospital. What's going to happen to them?"

"There are people who can help them."

"Like who?" she demanded.

"Like ... organizations. There are plenty of charitable groups that do nothing but help families with sick kids."

"Does it have to be an organization? A *charity*? Can't just a regular person help them, too?"

"Of course a regular person can help, but not if you're giving away money you don't have to give in the first place."

"If I had to wait to help until I could afford it, I'd never be able to help Brady or any of the other people who live in the building. That's my ministry, Mark; to provide a comfortable home and a sense of belonging for people who can't really afford to live anywhere else."

"There are other ways of accomplishing the same purpose. Have you ever heard of an organization called Harmony House? They do the same thing. They provide homes to people who can't afford a place to live through no fault of their own."

"Yes, I've heard of Harmony House," she said with a frown. "I think they have an office here in Denver. But they're just another big charity."

"Big charities aren't necessarily bad," he said, reasonably. "Big charities are able to pool resources and garner sponsors on a large scale. That way they can help many people at once."

She looked doubtful. "Sure, but I don't want to help a lot of people. I just want to make a difference in the lives of people who live in my building. Big charities are so impersonal. Their donors don't ever have to get involved. They just write their checks and go on about their lives, never seeing the people their money helps, never really having to get their hands dirty. Can you imagine seeing one of Harmony House's top contributors painting an apartment, like we're doing now?"

After a moment or two, Minda looked up at Mark, wondering over his sudden silence.

He was staring down at her from the top of the ladder, a frown lining his forehead and his blue eyes hard enough to bore right through her.

"Did I say something wrong?"

"No, you didn't." He smacked the paint brush in the tray a few times to coat it with paint and when he looked at her again, that hard look was gone and he had command of himself once more. He flashed his usual smile. "I think we're almost done here, don't you?"

Minda looked around the room and nodded. "That was

quick work. If it hadn't been for you, I'd still be working on the first wall. You're practically a pro. Where'd you learn to paint?"

"Painting houses was one of the jobs that helped me pay my way through college."

"*You* worked your way through college?" she asked, surprised.

"Sure. Almost everyone does, to some extent. What about you? When you were in college, didn't you have to supplement your student loans with a job?"

"I didn't go to college. I had a baby to raise."

"Tracy."

"Yes, Tracy." She looked at him expectantly, waiting for him to say something else.

He climbed down from the ladder and nodded as his blue eyes surveyed the room. "Yup, I'd say we're done." He sounded satisfied.

"Tracy will be going to college herself next year. *After* she turns eighteen."

"I hope she enjoys the experience." He held up his paint brush. "What do you want me to do with this?"

Minda frowned slightly and her hazel eyes searched his face. She couldn't detect even a glimpse of interest in his expression.

She shook her head slightly as she went to the duffle bag she'd left in the kitchenette. She pulled out a plastic bag with a zipper closing, opened the bag and held it out to him. "Put your paint brush in this."

He followed her instruction but couldn't help asking, "Why?"

"It keeps the paint from drying on the brush until I use it again."

"Why not just clean the brush? Or, better yet, why not

throw it out and use a new one tomorrow?"

"The landlord's cheap, remember?"

"Ah," he said, with a new understanding. "You're economizing."

"Just being practical."

Minda went into the bedroom, giving Mark the chance to put his dress shirt on and tuck it neatly into the waistband of his trousers. He was rolling up his shirt sleeves when she came back into the room. She had slipped off the painter's coveralls and was wearing a pullover sweater and jeans and toting a big purse that looked like it weighed more than she did.

In the hallway she pulled an oversized key ring from her bag and fitted a key into the lock on the apartment door. "I'm going to stop down the hall to see Miss Whimple and give her a quick progress report. I know she's anxious to get back into her apartment but I want to make sure she stays away from the fresh paint tonight."

"I'll come along, if you don't mind."

She hesitated. "It's not that I mind, but I should warn you that Addy Whimple is . . . Well, she can be a little crusty sometimes."

"I promise to be on my best behavior."

She didn't try to change his mind. She led the way down the hall to the apartment the elderly woman was temporarily occupying.

Minda knocked on the door and opened it when a frail, thin voice ordered, "Come in."

Mark followed Minda into the main living room of the apartment. As soon as he stepped across the threshold, his gaze swept quickly around the room. From practice, he took in every detail, assessing in mere seconds the market value of the apartment and the sum total of Adelaide Whimple's life.

He saw a wheelchair in a corner and a cane close by the tall wing-backed chair in which the elderly lady was seated.

In the oversized chair, Miss Whimple looked small and frail. She was wearing a heavy sweater despite the relative warmth of the room and her legs were covered with a knitted throw. On a table beside her chair rested a leather-bound Bible that was gently but visibly worn.

As soon as Minda and Mark entered the room, Miss Whimple snapped, "There you are! Have you finished? Is my place ready yet?"

"Almost," said Minda. "We're done painting for the night, but there's still a little bit left to do in the morning. The furniture is still in the middle of the room and there's a little bit of a smell of fresh paint. You'll have to promise me you'll stay away from that apartment until I have a chance to put it all back together and it's safe for you to move back in."

Miss Whimple looked at her with disgust. "I'm past ninety years old, young lady. If I can make it this far through depression, war, and famine, I sure as shootin' won't be done in by a little paint smell. There's not much that can affect me!"

"Still, you can't go back to your apartment until I give the all-clear tomorrow morning," Minda said, patiently.

"I could be dead by then. If I am, no one will care. You might as well just stand me out at the curb next to the dumpster."

"Will do," Minda said, in a way that led Mark to believe that this was a conversation the two women had had before.

Miss Whimple caught him smiling at the thought. "Who are you?" she demanded.

"I'm Mark Cartier, ma'am. I hope you don't mind my coming along with Mrs. McAllister to say good-night to you."

"Mind?" She looked him up and down. "I don't suppose I

mind when a handsome man calls on me. Although you'd look better if you were wearing a tie."

"I was wearing one earlier," he said, shaking her hand with deliberate care for her fragile fingers, "but Mrs. McAllister made me take it off."

Minda's head came up with a snap. She hadn't made Mark take his tie off at all, but she sure had noticed when he did. Mostly because he'd also taken off his suit coat and dress shirt. In his white cotton tee shirt, his shoulder and arm muscles had pulsed each time he'd dragged the paint brush against the wall. She'd been mesmerized by the sight and had blushed when he'd caught her staring.

Against her will, the blushes came again. She tried to mask them by saying, quickly, "He volunteered to help. He was painting the apartment, that's all. He took off his shirt and tie so he could paint. Not that he didn't have a shirt on—He did, but it was his tee-shirt, not his dress shirt." Heaven help her, she was starting to babble.

Miss Whimple snorted inelegantly. "In my day a young man never called on a lady without a tie. And a hat, mind you! In my day a gentleman always wore a tie and a hat, *which* he removed when a lady was present, although you'd be hard-pressed to even find a store that sells such things, now-a-days."

Minda recognized the signs that Miss Whimple was about to launch into a full catalog of all the ills of the modern world. She decided that distraction was the best course of action.

"Miss Whimple, why don't I get the things you're going to need from your apartment for the night? I'll get your toothbrush and your bathrobe and nightgown. Is there anything else you need?"

"I need to move back into my apartment down the hall,

that's what I need." For emphasis she brought her palm down on the arm of her chair with a frail slap.

"But I've already explained that you can't sleep in there tonight. Besides, there's nothing wrong with this apartment and you should be very comfortable here for just one night. Now, what can I bring you from down the hall?"

"I don't need much," Miss Whimple said, in a martyred tone; then she rattled off a list of things that Minda was sure she couldn't possibly need or use in a week, much less a single night.

"Addy, I'm not bringing all those things. You're only staying here one night. Now, tell me the things you really need and I'll bring them to you."

Impatiently, Addy Whimple flicked the blanket off of her lap with enough force to send it flying across the top of the table beside her. "Just bring my toothbrush," she said, sullenly. "And my nightgown and slippers. And my Bible. I can't stay the night here if I don't have my Bible. Don't come back without it, because I refuse to sleep anywhere without my Bible."

"Then I'll bring it to you," Minda said. "Mark, if you don't mind staying here a minute or two, I'll run back down the hall to gather her things."

"I don't mind at all," he said, politely, "if Miss Whimple doesn't."

"You might as well sit down," Miss Whimple said, as soon as Minda left the apartment. She waved her thin fingers toward a small sofa on the other side of the room, but Mark pulled a chair from the dinette set and drew it close beside her.

"Tell me, Miss Whimple," he said as he settled onto the chair, "do you like living here?"

She threw an acid look at him. "Don't think you need to

make small talk with me, young man, because you'd be wasting your breath. I don't like small talk. Never have."

"Actually, I wasn't making small talk at all. To tell you the truth, I'm pretty interested in this building."

"Ha! In this building's *owner*, you mean."

He smiled slightly. "What makes you say that?"

"I've got eyes, haven't I? And I saw her blush just a minute ago. She's not the type to blush easily. She's a tough little thing—always working and her hands have been full lately with that daughter of hers." She eyed him shrewdly for a moment and noticed he didn't flinch under her sharp gaze, as so many others did. "She won't go out with you, you know. Hasn't been out on a date even once since her husband died."

"She'll go out with me. In fact, I plan to take her to dinner as soon as we've said good-night to you."

"Mighty sure of yourself!" she retorted, impressed. "Tell me, do you always get what you want?"

"So far, I have."

"That I can believe. No doubt that smile of yours has something to do with it, too."

"Why do you think Minda McAllister doesn't go out on dates?"

"Who knows? Maybe she doesn't think she should. Maybe she's afraid her daughter won't like it. All I know is, she'd rather work in that store downstairs or cover herself in dirt from her garden than go out on a date with a man. I don't think its right. Never have. And I've told her so until I was blue in the face, but she won't listen to me." Addy Whimple made that snorting sound again, this time with disgust.

Mark nodded solemnly, as if he were in agreement with every word she said. "And her husband? He's been gone a long time, I believe."

"Too long for her to still be mourning him. Although,

confidentially, I don't think she does. Mourn him, I mean. I think she clings to his memory because it's too scary to let go. Not that she's one of those women who fall apart at the drop of a hat. Not her!"

He nodded once again, taking his time with her, leading her gently. "How, exactly, did her husband die? What killed him?"

She leaned forward until her face was inches from his. She said in a low voice of great secrecy, "Marshmallows."

Mark looked searchingly into her eyes, forcing himself to keep a straight face and not let on that her answer made no sense. Perhaps Miss Whimple—who had already confessed to ninety-plus years—was having a senior moment, a momentary lapse of sanity that was understandable in a woman of her age.

"I see."

Without warning, her thin, claw-like fingers clamped around his wrist with surprising strength and her pale grey eyes bored into his.

"Don't hurt her," she commanded.

"I won't. You have my word."

She let go of his arm and leaned back in her chair, but her gaze was unrelenting. "That's a promise you'd better keep if you plan to visit me again. I don't care to associate with people who resort to tricks and chicanery."

"I know, ma'am. You're the kind of person who would never deceive anyone to get what you want." As he spoke, Mark lifted a corner of the blanket where she had thrown it over the table and drew her Bible from its hiding place. "How much longer should we let Minda search for your Bible in the apartment down the hall before we tell her it was here all the time?"

She snatched the Bible from his hands. "*You* didn't want

her to return right away any more than I did!"

He smiled. "You're right. But if she comes back before we finish our conversation, we'll just continue it another time."

"Are you telling me you plan to come back?"

"Certainly."

"And why, exactly, would you do that?"

"For starters, I have an interest in knowing whether your newly-painted apartment meets your standards."

"Hmph!"

"And I could use your advice."

"I already told you: she won't go out on a date with you. But if she won't, I will."

His smile grew. "I intend to hold you to that, ma'am."

The apartment door opened and Minda came in carrying a grocery bag filled with items from the other apartment. "I'm sorry, Addy. I looked everywhere but I couldn't find—"

"My Bible?" Addy Whimple thumped her finger against the Bible in her lap. "Sorry to send you on a goose-chase, deary, but I had it with me all the time. Mr. Cartier discovered it."

Minda eyed them both with suspicion. They were sitting so close together and exchanging such secretive looks, she half suspected they were somehow in cahoots.

Later, after they said their good-nights to Miss Whimple and she and Mark were waiting for the elevator to take them down to the lobby, Minda asked, "How did you know where to find her Bible?"

"I saw her cover it up with her blanket when we first arrived."

Minda gave a little gasp. "Why would she do such a thing?"

"Maybe she just wanted a chance to talk to me. She probably doesn't meet new people very often and she saw me as a fresh audience."

"A fresh audience? What, exactly, did the two of you talk about while I was gone?"

"You mean, when she wasn't snapping my head off or complaining about the ills of the modern world?"

Minda laughed. "Yes, other than that!"

"Well, I'd be happy to tell you all about our conversation. Over dinner."

As soon as the words left his lips, Minda's expression altered. The remnants of her light laughter quickly faded and that wary, distrustful look clouded her hazel eyes.

"I don't think I can. You see, Tracy will be home and I really don't like to leave her alone in the evenings—"

"Tracy's at Bible study."

That stopped her cold. "You remembered?"

"Yes." He waited, patiently giving her time to think about his offer. He could see the reluctance in her eyes and realized—with a good deal of satisfaction—that Minda's face was too open and expressive for her to ever be any good at telling lies. He cataloged that bit of information in his memory and said, gently, "You'll be home before Tracy gets there. I promise."

She didn't even try to hide the fact that she was thinking about it. He wasn't sure if his pride should be hurt or not. If he were in New York, he'd have his choice of several beautiful women to invite to dinner. Any of those ladies would have immediately accepted his invitation and the world would have known that he was somebody simply by walking down the street with one of those beautiful women on his arm. Yet the petite widow with the hazel eyes was still trying to decide whether or not to have dinner with him. The irony of it all made him smile.

At last she said, "All right. Dinner would be nice."

He pulled a cell phone from the inside pocket of his suit coat. "Good. I'll call the Palms and make a reservation."

"Oh, I can't go anywhere that requires a reservation." She looked down at her jeans and sneakers. "Couldn't we just go somewhere simple?"

"Do you have a place in mind?"

"If you don't mind Italian, there's a great pizza and pasta place on Broadway."

"I don't mind Italian at all," he said, at just about the same time he realized that pizza and pasta with Minda sounded ten times better than any dinner he could have at the Palms.

7

Mark opened the car door for Minda and she slid into the passenger seat. The sun had set. The street lamps were lit and cast enough soft light on the interior of the car for Minda to see Mark's profile as he started the engine.

"Which way to the restaurant?" He stretched his arm out along the back of her seat and backed the car out of its parking place.

His sudden nearness took her by surprise. Mark's luxury rental car suddenly seemed like a very small and intimate space. He was close enough that she could smell the light fragrance of his aftershave long after he swiveled forward in his seat to steer the car out of the parking lot and onto the street. It had been a long time since she'd reacted so strongly to a man's nearness and she was a little startled by the way her nerves suddenly fluttered.

She pulled herself together and calmly gave him directions to the Italian restaurant.

"So this place we're going is good, right?" he asked.

"The best pizzas and calzones in town."

"Good. I like Italian. In fact, I was wondering if we should have invited Miss Whimple to join us."

She looked over at him, surprised. "Really?"

"Why not? She tries to come across as all bluster and crust, but I have a feeling she has a good heart."

"You're right. She doesn't like to show it, but she's been a very loving and caring friend to me."

"Does she have any family?"

"No. She never married and unfortunately, she doesn't have any family left."

"What else do you know about her?"

"Well, she's deeply religious, but she refuses to go to church—despite my many invitations. She always keeps her Bible at her side, but she won't let people get close at all. I know she was a schoolteacher in her younger years, but she doesn't like to talk about her life or her past." She looked over at Mark. "I have to say, she certainly seemed to like you."

"And I liked her. She reminded me a little bit of my own grandmother. You'll never guess what she said about you while you were in the other apartment."

"I can't wait to hear," Minda said, with mock dread. "Tell me."

"We were talking about you and she mentioned your husband. She said he died from marshmallows." Mark laughed slightly and shook his head at the memory.

Several seconds passed before he realized that Minda hadn't laughed with him. He threw a quick glance her direction.

She was sitting rigidly beside him, her lips pursed together, her eyes fixed straight ahead.

"Minda?"

She didn't answer.

A red stop light gave him the chance to take his eyes off the road and take a good long look at her. "Minda, are you all right?"

"Yes, I'm fine. You just surprised me, that's all. It's nothing."

She didn't say anything more and after another few seconds of silence, he took a deep breath. "I could kick myself," he said, as he pulled the car into the restaurant parking lot. "I guess what I said just now was pretty insensitive—"

"That's not it."

"—because you never can tell how long someone will grieve over the loss of a loved one—"

"Mark, it's really okay."

"—and just because your husband's been gone now for seventeen years doesn't mean—"

"How do you know how long ago my husband died?" Her eyes locked on his face.

He maneuvered the car into a parking space and turned the engine off. What could he say? He couldn't very well tell her that back in New York he had a file on her as thick as *War and Peace*. He couldn't tell her that he knew all about her husband and her daughter and her business, and what information he didn't have before, he was now quickly gathering. He knew her credit card debt. He knew the nine-year-old car she drove had an "I miss John Denver" bumper sticker on the back window. He knew the store she frequented most often was the local home improvement warehouse. The file probably contained her shoe size, for pity's sake.

He knew all those things about her because it was his business to gather those kinds of details. It was part of his strategy: Know your enemy, find their weakness, then hit that weakness again and again until you get what you want.

The only problem was, Mark Cartier was the one who was developing a weakness. A weakness for a pair of wide hazel eyes with flecks of green and gold. He was looking into those eyes now and wishing the parking lot weren't quite so dark so he could read her expression.

He said, evasively, "Miss Whimple must have mentioned it. Listen, I'm sorry. I didn't mean to touch a wound and I didn't mean to pry."

"You didn't pry," Minda answered. Her voice was calm and soft. "My husband died in a car accident. It was late at night and the middle of winter. The roads were icy, a drunk driver ran a red light . . . It's the usual story."

"Except this time, the story is about you."

"Except this time, I'm the reason he was in the car in the first place. I was making hot cocoa at home and we were out of marshmallows and Dale—that's my husband—Dale decided to go to the store. I didn't want him to go but he insisted. Tracy was just a baby then and I had a bad case of new-mother exhaustion and I wanted the hot cocoa to help me sleep. I could have had the cocoa without marshmallows but he was so good to me. He was so loving and giving. He was a wonderful man. He put on his coat and went to the store to get marshmallows just so I'd be happy. I never saw him again."

She could feel her throat swell with emotion just as it had countless times since Dale died. Over the years she had learned some little tricks to tamp that emotion back down: blink several times, look up to the ceiling, swallow hard, take a deep breath. It was a regimen she employed over and over and it always worked. It worked this time, too.

"So you see, Addy Whimple was right, in a way. About the marshmallows, I mean."

In the dimly-lit car, the silenced stretched between them. Mark Cartier—the man who liked to think he could sell ice to polar bears—suddenly found himself unsure what to say next.

Finally, he said the only thing he could think of. "I'm sorry."

"About what?"

"About your husband. About dredging up painful memories. And about doubting Miss Whimple's sanity."

"Don't be. Sometimes it's easy to underestimate people when we meet them for the first time. That's not a crime." Minda unlatched her seatbelt. "The real crime is that we're sitting out here in a parking lot when we could be inside that restaurant eating the best Italian food in Denver. Let's go."

<hr />

Minda looked across the table at Mark and knew the time had come. Their waiter had already filled their water glasses and taken their dinner orders, so she knew they wouldn't be interrupted again for several minutes.

The only reason she'd accepted Mark's invitation to dinner was so she could talk to him about Tracy. In her heart she knew it was the right time to say what was on her mind. In her head she heard Pastor Walker's voice cautioning her to go slowly so Pastor would have a chance to meet with Tracy and talk to her about the choices she was making. Normally, Minda would follow Pastor's advice to the letter, but sitting across from Mark, feeling his soft, appraising gaze upon her, she felt a window of opportunity open that was too good to pass up.

She watched him spread his dinner napkin across his lap and take a sip from his water glass. For the first time, she allowed herself to accept the fact that he was a handsome man. Of course, that didn't matter to Minda. She was still going to interrogate him. She was still going to demand honest answers from him. But this time, when he looked at her and smiled slightly, she wasn't put off. Instead, she found herself thinking back to the way he looked on top of the ladder. She'd seen the muscles of his shoulders and arms flex beneath the snowy white cotton of his tee shirt and her breath had caught and held. Even now the thought of his well-developed biceps was enough to send a feeling of warmth to her cheeks. Just as it had earlier in Addy Whimple's apartment.

She saw his brows go up and knew she'd been staring too long, so she blurted out the first thing that came to her mind.

"Do you always wear a suit?"

"Most of the time. It's kind of my uniform. It's what I wear to work."

"But you're not working now. Are you?"

"No. That's why I'm not wearing a tie."

"So, this is your idea of casual clothes?"

He shrugged slightly. "I like wearing suits. I like the feeling of confidence they give me. And they show the world that I mean business."

"And you're here in Denver just for business reasons, right?"

"That's right."

"When will your business be finished?"

"I can't say yet."

"But you'll be leaving Denver as soon as it's concluded, right? I mean, you don't really have any other reasons to stay in town, do you?"

"None, except that I seem to be the newest member of the church baseball team. But I haven't decided yet whether I'll play." One of his dark brows went up. "You seem anxious for me to leave."

"I apologize. I don't mean that at all. I'm just a little curious about your plans." She decided to dive right in. "I want to talk to you about Tracy."

"All right."

"I don't have to tell you that she's very young. She's going to be eighteen in two weeks and she thinks that somehow makes her an adult, ready to tackle life-changing decisions."

"She sounds like a normal teenager."

"But she's still very young," Minda persisted. "She doesn't know about the world and she doesn't have the skills yet to figure out who she should and should not have in her life."

He nodded but he didn't act all that interested. He just looked at her, politely waiting for her to get to the point. She pressed on.

"Tracy is very rebellious right now. She's emotional and vulnerable and she isn't in a position to make decisions of any real substance. As her mother, it's my job to ensure she doesn't get hurt and no one takes advantage of her."

"I take it you think Tracy is in need of some special . . . care right now." He chose his words carefully. "Do you want to talk about it?"

She nodded, playing for time while she figured out what she should say next. Silently, she thanked God the man was still listening to her. She thanked God he wasn't being defensive or arguing his case or declaring his feelings for Tracy. At least he was listening.

"I think you'd agree, Mark, there are some big differences between you and Tracy."

His brows went up. "Minda, I don't have enough fingers and toes to count all the differences between Tracy and me. The fact is, we don't have anything in common at all."

"Exactly! That's because you're different. In fact, you're

really quite different from anyone I—I mean, *we* have ever known. You're so . . ." She struggled to find the right word, deeply aware that he was watching her expectantly. "You're so . . . *rich*."

His blue eyes widened. "Rich?" he repeated, unsure he'd heard her right.

"I'm not just talking about monetary riches, although that's a big part of it. Your expensive rental car, your condo in New York, your pricey suits that I'm sure cost more than my monthly take-home pay—"

Mark held up his hand to stop her mid-sentence. He smiled politely across the table at her. "I can't believe I'm about to defend my wardrobe choices, but here goes: In my line of work, appearance is everything. I have an image to maintain and, frankly, the car and the condo and the suits all contribute to that image. I work hard and I'm successful. I won't apologize for it."

"I'm not asking you to. I'm just saying that the car and the clothes and the lifestyle can be very dazzling to a teenager. "

"So I have money," he said, with a shrug of his shoulders. "I like money. I like what it does for me and the doors it opens. There's nothing wrong with that. I've been without money before, so I know that life is a lot sweeter and a whole lot easier when you've got it."

"There are some things that are more important than money."

"Only in books and fairy tales. In the real world, money is respect and freedom and power."

"Do you honestly believe that?"

"Sure. And you would, too, if you'd never had money before but had it now."

"Is that what happened to you?

He pursed his lips together in a way that told her she'd

touched on a nerve.

"Sort of," he said, dismissively.

"So you have money now. You're able to buy expensive suits and live in an expensive condo in New York."

"I also work very hard for the things I have. I just happen to have a talent for business."

"You have a talent for singing, too. I heard you in church on Sunday. You have a wonderful voice." She watched his blue eyes widen again. "Sorry. I didn't mean to embarrass you."

"You didn't. You surprised me, that's all. No one has ever said that before."

"Really? I'd expect people would compliment your singing all the time."

He hesitated. "Well, actually—"

"You mean people don't compliment you?"

"Not about—"

"Unless no one hears you sing. Is that it?"

"It's been a while—"

"A while since you last sang? Or a while since you've been in church?"

Mark's dark brows went up. "Is this interrogation going to last much longer? And am I going to need a lawyer?"

She laughed. "Sorry. I didn't mean to grill you like that but you have to admit, you're something of a suspicious character."

"Me? In what way?"

"You're not what you seem."

"I assure you, what you see is who I am."

"No, you're not. You're a complete enigma. Otherwise you wouldn't have surprised me so much on Sunday."

"I surprised you on Sunday? By singing?"

"By showing up. To be completely honest, I thought you'd

conveniently forget your promise to go to church with us."

"To be completely honest, I almost did."

He smiled. Not that polished smile that she thought was such a turn-off, but an odd half-smile that raised one side of his lips higher than the other. A smile she recognized as genuine.

"Want more honesty?" she asked. "Once you did show up and the church service began, you surprised me even more."

"How so?"

"I assumed you'd be a non-believer in unfamiliar territory. I thought you'd be out of your element and uncomfortable in church. But then you started to sing and it was clear you knew the first hymn by heart, as well as all the other hymns we sang during the service. And you knew the scripture reading from the Bible by heart, too."

She looked at him a long moment, waiting for him to say something that would give her some insight into his background and upbringing—anything that would give her a glimpse into the kind of man Mark Cartier really was.

He didn't say anything, but that didn't deter her. Just because Mark chose to remain silent, didn't mean she was going to let him off the hook.

"How did you know those hymns and scriptures, Mark?"

"Exactly how you'd expect. From attending church regularly."

"Were you raised in a Christian family?"

"Yes."

"What kind of a Christian family?"

Mark raised an eyebrow. "How many kinds are there?"

"You know what I mean. Tell me about yourself."

"I'd rather talk about you."

"Later. You first."

He took a long, deliberate sip from his water glass, buying

time. "There's not much to tell."

"Parents?"

"I have a mother and a father."

"Both living?"

"Yes."

"Any siblings?"

"One."

"Brother or sister?"

"Brother."

Was it Minda's imagination, or did Mark's answers get shorter with every question? She had no idea why he was so reluctant to talk about himself or why he'd want to deflect attention away from the truths of his life, but she was determined to find out about him.

"You said you attended church regularly when you were younger?"

"Religiously." That crooked smile touched his lips. "So to speak."

"Because you wanted to?"

"Because my parents expected me to. Especially my father."

"Was your father a minister?"

"Just a good Christian man."

"Were your parents rich?"

"No. As a matter of fact, my parents trusted the Lord to provide everything, from food to shelter."

Minda leaned back against the padded booth and studied him for a long moment. "I have to say, you've surprised me again. I would have pegged you for the old-money New York Brahmin sort."

He flashed that crooked little half-smile again. "Why is that?"

"Because you project an image of being worldly and

elegant."

"Are you suggesting good Christians can't be elegant?"

She shrugged her shoulders. "I guess I never thought about it before. But you're living proof that it's possible."

He raised his water glass. "On behalf of all the other elegant Christians in the world, I thank you."

She laughed and clinked her water glass against his.

"Are we celebrating?" asked the waiter as he placed a plate of three-cheese lasagna in front of Minda and a plate of veal parmigiana before Mark. "Is it your anniversary? Or birthday?"

"No, we're not celebrating anything special," Mark said.

"Then maybe you should just celebrate the fact you make a great-looking couple. You seem really happy together."

The waiter moved on to another table and Minda felt the beet-red heat of a blush cover her cheeks. A mere moment ago they'd been talking together so comfortably, she'd actually been enjoying herself. Now, she could hardly bring herself to look at Mark.

"Don't be embarrassed," he said, softly.

"He just surprised me, that's all."

"Forget him. Go back to interrogating me about my childhood."

She laughed and dug her fork into her lasagna. "Maybe later."

"Are you sure you won't have dessert?"

She shook her head. "I couldn't."

Mark handed the dessert menu to their waiter. "Just the check, please." He turned back to her and smiled.

It wasn't that loopy little half-smile that she now recognized as genuine. Instead, he flashed his I-can-charm-you-into-doing-exactly-what-I-want-you-to-do smile that had been such a turn-off when she first met him.

She braced herself for what was coming. "Is there something you want to ask me, Mark?"

"As a matter of fact, there is. I'm not sure how you'll take this, but . . . I'd like to see more of your building."

"My *building*?" She stared at him, unable to believe her ears. Had he really said, *building*? Shouldn't he have asked to see more of her *daughter*?

Throughout their meal Minda had given Mark plenty of opportunities to talk about Tracy, to declare his feelings for her or even ask Minda's permission to date her. He struck Minda as a man who was used to getting what he wanted just by asking for it, yet each time she'd given him an opportunity to do just that, he'd breezed past it. It was almost as if he didn't think of Tracy at all.

"Yes, your building." When she didn't answer, a flicker of annoyance crossed his face. "We were there earlier this evening. You do remember, don't you? Painting the apartment? Visiting Miss Whimple?"

"Of course I remember. I just . . . I didn't expect you to say you wanted to see more of my *building*."

"Any chance I could get a tour of the place?"

"You want a tour of the McAllister Building?" she repeated, just to be sure.

"Yes, I do."

"What about Tracy?"

"She's welcome to come along, if she wants."

Minda frowned and looked back at him as if he'd just suggested they all go bungee jumping together. She narrowed her eyes into two slits of suspicion. "*Why* do you want to tour the building?"

"Why not? I'm interested in architecture and the

McAllister Building just happens to be an exceptional piece of real estate with a lot of character. Is it on the historic register?"

"No, it's not," she said, confirming what he already knew.

"And since the building is named the McAllister Building, would it be safe to assume it belonged to your husband's family?"

She nodded. "There have been McAllisters in Denver as long as there's been a Denver. My husband's great-great-grandmother knew the unsinkable Molly Brown."

His brows went up. "Impressive."

"Besides the building, is there anything or anyone else you're interested in seeing more of?"

You.

The thought came to him immediately. Clearly. Unconditionally. He hoped his best smile masked how much that little word surprised him.

For Minda's benefit he slowly shook his head as if he were actually thinking over the question. "No, can't say that there's anything else."

Her hazel eyes searched his face for something that would confirm for her that he was telling the truth.

"About the building . . . can I let you know?"

"Sure."

"And about Tracy . . ."

"Yes?" His expression didn't hold even a flicker of interest.

Minda recalled her conversation with Pastor Walker, and how he'd forced Minda to admit that Mark didn't seem to treat Tracy with any particular attention. Based on Mark's behavior each time she mentioned Tracy's name over the last hour, she was beginning to think Pastor had a point.

"Minda? What about Tracy?" he prompted, gently.

"About Tracy . . . um . . . Thanks for listening," she said, feeling a little off-balance. "And thank you for dinner but I really do have to go home now."

"And I promised you'd be home before Tracy got there." He pulled his pocket watch out and flicked it open, allowing the watch to play its lilting melody. "Looks like I get to keep my promise."

They left the restaurant together and stepped out into the evening darkness. The night was cool but comfortable and a soft, fall breeze skittered a few dry leaves around the parking lot.

Minda held out her hand. "Good night, Mark. And thank you again for dinner."

"Good night? Not yet, Minda. Not until I've taken you home."

She shook her head. "No need. My house isn't that far away and it's a wonderful evening. I think I'll walk home."

"But it's almost nine o'clock and it's dark outside."

She gave him a challenging look. "We have street lights in Denver. I'll be very safe, I promise."

"Then I'll walk with you."

"You really don't have to."

"Of course I have to or my status as a gentleman will be jeopardized. You wouldn't want that on your conscience, would you?"

She smiled. "I wouldn't be able to sleep at night."

She started walking and Mark fell in beside her at a comfortable pace.

He took a deep breath of crisp, autumn air. Its coolness brought him back to his senses and erased the lingering pleasure he'd felt while looking across a candle-lit table at a lovely woman. For a short time during dinner, he'd forgotten himself and his purpose for wanting to charm Minda. In fact, for a few moments, he'd forgotten everything but the enjoyment of being with her. That, he knew, was dangerous.

Thankfully, the night air worked like a splash of water to his face. He was in control of his emotions once more.

He looked down at the top of Minda's head as she walked beside him. Even in the pale glow of the street lamps her brown hair looked shiny and soft and touchable. Another dangerous thought. If a man strings too many of those together, he realized, he can get himself into a whole lot of trouble.

H ow far did you say your house was?"

"Not far. Are you tired already?"

"Not at all. I'm actually kind of enjoying this."

"You say that as if you've never taken a walk before."

"Oh, I can walk. My knees bend and everything. But I don't take *walks*. Strolls. At least, I haven't taken a walk in a long time." He smiled down at her. "It's kind of nice."

In fact, it was more than nice. Walking down the sidewalk with Minda, Mark enjoyed the feel of the cool evening air against his face. It reminded him of a simpler time and a simpler life he left behind years before.

From the moment he met Minda McAllister he felt as if he had stepped into an alternate universe, where families walked to church on Sunday and every home had a front porch. Where kids played in tree-houses and couples took leisurely evening walks. It was all a lot of Norman Rockwell, so different from New York and his world of high-rise buildings, miles of unending concrete, and cut-throat business deals. It was almost like being on a different planet.

When they reached Minda's house, she stopped at the sidewalk and looked up at him. "Did I thank you for dinner?"

"Yes, you did."

"Well, I want to thank you again. And I should thank you once more for helping me paint Addy's apartment. If it weren't for you, I'd probably still be on that ladder."

"I'm glad I could help."

"I'd like to find a way to show my appreciation."

"What did you have in mind?"

"Coffee. I was thinking I'd invite you to come in for coffee."

Her invitation caught him off guard. Less than an hour ago she'd sounded like she couldn't wait for him to leave town and now she was asking him in for coffee?

At some point during dinner the tide had changed and he'd missed it. At some point, the wary, mistrustful light in her eyes had dimmed several watts. He hadn't noticed when it happened. He'd been too caught up in the simple pleasure of being with her. But now he realized that something he'd done or said during dinner had caused her opinion of him to change. She was letting down her guard and letting him in a little. He'd be a fool not to take advantage of her invitation.

He followed her up the steps to the porch and into the house. As soon as he stepped inside, the warmth and comfort of the place washed over him. He might live in a multi-million-dollar condo in the most desirable neighborhood in New York but at that very moment, he found himself wondering what it would be like to live in an old house with a huge back yard, a roll-top desk and an antiquated upright piano.

"Make yourself comfortable and I'll start the coffee." Minda went through the dining room and disappeared into the kitchen.

Mark took a long, steadying breath. The air was lightly scented and he saw a vase of fresh-cut flowers arranged on the dining table. He moved closer and bent over the flowers, drawing another deep breath.

"Are these from your garden?"

"Uh-huh."

He followed her into the kitchen. "Where you born with a green thumb or did you take gardening classes?"

"Neither. I learned to garden from a book."

His brows went up. "A book? You're kidding."

"Nope."

She went to the back door where an old baker's rack stored cookbooks and stockpots. She selected a slim book from the shelf and handed it to him.

It was obvious the book was old, but it was meticulously made. The binding was leather and the title, once embossed in gold, had long since worn away. Mark tilted the cover against the light to read the embossed letters.

Mrs. Plowright's 1908 Guide for
the Genteel Lady Gardener.

A tattered blue ribbon bookmark was woven into the spine and he gently opened the book to the marked page.

Do not consider cultivating flowers a waste of time. It is a good and just thing to develop a love of flowers, as flowers have a refining influence. Flowers never lead astray, but always upward to what is purer and better.

"What a funny little book," he said, gently flipping it's pages.

"It *is* odd, isn't it? It's a peculiar mixture of gardening tips, etiquette lessons and Christian affirmations. I've never seen anything like it."

"Have you had it long?"

She nodded. "When my husband passed away, I had a hard time adjusting. I had Tracy to take care of and bills to pay. I was really struggling. Then one day Addy Whimple stopped me and said I had to start taking care of myself and find an outlet for my own emotions. She gave me that book and said it would help."

"Was she right?"

"She was. I read the book and followed all the instructions. And in the process, I discovered that digging in dirt and planting flowers works better than group therapy, and it's much less expensive."

"Are you trying to tell me that you created your gardens and landscaped this property from the advice in this book?"

"I sure did." She took two coffee mugs down from the cupboard. "Originally I had a bush here or there and the lawns were healthy, but I didn't have any of the flower beds or plantings I have now. This book taught me a lot."

He flipped through a few more pages of the book.

A true lady never mentions the weeds in her neighbor's garden when her own is choked with the same.

He laughed softly. "I never would have believed it. I guess this crazy little book must have some merit because your gardens are wonderful. Frankly, I'm surprised anybody could ever learn anything out of something so old."

"You shouldn't be that surprised. Old things are wonderful. They're our heritage and our history. Our ties to where we came from."

"Old things are just that—Things. They start getting old, they break, they get older, you get rid of them." He handed the book back to her. "Give me the newest and the latest any day."

"You don't mean that," she scoffed.

"Sure I do."

"Are you telling me everything you have is new? *Every*thing? Mark, don't have you have something that's old and has some value to you?"

He leaned his hips against the kitchen counter and shrugged his shoulders slightly. "No, I can't say that I do."

"That's not true. What about your watch?"

"My watch?" he repeated, blankly.

"Your pocket watch. I've seen you pull it out several times and it doesn't look new."

"I guess you're right." He drew the watch from his pocket and examined it as if he'd never really looked at it before. "Yeah, I guess it is old."

"Is it an heirloom? Something passed down in your family?" she asked, as she readied the cream and sugar.

"No. I actually bought this myself. It came up at an auction and I wanted it, so I bought it." He smiled slightly at the memory. "It was funny, really, because it was one of those things where I just felt drawn to it, like it was meant to be mine. The odd thing is, I wasn't supposed to be at that auction in the first place. I was supposed to be on a plane back to New York but I was stuck in Chicago and my flight got cancelled and . . . Well, one thing led to another and I found myself at an auction, buying this watch. It was the craziest thing."

"It wasn't crazy at all. You just listened to your angel."

One of his dark brows shot skyward. "I listened to my

what?"

"Your angel. That's what my husband used to say whenever something like that happened. You know, when you do something that's totally out character just because you feel compelled, as if it were meant to be. My husband, Dale, used to say that when things like that happen, it's because God has planned something for us, something good and special, and He sends angels to guide us toward that good thing. Just because we don't see halos and wings and flowing robes, doesn't mean there aren't angels doing His work among us."

"Well, the secretary who screwed up my travel plans was no angel," he said. The smile he gave her softened the sharpness of his words.

And almost took her breath away.

She held out her hand. "May I see your watch?"

He reached out and handed it to her.

The watch was heavier than she expected. Its weight and the delicately ornate carvings on the case signaled its age and value. Carefully, she cradled it in her palm and examined it.

"How do you open it?"

"Press down on the crown."

"Where's the crown?"

Slowly, he moved closer until he was standing within inches of her. "Right here," he said softly, as he touched his finger to the tip of the winding stem.

Minda inhaled the light fragrance of his aftershave when he dipped his head a little closer to hers.

She pressed the crown. The watchcase opened and the sweet, lilting music she had heard in the restaurant filled the kitchen.

"It's a beautiful watch," she said, as she closed the case and carefully handed it back to him. "And I think it means more to you than you're willing to admit."

A soft smile played at his lips. "If it makes you happy to think so . . ."

"And the music it plays sounds familiar to me. I think it's a hymn. I'll bet I have it in one my music books."

Mark followed her through the dining room and into the living room.

She lifted the hinged top of the piano bench and pulled out an old, well-used book of hymns. She thumbed through the book and found the page she was looking for.

"I think this is it." She propped the hymnal up on the piano and sat down on the bench.

Mark stood behind her as she played the first few bars of the song.

"See? It's the same music." She swiveled around so she could look up at his face.

Mark frowned. "Play some more."

"Doubter! I'll prove it to you," she said, challengingly.

He didn't doubt her; he just wanted to hear more of the song. As soon as she had played the first notes on the piano, he knew the music matched the tune his watch chimed whenever he opened it.

He glanced over her shoulder at the music book and the words of the hymn came back to him in a rush:

Day by day, and with each passing moment,
Strength I find, to meet my trials here;
Trusting in my Father's wise bestowment,
I've no cause for worry or for fear.

It was a hymn he hadn't heard in many years, but—like most songs of worship—it was one he knew well. How, he wondered, had he never recognized that the song his watch played—the sweet tune that gave him a sense of peace and comfort every time he opened the watchcase—was a hymn he had sung countless times in his younger years?

Minda finished playing and looked up at him again. "Now do you believe me?"

"You're right, it's the same song. You have a good ear for music and you play well."

She stood up and closed the music book. "Thanks. I don't get to play now as much as I'd like to and I think the piano could use some tuning."

"Maybe you'd play more if you had a new instrument."

She shook her head. "No thanks. I love this old piano. It belonged to my husband's grandmother, so it's been handed down through the family."

"I suspect you have a lot of things that once belonged to your husband and his family."

Minda's hazel eyes swept over the large room and its contents, which had changed very little since Dale died. "I suppose to someone like you, this house is just filled with old, out-of-date furnishings. But just because they're old doesn't mean they don't have value."

"That's true. But at the same time, buying a new piano doesn't necessarily mean that you love or miss someone less."

She opened her mouth to reply, then thought better of it. She closed the music book and tucked it back under the hinged top of the piano bench.

He watched her, certain that her determination to hold on to everything her husband had ever owned was some kind of metaphor for her holding on to the man himself. For some odd reason, he was uncomfortable knowing that after almost eighteen years, Minda was still mourning her husband's passing and still clinging desperately to the man she'd been married to so many years before.

"Do you want to talk about it?"

She didn't look at him. "I don't think so."

"If you ever change your mind . . ."

The sound of the front door opening caught their attention.

"Mark?" Tracy stopped just inside the front door, barely concealing her happiness at finding him there. "Wow, this is a surprise! I wasn't expecting to see you tonight." She put down her purse and Bible and asked, "Have you been waiting long?"

"Actually, I just arrived," he said. "How are you, Tracy?"

"I couldn't be better! If I'd known you were going to be here, I would have come home sooner but Bible study ran a little late and then Pastor wanted to talk to me. So, what's going on?"

"Nothing's going on," Minda said, firmly. "I was just about to offer Mark a cup of coffee."

"Sounds good. I'd love some coffee," Tracy said, in her best adult voice.

Since Tracy had never taken so much as a sip of coffee before, Minda wondered what other little white lies her daughter was willing to tell Mark in hopes of impressing him.

She headed for the kitchen and pulled a third mug from the cupboard for Tracy. She heard Tracy's voice carry in from the living room, "At school I try to stay away from them. I mean, they're okay and everything, but we really don't have anything in common. They're so immature."

Tracy and Mark entered the kitchen and sat down at the breakfast table where Minda had arranged cups, cream and sugar.

As Minda poured out the coffee, Mark asked, "Didn't I meet some of your friends on Sunday morning?"

"You met some of the kids I go to school with," Tracy said, dismissively, "but I wouldn't necessarily say they're all my *friends.*"

Minda felt a tide of irritation sweep over her as she listened to Tracy's meager attempts to please Mark. She wasn't certain which of them she should blame, but when she looked at Mark, she had her answer.

His blue eyes locked with Minda's and he smiled slightly; a kind of adults-only smile that Tracy didn't notice and wasn't meant to. His smile held equal amounts of tolerance and amusement that made Minda wonder if he was seeing evidence of Tracy's youth for the first time.

"Unfortunately," Tracy continued, "I have to spend a lot of time with them. I mean, between school during the day and church activities in the evening, we're together a lot. But we don't really bond, you know what I mean? I mean, how can I be close to any of them when they're so immature? There's almost no one in my circle of friends who's my age emotionally. Wow, I just had this great idea," she said suddenly. "Tomorrow's choir practice at church. You should come."

Mark looked from Tracy to Minda and back again. "*Choir* practice?"

"Don't look so surprised," Tracy said. "After hearing you sing on Sunday, it would be a crime if you didn't join our choir."

"You can't be serious."

"Why not? You have a wonderful singing voice. My mom and I both think so."

Attending choir practice was the last thing he wanted to do. A hasty "No thanks," was on the tip of his tongue when he chanced to look at Minda. She was watching him, her expression speculative.

When she looked at him that way he thought he could almost give up everything he owned to know what she was thinking. He certainly knew what she thought of his singing voice; she'd mentioned it earlier at dinner and had apparently discussed it with Tracy. He had the sudden notion that he might score some big Minda Points if he accepted Tracy's invitation. Maybe it would help his cause and close his deal if Minda saw that he was being nice to her daughter.

"Choir practice, huh?" he asked, weighing his options, stalling his answer.

Minda watched him struggle for a moment and took a small amount of pity on him. "Mark, please don't feel obligated."

"I don't feel obligated—"

"But you don't understand. There's something you need to know—"

"Sure," he said, recklessly. "Choir practice tomorrow night. Why not?"

Minda could tell him "why not." She could tell him that the invitation he just accepted was to sing with a group of teenagers. Mulishly, she bit back the words and decided to let him find out for himself that the choir he had just joined was the church youth choir. After all, if a thirty-something man wanted to date a teenaged girl he had to expect that he'd end up doing things a teenager would do.

She poured a cup of coffee for herself and watched as Tracy dumped three spoons of sugar and a generous amount of cream into her coffee before she tasted it.

"I'll introduce you to everyone at choir," Tracy said, more as a fact than an offer. "And you'll probably also see a lot of the same people you met on Sunday. They'll all be at the church, too. Wednesday night is when everything happens at church. Besides choir, there are all sorts of meetings, like the deacons and different committees. Mom's on the committee planning the Orphan Train Riders Reunion."

Mark's blue eyes settled on Minda. "Then you'll be at church tomorrow night, too?"

"I wouldn't miss it."

"Neither would I."

"Is he gone?" Minda asked, as she loaded the coffee mugs into the dishwasher.

"Yes." Tracy sat down at the kitchen table and absently traced her finger along the wood grain of the table top.

"How was Bible study?"

"Fine."

"And how was your conversation with Pastor?" She hoped her question sounded casual, but as soon as the words left her mouth, she saw Tracy frown.

"How do you know about *that*?"

"You mentioned it when you got home. You said Pastor wanted to talk to you after Bible study ended and that's why you were late."

"Oh, yeah. It was nothing special." Tracy turned her attention back to tracing the pattern of the wood grain, but this time her expression was more thoughtful than dreamy.

"Do you want to talk about it?"

"No."

"Do you want to talk about Mark?"

Tracy's head came up, her expression hopeful but wary. "I'm not sure. Do *you*?"

"I'm willing to talk about anything that interests you."

"Mark isn't a thing, Mom. He's a person."

"I stand corrected."

"I was just thinking it was kind of nice of him to surprise

me tonight. I wasn't expecting him to stop by to see me."

"Actually, I invited him."

Tracy's head came up. "What?"

"I invited him in for coffee. I wanted to thank him for helping me this afternoon."

"What do you mean, he helped you? Helped you do what?"

"He helped me paint Miss Whimple's apartment."

"In a suit?" Tracy clearly didn't believe her.

"Yes, in a suit. And he did a good job. He said he worked his way through college by painting houses." She watched her daughter digest this information.

"What was he doing at Miss Whimple's apartment?"

"He said he had business in Denver. Maybe he was at a business meeting close by. As a matter of fact, he asked for a tour of the building."

"Are you going to give him one?"

"I'm thinking about it."

"Does this mean that you're changing your mind about him?"

"It means I'm thinking about giving him a tour of the building."

"So, you still don't like him."

"To tell you the truth, I'm not sure if I like him or not. But there is something I *can* say I don't like: I don't like the way you act when you're with him."

"What way?" Tracy demanded, bristling.

"The way you behaved tonight. The way you tried to act sophisticated and worldly. Instead of being yourself, I watched you try to be the person you think Mark will be interested in."

"There's nothing wrong with being sophisticated."

"There isn't, if that's who you truly are."

"You just don't understand."

"What is it I don't understand?"

"You don't understand that I'm growing up. Maybe I'm just a girl in high school right now, but someday I *will* live in New York. Someday I *will* travel and go to the theater and live the kind of life Mark talks about."

"If that's what you want, Tracy, I hope you get it. But in the meantime, you're seventeen and you have school tomorrow where you're going to see all the friends you trash-talked to Mark earlier this evening."

M ark took a deep, steadying breath before he pushed
 open the door to Fellowship Hall. For the majority of
his adult years he'd made it a point to steer clear of church
services and faith-based meetings of any kind, and yet—for
the second time in less than a week—he was about to do the
very thing he had long ago promised himself he'd never do
again.

He pursed his lips into a hard line and mentally shook his
head over the things he was willing to do for his career and
his employer. But that was about to change.

Once he closed the deal on the McAllister Building, he was
going to take that big, fat commission check and kiss his job
at Goble, Haines and Wyman good-bye. With that
commission check he'd have the remaining capital he needed
to start his own firm, be his own boss, and check off yet
another accomplishment in his long list of life goals—even if
achieving that goal meant he had to do the very thing he'd
once pledged he'd never do again. As long as Minda
McAllister signed on the dotted line, he was willing to show

up at Eternal Joy Christian Church every night of the week. Heck, he'd move into the place, if he had to.

It only took a moment for him to find Minda and Tracy among the crowd of people milling about the large room. Minda was drawing off her coat and he saw that she was dressed in a blue sweater set and skirt. Her flat-heeled shoes and the healthy hint of color in her cheeks told him she had walked to church.

Tracy spotted him first and her face lit up as soon as she saw him. "I'm so glad you're here, Mark. I just know you're going to love choir. Don't you just love singing?"

"I've never sung with a choir before," he said, deliberately ignoring Tracy's real question.

"You'll love it! Won't he, Mom?"

Minda looked at Mark in a way that told him she suspected he was up to no good. "It will certainly be an experience," she said, before she moved away to speak with Ellen, who was setting out refreshments on the other side of the room.

Mark's eyes followed her until he felt a touch on his elbow. He looked down to see Tracy tucking her hand through his arm.

"Come on," she said, "I'll show you where the choir room is."

He allowed Tracy to lead him down the hall and into the choir room. As soon as he crossed the threshold, he realized he'd made a huge mistake. At least fifteen people were in the room and—with the exception of the guy banging away on the piano—not one of them was over the age of eighteen.

He stopped in his tracks just inside the door. Tracy released his arm and continued on into the room. He watched her greet her friends and bask in the attention of having them close around her.

"Let's take our places, everyone!" the man at the piano called out at the same time he looked up and spotted Mark.

The man got up and immediately came over to him. "Hello, Mark. Nice to see you again. I'm Jim Dailey, Ellen's husband. We met on Sunday after church services. Welcome to our choir practice."

Mark shook hands while he mentally took stock of his surroundings.

For the second time in less than a week he was in a church building.

Inside that church building, he was in a room full of teenagers.

That gathering of teenagers was called "choir practice."

He looked over at the old upright piano and—just like the piano—he realized he'd been played. He wasn't certain which McAllister he should blame—Minda or Tracy—for thinking he was stupid enough to want to sing in a choir of teenagers, but he was about to set both of them straight.

Jim cocked his head to one side. "Are you going to be joining us?"

"No," Mark answered, emphatically, "I'm not. I'm just delivering Tracy. It was good seeing you again, Jim, and I won't keep you."

Mark waved his good-bye at Tracy and went straight to the door.

The sound of the piano and the teens' voices trilling warm-up scales taunted him as he purposefully made his way down the hall. He inspected every room on the corridor until he finally found Minda in one of the Sunday school rooms where a meeting of the Orphan Train Riders Reunion committee was about to begin.

He marched straight up to the front of the room, where Minda was seated with other committee members at a long table facing the audience. "I want to speak with you," he whispered, ominously.

"Can't it wait?"

"No, it can't." He took firm hold of her arm just above the elbow and led her out the door of the Sunday school room and down the hall to a quieter part of the building.

Randomly, he threw open a door and propelled her into an unoccupied, dimly-lit room. "You and I are going to have a talk."

"We can't talk in here," she said, sounding outraged.

"Why not?"

"It's the pastor's study. No one is allowed in here."

"Good. Then we won't be interrupted. Have a seat."

For a moment he thought she was going to refuse. Her body went rigid and she opened her mouth to speak.

The muscles in his jaw tightened.

Her mouth clamped shut.

On one side of the room a single lamp on top of a writing desk gave off the only light. Near a wall of bookshelves, a pair of comfortable upholstered chairs were arranged to form a reading area.

Minda took one of the chairs and said, defensively, "I know you're angry, but it's your own fault. I tried to warn you."

"Warn me about what?" He sat down in the chair opposite hers.

"About choir practice. I tried to tell you it was for teenagers."

"You didn't try hard enough. Why would I want to sing with a bunch of teenagers?"

"Why not? If you're going to hang around teenagers, you have to expect to do things teenagers do."

"In case you haven't noticed, I'm not a teenager. I'm a

grown man."

"Yes, I *have* noticed you're a man—"

"I can show you my driver's license, if you'd like."

"—which makes me wonder why you're so certain you want to date my daughter."

He sat up straight up in his chair. "*What?*"

"Certain! You are certain, right? I mean, you must be, a man like you. You seem so certain about everything. I just don't understand why—out of all the women in the world, teenaged or middle-aged—you had to fall in love with my daughter!"

Mark stared at her, stunned. A full fifteen seconds passed before he could form a single coherent thought. At first he wasn't even certain he had heard her right; but the look on her face assured him he had, and left him completely baffled.

No one had ever come close to leveling such a preposterous accusation at him before. After all, Mark Cartier could date any woman he wanted. He was a man who hadn't hit a dating dry-spell since he was seventeen. When he was home in New York, he never made a move in the evening without a beautiful woman on his arm. The thought that he could be romantically interested in some graceless seventeen-year-old kid—It was almost funny.

Almost.

His first instinct was to tell Minda McAllister she had rocks in her head, that she couldn't possibly believe such a thing. But then he saw the look on her face and stopped. Rocks or no rocks, it was clear to him she was serious. That wary, mistrustful look was once again in her eyes, but he also saw an odd rigidity to her expression, as if she were bracing herself for whatever was going to happen next.

He bit back the words that were so close to the tip of his tongue. He leaned back again in the chair, his emotions under tight control, just as if he were at the negotiating table for one of his business deals.

"What exactly convinced you I want to date your daughter?"

"It's obvious," she said, with an impatient wave of her hand. "Tracy can speak of nothing but you. Less than a week ago I had never heard of Mark Cartier, but now you seem to fill her every waking hour. Either you're at our house in person or showing up here at church or Tracy's constantly talking about you."

He took a deep breath and slowly shook his head. "Minda, I never intended—"

"I know, I know," she said quickly, before he could finish getting the words out. "No one ever plans these things. They just . . . *happen*."

He looked at her sharply. "Nothing has *happened*. I want to make that perfectly clear."

"Thank you. I appreciate your telling me that."

"Minda, you don't understand. I don't know what Tracy has told you—"

"She told me everything. About how you singled her out at school and paid special attention to her. She told me how you wanted to come home with her and spend time with her."

He almost groaned out loud. Minda's words now made sense and explained, at long last, why Minda had been so suspicious of him from the start. And he finally understood the reason Tracy was constantly trying to inject herself in between them.

She was sitting there, looking at him as if he only had to say a few magic words to clear everything up.

But what could he say? He couldn't very well tell her that he was at the high school by design; that he'd been trying for weeks to find a way to insinuate himself into Minda

McAllister's life and the easiest way to do so seemed to be through her daughter. He'd had feelers out in the community for months when he got word that Tracy's school was looking for Career Day speakers. That's when he decided to go to Tracy's School and contrive to meet Tracy. His plan was to use her to meet her mother. It seemed like such a simple strategy at the time.

It never occurred to him that a seventeen-year-old girl would make a crazy jump to the wrong conclusion . . . and take her mother flying off the edge of the cliff with her.

"Tracy told me the truth, didn't she?" Minda asked. "You did single her out at school, right? And you did flatter her and show her attention and convince her to bring you to our home? You did all those things, didn't you?"

"Yes, I did those things." His voice was calm but his brain frantically searched for an explanation he could offer her.

"Thank you for being honest with me," she said. "Now, I'm going to be as equally honest with you." She squared her shoulders and said, purposefully, "You cannot date my daughter."

He shook his head again, exasperated that she could think such a statement was even necessary.

"You should know, Mark, that I intend to fight you on this. In fact, I absolutely forbid you to date Tracy. There's nothing you can say —"

"Then I won't."

"—that could even tempt me to recon—" She blinked at him. "What did you say?"

"I won't date your daughter."

"That's it? You're not going to argue with me?"

"No, I'm not. When we were at dinner last night I could tell how concerned you were about Tracy. To tell you the truth, I just didn't realize your concern was directed at me."

"So that's it?" she asked again, doubtfully.

"Yes, that's it. I won't date Tracy. In fact, I won't even see her unless you or someone you trust is present."

"You'll give me your word?"

"Yes."

"And you won't see her behind my back?"

"Absolutely not."

Her eyes narrowed. "What about phone calls?"

"I won't make any one-on-one contact with her at all."

"Then you aren't in love with her?"

"No!" he said, barely concealing his outrage. "I'm *not* in love with Tracy."

She digested this bit of information. "But she's in love with you, you know. She's been head over heels about you since the moment she met you."

"Minda, I'm sorry. I had no idea. I guess I just assumed she thought of me as some kind of newly-found, older brother."

"She doesn't see you that way at all. She's in the throes of her first serious crush and you're it."

"I understand that now. And I'm sorry."

"I'm sorry, too, because when I get home tonight, I'm going to have to tell Tracy she can't see you anymore and she's going to hate me for it."

Mark frowned. "What are you talking about?"

"I've been through this before. It's a dance Tracy and I already know the steps to. She's strong-willed and stubborn. And being a typical teenager, she doesn't always want to do what I tell her to do. Last year we went through a rough time because she didn't want to abide by my rules and—Let's just say, it was very difficult and very hurtful."

"Minda, I'm not going to be the cause of conflict between you and your daughter."

She shrugged her shoulders and flashed a humorless smile. "That's the fate of parents: to be hated on a daily basis by their teenaged child."

"Stop talking like that. Anyone can see that Tracy doesn't hate you. But I'm not going to let you take the fall on this. I'll talk to Tracy."

"You? You're going to tell her you aren't interested in her and never were? And then what? Are you going to simply disappear as quickly as you appeared in her life?"

That made him stop. He couldn't disappear now. His reasons for wanting to meet Minda in the first place were not yet accomplished.

"Okay, so I won't talk to her, but I don't want you to, either."

"I'm Tracy's mother. Breaking bad news to her is part of my job description."

"But you don't have to break the bad news to her tonight, do you? Or tomorrow? What's the harm in waiting a couple of days?"

"The harm is that she thinks you're interested in her!"

"And if she continues to think that for a couple more days while we figure out how to solve this problem, what's the risk?"

"*We? We* solve the problem?"

"Yes, *we*. Seems to me I own a pretty significant share of this situation. Why wouldn't I have some responsibility for fixing it?"

"And how do you plan to fix it?"

"How? Well, I . . . I don't know yet, but I will."

She shook her head slightly. "It would be better if you weren't involved. Maybe it would be a good idea if you just disappeared."

"Number one, I'm already involved. Number two," he

leaned forward and took her hand, "having me disappear and leaving you behind to deal with Tracy's hurt and anger is not a good solution. Do you agree?"

Her attention focused on his hand holding hers. A light flush of color warmed her cheeks. "Yes. I mean, I don't want Tracy hurt."

"She won't be."

"Promise?"

"Promise."

At that one word, Minda looked into the soft expression in his blue eyes and felt her insides tie in knots. Not the messy kind of knots that signaled trouble, but the kind of knots that could pass for bows. The kind that made a woman think of moonlight and softly starry nights and holding hands the way Mark was holding her hand at that very moment.

He stood up and drew her to her feet. He was so close she could feel his breath on her hair and for one terrifying but tempting moment, she wondered what would happen if she moved forward and closed that small gap between them.

"Minda, you do believe me, don't you? I have to know you believe me when I say I never had feelings for Tracy. To me, she is simply your daughter."

"I believe you."

She saw him relax, as if he'd been holding his breath until he heard those three words.

His fingers pressed lightly against hers and he smiled slightly. "Let's get you back to your committee meeting."

He moved away to open the door. A shaft of bright, florescent light from the hallway spilled into the room, bringing Minda back to her usual good sense.

"You don't have to stay," she said, when she realized Mark was walking back to the Sunday school room with her.

"If I'm playing on the baseball team for this train reunion

thing, I might as well listen in on the planning session."

She smiled. "It's not a train reunion thing. It's a reunion of orphan train riders."

"Whatever it's called, I'm staying."

Minda didn't bother to argue when he followed her into the Sunday school room. She made her way up to the front while Mark slipped into a seat at the back of the room.

He settled onto a folding metal chair but his attention was focused on Minda. Their conversation in Pastor Walker's study had shaken him. He realized how close he'd come to disaster simply because of Tracy's immaturity and Minda's distrust.

How could he have missed the signs that Tracy had a crush on him? He cudgeled his brain, wondering what words he'd said or action he'd taken that had misled Tracy and Minda. Hopefully, he'd put Minda's fears to rest. Hopefully, she'd be more receptive to him from this point on and he'd be able to buy her building and get back to New York where he belonged.

Already his short business trip to Denver had stretched into more days than he had planned. Somehow, his resolution to never again set foot inside a church had morphed into attending Sunday services and weeknight committee meetings. And his strategy to use Tracy to get to Minda had badly backfired.

Clearly, he had lost control of his grand plan. He had to refocus; he had to redouble his efforts.

In the front of the Sunday school room, Coach Morgan was standing by the chalk board and about eight people, including Minda, were seated at the long committee table. Another thirty people or so were seated in the audience, listening intently to the meeting.

"What's the next item on our agenda?" Coach asked, as he

consulted the blackboard at the front of the room, on which a list of discussion topics had been neatly written in chalk. "Doug is next. Doug Peterson designed a new poster to advertise the reunion. Doug, will you stand up and show everyone what you and your printing company came up with?"

A man seated near the front of the room stood and held up a large poster. At the top of the poster, in oversized letters, were the words:

Wanted: Homes for Children

"Here's the new poster," announced Doug Peterson. "This design was inspired by a headline from the Denver newspaper back in 1929. Two weeks after that headline appeared, an orphan train arrived with 28 children on board. I'm proud to say, each one of those children found homes here in Denver. Now, we don't know who all those children were or what's become of them, but we're hoping these posters, along with these flyers," he held up a handful of similarly designed brochures, "will generate interest here in the community and help us find out what became of those children."

"Haven't Doug and the good folks at Peterson Printing and Graphics done a great job with these posters and flyers?" Coach asked.

The people seated in the room responded with enthusiastic applause.

"The posters are beautiful, Doug. Just beautiful," Coach said. "We need to get as many of them distributed as we can before the weekend. If you can help hand them out to businesses and stores in the area, see Minda McAllister at the end of the meeting to sign up. Now, remember, folks, we want these posters placed in shops and businesses with high traffic so they get maximum exposure."

As the meeting continued, Pastor Walker slipped into the seat beside Mark's at the back of the room and greeted him in a whisper. "Mark, it's good to see you again."

"Thank you, Pastor. Nice to see you, too."

"How's the meeting going?"

"Fine, I think," Mark whispered back. "I'm not really involved."

"Would you like to be?"

"Not particularly. To be honest, Pastor, my time in Denver is strictly temporary."

"I'm sorry to hear that. I know a couple other people who'd feel the same way."

Mark looked at him, surprised. "Like who?"

"Like Coach. He's counting on you to play in the fund-raising baseball game, you know. And Tracy McAllister."

Mark felt a tide of outrage explode within his body. He glared at Pastor Walker. "Not you, too!"

His voice carried out across the room and several people swiveled around in their chairs to eye him with interest.

Pastor nudged him with his elbow. "Shhhh. You're disrupting the meeting."

"Is *everybody* in this church crazy?" Even whispering, Mark managed to convey a strong level of disgust.

"Not everyone."

"Pastor, let me set the record straight right now. Nothing—and I do mean *nothing*—"

"I know."

"But you just said—"

"I said Tracy would miss you if you left," whispered Pastor. "That's because she's a love-struck teenager with a crush on you as big as Texas. I never said, though, that I thought you felt the same way about her."

"Good. Because I don't."

"So how do you feel about Tracy's mother?"

For a moment Mark felt his heart thump wildly in his chest. "Minda? I . . . um . . ."

"Mark, you don't have to tell me that you're not interested in Tracy. You don't have to tell me what you're doing here in Denver. In fact, you could get up right now out of that chair and leave and never come back. That would be easy. But, if you left now, you wouldn't be able to accomplish the reason you used Tracy to meet Minda in the first place. Am I right?"

Pastor's whispered words caught Mark completely off-guard. His brain began working at warp speed to catch up. He didn't know yet how much Pastor knew or guessed about his motives, but he hoped Pastor Walker wouldn't share his suspicions with Minda. He decided, in this case, his best defense was a good offense.

"Pastor, you've got it wrong. Minda invited *me* to attend church with her last Sunday."

"But she didn't invite you into her home. You manipulated that invitation out of Tracy." When Mark didn't respond, he whispered, "I'm sure you have your reasons, Mark, but one of those reasons better not be to hurt Minda in any way."

"It's not."

"Glad to hear it. Minda's a well-loved member of our church family. She deserves our care and respect."

Mark drew a deep breath. It had been a long time since he felt as if he'd been taken to the wood-shed over some misdeed. "I have no intention of hurting Minda. My motives are strictly business-related."

Pastor smiled. "If you ever decide you want to talk to someone about those motives—business-related or other-wise—I have a willing ear and I'm easy to find."

He gave Mark's shoulder a couple of encouraging claps then he slipped out of the room just as Coach Morgan pointed a finger in Mark's direction.

"And speaking of fund-raisers, our last event will be the baseball game on Saturday against our sister church from Colorado Springs," Coach announced to the people in the room. "The newest player on our baseball team is sitting in the back of the room tonight. Before you leave, say hello to Mark Cartier and welcome him to the team and to our church family."

Several heads swiveled Mark's direction again.

He raised his hand in a token wave and tried to muster a smile. But he was still reeling from his brief conversation with Pastor Walker and wondering what the consequences of it would be.

Instinctively, he looked at Minda and his eyes met hers. She smiled and he immediately felt the impact of her warmth and encouragement.

Well, he didn't need her warmth and encouragement. And he certainly didn't need to get any more involved in her life or her church or anything else. He just needed her to sign on the dotted line and sell her building so he could get back to New York.

Somehow, his simple business transaction had run completely off course for reasons he couldn't even explain to himself. It was time he got the project back on track. As soon as the meeting ended, he sought Minda out with renewed purpose.

"You promised me a tour of your building," he reminded her, with his most charming smile. "How about tomorrow evening? If we do it late in the day, I won't take you away from your work at the bookstore."

"Tomorrow is fine. But if you really want to appreciate the

building, you should see it in daylight."

He flashed a smile that was part triumphant, part relieved. He felt he had regained his ambition; his purpose was renewed. "Great. My hotel isn't too far from the building. Why don't I pick you up after breakfast?"

"You'll be going out of your way, if you do. It would be easier if I picked you up instead. At eight o'clock in the morning? We can tour the building before I open the bookstore at ten."

"Okay, you pick me up."

"Then I'll see you in the morning."

"Wait a second," he said, laying his hand on her wrist in a way that sent a warm tremor vibrating up her arm. "Are you saying, good-night? Won't you let me drive you home?"

"No. Tracy and I are walking home. It's better that she not see you again tonight."

He let go of her wrist. "I suppose you're right. I'll see you in the morning, Minda."

10

At precisely eight a.m. Minda called Mark's room from a guest phone in the lobby of the hotel.

"I'm downstairs. Are you ready?"

"I'm sorry, but I can't leave yet. I'm stuck on a conference call with New York and it's running a little long. Why don't you come up? I'm in room 1602."

Her heart stuttered a little. The last thing she wanted was to be in his hotel room. "I'll wait for you here in the lobby."

"I have coffee and this morning's newspaper. You'll be much more comfortable here than in the lobby. Come on up."

A short, sixteen-floor elevator ride later, Minda stood in the hallway outside room 1602. The door had been propped open with the security latch. Tentatively, she pushed the door open and stepped into the living area of a large hotel suite. On the far end of the room, near the windows, Mark stood at the desk. His laptop and tablet computer were both on, each displaying different graphs and bar charts, as one image after another flashed on the screens.

Mark muted his cell phone and motioned for her to come

further into the room. "I won't be much longer. There's coffee on the table. Help yourself."

She set her purse down and poured out a cup of coffee. She took a tentatively sip and immediately recognized the taste and aroma of an expensive brew. She took another sip as her eyes traveled around the large, elegantly furnished room. From the quality of the furnishings to the size of the flat-screen television, she could tell the suite was expensive.

It was also very neat, with no sign of wet towels, discarded shoes or signs of other bachelor behavior she half-expected to see.

Her eyes strayed toward Mark. His hair was still slightly damp and curled softly behind his ears. He was dressed in khakis and a sport shirt that emphasized the muscles of his arms and shoulders. She'd never seen him dressed casually before and she had the impression that even these clothes cost more than the yearly clothing allowance she set aside for herself and Tracy.

He looked up from his computer and smiled at her.

Her heart skipped a little. She moved to the opposite side of the room, hoping distance would make him look a little less attractive. She sipped her coffee.

From what she could hear of his side of the telephone conversation, the topic was strictly business. He used a lot of acronyms she didn't understand: ROI. PIQ. PLAT. And phrases like, *diminishing returns* and *risk appetite*. It was all a lot of Greek to her. Minda settled onto the comfortable sofa with her coffee and picked up the newspaper he'd left on the table.

Several minutes later, he ended the call. "I'm sorry I kept you waiting."

"No problem. I took advantage of your newspaper and your coffee. I'm just sorry I can't start every morning this way. This is quite a suite."

His answering smile was quick and bright and seemed to light the room. "It's the best."

"Do you always travel first class?"

"Always." He powered off his computers and packed them into their cases, then he reached for the room phone. "It'll just call for my car and we can be on our way."

"You don't need your car. We can take the bus."

"*Bus?*"

She bit back a laugh at his horrified expression. "Yes, *bus*. The bus goes straight down the 16th Street Mall and it's free."

"But my car—"

"It's rush hour. If we take your car we'll still be sitting in traffic long after the bus has dropped passengers off in front of the McAllister Building. Come on," she said, challengingly. "It's time you had a taste of what life is like for the rest of us."

A few minutes later they stepped out into the cool morning air. Minda led the way out to the curb of the cobbled street. The 16th Street Mall was bustling with pedestrians on their way to work. They joined a group of people standing at the bus stop.

"The bus comes by every five minutes," she explained, "so we shouldn't have to wait long."

A few minutes later a bus filled with passengers pulled up at the curb. The doors levered open. Only a few passengers stepped down to allow new passengers to board.

"This one's too crowded. Since we're not in a hurry, why don't we catch the next one?" Minda suggested.

The next bus proved to be just as crowded, with standing room only. "Come on," she said, determined. She climbed the steps of the bus and squeezed into the aisle already filled with passengers.

She looked over her shoulder and smiled up at Mark as he wedged himself into the aisle behind her. The bus lurched forward and sent her colliding against his chest.

He dipped his head and said in a low voice, close to her ear, "Hold on to the grab bar."

"I can't reach it. There are too many people in the way." She did her best to balance as the bus came to a stop at the next corner.

Some passengers exited and new passengers replaced them. The bus lurched forward and Minda again struggled to keep her footing.

She heard Mark chuckle softly behind her. Without warning, he encircled her waist with one arm, as he reached his other hand above her head to clasp the grab bar. For a moment, she was too stunned to react; then she felt the heat of an unrelenting blush flood her neck and face. He held her so firmly against the wall of his chest, she was certain he could tell she had stopped breathing.

"Better?" His breath tickled against her ear.

She didn't trust herself to speak. She nodded, reveling in the feeling of being held in the arms of an attractive man in the middle of a crowded, standing-room only transit bus.

A few blocks later she turned her head slightly. "Our stop is next."

"Follow me." Mark took her hand and shouldered his way through the other passengers, cutting a swath that allowed Minda to follow behind. He stepped down onto the pavement, then turned back to help her down, too.

"Thanks," she said, quickly withdrawing her hand. "The building's this way."

They walked in silence for a few minutes, giving Minda a

chance to compose herself.

"Now that you've been in Denver for a few days, Mark, how do you like it?

"I like Denver. I'd like it better if it kept up with the times a little more."

She frowned. "Denver isn't out-dated. Just because we have a healthy respect for our heritage and—"

"Cling to old things," he said, helpfully finishing her sentence for her. "This end of the Mall could be a vibrant commercial area if some of these old businesses were replaced by commercial stores that are proven to draw customers."

Minda shook her head. "I hope that never happens. These buildings may be old, but they're beautiful and their style and workmanship can't be replicated in today's economy."

They turned the corner and Minda pointed at a small antique store. "That's one of my favorite shops. Every time I go in there I feel like I'm embarking on a treasure hunt."

"To me it looks like a giant rummage sale of old, cast-off things."

"Like I said before, there's nothing wrong with old things. Sometimes our mementos and memories are all we have."

"Are we still talking about Denver?"

"Of course!"

"Just checking. I think you and I see the world very differently."

They stopped in front of the McAllister building and Minda opened her purse to pull out her keys.

"Do you mind waiting a minute?" he asked. "That flower shop across the street looks open."

"Why do you want to go in the flower shop?"

"I thought I'd pick up some flowers for Miss Whimple. Kind of a housewarming present for her freshly-painted apartment. What do you think?"

What did she think?

She thought that his sweet but unexpected suggestion just increased his value a couple of notches on her Attractive Man Scale.

She followed him over to the flower shop while her insides melted into a warm puddle of unexpected romantic notions. Notions about being drawn to a handsome man who was thoughtful enough to think of taking flowers to a lonely old woman he'd only met once before.

She watched him select a bouquet of fall blooms. He held it out for her inspection.

"How about these?"

She nodded approvingly. "They're beautiful. Miss Whimple will like them very much."

She led the way back to the bookstore and twisted the key in the lock. "I hope you won't be disappointed if Miss Whimple doesn't show a proper level of appreciation for the flowers. She can be a little crusty sometimes."

"I know," he said. "I had a taste of her crustiness the other night. But she reminds me of my own grandmother, who was the same way. It's been my experience that people who keep others at a distance do so to protect themselves. They don't want old wounds touched for fear they might hurt again."

"And you think that's the case with Addy Whimple?"

"Among others."

She looked up at him and saw that he was watching her reaction.

"But," he continued, quickly, "we can't know for sure. To me, Miss Whimple seems to be a woman who had some sadness in her life. Some experience that left her a little heart-sore."

Heart-sore. It was a term Minda hadn't heard before but

she instantly divined its definition.

Inside the store, Minda locked the door behind them, then lead the way to the back of the building where her office was located. She stowed her purse in her desk drawer. "Ready for your tour?"

"I am."

"Okay. Well, I'm not sure where to start. You see, I've never done this before. Given a tour, I mean."

"Why don't we start by visiting Miss Whimple so I can deliver these flowers?"

"Good idea. She's an early riser, so I know she'll be up."

Miss Whimple glared at them over the top of the reading glasses that were perched low on her nose. She was in her own apartment, sitting by the window in her favorite chair. Her Bible was open on her lap.

"You again!" She glared at Mark. "It's been so long since the last time you visited, I'd practically forgotten what you looked like!"

"Good morning, ma'am," he said, unshaken by her acid tone. "I've brought you a house-warming gift."

He held out the flowers and her eyes widened.

"Are these for me?" she asked, unsure.

"They are."

"I see." She took the flowers and stared at them a moment, examining their bright colors as if committing them to memory. She smiled slightly, then held the bouquet out toward Minda. "There's a vase of some kind in one of those kitchen cabinets."

"I'll put the flowers in water for you," Minda said.

Mark sat down in a comfortably upholstered chair near Miss Whimple. "I like this apartment better than the one I saw you in down the hall. This unit is on the corner of the building so there's a lot more natural light."

"I get sun in the morning and the afternoon," Miss Whimple said. "It'll be pleasant enough once the paint smell goes away. I *suppose*."

He looked at her, curious. "I don't smell any paint."

"Not now." Her tone was impatient. "At night, when the sun goes down and things get quiet. That's when I smell the paint."

Minda was at the sink, running water into a vase. She looked up and caught Mark's eye.

"What kind of paint did you use?" he asked.

"I never use anything but latex paint," Minda replied. "Flat latex paint on the walls and semi-gloss on the trim. We painted this room two days ago. I don't smell anything."

"I told you, you can't smell it now," Miss Whimple retorted. "Luckily, I open the windows at night to let in the cool evening air. Of course, if this apartment had air conditioning, I wouldn't have to do that, either," she added.

Minda recognized the signs that Miss Whimple was preparing to launch a litany of complaints, but the woman suddenly recalled something she wanted to know.

"Never mind that! Tell me how your dinner date went. *He* was certain you'd go out with him. Did you?"

Minda concentrated on arranging the flowers in the vase. "We had dinner, but it wasn't a date."

She looked over at Mark, expecting him to back her up. Instead, his cell phone rang. He pulled the phone from his pocket and looked at the caller ID.

"I'm sorry, but I have to take this call." He excused himself and went out into the hallway.

Minda set the vase of flowers on a table near Miss Whimple. "Can I get you anything while I'm up? Some tea?"

"No, thank you."

Minda claimed the chair Mark had vacated. Her gaze strayed toward the door.

After a long stretch of silence, Miss Whimple said, "I'd stay away from that one, if I were you."

"Which one?"

"The one you can't take your eyes off, even when he's out in the hall!"

Minda blinked at her in surprise. "I don't know what you're talking about." She tried not to sound defensive. "If you're warning me not to be charmed by Mark Cartier, you're not telling me anything I don't already know."

Miss Whimple snorted inelegantly. "Too late. Any fool can see you're over the moon for the man. It's written all over your face."

Minda stared at her a moment, too stunned to say anything. "No, you're mistaken! My face is—"

"An open book," said Miss Whimple, emphatically. "Just don't give *him* a chance to read it. He's one to stay away from."

"You don't have worry about that. I have no intention of getting mixed up with a bad apple like Mark Cartier."

"Bad apple? No, no, he's not bad. He's just troubled. And you've got your hands full already with that daughter of yours. You don't need a troubled man in your life right now."

"Why do you think Mark is troubled?"

Miss Whimple tapped the tip of one thin finger against her temple. "It's in his eyes. They're the mirror to a person's soul, you know. And his eyes tell me he's unhappy and he doesn't know why."

"That's funny. He said almost the same thing about you. He said you were a woman with a deep sadness and something in your life had left you heart-sore."

"Heart-sore?" Addy Whimple snorted again. "He has his cheek!"

Mark came back into the room in time to hear her last comment. "You must be talking about me."

"I am, young man! You take a lot for granted. And don't suppose that bringing me flowers will make up for it."

"How about flowers and dinner? Name a restaurant you like and I'll make a reservation." He pulled his phone out of his pocket.

"Now you're being silly."

"No, I'm not. I promised to take you on a date and I intend to keep that promise. We just have to decide where we'll go."

"Another time. I'm not going anywhere. If the Lord intends to take me tonight, I want Him to see that I'm waiting for him right here with my Bible in my hands when He comes to get me."

"I hope that's not the Lord's plan. Not when I'm just getting to know you."

She pointed a thin finger at him. "Don't try to flirt with me, young man! You may be good looking and I may enjoy the view but I won't be charmed. I know your type!"

He sat down on the upholstered arm of Minda's chair. "I have a sneaking suspicion I'll regret asking the question but I've got to know: What type, exactly, am I?"

"The type who doesn't stay around very long, that's what. There's no point in letting you cozy up to me today because you'll be gone tomorrow."

"It's true that I may not stay long but there's always the possibility that I'll return if I have something—or someone— to return for."

Miss Whimple sullenly digested this bit of information. "When are you leaving?"

"I'm not sure yet. But it seems I'm committed to stay

through next Saturday."

"Why next Saturday?"

"I'm playing on the baseball team at Minda's church."

"*You?*" she asked, disbelieving.

He smiled. "Are you surprised that I play baseball?"

"No. I'm surprised you've been to church!"

He laughed. "I admit, it doesn't happen often. Which makes me wonder: when was the last time *you* were in church, ma'am?"

"None of your business and don't change the subject."

"I didn't change the subject. We were talking about church. Why don't you go?"

"Why should I? I'm God-fearing and faithful. Have been all my life, I might add."

"But you don't worship with your brethren on Sundays."

She scowled. "You sound like a minister."

"Just a disciple. What if Minda picked you up on Sunday morning and took you to church with her?"

"No, I thank you."

"What if I picked you up?"

"No!"

"Don't you want to please the Lord?"

"Ha! I please Him every day. But the Lord hasn't done anything for me since 1929."

"What happened in 1929, if you don't mind my asking?"

"I *do* mind!"

He smiled gently at her and said in a soft, coaxing voice, "Tell me anyway."

Her eyes narrowed. "Don't you have a phone call you have to take in the hall?"

He laughed again and looked down at the phone he still held in the palm of his hand. "I wonder if I could search your name on Google and find out all I want to know about you?"

His tone was teasing.

Miss Whimple frowned again, confused. "Google?"

Minda lightly touched Mark's arm. "Miss Whimple doesn't own a computer."

Mark immediately recognized his mis-step. His expression softened as he stood up and moved over to crouch beside Miss Whimple's chair. He touched the phone screen to launch the internet search app. "I can look up anything on my phone, just the same as if I were on a computer. I'd be happy to show you. Is there something you'd like to search for?"

She still looked confused. "I haven't lost anything and I've got all I need. Why would I want to search for something?"

"Well, you don't necessarily have to search for something you lost or misplaced. Maybe you want to learn something new or find a store you'd like to shop in or locate a person's address."

"Locate a person?" Addy Whimple sat up straighter.

"That's right. If you give me a name, I'll—"

"Albert Whimple!"

"Okay, let's look for Albert Whimple." Mark tapped the name into the search field. "I'm sorry. I didn't get any results for that name."

Addy Whimple seemed to deflate a little as she let out a long breath.

"Sometimes," Minda suggested, "it helps to add a second search term."

Mark nodded. "That's right. For instance, a last known address or employer. Do you know anything else about Albert Whimple that we can add to the search?"

"Kansas. Try Kansas."

Again Mark typed on the screen. Again, the search returned no matching results.

Miss Whimple sighed softly and looked down at the Bible in her lap. Slowly, she closed the cover and rested her slim hands on the book. She sat very still, then she drew a deep breath and straightened in her chair. When she raised her head, the customary flint was back in her expression. "Well, that was a waste of time, wasn't it?"

"Not necessarily." Mark stood up and returned the phone to his pocket. "Just because we didn't find any information about Albert Whimple today doesn't mean we won't find something if we searched again in the future. That's the beauty of the Internet. New information is added every day."

"What good does that do me if I don't have a computer to search with?" she demanded.

"I'll keep looking for you."

She looked skeptical. "You will? Why?"

"Because now I'm curious to know who this Albert Whimple is. And because I can see that finding out about him is important to you."

"I never said any such thing. You presume too much, young man."

Mark let the subject drop. He stayed several minutes more with Addy Whimple and managed to charm her into smiling one more time before he said his good-byes.

As he and Minda walked down the hall toward the elevator, Mark was still replaying Miss Whimple's words in his head.

"Have you ever heard her mention Albert Whimple before?"

"Never," Minda answered. "In all the years I've known her, Addy's never mentioned him."

"Could he be a brother? A long-lost husband, maybe?"

Minda shook her head. "She told me once that she never married. Whimple is her maiden name."

"Well, whoever Albert Whimple is or was, it's clear that he means a lot to her. Maybe I can do some more research for her. You know, find out what happened to the guy."

"At the same time, maybe you can also find out what happened in 1929. From what she said, I think it may have been a significant year in her life."

She looked up at him, her expression clear and candid. Her hazel eyes showed none of the mistrust he usually saw in their depths. Instead, he saw a question in her eyes.

"Would you like to say hello to Brady?" she asked.

"Who?"

"Brady. The boy you met the other day. This is his apartment."

Mark had been so mesmerized by Minda's hazel eyes that he hadn't realized he had stopped walking right in front of an apartment door. He pulled himself together and vowed to pay better attention in the future.

"Sure, why not. As long as we're here, let's stop and say hello to Brady."

She smiled. A genuine, happy smile.

Mark's gaze locked on her face. Minda McAllister, he decided, was a very attractive woman when she smiled. If he wasn't careful, he could get pretty addicted to making her happy, just to see her hazel eyes light up again.

Minda knocked on the apartment door. A moment later Brady's muffled voice came from the other side of the door.

"Who is it?"

"It's Minda McAllister, Brady. I brought you a visitor."

The door cracked open. "Oh, wow," Brady said, when he saw Mark. "Hi! Come on in."

He opened the door a little wider and stepped back into the room. The apartment was larger than Miss Whimple's, but the room held more furniture. A long sofa was positioned at an angle in the center of the room. A bed pillow leaned against one of the sofa arms and a heavy blanket was scrunched up at the other end.

In front of the sofa was an old, worn coffee table. On one end of the table were stacks of business magazines and a white, three-ring binder. A pair of low-slung chairs faced the sofa and finished off the seating area. Against one wall, an old-fashioned media cabinet held a behemoth television that had to be fifteen or twenty years old. The TV was on and tuned to a financial news network, where a commentator was reciting stock prices.

Brady sat down on the sofa and reached for the remote to turn the television off. "I was just seeing how the markets opened. Do you guys want to sit down?"

"Sure, if you don't mind missing your TV show for a few minutes," Minda said. She sat down in one of the chairs and Mark lowered his tall body down onto the other. "How are you doing today, Brady?"

Although the room was warm, Brady was dressed in a heavy sweat shirt and sweat pants. He pulled the blanket across his legs for additional warmth.

"I'm doing okay."

"And how are the markets doing?" Mark asked.

"They took a little dip after the opening bell, but trading's been steady so they're up. Of course, the day's not over but I'm optimistic that all my stocks will see gains."

Mark's brows went up. "You own stocks?"

Brady flashed an embarrassed smile. "No. But I have a fantasy portfolio, kinda like a fantasy football team." He opened the white binder and turned it around to display its contents to Mark and Minda. On sheets of lined notebook paper were neatly drawn columns containing stock names, dates and buy prices. Each stock's gains and losses were meticulously charted in red or green colored pencil over a thirty day period.

"May I?" Mark reached out to take the binder. He thumbed through several of the pages and looked up at Brady with a good dose respect. "This is pretty impressive. If I'm reading this correctly, the Buy column is the per share price you would have paid if you had actually purchased the stock on that particular date. Right?"

"That's right. Of course, not all of the stocks I've pretended to buy have been winners, but I think a lot of them have done pretty well."

"A lot of them have done *really* well," Mark said. He handed the binder back to Brady. "You're a pretty shrewd trader."

"I'm learning. I mean, I'm totally self-taught so I'm still figuring things out. Do you follow the market? No, don't answer that. Of course you do!"

Mark smiled at him. "How are you finding the stocks you want to buy? Are you reading traders' blogs or searching the Internet?"

"No. I don't have a computer."

Mark's quick gaze surveyed the living room. Of course Brady didn't have a computer. The room was clean but shabby. The sofa was old, the television was an antique and even the dates on the financial magazines that littered the coffee table were several months old. Just like everything else he'd seen in the McAllister Building, there was nothing in sight that suggested twenty-first century technology. It was too bad, too, because if any kid deserved a computer and a decent TV, it was Brady.

"I used to search for stocks on the computers in the library at school but I haven't been able to go there lately."

"Well, if you ever do get a computer, you'll be on fire."

"Thanks. That means a lot, coming from you. I was thinking . . . maybe you could you pass some stock tips on to me? You know, if you get any?"

"Sure. If I get any." As soon as the words left Mark's mouth, he realized how harsh they sounded. His first instinct, as always, was *never commit*; but it was the wrong instinct for this situation. He smiled slightly and said, in a friendlier tone, "Ten years from now, I want to be able to say I helped you make your first million."

Brady grinned. "Ten years from now I'll be worth *five* million."

"I don't doubt that," Mark said, laughing. "Listen, we just stopped by to say hello. I'm afraid we've got to get going. We're kind of on a tight schedule and Mrs. McAllister promised to give me a quick tour of the building."

Brady's expression fell a little. "Oh. Are you closing some big business deal today?"

"Nothing that exciting."

"Maybe you could come back later. My mom will be home from work around six-thirty and you could meet her."

"I'd love to, but not tonight. I have baseball practice tonight."

Brady's eyed him with interest. "You play baseball?"

"Well, I'm going to find out tonight. I used to play many years ago. Mrs. McAllister's church is having a baseball game for a fundraiser and I sort of ended up on the team."

"Wow, I didn't know that. When's the actual game?"

"A week from Saturday."

"I bet you'll be the star player," Brady declared.

Mark usually made a rule of ignoring flattery. He'd seen plenty of ambitious young men and women try to get ahead in the business world by heaping compliments on him like slobbering puppies. He made a habit of quickly and ruthlessly squashing them. But he recognized Brady's words weren't mere flattery; they were heart-felt. There was a worshipful look in Brady's eyes that touched him in a way he hadn't expected.

Impulsively, he asked, "Why don't you come to the game and see for yourself?"

"I'd like to. I really would, but my mom has to work so I don't have any way to get there."

"Yes, you do. I'll pick you up."

Brady's eyes widened. "Are you kidding? Geez, this is great! I mean, nobody's ever asked me to go to a game before."

"Then it's time you went to one. Just make sure your mom says it's okay."

"Oh, yeah. I'm sure she'll say it's okay. She always wants me to do stuff like that but she can't take me because she's always working and—Wow, I can't believe I'm going to a baseball game!"

Mark stood up, anxious to be gone before Brady's worshipful glances drove him make any more rash promises. "I'll pick you up on Saturday. Be ready at one o'clock."

"Yeah. Yeah, okay. See you Saturday. And thanks!"

11

Minda pushed the elevator call button and looked up at Mark. "That was a very nice thing you did for Brady."

"Inviting him to the baseball game?" Mark shook his head. "I didn't do it for him. I figured if I'm going to make a fool of myself playing baseball, I need at least one person in the stands cheering for me."

"Now you're being silly."

"No, I'm not. You haven't seen me play baseball."

She laughed, softly. "I'm sure you play as well, if not better, than everyone else on the team. And even if you don't, Brady will still enjoy going to the game."

"He seems like a good kid. He deserves a baseball game or two. He probably deserves a lot more."

"Don't let him hear you say that. He hates talking about his illness. That's probably why he likes you; because you were nice to him without being too nice, if you know what I mean. He gets embarrassed when people try too hard to be upbeat and happy, just because he's sick. You spoke to him in the same way you'd speak to anyone and I think he appreciated that."

Mark saw a gentle smile play on her lips. Lips that looked soft and velvety. Lips that looked downright kissable.

Instantly, he looked away and told himself he didn't want to kiss Minda. He didn't want physical attraction to get in the way of his business goals. He marshaled his willpower and forced himself to look at the inlaid pattern of the elevator doors. He punched the call button with more force than he intended.

"Sorry about the elevator." Minda moved over to shield the call button from any further attack. "Like a lot of things in this building, it's really old. I know the elevator needs updating, but I just haven't been able to get to it. There are always a million other little repairs that take priority."

"Which reminds me, we started out this morning with a different purpose in mind than visiting your tenants."

"We did get a little side-tracked, didn't we?"

"Should we start that tour now?" He was starting to feel more in command of his emotions. Focusing on his business goals had a way of doing that.

"Sure. Where shall we start?"

"Does this building have a basement?"

"Yes."

"Then why don't we start there and work our way up?"

"Okay," she said, doubtfully, "but there's nothing very exciting about the basement."

The elevator doors slowly opened and Mark stood aside to allow Minda to enter the car first. "Don't be too sure of that. You never know what you'll find in a basement. Let's go."

The basement held no surprises for Mark. In fact, it

contained exactly what he had expected to find there: an antiquated heating system and a hodge-podge of electrical panels and hot water heaters.

Mark studied the jumble of vents and pipes and whistled through his teeth. "How does your plumber ever make sense of this?"

"I have to admit, it's a challenge. Some of these fixtures were in place at the turn of the twentieth century, when gas lights lit the building."

"This can't possibly meet building codes," he said, pessimistically.

"According to the city inspector it does. But I have to admit, I hold my breath every winter when I have to fire up the heating system."

"Have you priced a new one? Some of today's energy-efficient units start paying for themselves within two years."

She shook her head. "I could never get the money together to have the entire heating system replaced."

His eyes focused on a knot of electrical conduit tacked to an overhead beam. The entire building was a handyman's nightmare. Clearly, the plumbing and electrical systems had been updated in piece-meal fashion over the last century, with no plan or anticipation of future needs. To Mark, the whole mess was unsalvageable. The only sensible thing to do was raze the building and start all over. And that's exactly what he intended to do once Minda signed her name on the dotted line of the sale contract.

"You know, it only takes one little thing to go wrong and this place will fall like dominoes."

"Don't say that."

"Are you seriously telling me that no one has ever told you that before?"

"Well . . . yes. To be truthful, every person who has ever

come down here has said something like that. But this is an old building. You have to expect some remnants of its history."

"Not in the mechanical systems. They're too important. Plumbing, heating and electricity are the core systems that make your building habitable."

"But this building passes all the city inspections."

"But barely, right?" When she refused to meet his eyes, he had his answer.

She shrugged her slim shoulders. "There are always things I'd like to do around here; things I'd like to update or repair. But it always seems that just when I have the money together, the roof needs attention or something else happens."

"What's wrong with the roof?"

"The same thing that's wrong with this." She waved her hand at the maze of pipes. "The roof is a hodge-podge of six different roofs. When it rains or snows, this place averages one roof leak per month. It's hard to keep up."

He slipped his hands into his pockets and looked at her. His expression was gentle and sympathetic. "Minda, don't you ever feel overwhelmed? There's so much to do and you have so many people depending on you. That's a pretty daunting responsibility."

"Sometimes." She wasn't willing to say more for fear that she wouldn't be able to stop once she started. That daunting responsibility Mark so casually mentioned was attached to a list of repairs and overdue maintenance tasks that was longer than her arm. And each one of those things to do had a price tag attached to it.

She decided to change the subject. "Shall we see some of the other floors?"

"Sure." He took another long look around the basement,

as if committing the sight of it to memory, then he led the way to the heavy fire door. He started to open it and slammed it quickly shut again, nearly causing Minda to crash into him.

"Why do you care so much about this building?" He sounded exasperated.

She already knew he wouldn't understand but she'd answer his question anyway. "I don't just care about this building, I love it. It's part of my family and part of my ministry. It belonged to my husband and he left it to me, knowing I would care for it as he did. I could never do anything but my best for him."

"Even though your best isn't enough? You're so far behind in maintenance right now, you'll never catch up. Even with all the sacrifices you make to keep this place running, your efforts are only postponing the inevitable. The building is crumbling around you."

She looked away, uncertain which was more uncomfortable: the deadly serious tone in his voice or the troubled look in his eyes. Somehow he had accurately gauged the state of the building and her situation, and he didn't like what he saw. She could tell he thought she was foolish or at least misguided; but that only convinced her that he didn't understand how important the McAllister Building was.

"I haven't sacrificed any more than God asks me to," she said. "And so far, God has met my needs. He's kept this building going for me and for the people who live and work here. I can't ask for more."

"Or won't."

He opened the door and stepped aside so she could pass ahead of him into the hallway.

She used a key from her big key ring to lock the door and when she looked up again at Mark, his expression had changed. His exasperated look was gone.

"Should we continue our tour?" he asked, softly.

"Sure." She didn't feel as enthusiastic about showing him around as she had earlier. "Would you like to see the bookstore?"

"I'd love to see your bookstore."

The corner of his mouth tipped into that lop-sided smile that she was quickly growing to love. Instantly, her defensiveness was gone and she smiled back at him.

"Follow me." She led the way toward the stairs.

For the next hour Mark followed Minda from one floor of her building to another. He asked plenty of questions about the location, the tenants and the cost of keeping the old building maintained. Minda answered his questions willingly, with soft smiles and a light in her eyes that conveyed to him just how much she cared about the building and people who lived in it. He could tell she was pleased to show the old place off. And she was pleased by his interest.

The only problem was that any interest he showed was simply for the purpose of gathering information. Information he planned to use against her when the time was right.

Determinedly, he tamped down the twinge of regret he felt when he realized how much he was deceiving her. It was her own fault for investing all her time and energy in a crumbling old building that should have been demolished years ago. A dinosaur of a building that—if all went according to his plan—would be nothing but a memory by the time New Year's day came around.

He made his way back to the 16th Street Mall and caught the bus that would take him back to his hotel. Unlike earlier that morning, the bus was virtually empty. The rush hour commute was over and he was able to sit down on one of the molded benches. He studied an overhead sign that displayed the bus route and the connections to other public transportation. On an impulse, he stayed on when the bus came to a stop in front of his hotel and rode until he was within a block of the high-rise building where Harmony House's offices were located.

The building was filled with plush suites and expensively-decorated corporate headquarters. By contrast, Harmony House's donated suite was modestly furnished. Mark knew that his brother worked hard to strike a balance between having offices that were efficient and inviting for his employees, yet budget-minded and sensitive to the donors' expectations. He pulled open the door and entered the reception area. Beyond the reception desk, he saw his brother speaking with an employee near a row of cubicles.

"Mark?" Paul Cartier's brows went up. "This is a nice surprise."

"Sorry I didn't let you know I was coming. Do you have a minute?"

"Sure." He ushered Mark into his office and sat down behind the desk. "What's up?"

"I can't stay long, but I neglected to give this to you the other day and I've been carrying it around ever since." Mark pulled his wallet from his back pocket and extracted a check.

Paul took it and whistled through his teeth when he read the amount. He looked up at Mark and smiled. "Generous, as always."

Mark sat down in one of the guest chairs and looked across the desk at his brother. "Don't spend it all in one place."

"I never do. By the way, I tried to call you last night but you didn't answer. Where were you?"

"At church."

"What, again? That's twice in one week. Are you sure you're going strictly for business reasons?"

"Strictly. Why were you trying to reach me? And why didn't you leave a message?"

"I wanted to ask you to have dinner with us. Come tonight. Sarah and the kids would love to see you."

"I can't tonight. I have to be at baseball practice at seven o'clock."

Paul stared at him. "*Baseball practice*? Did I hear that right?"

"Why do you look so surprised? I used to be a pretty good baseball player."

"You used to be a *great* baseball player, but—just like going to church—you haven't had anything to do with baseball in years. Why are you suddenly playing baseball here in Denver, if you don't mind my asking?"

"It's no big deal. The baseball game is a fund-raiser for an organization."

"Another surprise. Would you mind rolling up your sleeve?"

"What for?"

"My brother has a birthmark just above his left elbow and I'd like to make sure I'm talking to the genuine Mark Cartier."

"Yeah, you're a real comedian," Mark said, with brotherly disgust.

Paul laughed. "You can't blame me. I've run a charitable organization for decades. And for decades, I've tried to get you involved in it, with no luck. So you'll understand if I'm a little surprised that all of a sudden you're willing to play baseball for a charity."

"It's not a charity. It's just a baseball game. Besides, I have to. I'm trying to close that deal."

"Ah, that explains it. You're going to church and involving yourself with this baseball fund-raiser simply for business reasons."

"That's right."

"A sense of giving never even factored into your plan."

"Right again."

"In that case, couldn't you have just paid someone to play on the team for you? You've got enough money and I hear the Rockies are in town," he said, referring to Denver's professional team.

"Again with the funny man."

"Sorry, that wasn't a fair thing to say. So, where's the baseball practice?"

"At the high school."

"I'll come and watch."

"I told you, this is business. No one involved in the deal knows anything about me or my—"

"I won't blow your deal!" Paul said quickly. "I'll be careful not to say anything that will make anyone suspicious or reveal anything about you personally. I know the drill. Have dinner with the family and then you and I can go to the high school together."

"Okay."

"So, tell me how your plan is faring. Has the Widow McAllister succumbed to your charm? Is she ready to sign on the dotted line yet?"

Mark ignored the hint of sarcasm in Paul's question. "Not yet. But I haven't given up and I'm not prepared to take no for an answer. Actually, that's the reason I stopped by to talk to you."

"Okay." Paul laced his fingers together behind his head and leaned back in his chair, ready to listen to whatever his younger brother had to say.

"I really need your advice on this McAllister Building deal. Something happened . . . something unexpected. I realize now that I got off to a bad start with Min—I mean, Mrs. McAllister. I'm trying to repair the damage and I think, ultimately, I'll be able to close the deal on her building, but I have to be careful."

"Careful of what?"

"I can't go into details."

"Okay. How did you get off to a bad start?"

"I can't really say."

"You just told me a whole bunch of nothing."

"Let's just say she made some wrong assumptions about me. I'm trying to rebuild her trust but I'm not sure how to do that."

"And you want me to help . . . how?"

"You've got daughters."

"Right."

"And the oldest is how old?"

"Thirteen."

Mark frowned. "She's probably too young."

"Too young for what?"

"To like boys."

Paul let out a bark of laughter. "Girls are *never* too young to like boys. It's like they're born with a sixth sense or some kind of gender radar. Molly may be only thirteen but she's very aware of boys."

"What kind of boy does she like?"

Paul unhooked his fingers to throw his hands up in a helpless gesture. "It's a mystery to me. Sarah would know. Molly's pretty close to her mother and talks to her about all sorts of things. Ask Sarah when you're at the house tonight."

"Never mind. It was just a thought."

"Why the sudden interest in teenaged girls?"

Mark felt a flicker of annoyance kindle. "I have *no* interest in teenaged girls. None. Nada!"

"Okay, I believe you. Geesh, you're getting touchy."

Mark took a deep, steadying breath. "Sorry. I shouldn't have snapped at you. Forget I said anything, okay?"

"Is something going on I should know about?"

"No."

"Anything on your mind you want to talk about?"

For a fleeting moment, Mark was tempted. Tempted to tell his brother about Tracy's crush and Minda's distrust. About Pastor's lecture and how crazy each one of them was for misjudging him. Paul would understand. Paul had always been the perfect older brother. A rock of stability and sound advice. He was tempted to tell Paul, but he couldn't. It was too . . . embarrassing.

Mark shook his head. "No, thanks. But about this building deal. If it goes through—and I feel pretty confident it will—it could mean a big change for me. It's the last deal I have to close in order to reach my goal of starting my own company."

Paul nodded, impressed. "You're ahead of plan."

"I've saved every penny I could get my hands on to come up with the capital to make this move. All I need is the commission from the McAllister Building and I'll have enough money to kiss Goble, Haines and Wyman good-bye and set up my own real estate investment company."

"And would it be safe for me to assume the letterhead will have the name Cartier somewhere in the title?"

"Cartier Investments."

"It has a nice ring to it." Paul smiled approvingly.

"It's more than that. It means I've arrived. It means I've reached the goal I set out to achieve. But there's one more thing. If I make this deal and I start my own firm, the first year will be rough. I just want to warn you that the checks I write in the future may not have as many zeroes on them as they've had in the past."

"You sound like you're apologizing and you shouldn't. You've been a reliable and generous donor to Harmony House since it first opened its doors. Any success this organization has had is because of your donations and the business advice you've given me. "

"I'm pretty certain your dedication and hard work had a lot more to do with Harmony House's success."

"We always did make a good team."

Mark smiled at him and stood. "I've got to get going. I'll see you later."

"Come by the house at 5:30."

"I'll be there. Now, I've got to run so I don't miss my bus."

"*Bus*?" Paul repeated, astounded. "*You're* riding a *bus*? Hey, can I see that birthmark?" he called out, but Mark had already left his office.

"The cash drawer's not ready," Ellen Dailey muttered to herself. "And the new delivery hasn't been added to the inventory yet." She frowned and looked around the immediate area of the bookstore for Minda. When she didn't see her she called out, "Hey, Minda!"

Minda joined her in the front of the store, pulling the book-laden cart behind her. "What's wrong?"

"The new delivery of books hasn't been entered in the inventory yet. I thought you wanted those new books in the window display before we opened today."

"I do. The books are right here. There's still time to set them in the window before we open."

"But they're not in the inventory," Ellen repeated, in case

Minda had missed the point.

"They will be. I'm working on it right now."

Ellen helped her take the books from the cart and arrange them in the store window. "I thought you were going to take care of this as soon as you got in this morning. It's not like you to oversleep. What happened?"

"I didn't oversleep. I was just busy."

"Busy doing what?"

Minda knew Ellen was just like a hound dog with a bone when she wanted to know something. She could be tenacious until she got the information she wanted. She said, carefully, "I was giving someone a tour of the building."

"No kidding? A tour? Who on earth would want a tour of this old place?"

"Mark Cartier."

Ellen stopped what she was doing and looked happily over at Minda. "That gorgeous hunk of masculinity asked for a tour of the building?"

"Yes. And you can stop grinning at me."

"I'm not grinning, I'm smiling. Can I assume you worked out that whole thing about Tracy having a crush on him?"

"Not yet. She still has a crush on him. But he promised he won't see Tracy or encourage her in any way and I intend to make sure he keeps that promise."

"And what about you?"

Minda's jaw tightened slightly. "What about me?"

"Is he going to keep seeing you?"

Minda set a short stack of books down on the cart with a challenging thud. "Meaning what?"

"Meaning . . . the guy is obviously interested in you. Why else would he come up with lame excuses to see you? Don't tell me you really thought he wanted a tour of this building. Puh-leeze."

Minda tamped down the words that were on the tip of her tongue. Instead, she said, calmly, "You're jumping to the wrong conclusion."

"I don't think so. I've seen how he looks at you. Last night when you helped me set up the refreshment table at church, he could hardly take his eyes off you. If you ask me, he's crazy about you."

"I didn't ask. And I'm not going to argue with you about this. But even if what you said were true—And I'm not saying that it is!" she added, quickly, "the feeling is not mutual. I'm not interested in Mark."

"Why, what's wrong with him?"

"Nothing that I know of."

"Then, why aren't you interested in him?"

"Is there some rule I don't know about that says I *have* to be interested in him?"

"No, but I don't know any single woman who'd pass on a guy who's handsome, charming, and has some serious coin in his bank account."

Minda looked up from her work. "Maybe you just hit on the one thing that *is* wrong with him. When you were naming his assets just now, you never said anything about his faith."

"He obviously goes to church," Ellen suggested.

"No he doesn't. He showed up at church on Sunday because I invited him. He showed up last night because Tracy invited him. If it were up to him, I'm pretty sure he wouldn't set foot inside a church."

Ellen's eyes brightened, along with her smile. "You mean he's going to church just to please you?"

"You say that is if it were a good thing."

"Well . . . yeah. Isn't it?"

"No, it's not. Ellen, don't you see? Dale was so strong in his faith, so unshakeable. That was one of the things that drew me to Dale in the first place. How can I possibly be attracted to a man like Mark who only shows up at church—not because he wants to rejoice in the Lord and worship Him—but because he thinks that's what it takes to please me?"

"Honey, you can't compare every man you meet to Dale," Ellen said. "You know I love you like a sister. And you know I loved Dale because he was my brother. But Dale's gone. He's been gone for seventeen years. Isn't it time you let him go?"

"Of course not! Ellen, how can you say such a thing? Dale was my husband. He was the love of my life. He was my knight in shining armor."

"But you're grieving over a knight who's not coming back. Meanwhile, there's a prince knocking on your door that you won't let in."

Minda stared at her. "How long have you felt this way?"

"We're talking about your feelings, not mine."

"I don't want to talk about feelings at all," Minda muttered, feeling uncertain. "Besides, it's time to open the store."

Ellen wrapped a comforting arm around Minda's shoulders. "I didn't mean to upset you but don't you think it's time you let Dale go? You've proved you were a good and loving wife to my brother. You've mourned him for seventeen years and no one will think less of you for being interested in another man. It's okay if you fall in love again."

"Ellen!"

"Just think about what I said, okay?" Ellen gave Minda's shoulder a reassuring squeeze. "*Think* about it."

She was thinking about it. More than she wanted to, but she wasn't willing to admit that to Ellen or anyone else. Minda watched Ellen push the cart toward the back room and frowned.

It was just like Ellen to read too much into her relationship with Mark. It was just like Ellen to get carried away with thoughts of romance and a handsome prince. If Minda wasn't careful, she could find herself believing in Ellen's fairy tales.

She went to the front door of the shop and deliberately planted her feet firmly on the floor. Minda McAllister was much too practical to be carried away by a handsome man with blue eyes. She had a daughter to raise and a business to run. She had tenants to care for and an orphan train reunion to plan. There simply wasn't room in her life for Mark Cartier.

With that determined thought, Minda squared her shoulders and unlocked the front door of the shop to admit the morning's customers.

12

"Why can't I go to the baseball practice?" Tracy demanded.

"I didn't say you couldn't go. I simply said I'd take you," Minda answered, in a calm voice.

"You mean you're going to watch the practice, too?"

"Yes, I am. It's a beautiful night and it'll be nice to spend some time outside."

"But you've never been interested in baseball before."

Minda ignored the sullen tone in Tracy's voice. She also ignored an impulse to remind her daughter that she was no baseball fan herself; that she didn't know a first baseman from an umpire. Instead, she gathered up her purse and car keys. "That's true, but since the game is one of the major fundraisers for the orphan train reunion and I'm on the reunion committee, I think it would be a good idea for me to attend at least part of the practice."

Tracy's expression cleared a little. "So you're not going to stay for the whole thing?" she asked, hopefully.

"I haven't decided yet," Minda said, although she was

definitely staying as long as she needed to in order to ensure Tracy kept away from Mark.

Mark had promised he wouldn't see Tracy or communicate with her without Minda's approval, and in the soft dimness of the Pastor's study, she had believed him. But in the light of day, she wasn't so sure she could trust him. She couldn't shake the sneaking suspicion that she had been conned by Mark's dazzling smile and deep voice. What if it had all been an act? What if he had held her hand and spoken to her so comfortingly simply to disarm her?

Her heart rebelled against the thought. She wanted to believe in Mark's sincerity, but she was still a mom with a job to do. Clearly, Tracy didn't want her to go to the baseball field. As a mother, she had no choice but to do the exact opposite of what her teenager wanted.

They got in the car and Minda started the engine. "Why don't we stop at the store on our way to the ball field? We can pick up some bottled water for the players."

The last of Tracy's scowl disappeared. "And maybe some energy bars?"

Minda mentally calculated the amount she had budgeted for groceries that month. "Let's see how much they cost before we decide."

In the end they arrived at the baseball practice with the car trunk loaded with cases of bottled water and several boxes of snack bars.

Daylight was fading but banks of lights illuminated the playing field and sidelines. A small group of people was already gathered at the metal bleachers erected on one side of the baseball diamond. Minda recognized Pastor Walker and Jim and Ellen Daily. Josh Stuart was there, too.

And Mark.

As they got out of their car, Josh left the group and came

over to greet them.

"Hi, Tracy. Hi, Mrs. McAllister."

"Hello, Josh." Minda popped the trunk open. "We brought some water for the players. Can you help us carry it to the dugout?"

"Sure thing." He went with Tracy to the rear of the car and hoisted up one of the cases of bottled water. "I didn't know you were going to be here tonight, Tracy."

"I didn't decide to come until just a little while ago."

"Still trying to pretend to like baseball?" he asked, teasing.

"Almost as much as I try to pretend to like you," she retorted.

Josh frowned as he watched Tracy walk toward the bleachers, swinging the grocery bags filled with snack bars.

"Women," he muttered. "I'll never understand them."

Minda took pity on him. "I'm sorry, Josh. If it's any consolation, sometimes we don't understand ourselves very well, either."

"Why does she have to act that way? Like she's better than everybody else and sophisticated or something. She acts like she's twenty-five. She acts *old*."

Minda smothered a smile. "I think she's just trying to find herself and maybe she's trying to impress someone. Someone she's attracted to."

"Yeah, well, I've been trying to do the same thing." He shook his head slightly, then he hoisted the cases of water a little higher against his chest and headed for the dugout.

Coach was organizing the players on the field for warm-up when Minda joined the small group of spectators near the bleachers.

Her gaze naturally fixed on Mark. He was dressed in long athletic pants and a heather-gray tee-shirt that hugged his muscled shoulders and the planes of his strong chest. He was standing with Tracy, Pastor Walker and another man Minda didn't recognize. They were smiling and chatting together; but when Mark saw Minda, he tucked his baseball glove under his left arm so he could extend his hand to her.

Without thinking, she put her hand in his, allowing him to draw her closer to the group.

"Minda, I'd like you to meet my brother, Paul. Paul, this is Minda McAllister."

So this was Mark's brother! A real member of the very same family Mark was so reluctant to talk about. She smiled at him and saw that Paul shared the same blue eyes as Mark, the same dark hair; but his body wasn't as lean as Mark's and her quick assessment noted a wedding band on his left ring finger.

"*You're* Mrs. McAllister?" Paul asked, surprised.

"Yes, I am."

"The same Mrs. McAllister who owns the McAllister Building?"

"That's right. But please call me, Minda." She realized he was staring at her. "Do I know you? I'm sorry but I don't recall—"

"Oh, we've never met," Paul said, quickly, "so please don't apologize for not recognizing me. I know you only by reputation. A reputation my *dear brother* might have corrected." He made a fist and took a swipe at Mark's arm.

Minda valiantly kept the smile on her face. "I'm sorry. I don't understand."

"I was expecting Mrs. McAllister to be—I just hadn't expected to meet you here today," Paul said.

"Where's my short-stop?" Coach called from edge of the field.

"That's my cue." Mark pulled his baseball glove on and jogged toward the infield to take his position.

Minda sat down on the bleachers between Paul and Tracy and watched the players warm up. Her attention naturally focused on Mark. She watched him catch balls and toss them to Josh in left field or to Jim Dailey at first base with the ease of a natural athlete. Some of the balls the other players threw to Mark were wildly off-course, but he always managed to catch them; and when he threw the ball to another player, his aim was unerringly accurate. Minda realized that his ability was far above the other players on the field, and she could tell that Tracy was equally impressed by his performance.

Tracy clapped her hands together each time Mark caught the ball. "Good catch!" she yelled.

"Mark's a good player," Pastor Walker said as he climbed up to sit on the bleacher row directly behind Minda and Paul.

Paul nodded. "He played all through high school and college. He actually had an athletic scholarship for baseball. He could have played pro, if you ask me. Or maybe that's just brotherly pride talking."

Tracy pulled her attention from Mark's performance to stare at Paul with wide eyes. "You mean, he could have been a professional baseball player?"

"Among other things," Paul said. "Mark's one of those guys God blessed with all the talents."

"We already know he can sing really good. My mom and I heard him sing in church."

"Yes, he's a very good singer," Paul agreed. "He can also play the guitar and he's a pretty decent artist. When he was a kid he used to draw comic-book characters all the time."

Tracy's nose wrinkled. "Comic-book characters?"

"Super heroes. Boys like that stuff."

Ellen Dailey joined them on the bleachers, taking a seat next to Pastor Walker on the second row. "Have you all noticed how well my Jim plays?" As if on cue, Jim stuck his glove out to catch a ball but missed. Ellen smiled proudly. "He could have caught that one if he really wanted to. I think his glove is defective. And the other player should have thrown it better."

Tracy swiveled around to scowl at her. "Mark threw the ball right to him!"

"Exactly!" Ellen said. "Anybody can catch the easy ones. My Jim likes a challenge."

Tracy shook her head in disbelief and refocused her attention on Mark. "I don't think you should be making fun of the best player on the whole entire team, Aunt Ellen."

"I'm not making fun of him, honey. I'm just trying to encourage your Uncle Jim. I could use some help with that." Ellen looked hopefully at the back of Tracy's head. Instead, Tracy concentrated on gathering more information about Mark.

She leaned forward so she could look past Minda to see Paul. "Mark told me about his condo in New York. Have you seen it?"

"I'm afraid not."

"Do you live in New York, too?"

"No, I live here in Denver. My work here keeps me pretty busy. I don't get to travel much and over the past few years, the only time Mark and I ever get together is when he comes to Denver."

"Oh." Tracy sounded disappointed. She leaned back and refocused her attention on the players on the field.

"Minda," Pastor Walker said, "do you remember our conversation earlier this week? I mentioned a news article about a Denver man named Cartier? Well, Paul is the man I was talking about. Paul runs a local faith-based charity here in Denver that does some wonderful work."

Minda asked, politely, "What is the name of your charity,

Paul?"

"Harmony House. We offer a broad range of ministries, but our main focus is finding homes for individuals and families who can't afford housing through no fault of their own."

Minda blinked. "Did you say, Harmony House?"

"That's right. You might have heard Mark talk about it. He's on the board of directors."

He certainly had talked about it. In fact, Minda clearly recalled Mark mentioning Harmony House the night he helped her paint Addy Whimple's apartment. She also recalled how she had scoffed at his suggestion that a charitable organization could be anything but impersonal.

"Yes, he did mention Harmony House, but he never told me he was involved in running it."

"He doesn't really run it. He leaves the operations to me but he's a strong supporter, just the same. There wouldn't be a Harmony House if it weren't for Mark."

"You and Minda have something in common," Pastor Walker said. "Minda's personal ministry is along the same lines. She owns the McAllister Building in lower downtown. The apartments in her building are rented to individuals and families who are just getting on their feet. I know first-hand that if weren't for Minda, some of her tenants wouldn't have a roof over their heads."

"I know all about the building," Paul said. "You may not remember, Minda, but a couple years ago I sent you a letter offering to buy the McAllister building. Most of Harmony House's clients are in the downtown and lower downtown areas of Denver and I thought your building would be ideal for the ministry."

"I'm sorry, I don't remember that. But I would never sell the McAllister Building. That building belonged to my husband's family for generations and now it belongs to me. It's too important to my tenants and to my family to ever consider selling it."

Tracy made a face. "She never gets rid of anything that belonged to my dad."

"That must be why she holds on to you," said Ellen, as she gave a strand of Tracy's hair a playful tug.

"Not for long." Tracy twisted around so she could look back at Ellen and Pastor Walker. "I'll be eighteen soon. I'll be an adult and I can do whatever I want. I've got a whole list of things I'm gonna do."

Ellen cocked her head to one side. "Is getting a job and supporting yourself on the list?"

"No, but going to New York is."

Coach blew his whistle to call all the players into the dugout. He quickly divided them into two practice teams; one team took the outfield while the other team—which included Mark and Josh—remained in the dugout for batting practice.

Tracy got up from the bleachers and went over to stand against the chain-link fence that surrounded the dugout.

Minda watched Tracy speak to Mark through the fencing. She was too far away to hear what Tracy said. She was too far away to read Mark's expression. But she didn't see Mark do anything to discourage Tracy's attention. She frowned.

Josh was frowning, too. He was on the first step of the dugout watching Tracy thread her fingers through the chain link as she spoke to Mark.

Coach caught Josh's attention by thrusting a bat into his hands. "You're up, son." He clapped a hand on Josh's shoulder and led him toward home plate.

Josh crouched into his batting stance. The pitcher wound up and threw a strike over the plate. Josh watched it go by.

"Hey, son, that was a strike!" said Coach, from his place near the dugout. "You've got to swing at those."

Josh stepped out of the batter's box and took a few practice swings. His gaze strayed toward the dugout, where Tracy was still at the fence, trying her best to capture Mark's attention.

"Batter up," prompted Coach.

Josh stepped back into the batter's box. The pitcher threw the ball directly over home plate. Again, Josh let it go by without swinging.

"Josh!" Coach sounded exasperated. "Pay attention to the pitcher, not the dugout!"

Josh muttered something beneath his breath as he backed out of the batter's box. He took a couple of deep breaths and stepped back up to the plate. The pitcher wound up and released the ball. Josh swung hard and missed as the ball sailed smoothly into the catcher's mitt.

"Next time!" Ellen called encouragingly from the bleachers, as Josh stomped back toward the dugout. "Shake it off!"

Mark batted next. He took a few warm-up swings as he strode toward the batter's box.

"Time!" called Coach. He walked over to Mark. "Son, you can't run bases with that."

Mark looked down and saw the gold chain of his watch hanging from his pants pocket. "Sorry, Coach. I guess I'm so used to carrying it everwhere, I forgot all about it." He pulled the watch from his pocket and held it out. "Will you hold it for me while I bat?"

Mark stepped into the batter's box, held the bat up near his right shoulder and stared back at the pitcher. The pitcher wound up and sent a fast-ball over the plate. Mark took a big-league swing and drove the ball straight over the head of the right fielder. Mark rounded the bases and made it to third before the outfielder threw the ball back in to the second-baseman.

The next batter drove the ball down the first base line and Mark jogged easily into home.

Coach gave him an approving clap on the shoulder and walked toward the dugout with him. "Good at-bat, son." He drove his hand into the pocket of his sweatshirt and gently withdrew Mark's watch and handed it to him. "That's a mighty fine timepiece, son. Where'd you get it?"

"At an auction in Chicago a few years ago."

"Does it chime?"

"Sure does." Mark opened the watch so it could play its familiar tune, lilting and clear.

Coach cocked his head to one side and frowned. "I think I . . . Have I heard that song before?"

"It's a hymn."

Coached looked up and met his eyes. He was frowning with concentration, as if he were trying to conjure up a long-lost memory. "I know that, but . . . the tone of the chime and the way it plays the notes . . . I've heard it before. I can't seem to remember where, though." He shook his head slightly. He gave the watch one last look, then clapped his hands together several times. "Next batter!"

Another player stepped up to the plate and Coach focused on watching the batter and calling out instructions.

Mark went into the dugout and found Tracy still hanging on the fence.

"You're a really good baseball player, Mark."

"Thanks, Tracy. Do you like baseball?"

"I love it."

"Do you play?"

"No, not really," she said, without elaborating on the fact

that she'd never before shown real interest in any sport. "I'm afraid I'm not very athletic."

"Maybe you just need some help. Some lessons."

Tracy's eyes lit up. "Maybe someone who's really good at baseball could teach me."

"That's a great idea. You can't improve unless you practice. I'll ask Coach to give you some help."

The light in her eyes vanished. "Coach?"

"Sure. I bet he'd be happy to give you some pointers." He looked over to where Coach was standing at the top of the dugout steps; but instead of watching the batter and calling out words of encouragement, Coach was staring right at Mark.

"Excuse me, Tracy." Mark got up off the bench and walked to the dugout steps.

"Coach? What's up?"

"Can I see that watch again?"

Mark stepped up out of the dugout and withdrew the watch from his pocket. He held it out to Coach.

Coach took it reverently in the palm of his hand. He stared at it for a few moments. "We had a watch like this in my family. My *real* family."

Mark immediately felt the prick of goose bumps on his arms. "Real family? Are you talking about your birth family?"

Coach continued to look down at the watch and nodded slightly. "When I was a boy, I used to fall asleep at night hearing this watch. Or maybe it was a watch just like this one. I could be wrong, but I think my mother—my birth mother—used it like a lullaby when she put me to bed at night. Funny, I hadn't thought about it before, but seeing this watch and hearing it chime—it sort of brought the memory back."

Mark drew in a deep breath. He struggled to find the right

thing to say and realized that words weren't necessary. This was Coach's moment and only Coach's words and memories counted.

Coach looked up at Mark as he had a sudden thought. "My sister had the watch on the train. I remember it now. My oldest sister had the watch. At night we had to sleep in our seats on the train and it was pretty uncomfortable. But my sister kept telling us that we were together and that's what mattered. Every night on the train when it was time to sleep, she'd make sure we said our prayers and she'd open the watch and play the hymn for us just like my mother . . ." His voice trailed away as he battled back emotions that threatened to overcome him.

He looked down, taking one last, lingering look at the watch before he handed it back to Mark. His eyes were bright with moisture, but he quickly swiped his face with the cuff of his sweatshirt.

"That's a mighty fine timepiece, son." Coach clapped his hands together several times and walked toward home plate. "Batter up!" he called, gruffly.

Mark stared at the watch in his hand, feeling as if it had just taken on a profound meaning he couldn't begin to understand. Could Coach be right? Was this the very same watch that had been in Coach's family? He coiled the chain, fob, and watch in his hand and carried it over to where Minda was sitting in the bleachers.

"Would you hold this for me, please?"

Minda carefully took the watch. "Mark? Is something wrong?" She could see the change in Mark's expression. The joy she'd seen on his face as he'd played baseball had now been replaced with a distracted frown.

The sound of her voice brought him back to his senses. "Wrong? No, nothing's wrong. We're good."

He smiled at her and she knew that whatever had been bothering him was not something he was willing to share. *How many secrets could one man have?* she wondered, as she watched him walk back to the dugout.

"Not exactly an open book, is he?" Paul asked, quietly.

"I've noticed he doesn't like to talk about himself."

"That's because he doesn't usually stay in one place long enough for anyone to get too curious."

"I thought he had a condo in New York? He must have people there who are close to him."

"Maybe," Paul said with a shrug. "If he does, I've never heard of them. He travels a lot, goes from place to place. That pricey condo in New York is more like a home base than a home. It's just a place he keeps the things he needs to pack for the next trip."

A thousand questions leapt to Minda's mind and she wondered whether she could ask Paul about his brother without raising his suspicions. "Doesn't he have anybody special in his life? Like a girlfriend?" She hoped the question sounded casual.

"Not that I know of. He dates a lot, but I don't think he's ever been too serious about any of the women he sees."

"And his dates—those women—were they all around his age?"

"Give or take a year or two." Paul looked over to where Tracy was still hovering near the dugout, still trying to capture Mark's attention. "My brother's always been very focused on what he wants out of life. He always has a plan to accomplish. He checks off goals like you or I check off items on a grocery list while we shop. I don't think he's made any room in his life for serious romance. And he'd never do anything to jeopardize the life he's mapped out for himself."

Minda looked over at Tracy. She hadn't given up her

position at the dugout fence, but Mark didn't seem to be paying any attention to her. He was sitting on the team bench with his back to Tracy. His attention veered between exchanging small talk with the player sitting next to him and shouting words of encouragement to the players on the field. He was acting as if Tracy weren't standing right behind him.

He was acting as if he weren't the least bit interested in Tracy.

He was keeping his promise to Minda.

13

The sound of Coach's whistle called the players off the field and into the dugout. As the player's grabbed from the stock of water bottles Minda and Tracy brought, Coach praised their efforts. "You look like a real baseball team out there."

Josh waved his water bottle above his head to catch Coach's attention. "We'd look more like a team if we had uniforms."

"I know, son, but this is just friendly game between two churches. We don't have a budget for uniforms."

"What about tee-shirts?" Mark asked. "Couldn't we just get tee-shirts?"

"No budget for tee-shirts, either, I'm afraid."

Mark did some quick mental math. "I'll get the tee-shirts, Coach. Everybody likes blue, right?"

Coach frowned. "Son, are you sure?"

"Yes, I'm sure. On such short notice, they won't be anything fancy. I can probably get the name of the church printed on the front and a player number on the back, but that's it. Is everybody okay with that?"

The players on the bench all agreed. Except for Josh, who shot Mark a look of resentment before he crossed his arms over his chest and stared down at the dugout floor.

"That's mighty generous of you, son," Coach said. "We all appreciate it. Okay, let's get our heads back in the game." He clapped his hands enthusiastically, then pointed to a player at the end of the team bench. "I know you haven't played in a long time, son. We're all a little rusty," he said before he critiqued the player's performance; then, one-by-one, he did the same for all the other players, offering each one feedback and encouragement. The last player he turned to was Mark.

"I guess we've all figured out who our best player is. You had some great at-bats, son. Too bad you aren't a few years younger; I could have used about eight more of you on my varsity team this year."

Josh sputtered indignantly. "Wait a second, Coach! *I'm* on the varsity team!" His angry voice carried easily to the bleachers.

"And you struck out three times," Coach answered. "You're going to have to do better. You gotta get your head in the game and keep your eye on the ball. Okay, now, enough talk. Let's switch sides! Players who were in the outfield, stay in the dugout for batting practice. Those of you who already batted, take your positions on the field."

Mark followed Josh out of the dugout and onto the field. "You must be a pretty good player if you made the varsity team at school."

"Yeah, well, maybe I am," retorted Josh.

"Congratulations. It's a tough team to make. Do you play football, too?"

"None of your business!" Josh's voice rose, angrily. "I don't need you to rub it in—"

"Whoa! I didn't mean anything by it," Mark said, quickly. "I was just trying to make conversation."

"Well, maybe I don't feel like talking. Maybe you've been doing enough talking already tonight."

Mark wasn't sure if Josh's anger was the result of something he'd done or just a display of normal tortured teenaged angst. Either way, he could see that Josh was pretty riled up over something.

Mark took his position between second and third base just as the pitcher sent the first pitch toward home plate. The batter connected and sent the ball straight toward him. Mark caught it easily and threw it to the first baseman.

"Woo-hoo!" shouted Tracy from her place near the dugout fence. "Good catch, Mark!" She turned around to beam happily at the people on the bleachers. "Did you see that? Isn't Mark a great player?"

From behind him, Mark heard Josh sputter again and this time, the sound of Josh's indignation clicked in Mark's brain. This time, he didn't have to wonder over the source of Josh's anger. The five-foot-three-inch source of the trouble was standing at the dugout with her seventeen-year-old fingers curled around the chain-link fence.

Mark looked over at Tracy and she waved happily at him.

He looked over his shoulder at Josh, who immediately looked down and began kicking divots in the grass with the toe of his baseball cleat.

The next batter sent a ground ball hopping to Mark's left. He adjusted his position easily and scooped the ball up into the webbing of his glove. As if on cue, Tracy applauded enthusiastically. Mark threw the ball to first base then casually looked over his shoulder in time to see Josh scowl and shake his head.

Mark smiled slightly. So, Josh Stuart had a king-sized

crush on Tracy McAllister! He could have kicked himself for not noticing it before. Now Josh's resentful attitude made perfect sense to Mark. It also gave him an idea.

The next batter came to the plate. From his batting stance, Mark could tell he was aiming toward left field. The pitcher released the ball and the batter swung, sending the ball on a straight line just inches above the ground toward Mark.

He set his feet as if he were going to field it, but at the last minute he allowed the ball to go straight between his legs.

Josh rushed forward to scoop up the ball and throw it to the infield, but the damage was already done; the batter was safe at first base.

The next batter connected with the ball, as well, sending it hard and straight as a clothes-line toward the gap between Mark and the third baseman. It was an easy out, a back-handed catch Mark could have made in his sleep. For appearances sake, he made a half-hearted attempt to grab at it, but he let the ball sail by him toward left field.

Josh ran forward to field the ball and throw it to the third baseman. He looked at Mark with annoyance. "I hope this doesn't sound rude, sir, but for a guy who's supposed to be such a great short-stop, you sure suck at fielding balls."

Mark glanced over at Tracy. From the way her posture suddenly straightened, he was pretty sure she'd heard Josh's comment. In fact, everyone on the third-base side of the field must have heard it because the people on the bleachers and the players in the dugout almost turned as one to look at Josh and Mark.

Mark squared his shoulders. In a voice loud enough to carry over to the bleachers he yelled, "Oh, yeah?"

He walked purposefully up to Josh and stopped just inches in front of him. "Point at me," he commanded in a low voice.

"Huh?"

"You heard me. *Point* at me."

Josh looked doubtful. "Okay, I'll do it, but I don't know what for."

"And now take your finger and jab it into my chest a couple times."

Josh looked as if he wanted to back away. "This is getting kinda weird, Mr. Cartier."

"Just do what I say."

Confused, Josh did as Mark instructed. "Are you going to tell me why I'm doing this?"

"You're standing close to me and jabbing your finger in my chest because anybody who sees you do it will think you're telling me to shape up or ship out."

Josh frowned. "But everybody knows I wouldn't do that."

"You would if you had to take the lead on the team because I'm not as good a player as I claimed to be. After all, everybody here saw you make the plays that I blew."

"Yeah, I guess they did." Josh's frown slowly cleared. "But it's not like you're a bad player, Mr. Cartier. I bet you were pretty good when you were young."

"Thanks, Josh." Mark wondered how it would look to the spectators if he did some jabbing of his own. "Listen, you keep this up, okay? If I miss a play or overthrow first base or make any errors at all, I want you to call me on it."

"Okay."

"And make sure you do it loud enough so anyone near the dugout will hear."

Josh's eyes lit up. "Yeah, I sure will, Mr. Cartier."

And he did. Mark made several boner plays during the rest of the practice game, giving Josh plenty of chances to give him a good jawing in front of everyone on the team. And the best part was that he was pretty certain Tracy heard it, too.

After one of Mark's botched plays, Tracy backed away from the dugout fence as if the chain link suddenly burned her fingers. She sat down next to Minda on the bottom row of the bleachers.

"They don't look so good, do they?" She swung around to look worriedly at Minda, Ellen, Paul and Pastor Walker. "I mean, isn't he supposed to catch those?"

Minda was wondering the same thing. She'd heard Paul talk with pride about Mark's baseball skills, yet he seemed to be playing only slightly worse than the other players on the field. "Maybe they all need some encouragement," she said.

"Hey," Ellen suggested, "why don't the five of us do the wave?"

Tracy turned back in time to see Mark make another error by throwing the ball high above the head of the first baseman.

Coach sputtered from his position at the top of the dugout steps. "Turn down that heat a little, son! No need to throw it so hard. It's more important to throw it accurately."

"Will do, Coach," Mark said. But he didn't. He purposefully made several more errors and each time he did, Josh gave him a good jawing.

When practice ended, Mark walked up to the bleachers and stood in front of Tracy. "Pretty good practice, huh?"

She didn't answer but she didn't need to. Mark could easily see the disappointment in her face. She looked up at him as if he had just donned lederhosen and asked her to dance a polka with him. He tried not to smile but he was pretty certain his value had decreased in Tracy's eyes. His plan worked. He felt pretty proud of himself.

He walked back toward the field to help gather up the equipment. Paul followed him.

Mark scooped up the bats that were arranged near the

home plate fencing and turned to find himself toe-to-toe with his brother. Paul planted the palm of his hand on Mark's chest preventing him from moving away.

"What was that all about?" Paul asked, in a low voice.

Mark shrugged his shoulders disinterestedly. "What do you mean?"

"I'm talking about those boner plays you made . . . or *didn't* make," he amended, meaningfully. "You missed catching balls you could have snagged blindfolded."

"Listen, I can't explain it to you right now, but I had my reasons. Can we leave it at that?"

"I suppose, but I wish you had told me about your reasons before I bragged to everybody in the bleachers that you were good enough to have gone pro, if you'd wanted to. You made a liar out of me."

"I'm sorry," Mark said, and meant it. "I'll tell you all about it but just not right now."

"When you decide to share, maybe that would be a good time for you to also tell me why you decided to keep Minda McAllister a secret."

"She isn't a secret."

"She was supposed to be an *old woman*!"

"I never said that."

"You didn't correct me when *I* said it!"

An impish smile tugged at the corners of Mark's mouth. "No, I didn't. Sorry again."

"Are there any other secrets you have that I should know about?"

"No. Listen, I'll tell you all about . . . *this*," Mark tipped his head toward the baseball diamond, "on the drive home. I promise."

Paul held an equipment bag open and Mark dropped the bats into it. He looked over toward the bleachers and saw

Minda and Tracy gathering their things together. He thought it best to stay where he was, to keep some distance between himself and the McAllister women. He lifted his hand in a casual wave. They waved back and headed for their car. Josh followed them, carrying the left-over water.

Pastor Walker climbed down from the bleachers and joined Mark and Paul on the field. He extended his hand to Paul. "It was a pleasure to finally meet you. I've heard so many good things about Harmony House and the work you do. I'd like to talk more."

"I'd like that, too," Paul said. "Perhaps we could have lunch together this week, Pastor. Mark has told me a little about the excellent work your congregation has done reuniting orphan train riders with their families. Since Harmony House is devoted to keeping families together, I'd say we have a lot in common."

Pastor Walker's eyes lit up. "I wonder if there isn't some way we can join forces and really make a difference in some people's lives."

Mark smiled as he watched his brother and the pastor fall deep into conversation. They were like two peas in a pod, dedicated to a common cause.

He felt a hand on his shoulder. Jim Daily was standing beside him. "That was quite a show you put on."

Mark frowned. "A show?"

"Yeah, a show. You don't think everybody believed that bumbling ballplayer routine, do you?"

Mark darted a quick look around to see who might have overheard. Minda and Tracy were already at their car in the parking lot. Paul and Pastor Walker were deep in conversation. Ellen was still sitting on the bleachers, patiently waiting for her husband, but he saw her sit up a little straighter and look right at him. She'd heard.

Coach joined him, lugging more equipment bags laden with balls and gloves. "Just what was that all about, if you don't mind my asking, son? I figured you must have your reasons for suddenly turning into a Little Leaguer out there, but I can't for the life of me figure out why."

Coach's gruff voice carried and stopped Paul's conversation with Pastor Walker mid-sentence. Suddenly, Mark felt as if everyone's attention was fixed on him.

He scowled. "I did have a reason, but I'd rather not go into it."

"No need," Jim said. "Ellen told me all about it."

Mark's head swiveled toward Ellen, who was still seated on the bleachers. She flashed a smile and two thumbs up. "I told Jim all about it!" she called.

Mark's brain automatically went into damage control mode. "Listen, I don't know what she told you, but—"

"She told me about Tracy."

"What about Tracy?" asked Coach, mystified.

Mark felt more uncomfortable with every passing second. "This isn't the place to go into it."

Jim shrugged his shoulders. "You can trust us. It's just us four."

"Five!" yelled Ellen from the bleachers.

"Look, I can tell you don't want to talk about it," Jim said, "but I thought I'd bring it up in case you needed some help. Besides, I'd hate to see you throw an entire game if you don't have to. This baseball fundraiser means a lot to Coach and we all want to play our best for him. Think about that, will you?"

Mark felt his temper rise. "I'm not going to throw the baseball game. I'd never do that!"

Paul came over to stand beside him. "Let's all calm down a little, okay? Listen, we all know you deliberately played badly

197

out there today. I'm sure you had your reasons. Why don't we just talk about it now?"

That was easier said than done. With five pairs of eyes staring at him as if he were a carnival sideshow, Mark couldn't even figure out where to start. His gaze locked on Pastor Walker's face.

"Would you like me to tell them?" Pastor Walker asked.

Mark threw up his hands in defeat and looked down at the ground.

"A certain young lady," Pastor Walker said, "in our congregation has developed a little bit of a schoolgirl crush on Mark. Correct me if I'm wrong, Mark, but at some point during practice you realized that if you played badly, you might not look as attractive to her. Am I right?"

Mark nodded.

"Who's the young lady?" asked Coach, mystified.

Mark took a deep breath and muttered, "Tracy McAllister."

Paul whistled through his teeth.

"I think," Pastor Walker said, "your plan was somewhat effective but Jim has a valid point. It wouldn't be fair to Coach, to the rest of the team or the opposing players from the other church if you don't play your best at all the practices and at the fundraising game."

"I guess I didn't think of it that way before." Mark flashed an apologetic glance at Coach. The last thing he wanted was to hurt the man in any way.

Coach fiddled with the rope on the equipment bag. "We've sold a lot of tickets to the game, son. We want to give people a real competitive match-up. I expect everyone to play to the best of their ability, including you."

"Maybe it would be best if I didn't play on the team," Mark suggested, although he hated to say it. For some odd reason, he really wanted to play on a two-bit baseball team backed by a church he didn't even know existed two weeks ago. He really wanted to play and he really wanted to help Coach out.

Coach held up a hand as if he could stop Mark's thoughts. "Don't say that. We need you, son, and the team wouldn't be the same without you."

"Maybe there's a way we can help," Jim said.

Mark looked doubtful. "How?"

"Well, as the church youth minister I interact with Tracy a lot. Now that I'm aware of the situation, I can watch for opportunities to counsel her."

"I don't want anyone else talking about this. Frankly, it's a little embarrassing, and I'm sure Minda wouldn't want anyone else to know, either. She's pretty protective of Tracy, you know."

"We all are," Jim said. "I won't do anything unless you tell me to, but I do have a lot of experience dealing with teenagers. How much experience do *you* have?"

Instinctively, Mark's eyes locked on his brother's face.

"None," Paul answered for him.

Mark's level of discomfort rose a few notches. A week ago he'd felt like he was on top of the world, but now he recognized that he'd complicated the lives of these people, without even trying. When, exactly, had his plan gone so off course?

"I've got to get going," he muttered. "Thanks. Thanks to all of you. I appreciate your concern, but I really think I need to figure this one out on my own."

"I hope you figure it out soon," Jim said. "We don't have much time before the game."

"I promise, from now on, I'll play my best."

"And we promise to pray for you," said Pastor Walker. "We'll pray that God will give you the guidance to do the right thing."

Mark tucked his baseball glove under his arm and headed toward the parking lot.

Paul fell into step beside him. "Now I understand why you were asking questions earlier today about my daughters. You could have told me what was bothering you, you know."

"I almost did. Like I said, it's kind of embarrassing."

"So, what are you going to do?"

"I'm going to keep doing what I did here tonight. I'm going to look bad in front of Tracy. And I'm going to try to reroute her attention to a more appropriate target. A boy her own age."

"Do you have a boy in mind?"

"Josh Stuart."

"The kid who played left field?"

"He's the one. And the good part about it is that Josh already likes Tracy. He's crazy about her, so my work is already half done for me."

"Man, you lead a charmed life."

"Yeah? If my life is really so charmed, how come I'm in this situation in the first place?" Mark threw his baseball glove into the back seat of the car with unintentional force. "How come I'm spending my time and energy curing a love-sick teenager instead of closing my deal?"

"What are you so angry about?"

"Things aren't going the way I thought they would, that's all."

"Don't worry. You'll close the deal like you always do. It's just going to take a little longer than usual."

"Too long." Mark slid into the driver's seat. "I can't wait to get Minda McAllister's signature on that contract. As soon as she signs, I'm getting out of Beaver-Cleaver-land and back to New York where I belong."

14

I brought you something."

Mark set a slim white box on the coffee table in front of Brady and took a seat on the chair across from him.

Brady propped himself up on the sofa so he could reach the box. He was covered by a blanket from his waist to his toes and he wore a knitted cap to keep his head and ears warm.

Mark thought the poor kid looked sick. Too sick to show much interest when he picked up the box and examined it.

"What's this?"

"Open it and see."

Brady turned the box over in his hands and spotted the distinctive silver logo embossed on the lid. His eyes widened.

He threw a quick glance at Mark, then he adjusted the pillow behind his back so he could sit up a little straighter. He flipped the top of the box open and stared at the contents. "Is this for *me?*"

"Yes."

"Are you *kidding* me?"

"No, I'm not kidding you. It's a tablet computer."

"I know what it is! I mean, I've dreamed about having one of these." He looked up suddenly. "I can't take this. I mean, it's really nice of you and all, but this must have cost—"

"You have to take it. It's already been set up and personalized for you. I can't return it now."

"But . . . but this is one of the best tablets on the market."

"*The* best. You'll need top of the line technology in order to earn that first million. Go on," Mark coaxed. "Take it out of the box."

For the briefest of moments, Brady struggled with the temptation of holding such treasure in his hands. Carefully, he levered the thin tablet out of the box and held it up. He turned it one way, then the other.

"Hold it like a piece of notebook paper," Mark suggested. "The power button is on the top."

"You mean I can turn it on?"

"Absolutely." Mark tried not to laugh. "Fire it up and let's start tracking your stocks."

"But I don't have an Internet provider or Wi-Fi access."

"You do now. And before I leave today, we're going to set up an email account for you, too, if you don't have one already."

"Wow, this is great! I can't believe I have my own tablet now."

"The manufacturer offers user classes at their store. When you're feeling a little better you should attend a couple classes, so you'll learn to use the tablet efficiently. In the meantime, I can show you the basics and we can download a couple applications to get you started."

Brady's eyes widened again. "I can download apps?"

"You can download all the free apps you want but when it comes to the apps you have to pay for, you're on a strict budget. Understand?"

Brady nodded vigorously.

Mark reached into his coat pocket and withdrew a pen and a business card. On the back of his card he wrote a number. "That's your monthly budget. Don't go over it."

Brady took the card from him and gulped at the sight of the dollar amount. "Yes, sir! I promise. Wow, I can't believe this. This is the best gift anybody ever gave me. How can I thank you?"

"You can buy me dinner after you earn that million. And every once in a while, maybe you could offer to do some Internet searches for some of your neighbors who don't have computers. Do you know Miss Whimple down the hall?"

"Yeah. But she's kinda scary."

"Sometimes, when people are afraid or unsure of themselves, they act angry. But they're not really angry."

"She sure is a good actress."

Mark smiled. "The next time you see her, just let her know you have a new computer and tell her you'll be happy to do Google searches for her. She'll know what that means."

"Okay. I guess I could do that," Brady said.

"Thanks. I know I can count on you. Now, are you ready to start using that tablet?"

"Yes, but wait a second. I've got a surprise for you, too. Stay right there."

Brady threw the blanket to one side. He slowly got to his feet and disappeared into the back of the apartment. When he returned he had a magazine in his hand. He sank down on the sofa looking exhausted and pale, but he still managed to smile at Mark.

"Remember when we first met and I said you looked familiar to me? Now I know why." He held up the magazine. It was folded open on a well-read and dog-eared article on

New York real estate. There, on the left side of the page, in all its glossy glory, was a full-color picture of Mark.

"See? I *knew* you were famous!" Brady sounded triumphant.

Mark felt his heart thud in his chest. "Where'd you get that magazine?"

"My mom got me a subscription for my birthday a couple years ago. I've kept all the issues." He weakly waved his hand toward the stack of financial magazines on the coffee table. "I've got a bunch of them in my room, too. I'm really glad I never throw any of them away. That's you." He tapped his index finger against the glossy page of the magazine. "You're famous."

"I'm not famous, Brady."

"But you're here in the magazine. That's your picture. You're about as famous as you can get in the business world."

"But in the everyday world, I'm not famous at all. Most people have never heard of me or the company I work for, and they've never read that article."

"Well, *I've* read it and now you're here sitting here in front of me! I can't believe it! I must have read this article about a million times or more. It was really inspiring."

"Inspiring? Are you certain that article's about me?" Mark's tone was teasing, but he was also curious. No one had ever described him or his work in that way before.

"It's about you, all right. I've been reading business and news magazines for a long time and this was a good article. You know what made it so good? The way you described buying real estate nobody wants and turning it into valuable property. You made it sound like anybody can do it if they work hard. Anyone can be successful and achieve what you've achieved. That's really inspiring."

Mark felt an uncomfortable prick of conscience that made

him think he had to set the record straight with Brady. "You're right about that ... to a point. Anyone can be successful if they're willing to do whatever it takes to get what they want. But sometimes the business world can be pretty ruthless."

"Oh, I know you have to be tough to succeed and really smart."

"That's not what I meant. I meant that some of the things I've done to get what I want in my career aren't necessarily *inspiring*."

"You're talking about the back-room tactics the article mentions, right?" Brady scanned the familiar page of the magazine and cleared his throat before he read aloud: "'Mark Cartier is a man as cold and hard—and as perfect—as the diamonds his last name suggest.' What's wrong with that?"

"It's not that there's anything wrong with that, but sometimes in business when you're driving toward achieving a goal, sometimes you do things you wouldn't do under normal circumstances. Ethically speaking." He could tell from Brady's expression that he hadn't yet got his point across. "The truth is, if I had to do some of those deals over again, I might not use the same tactics."

"But you'd still close the deal," Brady said, confidently. "You'd get what you want in the end, and you'd still have magazines writing articles about you."

"I guess we'll never know for certain."

The longer Brady held the magazine, the more uncomfortable Mark felt. Funny, but when the article first came out, he'd been pretty proud of the way the author had described his ruthless business strategies. And just a few days ago, he'd felt a touch of irritation when Paul mentioned the article without offering a compliment to go with it.

But now, confronted by an admiring fourteen-year-old, he

felt almost ashamed of the article and he couldn't change the subject fast enough. The last thing he needed was Brady showing the magazine to other people. Like Minda. He reached over and took the magazine out of Brady's hands.

"What if I take this with me and replace it with a really great comic book or a computer magazine?"

Brady didn't take the bait. "No thanks. I guess I could read stuff like that, but I'm a pretty focused person, just like you. I have a plan and I'm educating myself to prepare for the future. I won't always be sick, you know. One day I'll be well and I'll go to work. First I'll go to college and get an MBA," he said, proudly. "I'm gonna earn a lot of money just like you and be rich enough to support my mom. I'm also gonna help kids like me so their mothers don't have to struggle so much."

"That's a noble ambition."

"It's more practical than noble. Besides, my mom works hard. She stresses out a lot because she has to be at work instead of taking care of me. I'll bet there are a lot of mothers with kids like me who are in the same boat."

"You're probably right. Sounds like you've given this a lot of thought."

"I have, and I'm going to accomplish everything I said I would. Unless my mom finds a rich husband." He looked hopefully at Mark. "You're pretty rich, aren't you?"

He almost smiled at Brady's poorly-disguised plot. "Are you going to ask to see my personal financial statement?"

Brady laughed. "Hey, that's not a bad idea. I should do a background check on any man who dates my mom."

"Does she date a lot?"

"No. She just goes to work and comes home to be with me. She's a pretty good mom. I mean, if it weren't for me she could be having a lot more fun, you know?"

"I have a feeling she doesn't mind too much. Hanging out with you is pretty fun."

"Yeah? You think I'm fun to hang out with?"

"Why else would I come by today to visit?"

Brady considered this for a moment. "Does that mean you'll visit me again?"

"When I'm in town. And when I'm not, we'll keep in touch, now that you have a computer tablet. You're somebody with a future in business, and I like to keep tabs on my competition."

"Kind of like a mentor?"

"Sure. Listen, about this magazine article—You haven't shown it to anybody else, have you?"

"Not yet. I forgot all about it until earlier this morning."

"Good. I mean, it's probably for the best that nobody else knows about it. I don't think most people would understand the content or the business deals the article describes. At least, not like you and I understand them."

"I guess I hadn't thought of that."

"I'd appreciate it if we kept the article just between you and me for right now. Let's not show it to anybody else, okay?"

Brady looked at him for a long moment, then his eyes widened. "You're gonna buy this building, aren't you?"

Mark felt his mouth go a little dry. "I never said—"

"You are! You *are* going to buy this building!"

"What a minute, Brady. Nothing's been decided—"

"That's why you were here the other day. That's why Mrs. McAllister was showing you around." He shook his head slightly. "Wow, I can't believe I was so slow picking up on that!"

"Brady, you're making some huge assumptions. I can assure you, I have not talked to Mrs. McAllister about—"

"You're going to buy the building and tear it down, aren't you?" Brady's expression darkened. "That's what the magazine said you do. You buy buildings and redevelop the property or you tear the building down and parcel off the land."

"Sometimes that's what I do," Mark said, slowly, "but not always."

"What's going to happen to everybody who lives here? What's going to happen to me and my mom? We can't afford to live anywhere else. My mom makes minimum wage plus tips and when I balance the checkbook every month, there's no money left."

"Brady, you're jumping to conclu—Wait, *you* balance the checkbook?" Mark repeated, astonished.

Brady shrugged his shoulders. "So? My mom's not good at math."

Mark dropped the magazine on the coffee table and got up to stand beside the sofa. He picked up the blanket in both hands.

"Lay down."

Brady didn't have the strength to argue with him. He swung his legs up on the sofa and leaned back, exhausted, against the pillow.

Mark covered him with the blanket. "Brady, this is really important. I want you to just listen to me for a minute. Don't talk!" he warned, when Brady opened his mouth to speak. "Just look at me and listen calmly to what I have to say. Ready?"

"Yeah, I'm ready." Brady's expression was a mixture of worry and distrust.

Mark sat down in the chair again, buying time while he decided how much he should actually admit. "You read the article, Brady. You know what I do for a living. I work for a company that buys buildings and makes them profitable. Sometimes the profits come after the building is renovated. Sometimes the profits come when the building gets torn down and the land is resold or rebuilt. You're right about that. But you were wrong about the McAllister building. I promise you, I have *not* talked to Mrs. McAllister about buying this building."

At least, he hadn't talked to her yet. He felt a twinge of guilt for not telling Brady the entire truth, but he took some comfort in the fact he hadn't actually lied, either.

He searched Brady's face, trying to gauge his reaction. "Do you believe me?"

"I guess so."

Mark felt the tension leave his body. "I'll make you another promise. If anything happens, and you can't live in this building anymore, I'll make sure you're taken care of. I'll make sure you do have a place to live."

"Where?" Brady demanded. "We can't afford anything else."

"You and your mother will be taken care of. Will you trust me? Please?" As soon as the words came out of his mouth, Mark recognized their irony: One of the country's most successful businessmen just begged a fourteen-year-old kid to trust him in a real estate deal. And in case he hadn't debased himself enough, he took it a step further, by adding, "*Please?*"

"I guess so." Brady looked away, refusing to meet Mark's eyes.

"I would never do anything to hurt you," Mark said, and meant it.

"I believe you. It's just that we've got a lot going on, my mom and me. She's working crazy hours and me sick and money's tight. We've got enough to worry about, you know?"

"I know. But having to find another place to live is *not* something you have to worry about. If it turns out that you can't live in this apartment anymore, I promise you'll have another place to live. And the new place may even be a little bit better."

"In this neighborhood? I mean, it has to be close to the hospital."

"I'll make sure you live close to the hospital. Besides, you won't always be sick. You said so yourself."

Brady focused on tracing his fingertip along the edge of the computer tablet as it lay in his lap. "Sometimes that's just talk."

"It better not be just talk. I'm counting on you to get well. Remember, you owe me dinner after you earn your first million."

Brady looked up at him. "I guess I did kinda say that."

"And I kind of said I'd show you how to use that tablet. Are you ready to search for some apps?"

"Yeah." Brady's worried expression softened. "Yeah, I'm ready."

"Good. Let's start earning your first million."

15

"Anybody home?"

At the sound of Mark's voice, Minda looked up from the fall leaves she had just raked together into a neat pile in the back yard. Instinctively, she took inventory of her appearance: jeans and a pull-over sweater. Appropriate clothing, she judged, for someone trying to get a little yard work done before the sun set, but she wished she were wearing something a little more attractive. She had to be content with the fact that her sweater wasn't smudged with dirt from the garden and her jeans weren't darkened with grass stains from crawling around on the lawn.

Seconds ago she'd been enjoying a quiet evening in her back yard, but now she felt like a nervous teenager with a crush on the quarterback. She dropped the rake and looked over at Tracy.

She'd been doing her homework at the patio table but, hearing Mark's voice, she immediately jumped up, making her metal chair scrape against the stone patio. Her eyes glowed bright with happiness and the algebra problems she'd been working were forgotten.

"Yes, we're home!" Tracy called. She closed her notebook and pushed her study materials aside. "We're here in the back yard! The gate latch is on the right. Come on through."

Minda heard the familiar creak of the gate opening and closing. A moment later, Mark came around the side of the house with Josh Stuart following close on his heels.

Mark was dressed in jeans and a blue sweater; nothing special about that except that he looked so handsome, Minda had a hard time dragging her gaze away as she joined them on the patio.

"I hope it's okay that we just dropped by," Mark said.

Tracy ignored Josh and directed her best smile at Mark. "It's no problem at all. I'm glad you did."

"We won't stay long. We just came to get the answer to a very important question."

Minda pulled off her gardening gloves. "What's the important question you want to ask?"

"Actually, it's an important question for Tracy. Tracy, how would you like to go to a Rockies baseball game tonight?"

Tracy's eyes locked on his. "I'd love to go!" she said, quickly.

"That's good, because I happen to have two tickets to tonight's game. I was really looking forward to going myself but at the last minute an important appointment came up that I can't seem to get out of. I'd hate to see a perfectly good ticket go to waste."

"Oh!" Tracy didn't hide her disappointment. "You mean *you* won't be going?"

"I wish I could. But I remembered that you told me how much you love baseball so, of course, I knew you'd help me out and use the ticket."

"I guess it would be okay." Tracy's expression was less

than enthusiastic when she looked over at Minda. "What do you think, Mom? Do you feel like going with me to a baseball game tonight?"

Before Minda could answer, Mark said, "Sorry, but this offer is only for you, Tracy. I've only got two tickets, and I've already given one of them to someone else."

"To who?"

"To Josh."

Tracy's eyes flew to Josh's face and he looked back at her, his expression unreadable.

"You mean, I'd be going to the baseball game with Josh? We'd go *together*?"

"That's the arrangement."

Tracy hesitated.

Mark waved the tickets in front of her. "The seats are right behind home plate."

Tracy shot a glance at her mother.

"It sounds like fun," Minda said. "I think you should go."

"Come on, Tracy," Mark said. "You'd really be doing me a huge favor."

"Okay," Tracy said, sullenly, "but I want to be clear that just because Josh and I are going together doesn't mean this is a date."

"Of course not," Mark agreed. "You're just helping me out because you know I'd hate it if these tickets went to waste. The game starts at seven, so you two better get going."

"I'll get my purse." Tracy walked toward the back steps and disappeared into the house.

Josh leaned toward Mark and said in a loud whisper, "That went just like you said it would."

Mark smiled approvingly. "You played it perfectly. Do you remember the instructions I gave you?"

"Yeah. Act respectful, but not too interested."

Mark winced slightly at Josh's over-simplification of the advice he'd carefully given Josh earlier. "That's close enough. For now. Remind me to give you some more dating pointers later." He handed the tickets to Josh, along with a couple of twenty-dollar bills. "The hot dogs are on me."

"Thanks, Mr. Cartier."

Tracy came back carrying a small purse and a pink hoodie.

"Have a good time, you two," Minda said. "And come home as soon as the game is over."

"Yes, Mothe-e-e-er," Tracy said, sounding very much like a normal teenager.

Minda watched them disappear through the gate and wondered if the evening would turn out as well as Mark seemed to think it would.

"All fixed."

Mark's voice was surprisingly close and low and soft. She looked up and saw he was wearing a confident smile.

"Fixed? You think that by sending Tracy to the Rockies game with Josh, you've eliminated her crush on you and everything's fixed?"

"I wouldn't say *everything*, but we're certainly headed in the right direction. Tracy just needs to refocus her attention on someone else. Someone more appropriate."

"And you think that's what just happened?"

"It's a start."

She smiled and shook her head slightly. "You don't know very much about teenage girls."

"Maybe not, but I don't see how my plan can fail. For the next three hours Tracy and Josh will be side-by-side, talking, eating, and cheering. They'll bond, believe me."

"Some girls aren't charmed by a big show. Some girls are a little more cautious and need to take their time when they start a relationship."

"Is that a family trait?"

Startled, her hazel eyes widened slightly.

"You don't have to answer. Besides, anyone can see that Josh is crazy about your daughter. He just needed a little help getting started in the right direction."

"So you gave him some dating advice?"

"A little."

"And are your dating skills better than your baseball skills?"

"By any chance, are you talking about my performance at baseball practice last night?"

"Yes."

"Did I disappoint you?"

"Disappoint? No. I think 'confused' would be a better word. Your brother told me you played so well, you could have gone pro."

He flashed that lop-sided smile of his. "And you don't think I looked like a professional player last night?"

She shook her head again. "Sorry, no."

"Don't be sorry. In a way, I should be apologizing to you."

"What for?"

"For deliberately playing badly and not telling you the reason why."

"I don't understand."

"I played like a Little Leaguer on purpose. In the middle of practice last night, I realized Josh liked Tracy. So, I thought that if I played really bad and Josh played really well, Tracy might reconsider how she felt about both of us."

"I see." She focused her attention on picking specks of dirt from the gardening gloves she still held in her hands.

"You think it was a bad idea?"

"It's not that. In fact, I think your plan may work out. But I wish you would have told me about it first. I'm Tracy's mother and I should be part of any decision concerning her. And, besides, you shouldn't have . . ."

He braced himself to hear her criticism. "I shouldn't have what?"

"You shouldn't have put yourself in a position to look bad in front of others. If God gave you have a talent, you should use it. You should never have to hide it."

"I thought at the time I was doing the right thing. But after you left last night, I came to realize I shouldn't have put on such a show. I should have played my best."

"Did your conscience tell you that?"

"No, Coach told me. And Jim and Pastor Walker. And my brother."

"Sounds like you took quite a scolding."

"Let's just say they explained how important the fundraising game is to the orphan train reunion and, in return, I promised to play to my best ability. The truth is, I don't want to disappoint Coach. The reunion means a lot to him. " He took a deep breath. "I hope he gets what he wants. I hope the reunion helps him find his family."

She could sense his compassion for Coach Morgan and when he smiled that loopy little half-smile, she could feel her insides melt a little. Did he know, she wondered, how attractive he was when his voice went soft and gentle? From the moment she'd met him, she'd admitted he was attractive in a polished, practiced kind of way. But when he let down his guard and allowed her to glimpse his real feelings, like he did now, she liked him so much better.

"You don't have to rush off tonight, do you?"

"I wasn't planning to."

"I just asked because . . . I thought you said you had an important appointment you couldn't get out of."

"I do. *You're* my important appointment."

Minda felt the tell-tale warmth of a blush creep up her neck toward her cheeks. She tried to find something to say in response, but her brain refused to cooperate. It was mortifying to know that it only took a few softly spoken words from Mark to make her mind go soft and squishy. She pulled her gardening gloves back on and self-consciously waved her hand toward the pile of leaves. "I have to . . . I was raking . . ."

"I'll help."

He must be used to women saying lame things, Minda thought, because he didn't seem to notice that she'd suddenly lost the ability to complete a sentence. Instead, he picked up the abandoned rake and looked at her expectantly. "Would you hold the bag open?"

Minda nodded, not trusting herself to speak, and opened the black garbage bag with both hands. With Mark's help, the leaves were gathered in the bag in no time.

"We make a good team," he said.

"Thanks for helping." She was relieved to find that her voice and brain were working together again. "Is it just me or does it seem that every time you show up, I put you to work?"

"I don't mind."

"I have your watch. I forgot to give it back to you last night after baseball practice. Come inside and I'll get it for you."

Mark followed her into the kitchen, where she pointed toward the sink. "Would you like to wash up? There's soap and a towel at the sink. Help yourself. I'll just be a minute."

She disappeared, leaving Mark alone in her kitchen. As he washed and dried his hands, he looked around the large kitchen and felt the same feeling of comfort sweep over him that he always felt whenever he stepped inside Minda's home. His critical eye told him that the appliances were old and the cabinets needed to be replaced. There wasn't so much as a sliver of granite countertop in sight, but, despite all that, he liked the kitchen. It felt homey and comfortable and peaceful.

He hung up the towel and walked through the dining room and into the living room, looking for Minda. She was nowhere in sight and the house was silent except for the soft ticking of a clock on the fireplace mantel. Mark drank in the quiet atmosphere of the room. He hadn't been in Minda's home that many times, but he'd acquired an appreciation for the place, from the large porch with the old-fashioned swing to the out-dated upright piano, to the huge roll-top desk.

Glancing at the desk, he spotted the envelope from his employer lying on the desk-top. The unopened envelope that was previously stuffed forgotten into a desk drawer had now made it to the top of the desk. He took that as a positive sign.

He picked it up and turned it over. The sealed flap had actually been opened. Another positive sign.

"You'll never guess what that is." Minda's voice was directly behind him.

He almost jumped. Every muscle in his body tensed as he turned around, the envelope still in his hand.

Minda looked back at him with a slight smile on her lips. She didn't seem to mind that she'd caught him going through the mail on her desk.

She was holding his out his watch, dangling it in front of him by the length of its chain.

He took the watch in his other hand and shoved it into his pocket, all the while keeping a careful eye to her expression. "You correspond with some impressive people."

"It's a one-sided correspondence, at best. That company writes every couple months asking to buy my house or the McAllister Building or both. I can't be sure because I've never really read their letters. They just keep writing anyway."

"Why haven't you ever read their letters?"

"I did the first time I got a letter from them but it didn't make very much sense. I couldn't figure out all the terms they were using but even if I understood every word, it wouldn't have mattered. Selling this house or the McAllister Building isn't something I'd ever do."

Mark stared at her, amazed by her words and even more amazed by the look of utter innocence on her face. He was having a hard time believing that what she said was true; that she actually admitted to tossing aside a multi-million-dollar offer simply because she didn't understand the phrases and terms in the proposal letter.

"Minda, if you didn't understand the letter or the offer they were making, you should have asked your attorney to explain it to you."

"I don't exactly have an attorney on my payroll."

"I understand that, but you're a business woman and when you receive a business offer, you might think about getting an expert's input. Just to be sure you have all the facts before you make a decision."

"That makes sense, Mark, but attorneys usually charge a fee up front and it's hard for me to justify that kind of expense right now."

"How about if someone who isn't a lawyer explained the letter to you?"

"Like who?"

"Like me. I'm not a lawyer but I have a pretty good grasp of real estate terms. Let's give it a try." He went over to the dining table and pulled out a chair for her. He looked at her expectantly.

"I guess we could, but I hate to waste your time. I already know I'll never sell the McAllister Building."

"I won't consider it a waste of time," he assured her as he sat down beside her. "If we come across any terms you don't understand, just say so, okay?"

"Okay."

He smiled as he pulled the contents from the envelope and forced himself to remain calm. This was his moment. The moment he'd been waiting for. The opportunity to talk to Minda about selling her building. He'd worked so hard to lay the foundation, to get her to trust him. If he handled the next few minutes correctly, he'd have her signature on the sale contract before the sun finished setting outside.

He knew the documents practically by heart but for Minda's benefit he pretended to scan through the cover letter, the five-page proposal and the contract that accompanied it.

"Let's start with the letter, okay? It's simply an offer to open a discussion about buying your building."

"The McAllister Building?"

"That's right."

She shook her head. "It's not for sale."

"That may be true, but this company—Goble, Haines and Wyman—wants to open a dialog with you about the building. You may not have thought before about selling, but they're hoping you're willing to at least consider their offer."

"I guess I'm willing to hear what they have to say, but I'm not selling the building."

"Fair enough." Mark read the first paragraph of the letter aloud. "Nothing that requires a law degree there, right?"

"I'm with you so far."

"Paragraph two." Mark read the next portion of the letter to her, and Minda's attention focused on the color of his vee-neck sweater. It was almost an exact match to the blue of his eyes. He had pushed the sleeves of his sweater up to just below his elbows, exposing the dusting of dark hair that accentuated the tanned, muscular strength of his forearms.

He stopped reading and looked at her, a question in his eyes.

"On to paragraph three," she prompted, knowing full well she hadn't listened to even one word he'd read so far.

As soon as he began reading she remembered that moment in church when he had first joined the congregational hymn. Sitting beside him, listening to him read the letter aloud, she realized his speaking voice had the same rich, melodic quality his singing voice had.

"Did you understand that part of the letter? Do you want me to go over it again?"

She shrugged slightly. "No, not really."

"Minda," he said with a touch of exasperation, "if you're not going to pay attention, how are you going to make a decision about this offer?"

"I am paying attention."

He started reading again and Minda resolved to take control of her thoughts and concentrate only on the documents. But then she noticed that Mark's hair curled just behind his ear in a very attractive way.

"That's the end of the letter." Mark laid the paper down on the table. "Any questions? Are you ready to go over the contract?"

"Sure."

It seemed a shame to make Mark review the documents when, in her heart, Minda knew she had no intention of selling anything to anybody, no matter what the offer. But she wasn't ready to tell him so. Selfishly, she wanted to enjoy the experience of an attractive and attentive man sitting close beside her, even if it was just for business reasons. It was nice to sit so close to him, to feel his nearness and appreciate the light scent of his aftershave. The little bit she had learned about him in the last few days told her he was confident and funny and smart. He was also wildly handsome and Minda found herself wholly and inexplicably drawn to him. It had been a long time since she'd felt that way; a long time since she'd had a man in her life in the romantic sense.

Mark started to read the contract aloud.

Minda started to pretend to pay attention. But her focus locked on the curve of his lips the moment he started reading and she found herself wondering how it would feel if he were to kiss her.

It was a pleasant thought. She'd already had a hint of what it would feel like to be held in his arms when they rode the bus together and he had wrapped his strong arm protectively around her. Even now, he was sitting so close beside her that when he paused from reading and turned his head to look at her, his lips were tantalizingly close. It would be easy enough for Minda to lean in just slightly and—

"Did you understand that part?"

She blinked, jolted into abandoning her daydream. She hadn't paid attention to anything he'd read, but a few of the words had somehow stuck in her brain.

"Um, what does 'restriction lease' mean?"

"Actually, the term is, 'restrictions on leasing.' It means that once you sign the contract, until the deal closes and the buyer takes possession of the building, any apartment leases that come up for renewal cannot be renewed."

She thought for a moment. "Does that mean my tenants won't be able to stay in their apartments?"

"That's right."

"What about my bookstore?"

"You'll have to find a new location for the store, too," he said, gently.

"That's a deal breaker."

"Why don't you wait until you've heard the balance of the offer?"

She shook her head. "I don't need to. They'd have to offer a million dollars for me to even consider selling my building under those conditions."

"How about twelve million?"

Her breath caught in her throat. "Twelve? Twelve million *dollars*?"

He didn't answer. He simply watched her reaction, his eyes locked on her face.

"Are you kidding? *Twelve* million doll—Give me that contract." She plucked the papers from his hand and scanned the jumble of printed words. "Where does it say that?"

"Paragraph four. Where it reads, 'In consideration of . . .'"

Minda's eyes focused on the paragraph Mark pointed to. There it was, as plain as day: A one and a two and a whole bunch of zeroes. Her breath caught in her throat. Twelve million dollars. It had to be a joke or a mistake. Maybe she should call the company and let them know that one of their employees had made a little ol' typo and accidentally added an extra zero to their offer.

"Minda? Are you all right?"

She drew a deep breath as she set the page down on the table and made a great show of smoothing it with her fingers.

"It's not what I expected." She looked at him then and saw gentle amusement in his expression.

"Were you expecting them to offer more money?"

"No, not at all. In fact, I think they offered *too* much money."

"Sweetheart, there's no such thing as too much money."

Minda looked down at the contract again. Funny, but when she got dressed that morning she never expected that her day would end with millions of dollars being thrust at her and Mark calling her *sweetheart*.

"I can't deny that it's an attractive offer," she said.

"Does that mean you're going to accept it?"

"I—No! I mean . . . I'm really not sure."

"But you're going to at least think about it, right? You'll give the offer some thought?"

"Yes, I'll think about." She couldn't believe those words had come out of her mouth. Was she really going to consider selling the building that her husband's family had owned for generations? The very same building that she'd always considered to be a brick-and-mortar reminder of her husband, Dale?

She took another deep breath. "I'll think about it, and I'll pray about it. I'll ask for God's guidance and the knowledge to do what's right for everyone."

"For *every*one? Don't you mean, you'll do what's right for you and Tracy?"

She gave her head a small shake. "Tracy and I won't be the only ones affected if I were to sell the McAllister Building. Mark, you were there. You saw the people who call that building home. You met Brady Blythe and Miss Whimple. They're just two of the people who rely on me for a place to live. There are over a hundred apartments in that building and each one is occupied. The people who live there are elderly or disabled or both. You met Ellen, too. She relies on the income she earns at the bookstore to supplement Jim's salary from the church. There are many people to consider in any decision I make."

"But what about you?" He turned slightly toward her and slipped his arm across the back of her chair. His handsome face was inches from hers and his voice was tantalizingly low. "Doesn't Minda McAllister figure in this decision somewhere? A few million dollars would make a big difference in your life, wouldn't it?"

That was a question she very much wished he hadn't asked. Of course the money would make a big difference. She thought about the bills she could pay, the old car she could replace, and the college tuition she could count on for Tracy.

Her chin went up a little. "I'd be lying if I said the money wasn't tempting, but—"

"With that kind of money, you can buy a new building. You can catch up on some bills or pay off that credit card debt that haunts you."

She frowned. "How did you know I have credit card—"

"Most people do," he said, dismissively. "Money doesn't have to be bad, Minda. Money can be a very good thing. It can make your life comfortable. It can open doors, give you a little freedom, help you forget past pains and hurts."

Mark's words were having an almost hypnotic effect on her. She struggled to answer him sensibly. "Has that been your experience? That money can heal old hurts?"

"We're talking about you," he said softly. "We're talking about Minda McAllister, who hasn't been dealt the easiest of hand in life. Minda McAllister, who probably can't remember what it's like to not have to struggle to pay the bills each month and run her business and raise her daughter and take care of her tenants. Minda McAllister, who juggles careers as handyman, landlord, and small-business owner. Who has time for her church and her child and her friends—but never has any time for herself. Don't you think it's Minda's turn now?"

His blue eyes were locked on hers and his voice was gentle and persuasive.

"I never thought about it that way before."

"Minda, isn't there anything that's always been just out of

reach in your life? What do you want more than anything right at this very moment?"

Two weeks ago she could have told him. Before he'd ever come into her life, she had wanted nothing more than to catch up on her tithe pledges and maybe pay off a credit card. Two weeks ago her goals had been simple and meager; but now they paled in comparison to the shiny new dreams of love and attraction that she wasn't even certain she wanted to recognize. But she had to recognize those dreams, now that they were staring her right in the face.

And the truth was, she wanted Mark. She wanted him to look at her with softness in his eyes and tell her she was pretty. She wanted to hear the warm timbre of his deep voice when he shared a secret meant just for her. She wanted to feel the ripple of reaction when he took her hand and held it in his. She wanted all those things even as she was afraid of them.

She quickly looked at Mark, afraid that if her eyes met his, he'd be able to divine what was in her heart. He looked back at her with an intense light in his blue eyes as if he were committing every inch of her face to memory.

"I . . . I don't know what I want."

She dragged her gaze away from his and tried to focus again on the contract on the dining table; but it was impossible to concentrate on anything while his handsome face was mere inches from her own.

"This is a lot to think about," she said. "The truth is that I never once considered selling the building before. I always believed God would provide whatever was needed to keep the building going. I never thought of anything but running the bookstore and taking care of my tenants."

"And now? What do you think now?"

"I think I need to pray about it. It's a big decision. I need to pray about it and ask the opinion of people I trust." She looked at him speculatively. "What would *you* do if you were offered this kind of a deal for the McAllister Building?"

"Why are you asking me?"

"Because you're smart and you know about real estate and I trust you."

"You *trust* me?"

"Yes. Oh, I know we got off to a rocky start at first, but that's in the past. I think you've proven my initial impression of you was wrong. I know now that I can trust you."

"You really mean that?"

"Of course. I don't think you'd ever let me sign a contract if you thought it would hurt me in any way. Would you?"

"No. Never." He looked down at the papers on the table and pressed his lips into a thin line that caused the muscles in his jaw to jump. Abruptly, he pushed his chair back and stood up. "Maybe this wasn't a good idea."

His whole demeanor changed right in front of her. With tight, staccato movements, he gathered the papers together, refusing to look at her.

"Why wasn't it a good idea?"

"You should have your lawyer go over this. A lawyer can advise you better than I can."

"I thought you were doing a pretty good job of explaining the documents to me."

"A lawyer will give you impartial advice."

"Aren't you impartial?"

"I—No. No, not as impartial as a lawyer would be."

In Minda's mind, his confession was a good thing. If Mark wasn't impartial, maybe that meant he cared about her. Maybe it meant he found her attractive. On the basis of those two maybes alone she felt her spirits lift.

She put her fingertips on his arm, stilling his movements.

"Thank you for explaining the contact to me."

He didn't answer but she saw the muscle pulse in his jaw again. He wasn't looking at her like a man who found her attractive. He wasn't looking at her at all.

She stood up and moved to the end of the dining table, putting a few feet between them before she turned back to face him. "Did I do something wrong?"

He shook his head slightly. His eyes were still focused on the papers but his expression softened. "No. You didn't do anything wrong."

Minda went into the living room, turning on lights as she went, banishing the last vestiges of attraction and romance that filled her senses moments ago. "I'll be at the bookstore tomorrow morning and at church in the afternoon for the orphan train meeting."

Her invitation was implied. She waited expectantly for him to acknowledge it.

Mark went directly to the front door. "I'll see you tomorrow. Good night, Minda."

16

In the dark interior of his rental car, Mark pushed the key into the ignition and started the engine. The evening temperatures had fallen dramatically since the sun had set and the car was cold. Mark shivered and was glad of it. Feeling cold was infinitely better than feeling guilty.

He leaned forward a little and lightly knocked his forehead against the top of the steering wheel a couple of times.

Idiot.

For almost an entire week he'd been acting like an idiot, mooning over a woman he barely knew; a woman he was supposed to regard as his enemy. She had something he wanted and he was prepared to use any means necessary to take it. He preferred persuasion and he'd started to see some success. Minda had opened up to him. But at the very moment he could have seduced her into signing her name and selling her building, she'd blindsided him. She'd looked at him with her beautiful hazel eyes and said those three words that had thrown him off his game: *I trust you.*

She trusted him. Wasn't that what he wanted? Hadn't he

been working his head off to get her to do just that? Yet when he finally had her trust, he couldn't follow through. He felt only guilt.

It was lunacy. He had nothing to feel guilty about. His offer to Minda was more than fair. He'd seen the stunned look of surprise on her face when she realized how much money she'd get from the sale. The amount was a bargain compared to what the property would be worth once it was properly redeveloped, but it was still a fair offer. All of his deals were fair, structured so the seller got plenty of money for their property, whether they wanted to sell or not. So nobody really got hurt, right? How could anyone find fault with too much money?

In his vocabulary, there was no such thing. In his world, money brought happiness. Money showed the world that you were somebody. Money bought respect.

But money didn't buy love. It didn't buy tenderness or romance and those were the emotions he'd felt sitting next to Minda at her dining table. The entire time he'd been reading the contract to her, he'd been keenly aware of how close she sat beside him. He'd tried desperately to concentrate on the documents, all the while fighting an impulse to pull Minda into his arms and kiss her. Her nearness had been an exquisite torture and then she'd delivered the final assault against his good sense: *I trust you.*

Those three words shattered him. They made him acknowledge what he'd been trying to ignore for days: he was attracted to Minda in a way he had never felt attracted to a woman before. He liked her determination and fierce loyalty to that tumble-down building she owned. He was drawn to her smile and compassionate nature. He admired her quiet faith and her dedication to her ministry. He was attracted to everything about her, even at the same time he sat at her dining table under false pretenses. It was the same as lying to her.

He'd entered her life for the sole purpose of charming her into selling her building. Instead, he was the one who was charmed; charmed by a gentle smile and beautiful hazel eyes.

He had to be strong. He had to keep his hands off her. He had to remember what was at stake and remember that his future depended on getting Minda to do what he wanted.

He took a deep breath and flipped the car heater on. The blast of warm air melted away the final traces of guilt he'd been feeling and strengthened his resolve.

When he put the car in gear and pulled away from the curb, he felt his good sense return. He was back to his old self: cool, analytical and focused only on his goal. Business. That's why he was there in the first place. That's why he was trying his best to get her to like him.

Business.

And once that business was accomplished, he'd be on the next plane back to New York, ready to collect that big, fat commission check.

He'd accomplish his goal. He'd have the money to start his own investment firm.

He'd go back to the life he knew before he ever met Minda McAllister.

Minda scanned the computer screen and frowned. Her search results listed only a few apartment buildings for sale in the city of Denver. Studying the search results, she noticed most of the buildings listed were small; only two buildings had more than thirty units and they were nowhere near the downtown area. Sighing, she sat back in her chair just as Ellen entered the office.

"Is the safe open?"

Minda nodded absently, her attention on the screen.

Ellen pulled the cash drawer from the old, antique safe and began counting out one-dollar bills. "The store opens in fifteen minutes. I could use some help."

"Okay, just give me a minute."

"What are you looking at so intently? It's not that dancing kitten video, is it?"

"I'm looking at apartment buildings for sale."

"Thinking of buying one? I never knew you were the tycoon type."

"I'm not. Owning one apartment building at a time is plenty." She looked up at her sister-in-law and said, cautiously, "As a matter of fact, I got an offer for the McAllister building. Someone wants to buy it."

"Interesting." Ellen pulled a wooden chair up to the desk and sat down across from Minda. "So, are you going to accept the offer?"

"I haven't decided yet. It's a lot of money, though. More than I ever thought this place would be worth."

"Hmmm. Someone's willing to give you a lot of money for a building that would fall down if it weren't for the termite colonies holding it up. Sounds like a real dilemma."

"Don't laugh. And it is a dilemma. That money would solve a lot of problems. But it would create new ones, too."

"Wait! Don't start talking yourself out of accepting the offer yet."

"I'm not. The offer is too tempting."

"How tempting?"

"I-can't-stop-thinking-about-it tempting. I was up all night praying about it." She took a deep breath. "They offered me twelve million dollars."

"Wow!" Ellen was too stunned to say more.

"I know. It's hard to believe that someone would be willing to give me that kind of money. I've spent my whole life counting pennies and scraping by. I can't imagine what it would be like to never have to worry about making money stretch anymore."

"Then why are you sitting here? Quick, sign the contract before they change their mind and realize this old relic of a building isn't worth that kind of money!"

"I wish it were that simple."

"Well, what's complicated about it?"

"For starters, I have to think about the people who depend on this building."

"Like who?"

"Like my tenants, of course. And don't look like you don't know what I'm talking about. You know each and every person who lives in those apartments upstairs."

"Yes, I do know them all because I've had to listen to each one of them complain ... *about the building*," Ellen said, meaningfully. "If it were me, I'd jump at that offer. Twelve million dollars? Bam! Done deal."

"It's not that easy. If I sold the building, I'd have to find new homes for my tenants. I just did a search for apartment houses for sale in Denver and none of them will do. The largest building has only sixty-two units and it costs a fortune."

Ellen frowned slightly. "I don't understand. Why would you sell one apartment building, then turn around and buy another?"

"I have to make sure my tenants have a place to live. I can't just put them out on the street."

"Honey, that's not your responsibility. As long as you give your tenants sufficient notice they should be able to find a new place to live. Sure, some of them may need special help, like Brady and his mother or Addy Whimple, but they're the exceptions. Your tenants are adults. They can find new places to live."

"I've been taking care of them and this building for so long, I guess I've become more personally involved than I should be as a landlord."

"There's nothing wrong with that. You're a compassionate person and you've done your best to make this a pleasant and comfortable place to live. But, honey, you can't mother all the people who live here."

"Or work here."

"What do you mean?"

"If I sell the building, I'll have to close the bookstore or move it to a new location."

"Another big decision to make."

"You don't sound very concerned."

Ellen shrugged her shoulders. "I'm not. But I will be if you decide to move the store and I have to pack all those books up."

"On the other hand, if I decide to *close* the store, you and the other people who work here will be out of a job."

"I'll find another one. I only keep this job to help you out."

Minda sat back in her chair and stared. "Well, *that's* a revelation. I distinctly remember offering you a job because you said you needed the income. You said Jim didn't earn enough as a youth minister."

"That was the situation years ago when Jim and I first got married, but not now. Don't get me wrong, the extra money is nice, but I can always get a job somewhere else, if I need to."

"I don't understand. I thought that providing homes for people in need and running the bookstore—I always felt those were my ministries to others."

"They are. Just like Romans says, you've used this building to meet people's needs with love and humility on Christ's behalf." She studied Minda's puzzled expression. "Want my opinion?"

"Yes."

"I think you've confused the building with the ministry. It isn't the McAllister Building that helps people. It's you. And if you sell the building, you can still help people. You'll just do it in a different way and in a different place."

Minda looked away. "I really don't think I can sell this building."

"Why?"

"You shouldn't have to ask. You're a McAllister. This building has been in your family for generations. It's part of your heritage."

"And my entire family thanks you for taking care of it as well as you have. But no one in the McAllister family is as attached to this building as you are. To us, it's just a building. A bunch of bricks stacked in a neat pile." She cocked her head to one side. "But this building used to mean a lot to my brother, Dale. Is that why you hang on to it so tightly? Because you think that's what Dale would have wanted?"

"It's more than that," Minda said. "I feel that if I give up this building, I'm giving up Dale. I know it doesn't make sense, but I always felt that holding on to this place was like holding on to a piece him. I just don't want to let him go."

"You don't have to let him go. You can still hold on to him, but you've got two hands, don't you?"

Minda frowned. "Yes."

"So, hold on to Dale with one hand, but use your other hand to reach out for something new. It won't hurt, I promise. In the meantime, why don't you talk to someone who can help you decide whether or not you should sell the building? You know, talk to someone who can give you some good advice. What about Mark? He's in the real estate business, isn't he?"

"I already talked to him. He read the contract and explained the offer to me."

"Really? When?"

"Last night. He sent Tracy to a baseball game with Josh and then he offered to go through the documents and explain—What are you smiling about?"

"He got your daughter to leave so he could be alone with you?"

"It wasn't like that."

"Yes, it was. You just don't see it. You're the *only* one who doesn't see it. Minda, the man's crazy about you. Why else is he hanging around?"

Minda felt the warm fingers of a blush creep up her neck toward her face. Leave it to Ellen to say out loud the very thought Minda had been secretly nurturing.

Mark was attracted to her. She allowed the idea to blossom and felt its warmth slowly radiate through her core.

And she was attracted to Mark. For the first time, she allowed herself to fully admit the attraction. She braced herself, waiting for the usual feelings of guilt to push the notion aside, but the guilt didn't come. Nor did the tearfulness or the tightness in her throat that she usually felt every time she thought about Dale and the fact that he wasn't coming back. Instead, she felt . . . okay. Maybe even hopeful. And a little bit happy.

She looked at Ellen. "Do you really think he likes me?"

"Likes you? Are you kidding? He's so smitten he can't see straight. Now, the only question remains, what do you think of him?"

"I . . ." She hesitated only a second or two. "I like him. A lot."

She was immediately rewarded with Ellen's smile. "Oh, Minda, I'm so happy for you!"

"Don't get carried away! I like him and I really enjoy his company, but we don't have very much in common, I'm afraid."

"Why do you say that?"

"Well, for starters, his priorities are so different than mine. He's motivated by material possessions and having expensive things. But on the other hand," she added, her voice softening as a light smile touched her lips, "you should have seen how sweet he was to Brady. He was gentle and kind. He's so good with Miss Whimple, too. And I think he was really moved by Coach's story and that's why he's playing on the church baseball team. When I see him do things like that, I realize he has a good heart. I just wish his priorities were different. "

"The funny thing about priorities is the way they can change. He seems like a smart guy to me. He probably is used to shifting his priorities around, if needed."

Minda looked at her with a hopeful expression. "Do you really think so?"

"He'll have to, if the two of you are going to stand a chance at building a future. Long-distance romances never work, you know, especially when the guy lives half-way across the country. He's going to have to pack up his life and move to Denver and—"

"Wait!" Minda's voice was a mixture of alarm and laughter. "He hasn't even asked me out yet and you're talking as if we were already engaged."

"He'll ask you out," Ellen predicted, with confidence. "Mark my words, he'll be taking you on a real date by the end of the week."

"I hope so. I'd love for him to ask me on a real date but at the same time, I know I'll be a nervous wreck when he does." She touched her hands to the sides of her face and laughed. "It's funny, but I feel like I'm in high school again, hoping the boy I like will ask me to the prom!"

"It's nice to be in love, isn't it?'

"Yes. I mean, no! I wouldn't call it love. Not yet. But I'm really, deeply in like."

Ellen reached across the desk to grasp Minda's hand and give it an encouraging squeeze. "After all these years, it's nice to see you let go of the past a little."

"What do you think Dale would say if he knew that—Just hypothetically, let's say I started dating?"

Ellen flashed a dazzling smile. "He'd be very happy for you. And, Minda? I think he *does* know."

The bell above the door lightly jingled as Mark stepped inside the bookstore. Ellen looked up from her place behind the counter and gave him her best smile.

"Good morning!"

Wary, he pinned a polite smile to his lips and approached the counter. "Good morning."

"She's in the back, in her office. Do you know where that is?"

"Yes." He caught himself before admitting that he'd been in the office before. He didn't want to reveal to Ellen, even indirectly, how much time he spent pursuing Minda.

Her smile broadened. "Right. So, have you cleared everything up? Are you still planning to play in the baseball game?"

"Yes, I'm still on the team."

"Great! That means you're sticking around for at least

another week."

"Actually, I'm not certain of my plans at this time." He sounded so formal and business-like, he wasn't surprised to see Ellen's brows rise in response.

The truth was that Ellen worried him. She had a way of looking at him that sent alarm bells off in his head. She looked at him as if she knew more about him than she was willing to let on. It was a stupid feeling. He told himself that the woman couldn't possibly know that he was being nice to Minda for the sole purpose of convincing her to sell her building. And she certainly couldn't know that he liked Minda more than he ever intended.

And she certainly couldn't know that he'd come within seconds of kissing Minda last night as they sat at her dining-room table with the contract spread out before them.

Thankfully, he had come to his senses in time. He hadn't kissed her nor had he allowed his emotions to take over. And he wouldn't. Not until Minda signed the contract.

"I just asked," Ellen persisted, "because Tracy's birthday is this week. The party's Thursday night. You'll be there, right?"

"Can I get back to you about that?"

"Sure. But you're going to be in town, right?"

"I'll let you know. Good seeing you again." He flashed his best smile at her and headed toward the back of the store.

He remembered the cramped room Minda called an office from the building tour she'd given him. The office was only about ten feet square, with a desk in one corner, a huge antique safe in another corner, and boxes of books and office supplies piled everywhere else. It was organized but uninviting. In his opinion, Minda deserved better. At the very least she should have some sturdy shelves to hold the boxes. She should have a window that looked out on a pleasant view and a desk that wasn't older than she was. And she needed a new computer and a decent printer.

She was working at her computer when he paused at the doorway. He stood there quietly for a moment, watching her frown in concentration over whatever she was looking at on the screen. She had so many things to worry about and people to take care of. In his opinion, she had more than her fair share of responsibilities. He liked to think he could lessen her load a little bit. All she had to do was sell her building and Minda's road would be so much smoother. He intended to convince her to sign the contract by the end of the day. If she did, her worries would be gone and her only problem would be figuring out to spend a few million dollars.

Last night he'd blown it. He had failed to get her to sign. He'd been blindsided by those three simple words she'd uttered: *I trust you.*

Last night he'd allowed his emotions to rule his head but it wouldn't happen again today. Today he would accomplish his goal. Today he would convince Minda to sign the contract to sell her building.

And once he accomplished that goal, he'd get on the next plane back to New York, and he'd never look back.

"Good morning."

Minda jumped at the sound of Mark's voice. "Oh! Good morning."

He stepped into the room. "Sorry. I didn't mean to startle you. You were really concentrating on your work."

"It's not work, exactly." She flashed a self-conscious smile at him and quickly clicked her mouse on the red "x" in the corner of the screen, closing the search engine she'd been working in.

"Any chance you're looking up some of the terms from the letter we read last night?" He skirted the desk and crouched down beside her chair, causing her heart to gallop in her chest. He frowned. "Your browser isn't open."

She clicked on the browser icon and watched the search engine's home page fill her screen again.

"That's better. Now, what term do you want to search for?"

He was looking at her so expectantly and his handsome face was so close to hers, she thought it wouldn't be a bad thing to come up with enough search terms to keep him crouched beside her for the remainder of the day. She forced her gaze to lock on the safety of the computer screen.

"I wasn't searching for real estate terms. I was looking for apartments. If I were to sell the building, my tenants would have to move so I was looking for information on what's available for them."

"That's a good idea."

"Really? Ellen doesn't think so. She thinks I *mother* my tenants. She says I'm too involved in their lives."

"That's because they're not just tenants to you. You see this building and the apartments as your ministry to others out of your devotion to Christ. Am I right?"

She allowed herself to look at him and saw an expression in his blue eyes that was encouraging. "Yes, that's exactly right. I'm glad you understand because I can't help thinking that maybe God wants me to continue what I've been doing. Maybe He wants me to keep the building."

"Or maybe God wants you to have the money."

She shook her head slightly. "I don't think God cares that much about money."

"What makes you think that?"

"Because of some of the people he gives it to."

"Perhaps he's trying to give some to you."

She willed herself to block out his nearness, the warm scent of his aftershave, and the soft, intimate sound of his voice. "Is that what you think? Really?"

"It's a distinct possibility."

"I was awake all night praying about it and asking God to tell me what to do."

"And were your prayers answered?"

"I don't think so. Not yet, anyway. I wish we hadn't read the contract last night. I wish I'd never opened the envelope. When I didn't know what it said or how much money they were offering, it was so easy to just go about my daily life. But now . . . everything's changed."

"Change doesn't have to be bad, Minda. It can be the beginning of a new adventure or an opportunity to expand your life in a way you never thought before."

"I don't need my life expanded."

He smiled softly. "Why are you so resistant to change?"

"Why are you so disrespectful of the past?"

"I'm not disrespectful at all. In fact, I have a heritage and history myself. But I balance it with my present life and future goals."

She realized that she knew virtually nothing about the man crouched beside her. She knew only that he had a brother, he dabbled in real estate, and he played baseball. That's all she knew. But despite his reluctance to reveal anything about himself, she felt herself drawn to him in a way she hadn't felt in seventeen years. She'd witnessed his kindness to Brady and she'd sensed how much he enjoyed spending time with Addy Whimple. She felt the sincerity of his promise to set things right with Tracy. Weren't those things proof enough of the kind of man he was?

"You never talk about your history. Where you came from or what your goals are."

"That's a topic for a different time," he said. His voice was low and intimate, underscoring how near his face was to hers. "Right now, we're talking about you. Last night you asked for my advice."

"Yes, I did. And I'd still like it."

"Okay, I'll give it to you. But first, I have to make a couple disclaimers."

She giggled. "You sound like a lawyer."

His eyes locked for a moment on the curve of her lips. "It's important you know where I stand. Disclaimer number one: my priorities are different than yours."

"I know that."

"Disclaimer number two: I don't have any personal relationships with the people who would be affected by the sale of the building."

"But you know some of my tenants. You've met Brady and Miss Whimple."

"But I don't know them like you do."

"That's true. But I'd still like to know what you think I should do."

"Okay, then." He hesitated for a moment. "If I were in your situation . . . I'd sell the building."

For the first time since entering her office, Mark didn't look at her. He told himself that he looked away because he knew his advice would be hard for her to hear. But the truth was, he couldn't bring himself to look at her.

Instead, he concentrated on a loose paper clip on the desk. He picked it up and studied it as if he'd never seen one before.

"I see. Thank you for telling me."

"Does knowing my opinion help move you closer to making a decision?"

"A little, but I can't decide yet. I was thinking of talking with Pastor Walker about it this afternoon. There's an orphan train committee meeting at the church and I'm sure he'll be there. Pastor Walker ministers to a lot of my tenants and knows their needs."

"Would it help if we went over the contract again?"

She shook her head. "No. I just have to ask for God's guidance and make a decision the best I can. The funny thing is, if I decide to sell the building, I won't know what I'll do with myself. Between running the bookstore, and maintaining the building, and keeping an eye on my tenants, the McAllister Building takes up a big part of my life. If I sell, I think I'll feel as if there's a hole in my heart."

He looked at her then. "You're heart is so open and giving, I guarantee it won't take long for that hole to be filled." As he spoke, he put his hand over hers as it rested on the computer mouse.

It was a small gesture, but it had a stunning effect on her senses. Her breath caught. Her hazel eyes flew to his and held.

"What time do you have to be at the church?" Mark's voice was low and soft but held an urgent quality that told her how important her answer was.

"Two o'clock."

"Have lunch with me first, then I'll drive you to church."

As much as she wanted to say yes, Minda knew she couldn't. She had responsibilities and promises to keep. She felt a bit of the real world intrude on the magical world Mark had created in her office.

"I can't. I'm taking Tracy shopping this morning for a dress to wear to her party."

"Then have dinner with me tonight."

She held her breath for a moment, reveling in the knowledge that this man—the man she found so impossibly attractive—was asking her to have dinner with him.

Asking her for a *date*.

"Okay. I'd like that."

He smiled. "Okay, dinner tonight. And in the meantime, I'll see you at the church."

"Does that mean you plan to be at the committee meeting?"

He nodded. "There's something I want to talk to Coach about." He stood up and impulsively drew her hand up to his lips to lightly kiss her fingertips. "See you at two."

17

Minda adjusted her hold on the heavy tray laden with food and drinks. Her hazel eyes scanned the crowded mall food court. She spotted Tracy sitting at a small table in the middle of the court, patiently waiting, her shopping bags piled on a chair beside her.

Minda made her way through the maze of tables and chairs and deposited the tray on the table.

"Thanks, Mom. I'm starving." Tracy claimed one of the sodas and a plate of food from the tray.

Minda sat down on the chair across from her daughter and arranged her own food on the table. "As soon as we're done eating, let's get to the shoe store. Remember, I have to be at the church by two o'clock."

"Yeah, I know. I was thinking that if we aren't done shopping, maybe I could take the car. I could, like, drop you off at the church and pick you up later."

Minda nodded as she unwrapped a straw and drove it through the hole in the lid of her soda cup. "That's a good idea, if we run out of time. But you should be able to pick out a pair of shoes from the mall store in the next thirty minutes, don't you think?"

Tracy swallowed a mouthful of food. "But the shoe warehouse will have a *better* selection."

Minda frowned. "There's no shoe warehouse here at the mall."

"But there is one about eight miles from here. I probably have a better chance of finding a pair of shoes there that will match my dress. They have more variety. I think I want a high-heeled sandal."

"That will look nice. But let's try the shoe store here in the mall first."

"Can I get a new purse, too?"

"Sure." Minda tried not to think about the amount of money that had already been charged on her credit card that morning. Between the cost of Tracy's birthday party as well as a dress, earrings, necklace, hair accessories and a yet-to-be-chosen pair of shoes and purse, she was really feeling the financial pinch. She pushed the thought from her mind. Tracy would turn eighteen only once in her life and Minda wanted it to be special for both of them. "But you have to stick to the budget I gave you."

"I will. You know, Mom, I think I've been pretty responsible about the money thing. I mean, you told me how much I could spend and I haven't even asked to spend more. I'm keeping to the budget."

"That's true," Minda agreed. "You've been very considerate of my wallet today."

"I'm considerate of your wallet *every* day. I know we don't have a lot of money, but—" Tracy suddenly clamped her lips together and stared down at her plate of food.

"Is something wrong?" Minda tried to keep the confusion out of her voice, but she couldn't make sense of Tracy's sudden change of mood. Their day had been going so well; shopping and talking and now eating together. What on earth was Tracy upset about?

"I really wish you would stop treating me like a child, that's all. My birthday is just a few days away and I'm going to be *eighteen years old*."

"I know that, Tracy."

"Can't you start talking to me like an adult? Can't you trust me a little bit?"

"I do trust you, but the problem is, for the last seventeen years I've been your mother. I've fed you and protected you and worried about you and cared for you. After seventeen years, I can't just turn that off. I can't flip a switch and stop being your mother."

"I'm not asking you to stop being my mother. I just want you to trust me. Like the money thing. Couldn't you just give me the benefit of the doubt? I mean, I know what a budget is. I know there's only so much money, and I've been really careful to spend no more than what you said I could. I didn't even *look* at most of the dresses in the last store that were super cute because I knew they'd cost too much. I'm a very responsible person, and you just don't see it."

For a long moment Minda sat in silence, unsure what to say.

"And that's just one example," Tracy said. "I'm very responsible in other ways, too, Mom. Like, I know that paying for a party and buying me a new outfit means you have to sacrifice other things. I know you go without stuff so you can pay for all of this."

"Tracy, I don't want you to think about that."

"I can't help thinking about it. But when you say stuff about me spending more money than you have, you make it sound like I don't care that you have to make sacrifices. You make me sound *selfish*."

"I don't think you're selfish, Tracy. I never thought that."

"But can you see how the things you say might make me feel that way?"

"Now that you mention it . . . yes, I guess I can."

"I don't want to hurt your feelings or anything, Mom, but I just think that if you saw me as more of an adult and trusted me a little, you wouldn't have so much to worry about. You'd see that I'm really responsible, and then you wouldn't have to worry about me."

"I'll always worry about you, whether you're eighteen or eighty."

"But you'd worry about me less if you recognized that I make good decisions, right? I mean, wouldn't that make a difference?"

"Yes, that would make a difference."

"And instead of you always taking care of me, maybe I could help you once in a while, you know?"

Minda leaned back in her chair and looked at Tracy. When had her daughter grown up? In the last month Tracy had talked of almost nothing else but her eighteenth birthday. But Minda had never stopped to think about what it meant. She'd spent her whole adult life caring for Tracy and now Tracy was offering to help her. As one adult would help another.

"I see what you mean. I've been treating you the same way I treated you when you were twelve, haven't I?"

"Yeah, you have."

"And I haven't even acknowledged—to you or to myself— that you've grown up into a smart, lovely, and caring young woman."

"No, you haven't."

"I'm sorry, Tracy. I didn't realize I was hurting you." She felt a lump of emotion rise in her throat as she studied her daughter's expression. She was staring down at her plate of food but there was no sign of the sullen teenager look that Tracy wore so habitually of late. Instead, she seemed thoughtful and a little sad.

"I know you didn't mean to hurt me, and I probably should have said something sooner. I mean, I used to, like, tell you how I felt about stuff, but I haven't been doing that lately, have I?" Tracy looked up.

Minda thought she saw a little bit of regret and lot of apology in her daughter's eyes.

"I promise to try harder to treat you more like an adult. But please remember, I'm still your mother."

"I know. It's enough for me to know that you're willing to try. And I promise to tell you when something's bothering me. Like I used to before."

"Good. I'd like that." Minda smiled softly at her as she tried to fight back the sudden tears that threatened to well up in her eyes. "Your father would be so proud of you."

"You always say that."

"That's because it's true."

"What about you? Are you ever going to be proud of me?"

"I *am* proud of you!" Minda said, shocked.

"Oh. I wasn't sure. I mean, you never said so. You just always say that Daddy would be proud, so I didn't know."

"Then I'll make it clear: I'm very proud of you, Tracy."

"Thanks, Mom." Tracy's eyes shone bright and she smiled in a way that reminded Minda of a happy time before teenaged rebellion and rampaging hormones changed her daughter. She sniffled and smiled back.

Tracy looked down at her plate again. "Can we, like, change the subject before we both start bawling in the middle of the mall?"

Minda laughed, driving back the mist of tears that had formed in her eyes. "Yes! Let's change the subject! Tell me how the Rockies game was last night."

"The seats were really good."

Minda waited for her to say more. "Did they win?"

"I think so. Mom, how do you know if a man likes you?"

Instinctively, Minda's body braced for what promised to be another discussion about Mark. She forced herself to remain calm. "Are you asking how you know if a man likes you in a romantic way?"

"Yeah. I used to think Josh liked me."

Josh? Tracy wanted to talk about *Josh* instead of Mark? Minda fought back the urge to hug her daughter. "What made you think so?"

"I dunno. He used to, like, follow me around. And he always tried to do things to help me."

Minda nodded. "That sounds like the actions of a man who's interested."

"Yeah, well, he stopped doing those things. I'm not sure when. All of a sudden I realized it last night at the game. I mean, he paid for our sodas and nachos and he was really polite and stuff. But he didn't act like he was trying to please me. Not like he usually does."

"Well, maybe he decided that trying to please you didn't work. Maybe he came to realize that—as much as he liked you—you didn't like him back in the same way."

"Well, he shouldn't have. I mean, how could he know that?"

"True. I guess, when people don't talk about things, it's easy to jump to the wrong conclusion." Minda watched Tracy wrestle with that concept. "Sounds like you miss the old Josh. The Josh you knew and counted on."

"Yeah. Sorta."

"Why don't you talk to Josh about it?"

"You mean, tell him what I just told you? No way!"

Minda thought for a moment. "It seems to me that if you want the old Josh back, you need to give him a little bit of encouragement."

"How do I do that?"

"You could invite him to do something with you."

"Like what?"

"Well, I'm not sure. Let's see . . . Your birthday party is Thursday night. What if you invited Josh to go for pizza afterward?"

Tracy looked a little horrified. "You mean, ask him for *a date*?"

"No, not a date. You've known Josh for a long time. He's one of your oldest friends. It seems natural that you'd want to celebrate an important birthday with the people who have meaning in your life. You could ask a couple other friends to go, too. Keep it casual . . . Just a small party with your closest friends."

Tracy gave it some thought. "Kinda like a mini-party with my best friends right after the big party's over. That's a good idea, Mom."

Thank you, Lord, Minda prayed. *Thank you!*

She watched Tracy turn her attention back to her plate of food and picked up her own fork. She wasn't hungry, though, and her food held no appeal. The only thing she could think about was telling Mark that Tracy's interest seemed to be shifting toward Josh. Mark's plan had been right all along.

Mark's blue eyes scanned the Sunday school classroom,

searching for Minda. He didn't see her seated in any of the folding chairs arranged in neat rows or in the small knots of people laughing and talking together in one corner of the room.

Coach Morgan was at the front of the room writing a brief agenda on the chalkboard in neat capital letters. When he turned away from the chalkboard, his gaze landed on Mark. He went directly toward him with his hand out.

"Good to see you again, son." He clasped Mark's hand in a hearty shake.

"I'm glad I caught you before the meeting, Coach. Do you have a minute?"

"I sure do, but there's no need to apologize again about the baseball practice. I understand why you played the way you did."

"Actually, that's not what I wanted to talk to you about."

"No? What, then?"

Mark reached into his pants pocket and withdrew the pocket watch. "I want you to have this."

Coach stared at the watch. He made a choking sound that he quickly masked by clearing his throat.

"I couldn't take your watch, son."

"I wish you would. I'm pretty certain it has more meaning for you than it does for me."

Coach shook his head, slowly. "Well, it certainly brought back memories. Memories I hadn't thought possible. I'll always be grateful to you for that. But what are the chances that watch in your hand is the same watch my sister had on the train?"

"I don't think there are many watches like this."

"Maybe not. Where'd you say you got it?"

"In Chicago. Did you ever live in Chicago, Coach?"

"No. The trains went through Chicago, but I grew up in

Kansas."

"Then it's probably not the exact same watch that was in your family. But I'd still like you to have it."

Coach smiled and clapped him on the shoulder. "I appreciate your willingness to give it to me, but I can honestly say I don't need it. What I mean is, seeing that watch the other night brought back a lot of memories I'd lost, especially memories of my sister. She was so protective of us—of me, especially. *She* was the real keeper of the watch."

"I'd really like you to have this," Mark persisted. "You'd be doing me a great favor by taking it."

"I wouldn't feel right," Coach said, shaking his head slightly. "But I'll make you a deal. If this reunion is a success and if I find my sister, I'd like you to offer the watch to *her*."

"You've got yourself a deal, Coach." Mark tucked the watch back into his pocket.

"You're staying for the committee meeting, I hope."

"Sure. I'll stay. And Coach, I'm . . . I'm praying for you." He watched for Coach's reaction, wondering if Coach could tell just how unaccustomed he was to saying those words. "About the reunion, I mean. I'm praying that everything works out."

Coach smiled. "Thanks, son. I appreciate it. And, by the way, I'm praying for *you*." He headed up to the front of the classroom where the committee members were gathering.

Mark's eyes strayed toward the door just as Minda came in the room.

She saw him and immediately went to him. "I'm glad you're here," she said. "I have some news for you."

"Can we have all the committee members up here at the front of the room?" Coach called above the noise of people milling about. "Let's get the meeting started."

"Just my luck," Minda said, ruefully. "I'll tell you all about it after the meeting. You're staying, right?"

"Yes, I'm staying."

The smile she flashed at him was almost dazzling. "Good. I'll talk to you later."

She went to the front of the room and took her place beside Coach Morgan at the long table. Her attention locked on Mark. She smiled at him, her expression light and carefree as she watched him claim a place in the last row of chairs at the back of the room.

Coach Morgan stood up and pointed to the meeting agenda he had printed on the blackboard. "This will be our last formal meeting before the baseball game, so we have a lot of territory to cover today. But before we start, I'd like to say something. Something personal. You've all known me long enough to know that I don't believe in dwelling on the past. There probably isn't anyone in this room who hasn't experienced trials in their life and I'm no exception. But I always believed that if I worked hard and lived my life according to Christ's teachings, I'd be blessed and happy, with no memories of those past troubles. But a few days ago, a young man—I won't tell you his name—convinced me that it may not be such a good thing to erase all memories of past trials. Because sometimes—in the middle of the memories of awful things that happened—there can be good memories, too."

Coach paused for a moment, considering his words. "Because of that young man, I was able to recall a good memory. It's a memory that explains what this reunion is all about."

"Share it with us, Coach!" Pastor Walker's voice rang out from where he stood in the doorway.

"I see I have a heckler," Coach said, and everyone in the room laughed.

Pastor Walker held up his hand as if he were taking an oath. "I promise to be quiet. Don't mind me." He sat down in the back row of chairs near Mark.

"I'll try to make this short," Coach said. "You all know I was adopted when I was young. Five years old, as a matter of fact. I was put on a train somewhere in the East and sent to Kansas, where I was adopted by the Morgan family. But I didn't ride the train alone. There were other children like me on the train. And you all know that it's my belief I had three older sisters who were with me. Sisters I've looked for all my adult life, but never found. I was too young at the time to remember very much about them. I can't even remember their names. That's where you good people come into the picture. You've always been supportive and caring in my search for my sisters. You've helped me with my research and prayed for me. And I especially want to thank Minda for coming up with the idea of hosting a reunion of other orphan train riders who were adopted like I was. I'm hoping—I'm praying—that God will grant me one more blessing and see to it that one of the train riders who attends the reunion will know something about my sisters."

Several people in the room murmured, "Amen."

Coach nodded. "Amen. But even if that doesn't happen, I can take comfort in knowing that God already answered another of my prayers. That young man I mentioned earlier? Because of him, I know that my mother—my birth mother— loved me. That young man gave me a memory I hadn't recalled before, but I remember now. I remember my mother putting me to bed at night and teaching me to say my prayers. And I remember that she gave my oldest sister a memento to take with us on the train that she thought would bring us comfort. And maybe . . . maybe she meant it to be a reminder so we wouldn't forget about her." Coach's eyes shone bright with emotion. "I guess every adopted kid struggles to understand *Why*? Why was I adopted? Why didn't my parents keep me? But in my case, I have the answer now: My mother didn't put me on the train because she didn't want me anymore. She put me on the train because she loved me so much and wanted me to have a good life." Coach looked down at the table and quickly wiped his eyes. He looked up again, his emotions controlled. "And I *have* had a good life. Thanks, in large part, to having good friends like you. Thank you all for working hard to put this reunion together. With God's help, this reunion will be a success and other orphan train riders will find a little bit more about themselves and their histories, like I did this week." He sat down.

The room was quiet. Several people in the audience sniffled.

Minda reached into her purse and pulled out a tissue to dab at her eyes.

"God bless you, Coach," said a woman in the front row.

"Amen," said Pastor Walker from the back of the room.

"Are all committee meetings at this church so emotional?" Mark asked Minda, in a low voice.

She was alone at the table in the front of the room, gathering together the papers and notes she had used during the meeting. She looked up at him and smiled.

"No, they're not. But Coach is very special and very well loved. And I have a sneaking suspicion I know who the young man was who helped him remember his mother."

Mark eyes quickly scanned the room to see if anyone was close enough to overhear them. The meeting had ended several minutes before. There were few people left and those that remained were moving in groups toward the door.

He gave Minda look of innocence. "He sounds like a very impressive young man."

She laughed. "That's debatable. But I did see you and Coach talking about your watch when we were at baseball practice the other night. Coach looked upset. And later, when you asked me to hold the watch for you, I could tell something was bothering you."

Mark drew the watch out of his pocket. "This," he said, holding it in his palm, "reminded him of a watch that was in his birth family. I don't suppose there's a way to tell if this was the actual watch or just a reminder of the one he saw when he was a child. But it's still pretty amazing that something like this—an old pocket watch—could affect someone's life like it did Coach's."

"And yours. I know you want to deny it," Minda said, "but I still think that watch means more to you than you're willing to admit."

"Is that the news you wanted to tell me?"

"No," she said, feeling a little disappointed. By now she should be used to Mark's reluctance to talk about himself. But it bothered her that he wouldn't open himself up even a little, especially after his behavior that morning in her office. When he'd taken her hand and held it, she knew he was attracted to her. She knew it in her heart. Why, then, was he still so reluctant to open up to her?

She stuffed the papers into her tote bag and looked quickly at the doorway. "I don't want Tracy to hear this. I gave her the car so she could go shoe shopping but she'll be here any minute to pick me up."

"You left a teenaged girl alone in a shoe store? You're a brave mother."

"Finding the right pair of shoes is the last thing she has to do to get ready for her birthday party."

"Did Tracy tell you that she invited me to the party?"

"Yes, she did. And speaking as her mother and given the circumstances, I don't think it would be a good idea for you to come."

"I already told her I won't be there. But, at the same time, turning eighteen is an important birthday. Do you think I'd be making things worse if I gave her some small gift? What about a gift card?"

"I think that will be fine. You can drop it off before or after the party, if you'd like."

"I'll do that. What's the news you wanted to tell me? I hope it's good?"

"Very good. I think your plan is working. Tracy told me she had a good time with Josh at the baseball game."

His brows went up. "Glad to hear it."

"She also mentioned that Josh was polite, but he didn't seem quite as interested in her as he was before. And that, of course, made her more interested in Josh."

"You don't say?"

"I do say. And I suspect that someone gave Josh advice about how to treat women."

Mark remained silent, but looked down at her with an expression of abject innocence.

She laughed and shook her head. "I don't expect you to admit to it. But I noticed you don't *deny* it, either."

"I'm just glad to hear their evening together was a success. I'll keep encouraging Josh if you'll keep encouraging Tracy."

"Deal." Automatically, she held out her hand.

He took her hand in his, then covered it with his other hand. "Deal," he said, softly.

The warmth of his hands enveloping hers traveled up Minda's arm on a direct course to her heart. For the second time that day she found her hand in his. And for the second time, she felt the same reaction: she hoped he never let her go. She hoped he'd hold her hand all through their dinner date and every moment they were together.

"Mom?"

Minda looked over and saw Tracy in the doorway, a look of indignant anger on her face.

"Mom, what are you *doing*?"

"Striking a deal." Minda pulled her hand from Mark's grasp.

"Hi, Tracy," he said, casually.

Tracy ignored his greeting. "What kind of a deal?" she asked, suspicious.

"I can't be at your birthday party," he said, "but we just agreed I'll drop off a gift for you."

"Oh." Tracy's expression relaxed slightly, but she was still frowning.

"He can't back out of giving you a gift now," Minda said, trying desperately to sound as casual as Mark. "We shook on it."

Tracy didn't smile. "So, are you ready to go?"

"In just a minute." She scooped up the last of the papers on the table and stuffed them into her tote bag. "Okay, ready."

"Good. I didn't get any shoes this afternoon, so can we go back to the shoe warehouse? There were a couple pairs there I liked, but I couldn't decide what to get. Will you go with me?"

"Sure."

"And then, maybe we can talk some more at dinner. You know, about what I told you earlier?"

Minda's eyes flew to Mark's face. "I'd love to, honey, but I—"

"Sounds like you two ladies have a lot to do tonight," Mark said, cutting her off.

Minda's mental image of a date with Mark shattered into a thousand pieces. "But, Mark—"

"It's okay. I'll see you tomorrow. Have a good time shopping, ladies."

He left the room and Tracy shot an accusing glance at her mother. "What did he mean, *it's okay*?"

"Nothing." Her tone was flat as she tried to hide her disappointment. She wouldn't be having dinner with Mark, after all. "He didn't mean anything."

18

ood morning, Minda!" Pastor Walker clasped her hand
as he greeted her. He was in his usual place after Sunday
service, standing at the threshold of the sanctuary's heavy
oak doors, speaking words of greeting to each congregant as
they stepped out into the sunshine. "And Tracy! Good
morning, how are you?"

"Fine, Pastor Walker. I liked your sermon this morning. It
was very insightful and when I get home, I'm going to reread
the Bible verses you used."

"Thank you, Tracy. That's exactly the response I pray for
every Sunday." He smiled at Minda. "Things appear to be
going well for you."

Instinctively, Minda knew he was referring to the talk
they'd had about Tracy. "Things *are* going well, Pastor. I
think we're headed on the right track."

"Glad to hear it." He pressed her hand encouragingly
before he turned to greet the next person exiting the
sanctuary behind Minda.

She went down the steps and walked with Tracy to the

patio area near Fellowship Hall. Josh Stuart was standing with a group of Tracy's friends. He looked over and waved, but instead of coming to Tracy's side as he usually did, he simply turned his attention back to the group of teenagers.

Tracy let out a short, frustrated breath. "See what I mean? That's what I was telling you last night at dinner. He did the same thing at the Rockies game. He acts like he doesn't even like me."

"He must like you a little. He did look over and wave at you."

"That's not the same."

"Have you invited him to have pizza Thursday night after your birthday party?"

"Not yet."

"Why don't you do it now?"

"Now? I can't. He's standing with all our friends. I can't ask him in front of them."

"Then call him over here." When Tracy hesitated, Minda said, "I'll do it."

She caught Josh's attention and waved him over with a subtle sweep of her hand.

"Hi, Mrs. McAllister. Hi, Tracy." Josh's voice was polite but controlled, with no hint of his usual exuberance. "Where's your friend?"

Tracy frowned. "What friend?"

"Mr. Cartier."

She gave him a challenging look. "How should I know?"

"He's been coming to church with you lately."

"That doesn't mean he has to come with us again today."

"I guess not. He seems pretty inconsistent, though. "

"No, he doesn't."

"Sure. I learned all about it in my psychology class last year. It's not uncommon for older people to get a little flaky when they age, you know. There was a whole chapter about it in the textbook."

"I thought the only book you ever read was a football playbook," Tracy retorted. "Besides, Mark isn't *that* old."

"I'm pretty sure he had a couple grey hairs," Josh said, confidently.

"I never saw them."

"Yeah, they were there. I'm pretty perceptive about those things."

Tracy searched his face. "Is there something different about you? Have you changed something since we went to the Rockies game?"

"No."

"You seem different."

"That's because I'm cultivating an aura of mystique."

Minda put her fingers up to her mouth to hide a smile. She was pretty sure that *cultivating an aura of mystique* was not a concept Josh came up with on his own. She was going to take a lot of pleasure teasing Mark about the kind of advice he was handing out to teenage boys.

They chatted with Josh for a few more minutes. Minda carefully guided the conversation to the subject of Tracy's birthday party so Tracy could invite Josh to have pizza after the party.

Josh's eyes lit up but he thrust his hands into his pockets and looked off into the distance, as if he were deciding whether or not to accept the invitation. After a moment, he said, "Pizza, huh? Sure, that sounds okay, I guess."

"Good." Tracy's voice held a hint of relief. "I'm glad you can make it. See you later, Josh."

Minda and Tracy began their walk home. As soon as they were safely away from Josh, Tracy asked, "Mom, did you hear what Josh said?"

"Which part?"

"About Mark. Did you ever see any grey hair? On Mark, I mean."

"Not that I remember."

"Do you think he could have some? I mean, he is kind of old. Thirty-two is middle-aged, right? And isn't that when you start getting grey hair?"

"Some people do. Not everyone." Under normal circumstances, Minda would have defended a man in his early thirties as still young, but since Tracy was doing a good job of talking herself out of her attraction to Mark, she decided to keep quiet.

"Why do you suppose Mark didn't show up for church?"

Minda was wondering the exact same thing. For Tracy's sake, she was glad Mark hadn't joined them but she couldn't deny she felt disappointed, too. She already knew he wasn't a man who attended church regularly, but she thought—she *hoped*—that last Sunday's experience had inspired him; that he'd been filled by the Holy Spirit to attend church of his own accord because he wanted fellowship with his brethren; because he wanted to worship the Lord.

But was he a Christian? Minda thought so, especially after he told her that he'd been raised in a Christian home, but he never seemed to openly profess his faith. Even Ellen realized that he only attended church because Minda invited him. None of it made sense.

She sighed softly. "I don't know."

"I thought he liked going to church with us. He knows practically the whole congregation now."

"He's certainly made some good friends here," Minda agreed.

"Do you think Mark's a Christian?"

"I haven't heard him say so. But on the other hand, I

haven't asked him."

"I don't think I could date a man who isn't a Christian. I mean, religion's a pretty fundamental thing you should have in common if you're gonna date, don't you think?"

"I absolutely agree with you."

"But even without knowing that about him, you still like Mark, right?"

"He's nice enough."

"No, Mom. I mean, you *like him*."

Those last three words surprised Minda, leaving her almost breathless. Her steps slowed as she looked at Tracy.

Tracy looked unflinchingly back at her. "I saw, Mom. Yesterday, when I picked you up at church. I saw the way Mark looked at you when he was holding your hand. And you looked the same way back at him. You *like* him."

Minda stopped walking. She stared at Tracy and swallowed hard, even though her mouth had gone dry. She wanting to say something but no sensible thoughts came to her mind. She felt almost as if she had been caught in some misdeed, but she knew in her heart she hadn't done anything wrong. Yes, she liked Mark. Yes, she was attracted to him, but she hadn't acted on that attraction. And since their plans for a first date had died a tragic death before they could be realized, Minda doubted her attraction to Mark would ever get a chance to play out.

"I think Mark is a nice man." Minda spoke slowly, alert to her daughter's reaction and any signs of a possible meltdown. "But he has made it very clear to you and me that he's not staying. He lives in New York and that's where he's going as soon as he finishes whatever business he has here."

"I'm not angry about it," Tracy said, in a calm voice. "I kinda was at first. I was angry 'cause I thought you stole my boyfriend, but then I realized he was never really my boyfriend. It was just a crush I had. I mean, he never liked me back and he didn't want to hang out with me. He acted like I was his little sister."

Meltdown averted. Some of the tension left Minda's shoulders.

Together they began walking again at a slower, more thoughtful pace.

"Are you saying," Minda asked, "that you don't have a crush on Mark any more?"

"I don't think so. "

"When did your feelings change?"

"When I went to the baseball game with Josh. We had a good time together. Josh was nice to me and I felt like I could be myself with him. That's when I remembered what you told me—that the man I'm with should like me for who I am."

"After seventeen years, you finally listened to something I said?" Minda asked, in a teasing tone.

"Yeah. For, like, *once*." She threw her mother a saucy look.

"What if Mark had been at church this morning? Would you have been okay? Would you have been embarrassed to see him?"

"No. I don't think so. It's not like we were dating and broke up or anything. Besides, he's still kind of a cool guy, and he still looks like a movie star. I still like him and all, but just in a different way."

Minda's spirits lifted. She felt carefree, as if a heavy weight had been lifted from her back. Tracy was no longer interested in Mark. Her prayers had been answered.

Wait until Mark hears this, she thought. For the second day in a row she had good news to tell Mark. And she couldn't wait to see him again to share the news.

Mark and Paul arrived at the high school for the last team practice before the baseball game on Saturday. Mark pulled his rental car into a parking space. He turned off the ignition and looked over at his brother. "Listen, before we meet up with everybody, I need to ask you for a favor."

"That's a switch. It's usually the other way around." Paul unlatched his seat belt and opened the passenger door. "I'm usually the one begging you for help."

"I'm glad you see it that way. Maybe you'll feel obligated to me and you won't say *No*."

Paul chuckled softly and shook his head. "You never stop working the angles, do you? Go ahead, then. Ask your favor."

"There's a kid named Brady Blythe. He's sick."

"Sick? You mean, like the flu?"

"No, I mean sick, as in something's-wrong-with-him sick. He has to receive some kind of treatment at the hospital on a regular basis. He's lost his hair and he's pretty pale."

"Sounds rough."

"I think so, too, because he's really a cool little guy. So, will you help him out?"

Paul looked back at him with a blank expression. "Help him out?"

"Yeah, help him."

"What, exactly, do you want me to do?"

"You minister at the hospital. You have contacts there. Find out about him. What's it going to take to make him better? How does he get moved to the top of whatever waiting list he's on?"

Paul looked at him for along moment. "You've been on the board of directors of Harmony House since Day One and you've never shown the least bit of interest in its work or its clients. Why the sudden interest in this boy?"

Mark pulled the key out of the ignition and focused all his attention on the remote button that opened the trunk. He was careful not to reveal any of the feelings he had a hard time understanding himself. "I met the kid."

Paul's expression softened. "I see. It makes a difference when they look you in the eye, doesn't it?" He got out of the car and closed the door.

Mark got out of the car, too. "Don't start preaching," he said, with a scowl. He went to the open trunk and grabbed his baseball glove. "Just find out what you can about him, okay?"

"And then what?"

"And then . . . *help* him. That's what you do, isn't it? Isn't that what Harmony House is all about?"

"It is," Paul said, patiently. "I assume you know that *everyone* Harmony House helps is just like Brady. Each person is real with a real story and a real need. Just like Brady."

"I know that." Mark's tone was curt. "Sorry. It's just that I—" *What?* It was just that he had never thought about the actual lives Harmony House touched? Or that he'd chosen to think of Harmony House as just his brother's pet project? Or that he realized maybe Minda was right about donors who never get involved with the charities they support?

Of course she'd been right. He'd always stayed detached and disinterested; writing big donation checks to assuage his conscience but never becoming emotionally involved with the clients Harmony House served. He was exactly the sort of person Minda had spoken of with disdain and, at that very moment, he hated himself for it.

"I guess I always thought it was enough just to write the check," he muttered.

"Don't sell yourself short. If it hadn't been for you and

those checks you send, there would be no Harmony House."

"Yeah, well . . ." Mark allowed his thought to go unfinished, but the unaccustomed prickling of conscience he was showing moved his brother to wrap his around his shoulder and give him a couple of gruff, man-style claps on the back.

"Don't get sentimental on me," Mark said, brusquely. "Just do what you can about Brady, okay?"

"I'll see what I can find out, if you'll stop pretending that you don't have a heart. It's okay to care about the kid. It's okay to get involved."

"I seem to be involved in a lot of things I wouldn't normally care about," Mark muttered. "It must be the high altitude or Denver's thin air."

"Or maybe you actually have a heart buried under that tough businessman's shell."

Mark shook his head as he stuffed his hand into his baseball glove. "I never should have brought it up."

He couldn't tell which was more annoying: Paul's sympathetic smile or his own weakness. A weakness that caused him to become dangerously involved in the emotions and needs of Minda and the people in her orbit. A weakness that caused him to care about Minda when he was supposed to be wearing her down, bending her to his will, inching her toward signing on the dotted line and selling her building.

He wrestled with the thought as he and Paul walked toward the field. Ellen was sitting in the bleachers, ready to cheer for her husband, Jim, but there was no sign of Pastor Walker or Tracy. Or Minda.

Mark left Paul at the bleachers and joined the team on the field for warm-up. He threw the ball to Jim and easily caught it when Jim threw it back. Eventually, he felt himself relax, finding pleasure in the exercise of a simple game of catch.

He'd unexpectedly found pleasure in a lot of simple things since he'd arrived in Denver; like evening walks and affordable Italian dinners; peaceful gardens and clunky old roll-top desks.

And now he was playing baseball. He hadn't played since college, but all the skill and talent had come instantly back to him. Just like riding a bike. He gave himself up to the sheer pleasure of it.

Coach blew a whistle, calling the team together. Mark headed toward the dugout. His gaze instinctively strayed toward the metal bleachers as if drawn by a force not his own.

Minda was there. She was sitting beside Ellen and Paul, but she was looking straight at him.

His eyes locked on hers. She smiled softly. It was a small gesture that impacted him in a big way. A rush of happiness swept through his body, energizing him, as if the sun had just come out from behind a bank of clouds. In that moment, Minda's presence pushed every thought from his mind. Tomorrow would be soon enough to think about the job he had yet to do or the goals he had yet to accomplish. For right now, he only wanted to play baseball and know that Minda's beautiful hazel eyes were watching him.

Mark kept his promise to Coach Morgan and played to the best of his abilities. At one point, Josh fielded a long ball and threw it hard and straight to Mark, who caught it and threw it unerringly to the catcher behind home plate to force an out.

Coach whistled and clapped from his place at the top of the dugout steps.

"Great teamwork!" he called. "You look like pros out there!"

Mark put his hand in the air as Josh jogged up to him;

then Josh smacked Mark's palm with the stinging force of a young man who didn't know his own strength. It was a good moment, and Mark reveled in it.

When practice ended, he headed straight to the bleachers and Minda's side, not even bothering to hide his interest in her. The loud talk and laughter from the other players subsided as they moved as a group in the direction of the parking lot. Eventually, only Mark and Paul lingered near the bleachers. And Minda.

"I have some news for you," she said, in her soft voice.

His brows went up. "More news? Is it as good as the last news you gave me?"

"Even better."

"I can't wait to hear it." He saw her hesitate and knew she didn't want to talk in front of Paul.

He put one hand on his brother's shoulder and held out his car keys with the other. "Would you mind driving yourself home? I'll get the car back from you later."

"Sure, no problem." The light in Paul's eyes showed he knew the reason he was being dismissed and he didn't mind at all. "I've got to get going anyway, if I'm going to start on that homework assignment you gave me."

"Homework assignment?" Minda asked, after Paul said good-night and headed toward the parking lot. "You gave your brother a homework assignment?"

"Paul needs to keep busy so he stays out of trouble," he said, lightly. He looked off across the darkened parking lot. Only Minda's car was left. "We're all alone. Is it safe to tell me your news now?"

She reached into her purse and dug out her keys as she walked beside Mark toward her car.

"Tracy talked to me about you on Sunday. She said her feelings about you have changed. She realized the only emotion she felt for you was a crush. A crush that no longer exists." She told Mark about her conversation with Tracy, but not all of it. There was no reason, she decided, to share the part where Tracy accused her of liking Mark. Those feelings—while she could admit them to herself—were not feelings she was ready to express to anyone else. Not yet.

"That's good news," Mark said. "In fact, that's great news!"

She smiled. "I thought so, too. She even acknowledged that you never treated her as anything more than a sister."

"No, I sure didn't."

"She's still going to need a little time, though. What her brain recognizes as the truth is still a little hard for her heart to understand, I think."

"Did she say . . . Did she tell you if my actions hurt her?"

"I don't think you hurt her, but I think her ego took a bit of a beating."

"How do we fix that?"

She laughed softly at his reaction. "We don't need to fix it," she said. "We just need to give her a little time to heal the wound. She'll be fine, I promise."

"What are you laughing at?"

"You. I can see why you're so successful in business. You're very direct. You identify obstacles and immediately come up with a strategy to overcome them. You like to fix problems and move on."

"That's how I roll. It's a strategy that has worked for me so far."

"And would it be safe to assume that homework assignment you gave Paul has something to do with fixing another problem you've uncovered somewhere else?"

"You're pretty perceptive. Yes, I'm trying to solve another problem."

"Care to share?"

Why not? he decided, after hesitating only a second or two. "Paul ministers at the hospital. He visits patients, prays with them, makes sure they have resources and support. He knows a lot of the doctors and administrators so I asked him to look into Brady's situation. He's going to see if something can be done."

"You really care about Brady, don't you?"

Mark shrugged his broad shoulders. "He seems like a good kid."

"Sometimes the people we meet can touch our lives in unexpected ways."

"I know." Boy, did he know.

"Brady showed me the computer tablet you gave him. I think you must have made him the happiest boy in Colorado. He never dreamed he could actually own one. It's hard, I think, for a child to want something they know they can never have."

"I know," he said, again.

"You do?"

He looked at her. "Don't sound so surprised."

"But I am," she said, candidly. "You have everything a man could possibly want in life. An expensive condo, an expensive car, expensive clothes. You have everything."

"But I didn't always have those things."

"Meaning what?"

"Meaning that I earned them. I've worked hard to make the money to buy the things I want."

She drew a deep breath as they stopped beside the driver's door of her car. She wasn't sure she wanted to have the same discussion again with Mark. Why underscore what she already knew? "We're polar opposites, aren't we? When it comes to how we feel about money and material possessions, we couldn't be further apart."

"That's because I've been without them before and it wasn't any fun. Do you think everyone should have to struggle to pay their bills like you do, Minda?" he asked. "Or worry about making ends meet like Brady and his mother?"

"No, but—"

"Do you know that Brady has never read a comic book or seen a super-hero movie? When I was his age, I couldn't get enough of them. They were like gold to me."

"A comic book?" she repeated, doubtfully. "How could a comic book be like gold to you? They're everywhere you look. You can find them at drug stores and supermarkets and—"

"I didn't grow up near drug stores and supermarkets."

"Where did you grow up?"

In the dim light of the parking lot, Minda could see the indecision in his expression, as if he were debating whether he should answer her.

He reached over and took her keys out of her hand and unlocked the car. For a moment, she thought he was going to open the car door and push her inside, anything to keep from having to answer her.

"You're not going to tell me, are you?" She said the words more as a statement than a question.

He shook his head slightly as he stared at the keys in his hand. "You don't know what you're asking."

She leaned casually against the car. "I thought I asked a simple question. 'Where did you grow up?' It's a pretty common thing to wonder when you're just learning about someone new in your life."

"I never talk about myself. It's kind of a rule with me."

"I figured that out ten minutes after I first met you." She smiled up at him. "On the other hand, you know everything about me. I'm the same person I was ten years ago. Not much in my life has changed."

"My life, on the other hand, is the complete opposite of where I started. Anything that happened before I moved to New York is buried history."

"It's not *that* buried. You have a brother who clearly loves you."

"Paul. Yeah, he's a good brother."

"And you told me once about your parents. Are they still alive?"

"Yes."

"Do you see them often?"

"Never."

Minda recalled that Addy Whimple once said Mark was unhappy and didn't know why. Perhaps he had argued with his parents, she thought. Or maybe something had happened to drive a wedge between them.

"*Never?*"

"I told you a little bit about my parents when we had dinner together last week."

"I remember. You said they were good Christian people."

"And when I told you that, I told you the truth. But I didn't tell you the *entire* story. My parents were good Christian people—that much is true. But the part I didn't tell you is that . . . my parents are missionaries."

"Missionaries!"

"I can see I've surprised you."

"That's an understatement. I'm sorry, but I never thought . . . I expected your parents to be titans of business who raised you to be the same."

"No. As it turns out, I'm the member of the family who's out of step. Everyone else is involved in ministry of some kind. We call it the family business."

"And since you never get to see them, should I assume they serve somewhere overseas?"

"Yes. They're both talented linguists and they both speak several languages so they're in demand. They love going to the most remote places in the world to preach the Gospel."

"When you were a child, what did you and your brother do while your parents were off on their missions?"

Mark leaned against the car beside Minda and looked into the dark night instead of at Minda. It was easier to talk that way. "We went with them. I grew up in a lot of different places, none of which were here in the U.S. Most of those places didn't have running water or electricity or indoor toilets. And they certainly didn't have drug stores or supermarkets."

Of all the things Mark could have told her about himself, Minda never could have guessed the background he described. A hundred different questions popped into her mind. "How long did your parents serve as missionaries?"

"All my life and they're still serving. They're still ministering in some remote place in the world. When I was old enough to attend high school, they sent me back here to the States and I've been here ever since."

"Was that a hard decision for you? To stay here and not return to your parents?"

"It was the easiest decision I ever made. I'm not like them, Minda. I'm not the kind of person who can sustain their lifestyle. When I think about the way we lived—wearing clothes out of the missionary barrel and not having enough to eat sometimes because all the support funds didn't arrive—that wasn't for me. I couldn't live that way."

"I suppose that would be hard for a child."

"Actually, when I was a kid it was easy. I didn't know anything different because it was all I knew. My dad taught me to play baseball in a dirt field with local children. We were all barefoot and we all wore patched clothes. At the time, I thought it was great fun. It was just how we lived. But when I came back to the States to go to high school, everything changed. I lived with a family in a real home for the first time in my life. I ate real food and went to a real school. I looked around at all the other kids at school and saw what they had. It was the first time I ever felt *envy.* By the time I got to college, I knew I couldn't go back to the way I'd lived with my parents. I knew that my future was here. I made goals and worked hard, and so far I've achieved everything I've wanted to accomplish. "

In the quiet the followed Minda silently played back everything Mark just told her. She felt as if a door had opened into his soul, revealing the hidden motivators that drove him to succeed in a world that valued money and possessions above all else.

"I'm glad you told me. And you should be proud of what you've accomplished . . . if it makes you truly happy."

"It does."

Or at least, it did. Now he wasn't so sure. He'd driven himself to achieve one goal after another, each step more difficult, each achievement more risky; but any sense of accomplishment he'd felt had been fleeting. He'd only felt pressure to achieve more, to reach the next rung on the ladder of success.

"Have you ever thought about joining the family business?" she asked.

"No."

"But when you were younger, before you returned to the States, you helped your parents in their ministry, didn't you?"

"Yes, but that was a thousand miles and a hundred lifetimes ago. I'm not that person anymore."

He stole a glance at Minda's profile, hoping he could see

some indicator of what she was thinking. She wasn't frowning and there was no sign of judgment in her expression. She was simply listening to him.

He drew a deep breath and when he released it, he felt his body relax. It was easy to talk to Minda. There was something about her that invited confidences and trust. She was the kind of woman a man could tell his secrets to, knowing she wouldn't turn away.

"I never meant to tell you about myself. I've never shared my background with anyone before. But there's just something about you ... I don't know how to explain it. Since the moment I met you, I've found myself doing things I never imagined I'd do."

She looked up at him, a curious smile on her lips. "Like what?"

"Like going to church again." He smiled back at her. "Like flirting with a ninety-four-year-old woman. Like playing on a baseball team and worrying about a sick kid and caring about a high school coach searching for his family."

"That shows what a good heart you have. No matter how many goals you create for yourself, you can't really change who you are as a person."

They stood quietly for a while, side-by-side, leaning against the side of the car.

"I'm glad you told me. When you wouldn't answer any questions about yourself, I started to wonder if you were a spy with the CIA or something."

He laughed softly. "You've got a good imagination."

"I changed my mind when I realized a spy for the CIA probably wouldn't buy a child a computer tablet. His government superiors would never approve the expense. But that just made me more curious about you, especially once I realized you came from a Christian background. You knew the Scriptures and you sang hymns in church as if you'd done it every day of your life. I wondered if maybe something happened that made you lose your faith."

"I never lost my faith. I just haven't called upon it in a good number of years."

"I'm glad to hear it. I mean, I'm glad that you still believe. You do, don't you?" She waited, feeling the importance of his answer.

"Yes, I'm still a believer."

She smiled with relief. "I knew it. You couldn't sing those hymns as beautifully as you did without meaning every word."

"Do you always look for the best in people?"

"I try."

They lapsed into silence again, a peaceful, companionable silence that he only felt when he was with Minda. He just stood there beside her, leaning against the side of the car, staring off into the starlit Colorado sky. No talking, just a feeling of easy calm. A calm he hadn't felt in years.

"A month ago," he said, in a low voice, "I never would have dreamed that I would enjoy standing in a dark high school parking lot looking at the stars. I would have thought it was a waste of time."

"What do you think now?"

"It's nice."

"You said that about going for a walk, too. I take it you don't lead a life of peace and tranquility in New York."

He shook his head. "I don't have much down time in New York or anywhere else."

"You could, if you wanted to. Don't you ever think about adjusting any of those goals you're always talking about? Would the world really come to an end if you postponed a due date every once in a while?"

He wanted to answer her, but decided against it. How could he talk to her about his goals when she was the major obstacle in accomplishing them? And now, because of her, he wasn't even certain he wanted to accomplish them.

He had arrived in Denver with a purpose, determined to charm her into selling her building. Instead, she had charmed him. Charmed him into caring about her, almost against his will. He'd fought against his feelings, but he now knew he was quickly losing the battle. He'd been sucked into the vortex her life. A life filled with tenants whose lives were a lot tougher than any hardship he had ever endured; a life centered around church and an old house and a crazy, outdated building that should have been torn down decades ago.

But instead of wanting to take advantage of her, he now wanted to fix her problems and make her life a little easier. And he wanted to make the people close to her happy, too. In short he'd turned into the kind of man he had always viewed in the past with scorn: An unfocused businessman. The kind of businessman who left his job or rearranged his career so he could spend more time with his family. He'd always thought those were weak men who lacked vision. Those were the men with skewed priorities.

Now he was one of them. He'd lost his sense of direction and was perilously close to abandoning his goal altogether. And that would mean abandoning his dream of opening his own investment firm.

It took every ounce of willpower he possessed to leverage his hips away from the car.

He took Minda's hand and turned it over so her palm was up; then he placed her keys in her hand and covered it with his own. "Thanks for listening to my tale of woe."

"That's what friends are for. After all, you listened to my

story about losing my husband." The warmth of his hands as they encircle hers seemed to intensify.

"Friends, Minda? Is that what we are? What would you think if I said I want to be more than a friend to you?"

19

Minda's breath caught and held. She thought there was a strong possibility she might never take another breath again. Without even realizing it, she'd been waiting to hear him say those words since the first moment she had acknowledged her attraction for him. And now she found herself almost trembling with anticipation of what was to come.

"I want to be more than a friend to you, Minda."

His voice was soft and low and urgent. Even in the dim light of the parking lot, she could tell his blue eyes were searching hers as he waited for her response.

She smiled softly up at him. "I would like that, too."

He leaned slightly toward her. She did the same, meeting him half-way, as ready to receive as he was to give.

He bent his head closer and his lips brushed, light and soft as suede, across hers. Then he drew back slightly, leaving her wanting more.

She was to have it. He let go of her hand and reached for her. Automatically, she responded, melting comfortably into his embrace.

She closed her eyes, savoring the feeling of his arms encircling her shoulders and waist. She allowed the magic of the moment to wash over her, marveling that one fleeting kiss, one protective embrace, could make her feel so cherished.

Her cheek nestled against the soft fabric of his shirt. She felt his strong chest rise and fall as he took a deep, steadying breath.

"You have a strange affect on me, Minda. First you have me confessing my secrets to you and then you erase every thought from my mind except the impulse to kiss you." His breath whispered gently against her forehead. "I hope you don't mind that I acted on that impulse."

A rush of warm emotions flooded her. Mind? How could she mind, when that brief touch of his lips against hers brought her so much happiness? She felt as if his kiss unlocked the door to her soul and for the first time she felt ready to embrace the promise of his kiss.

"I don't mind at all," she said, happily.

His arms tightened subtly around her. "You and I were supposed to have dinner on Saturday and it didn't happen. Have dinner with me tomorrow."

A little bit of reality intruded on the heaven of his embrace. "I can't," she said, reluctantly. "I have to be at church."

"What about Thursday?"

"Tracy's party is Thursday night. But she's going out with friends afterward. We can sneak away then to have dinner, if you don't mind eating late."

"I'll take any time I can have with you. I'll pick you up after the party, and we'll go back to that Italian restaurant. I want to hear that waiter tell us again what a good-looking couple we make."

She smothered a happy laugh against the soft fabric of his tee-shirt. "And this time I promise not to blush."

"I like your blushes." Mark tucked a fingertip beneath her chin and gently lifted her head so he could look into her eyes and kiss her once more.

The next morning, Mark's breakfast order was delivered to his hotel room on a wheeled table draped in crisp, white linen. He lifted the silver dome from the largest plate. His omelet was cooked just the way he liked it. He lifted another cover and found lightly-toasted bread, buttery and warm. There was a third plate on the table that he was pretty certain wasn't part of his order. He lifted the cover. On the plate was a warm, freshly-baked beignet.

He stabbed his fork into the pastry and released a tide of apple filling onto the plate. He took a bite and closed his eyes, enjoying the flavor of the apple mixing with the sweetness of the light pastry.

Minda would enjoy one of these, he thought. In the next moment, he was on the phone to room service, ordering two more of the pastries to go.

An hour later, he pushed open the door of Minda's bookstore with one hand, while the other hand held a small container from the hotel kitchen stuffed with two pillowy beignets.

He waved to Ellen as he passed the front counter and began searching between book shelves for Minda. He found her helping a customer near a display of devotional books. He watched Minda nod and smile as the shopper explained what she was looking for.

"I'm sure you know what book I'm talking about," the

woman insisted. "It had a cat on the cover but it wasn't about a cat."

Minda continued to smile even as her eye caught sight of Mark standing just beyond the woman's shoulder. "Is there anything else you can tell me about the book?"

"It was about a man and a woman."

"That helps narrow it down. Anything else?"

"It was on that shelf right there last month." The shopper pointed to the display of devotional books.

Mark felt pretty certain the conversation was going to take some time. He held up the box of pastries to catch Minda's attention and pointed toward the back of the store.

In her office, he picked up a marker from the desk and scribbled on the top of the box:

Something sweet
   To remind you of last night.
Until tomorrow,
   Mark

What a goof, he thought. *What a complete goof I've become.*

All it took was a few kisses to make him go all sappy and giddy and willing to write love letters on pastry boxes. But what sweet, perfect kisses they were.

He smiled as he removed one of the pastries from the box and carefully wrapped it in a napkin. A few minutes later, he was carrying the pastry up to the third floor apartments.

He knocked at Miss Whimple's door.

"Come in!"

She was in her favorite chair by the windows. As usual, her Bible was in her lap and a cup of tea was on the small table beside her chair.

"Good morning." He went straight to her kitchenette and opened one cabinet after another until he found a plate.

"Make yourself at home, by all means," she said, testily.

"I brought you something to have with your tea." He presented her with the plated pastry, along with a fork, knife and napkin.

A hint of a smile touched her lips. "I haven't had one of these in years." She closed her Bible and placed it on the table, then took the plate into her lap. "It's a beignet, isn't it?"

"Yes. I hope you like apple." He noticed the heavy blanket across her lap. "Are you cold, ma'am?"

"Not now but if you'd been here an hour ago you would have found me with my teeth chattering. It was chilly last night. I'm sure the temperatures fell below freezing and this place was an icebox when I woke up this morning."

He saw that the window was open a few inches. "Why didn't you close the window? Is it stuck? Should I close it for you?"

"No, it's not stuck."

"Then why didn't you close it last night, if you were cold?"

"Because of the paint smell. I have to have fresh air. I can't sleep with that smell. It's enough to make a body sick."

Mark frowned. It had been almost two weeks since he and Minda had painted Miss Whimple's apartment and he could detect no trace of paint smell. He was beginning to wonder if there were something else wrong. Maybe Miss Whimple's advanced age was making her confused or maybe she had an illness or medical condition that affected her sense of smell. He made a mental note to talk to Minda about it later.

He felt his phone vibrate against the pocket of his coat. He glanced quickly at the screen and saw a text message from Paul.

Brady is high on waiting list. Can't move up. Strict protocol for those things. Source says he's a good candidate and should have donor soon. Local charity raising funds to pay for expenses while he's hospitalized. Will text more soon.

He smiled up at Miss Whimple. "I just got some good news."

"From Gaggle?"

"Google," he corrected. "Actually, the news was from my brother. But speaking of Google, I wanted to talk to you about that computer search you asked me to do. I'm afraid I haven't had any success so far. I haven't been able to find any information about an Albert Whimple from Kansas."

"Oh." Disappointed, she slowly set her fork down on the plate and looked at him earnestly. "But didn't you say new information is added to computers every day?"

"Added to the Internet. Yes, I did, so we'll keep looking. And it just so happens that I have a pretty good research team in my office in New York. I'll get them busy searching, too. If anybody can find anything, they can."

She nodded. "Thank you."

He smiled, feeling as if she'd handed him a treasure with those two simple words. "It would help a lot if I had some more information about Albert Whimple. Is there anything else you can tell me?"

She looked away, focusing her gaze on a point just outside the window. "I don't know anything."

"You mentioned 1929. You said it was the year your life changed. Is that year significant for Albert Whimple, too? What happened in 1929?"

She dabbed at the corners of her mouth with her napkin,

then she set it and the plate on the table beside her tea cup. "1929 was the last year I saw him. I don't know what happened to him after that."

"What happened to you in 1929? Don't pretend it wasn't significant. I already know your life changed that year. Just tell me what happened."

"In 1929 I was just a girl. My family was poor. Very poor. But that was true for a lot of families. Times were hard then, with the Depression and all, and we didn't always have the barest essentials. Sometimes, we didn't even have enough to eat." Her pale eyes settled on the soft fabric of his expensive suit coat. "I don't expect you to understand."

"I do understand," he said, quietly. "More than you know."

"I doubt that."

"That's a subject for another day. Right now we're talking about you and what happened in 1929. You said you didn't have enough to eat?"

"That's right and I didn't like it one bit. No child likes to go to bed hungry! But I was raised a good Christian girl and taught to always turn to the Lord in prayer. So I prayed to God to help my family. I prayed with the trust and innocence of a child that He would give us enough food to eat and make sure we were never hungry again."

"And did God hear your prayers?"

"Yes, he did. But sometimes," she looked out the window again, "sometimes God's greatest punishment comes when he answers our prayers. That was a lesson I hadn't anticipated."

"What do you mean? What happened?"

"The Lord answered my prayer. I wasn't hungry anymore. In fact, I was never hungry again. And as far as I know, none of my kin were, either."

"As far as you know?" He was having a bit of trouble

following her story. "What happened to your family?"

"I don't know." She shrugged her thin shoulders. "But I started a whole new life in 1929. I got a job. I worked hard. I made something of myself. And I was never hungry again."

Mark did some quick math in his head. "You couldn't have been more than twelve years old in 1929."

"I was ten. Of course, times were different then. Children worked. I went to work in a clothing factory. I was a seamstress and I was good at it, but I didn't earn enough to live on. So at night, after work, I studied hard and became a teacher. But I was lucky. I'd been to school before. I could read and write and I was smart. Other children at the factory weren't as lucky."

"You worked in a factory when you were ten years old?" He didn't bother to hide his indignation.

"It wasn't so bad. I had three meals a day and a bed to sleep on."

"And Albert Whimple . . . what happened to him?"

"If I knew that, I wouldn't need you to help me look for him, now would I?"

"Can't you tell me anything more about him?"

"No, I can't. Maybe you should just forget I ever brought it up," she said, pessimistically. "A lot has happened since 1929 and the world is a big place. He could be anywhere."

"I'm not ready to give up yet. Wherever he is, I'll find him. But I should warn you, it might take some time."

"I'm not going anywhere . . . unless the good Lord takes me home. But as long as I draw breath, you can find me right here in this chair."

"Don't you ever go out into the neighborhood? Minda told me you went up and down the alley gathering paint not too long ago."

"No. These old legs of mine don't hold me up like they

used to."

"Would you like to go outside with me now? I'd be happy to take you."

"And do what? Besides, if I go any further than the bedroom, I have to use that." She pointed disdainfully at a wheelchair in the corner of the room.

"It's not a very attractive accessory," he conceded.

"No, it's not.

"So instead of using it, you simply refuse to leave this building?"

"I don't have any reason to go beyond its doors."

"Actually you do. You promised me a date. How am I going to take you out to dinner if you can't walk and you refuse to use your wheelchair?"

"You don't want to take an old woman like me to a restaurant. Take Minda instead. She'd like that."

"I've already taken Minda to dinner and I probably will again. But I'd also like to take you when you feel up to it."

"If you aren't the biggest flirt!" she said with a laugh and a shake of her head. "You could make a dog meow and like it."

It was the first time he'd heard her laugh and he found himself smiling back at Addy Whimple. He stayed with her a few minutes longer, then left her to finish eating the pastry while he went back downstairs to the bookstore.

He found Minda in a quiet corner of the store, inspecting the shelves for mis-shelved books. His eyes quickly scanned the area for customers. There wasn't another person in sight. He took that as permission to slip his arms around her slim waist.

"Have you been in your office lately?" he asked.

"I have. Thank you for the pastry."

"Did you taste it?"

"Um-hmm. It was delicious."

"I thought so, too. The hotel served me one for breakfast and I thought of you with the first bite."

"An eight-hundred-calorie pastry stuffed full of baked apple reminded you of me?" she teased, with mock offense.

"Everything reminds me of you."

He was turning into a goof again. A grinning, idiotic, love-struck goof.

He kissed her lips lightly and immediately recognized the danger of wanting more. "I'm looking forward to tomorrow night."

"Me, too."

Her confession, he decided, deserved to be rewarded with another kiss. Mark pulled her gently against his lean body. Her head fell back against his shoulder as she looked up at him and in the next moment, his lips claimed hers with a slow, tantalizing pressure.

She surrendered, matching kiss for heavenly kiss. Her hand rested on the hard plane of his chest but as the tenor of his kisses deepened and carried her to dizzying heights, she grabbed a fistful of his shirt and held on for dear life.

He lifted his head and looked down at her with that lop-sided smile that was for her alone.

"I didn't mean to do that," he whispered. "Not here. Not in the middle of your store."

"It was probably a little unprofessional," she whispered back, "but at least we're in the right section of the store."

He lifted his eyes to read the label on the bookshelves:

Christian Romance
Alphabetical by Author

"We're in the right section, all right." Mark drew a deep, steadying breath. His hands left her waist to grasp her shoulders, holding her firmly as he took a purposeful step back. "I have to get out of here before I drag you back to the office and lock the door. Remind me tomorrow night where we left off, okay?"

Her responding smile was light and carefree and full of happiness. "Oh, I'll remind you, all right."

"Good. I'll see you tomorrow night, after the birthday party."

He kissed her lightly on the forehead, then his hands dropped from her shoulders. With a last look and a final lop-sided smile, he was gone.

Minda leaned back against the shelves. Her knees were like water and she felt as if she'd just come through a windstorm of emotions and feelings. It was a windstorm she didn't want to end.

20

Mark made his way up the walk toward Minda's front porch carrying a small gift bag that contained Tracy's present. He gave the bag a light swing that matched his mood. Tonight belonged to Minda and he didn't plan to waste one precious, carefree minute of it.

All day he'd imagined himself with Minda at the restaurant, looking across the table into her beautiful hazel eyes, maybe even holding her hand on top of the red and white checkered table cloth. He felt a little goofy again, like a teenager on his first date, or like a character straight out of a romantic, chick-flick-type movie, but he didn't care. The only thing he cared about was spending the evening with Minda and learning together what the future may hold.

His goals for the night were simple: Enjoy Minda's company. Get to know her better. And tell her the truth about himself.

It was a simple plan but one that had the potential for enormous risk. He wasn't at all certain how Minda would take the news that he'd been actively deceiving her since the moment they met. He told himself that Minda was a fair woman; an intelligent woman, who would realize that business was business. Surely Minda would listen to what he had to say and understand his reasons. Surely she'd see that those old reasons didn't exist anymore. Since meeting her, he'd changed his mind about a lot of things. Most importantly, he'd changed his mind about Minda. He'd been on the verge of betraying her completely, coercing her into parting with something that meant a lot to her, but he'd caught himself just in time. Surely she'd see that.

Tonight he'd come clean to her. Tonight he'd put an end to his deception. He hoped she'd forgive him, although, in his heart, he knew he didn't deserve her or her forgiveness.

He took the porch steps two at a time. The front door was open and he stepped inside.

The living-room looked like a swarm of party-goers had come through, leaving behind the litter of their celebration. Red plastic cups, paper plates, and colorful party streamers littered the room. In the dining room, the remnant of a well-dissected birthday cake was in the center of the table. Jim and Ellen Dailey were there, helping clean up. Near the fireplace, Brady Blythe was sitting in a wheelchair, watching their efforts through happy but exhausted eyes.

Ellen looked up. "Mark! It's nice to see you. Did you come to help?"

"I came to drop off a gift for Tracy, but I wouldn't mind helping. What can I do?"

Minda came in from the kitchen and stopped short when she saw Mark.

"Hi." There was no warmth in her voice nor did she flash a smile of welcome.

Mark didn't expect her to greet him with open arms, but he didn't expect a cold reception, either. He quickly flipped through his memory. He was pretty certain they'd agreed he would take Minda her to dinner after the party. Yet he got the distinct impression she wasn't happy to see him.

"Hi." He held out the gift bag containing Tracy's present. "Where should I put this?"

"I'll take it."

She held out her hand and as Mark passed the ribboned handles of the bag to Minda, he deliberately twined his fingers around hers.

Instantly, she pulled her hand back and quickly looked away. "Maybe you should just put that on the dining table. Help yourself to some cake." She picked up a black plastic garbage bag and focused all her attention on opening it.

He caught her wrist, stilling her movements. "What's wrong?" he asked, his voice concerned.

"Nothing."

About five different alarm bells went off in his head. He'd had enough experience with women during his lifetime to know what it meant when a woman said, *Nothing.* He knew that one-word reply meant something was really wrong. Really, really wrong. What could have happened in just one day to upset her so much?

"What is it?" His eyes scanned the room, looking for signs of trouble. "Is Tracy okay?"

"Yes."

"Is something wrong with Brady?"

"No. He's fine."

"He looks pretty tired."

"He's been here since I picked him up this afternoon. Ellen and Jim are taking him home in a few minutes."

She pulled her wrist from his grasp and began to gather plastic cups and paper plates, stuffing them into the garbage bag.

He frowned. There was no denying the tension in the room; it was thick enough to cut with the cake knife. Something was going on, something he couldn't quite comprehend.

He looked over at Ellen. In between gathering red plastic cups into a black trash bag she shot him a couple quick, furtive glances. He also thought he detected a little sympathy in her expression, but that didn't help him understand why Minda was upset with him.

He hoped he had at least one friend left in the room. He went to Brady and crouched down beside his wheelchair.

"Doin' okay, buddy?"

"Yeah."

"I haven't seen you in this sports car before." Mark thumped his palm against the arm of the wheelchair.

Brady smiled weakly. "That's because I hate it. But it comes in handy sometimes. Like now. To tell you the truth, I'm pretty tired."

It was an unnecessary comment. Mark only had to look at the dark bruising around Brady's eyes to see that the kid was exhausted.

He looked over at Jim, who was on a step stool pulling crepe paper streamers down from the dining-room chandelier. "I'll do that, if you'll take Brady home."

Jim shot a quick look over at Minda. "Be glad to. We've kept Brady here a lot later than we thought we would. It's time we got him home. Ready, Ellen?"

Mark watched as first Jim then Ellen hugged Minda and wished her a good night. It looked to him as if Ellen whispered quite a bit into Minda's ear, and he could see Minda's lips purse together in response.

Minda gave Brady a kiss on the cheek. Then, with Mark on one side and Jim on the other, they carefully carried Brady in his wheelchair down the front steps of the house.

Ellen went ahead of them to unlock the car doors and open the trunk.

Mark scooped Brady up out of the chair and deposited him in the back seat.

"We're still on for Saturday, right? You're still coming with me to the baseball game?"

"Yeah, I sure am. One o'clock."

"That's right. I'll see you then. Take care of yourself in the meantime."

Mark stepped back to shut the car door and nearly collided with Ellen.

"Something's wrong," Ellen said, in a hushed, urgent voice. She glanced over to make sure Jim was still busy stashing the wheelchair in the trunk.

"I know that. What I don't know is, *what* is wrong?"

"Minda's upset, but she won't say why. Be careful, okay?"

Jim closed the trunk with a thud and went to the driver's side of the car. "See you later, Mark."

Ellen opened the passenger door as she shot Mark a pleading look. "Be careful," she said, again, enunciating each syllable.

Mark stepped away from the curb and waved as they drove away. He turned toward the house. He had no idea what could have upset Minda, but he felt confident he could fix whatever was bothering her. That's what he did best: identify a problem, determine the remedy, and fix it.

When he went back into the house, Minda was carefully putting the remains of the cake back into a large, pink bakery box. He shut the front door and saw her jump slightly at the sound.

"Are you going to tell me what's wrong?"

She pursed her lips and looked up at him. He could tell

she was keeping her emotions under tight control.

"What do you do for a living, Mark?"

"I told you. It's a little hard to explain, but—"

"Who do you work for?"

He'd never seen her this way before. She seemed angry and hurt and almost daring him to answer her.

"Are you asking for a name? I work for a guy named Robert."

That big, oversized tote bag he often saw her carry was propped up on one of the dining chairs. She opened the bag and withdrew a glossy magazine.

"And do you and Robert just happen to work for a company called Goble, Haines and Wyman?" She held up the magazine.

He recognized it instantly. It was the same dog-eared magazine Brady had showed him a few days before. The very same magazine that contained his picture and an article about his career. He felt his heart drop to his knees.

"Where did you get that?"

"I saw it on the coffee table when I picked up Brady this afternoon. He doesn't know I have it." Her voice was deadly calm as she thrust the magazine closer until it was practically under his nose. "You work for that company, don't you? The company that wants to buy the McAllister Building."

There was no use denying it. Still, the words didn't come easily to him. "Yes. I work for that company."

She flinched slightly and lowered her arm. "Didn't you think that was an essential fact to tell me? Or were you too busy trying to convince me to sell to include something as unimportant as *ethics* in the conversation?"

"I know it's too late now, but I honestly planned to tell you at dinner tonight. I swear to you, Minda, I was going to tell you everything."

He could see how hurt she was. The wounded expression in her eyes was beginning to blur with gathering tears.

She looked down at the magazine and struggled to focus on the words in the article that were the most inflammatory. "'Mark Cartier,'" she read aloud, "'is a man as cold and hard—and as perfect—as the diamonds his last name suggests. He is a man who doesn't just achieve, he conquers. His charm, good looks, and knowledge of real estate are unsurpassed, but it's his cunning and willingness to do whatever it takes to close a deal that makes him a force to be reckoned with.'" She looked at him. "That's you, isn't it? You're the man this magazine is describing?"

"Yes, that's me. But, Minda—"

"And what about the rest of the article? Is the rest of it true, too? Have you convinced city officials to foreclose on people's homes so you could have the land? Did you force people out of the homes they loved just to build *a mall?*"

"It's not that simple, Minda. That was a very complicated deal, but I can assure you, no one was hurt in that transaction. None of those people were harmed in any way."

"And did you actually say that you can close more deals with female property owners just by using charm than you can with dollar signs?"

He winced. For the first time, he wished with all his might that he'd never given that interview; that the article had never been written. He shook his head, hoping the movement could somehow clear his thoughts and help him find the right words to say. "It was just talk, Minda. It was just my ego talking."

She set the magazine down on the table. Only a few hours before, she'd picked up the magazine from Brady's coffee table while he was in his bedroom. At first, she couldn't believe her eyes. A magazine had written an article about

Mark? *Her* Mark? The same man who zealously guarded his privacy and declined every opportunity to talk about himself? She scanned the first few paragraphs of the article, then quickly slipped the magazine into her tote bag when she heard Brady's bedroom door open.

The magazine haunted her all evening, calling to her like a siren song. It wasn't until the gathered guests had sung Happy Birthday to Tracy and the cake had been served that she finally snuck away from the party. She made certain no one saw her tuck the magazine under her arm and escape to the back yard, to her haven, to the one place she relied on for serenity. She sat down on the swing under the oak tree. In the dim light of evening she read the article from the beginning, eagerly devouring each word; anxious to discover what Mark might have done to attract such attention. She felt a swelling of pride in her chest, knowing that whatever he'd done, it had to be good and worthy of recognition.

She didn't have to read beyond the second paragraph to realize her pride was misplaced. She quickly mastered the theme of the article and felt the color drain from her face.

Although she didn't move, she felt as if the swing had begun to career wildly beneath her. The article made everything clear: the reason he wouldn't talk about his work or his life in New York; the reason he had initially come into her life; the reason he had been so attentive and romantic. He wasn't falling in love, she realized, bitterly. He was just engaging in tried-and-true business tactics.

She forced herself to look at him now without emotion. "Those women you charmed into selling their property . . . did you take *them* to dinner, too?"

"That was business. You can't compare a business dinner with—"

"And did you go to church with them? Did you hold their

hand? Did you . . .?" She clamped her lips together but it was too late. A single tear escaped down her cheek. Then another.

"Kiss them? No. No, I didn't kiss them." His voice held an urgent tone as he took a step toward her. "You have to believe me, Minda."

"*Believe* you?" she repeated, incredulous. "Believe you? The only thing I believe right now is this." She tapped her finger on the magazine. "It says right here, 'The deal is all that matters.' That's a quote, Mark. That's *your* quote."

"Please let me explain."

"What is there to explain? Are you going to deny that your employer sent you here to charm me into selling my building to them?"

A look of desperation crossed his face. "I—Yes! No! I can't deny that, but—Minda, please sit down."

He pulled out a chair at the dining table. Just like he did a few nights ago when he read the sale documents to her. The night she realized her attraction for him. The night she first allowed herself to dream of his touch and his kisses and a future together. It seemed so needlessly cruel of him to taunt her with the same gesture now. "No," she said. "I don't want to sit down. I don't even want to see you."

She put her hand to her face and angrily swiped at a tear before she marched to the front door. She held it open expectantly. "Please leave."

He hesitated for a moment then walked toward her, his blue eyes clouded with caring concern. Concern she knew to be a complete lie.

He stood very close to her. Too close. She wished she could summon the courage to tell him what she thought of him and his betrayal, but she knew she'd never be able to control her emotions long enough to utter even one sentence before breaking down. Already the knowledge of his treachery caused more threatening tears to gather just behind her eyes.

"Minda, I'll call you tomorrow."

She turned her head away, refusing to look at him. Her breath caught on a sob. Just as she doubted whether she could hold on to her emotions any longer, Mark stepped out onto the front porch.

She closed the door on him and let loose the flood.

———⊙———

Minda hated to look in the mirror after she'd been crying. She'd had never been one of those women who could cry pretty. She'd spent the entire night bawling like a baby, but quietly, so Tracy wouldn't hear. By morning, she had nothing left but puffy eyes, a red nose, and a sinus headache that could drop Goliath to his knees.

Splashing cold water on her face didn't help. She vaguely recalled reading once that cucumbers were a natural remedy for reducing eye puffiness. Or was it tea bags?

She splashed more cold water on her face and gave up any pretence of trying to rectify her appearance. Tracy had already left for school, and Minda wasn't due at work for another hour. She could only hope the rest of the puffiness would subside by then.

In the kitchen she poured herself one last cup of coffee and sipped at it without even noticing its flavor. Her taste buds were dulled and her demeanor was deadly calm. Too calm, she thought, for a woman who had cried nearly all night long. But that, undoubtedly, was the problem. She had no more emotion left in her. She had spent it all in grieving over Mark's betrayal and mourning the loss of what might have been.

How could he have done that to me? He must have

thought her an easy mark; a lonely widow, desperate for a little masculine attention. A pathetic creature who'd do whatever he wanted as soon as he flashed his megawatt smile.

She took her coffee cup to the kitchen table and sat down, unable to drive thoughts of Mark from her mind.

"Stupid, stupid, stupid," she said aloud in the empty kitchen. Stupid to have let her guard down over a man she knew nothing about. Stupid to have opened her heart up to a materialistic, non-church-goer who—

The slapping sound of the kitchen screen door closing interrupted her thoughts and made her jump slightly. She looked up to see Mark stride into her kitchen as if he owned the place.

"Sit down," he ordered.

She frowned. "I *am* sitting down."

"Okay. Good. We need to talk."

"I have nothing to say to you." She laced her arms across her chest.

"Then you can listen while I talk." He pulled out the chair next to hers and sat down. "There are some things you need to know."

"About what?"

"About me."

"I already know about you, Mark. I read the article, remember? I already know you'll do anything to close a deal. I already know that seducing lonely widows is just another tactic you use to get what you want." She looked at him coldly. "I have to admit, your methods were somewhat successful. You must have had a lot of practice."

"You're wrong about that but you're right about everything else. Will you listen if I tell you *why* I did what I did?"

"I already know the history," she said, impatiently. "I was there, remember? In the parking lot? I actually fell for that story you told me about growing up poor. I actually felt sorry for you."

"I'm not talking about my history. I'm talking about yours."

She eyed him with distrust. "What about my history?"

"I knew about you. *All* about you. Before I ever came here I did my research and found out everything I could about you. It was my way of preparing to do battle, to find your weakness. I approached this deal like I did any other. Until I met you."

"But . . . I thought you met Tracy at school."

"I did. It was part of my plan."

"Are you telling me you deliberately attended that Career Day at Tracy's school just so you could use her to meet me?"

"That's right. I wanted to meet you so I could beguile you into selling the McAllister Building."

She couldn't bring herself to look at him. Instead, she focused on her coffee cup, feeling incredibly foolish. How could she have ever thought he was actually attracted to her?

"You're quite clever, aren't you?" she asked, in a wooden voice.

"No, I'm not, because the plan backfired. *Badly.* It didn't take long for me figure out that you meant more to me than just a business rival. That wasn't something I anticipated."

"You don't give up easily, do you?"

"No, I don't. Especially now that I realize the reason I came here had nothing to do with the reason I stayed."

She didn't believe him. Not one bit. "I know why you stayed. You stayed because you had to. You stayed because I wouldn't look at the contract or talk about selling the building."

"I could have pushed you. I saw that unopened contract in your desk the first night I was here for dinner. I could have created an opportunity to talk to you about it."

Instantly she recalled the day they'd met. How cocky he had been. He'd flashed that self-possessed smile of his like he was doing her some kind of favor. She also recalled the night he sent Tracy and Josh to the baseball game. She had found him going through her desk with the contract in his hand. At the time she'd been too blinded by his charm and handsome face to have felt any alarm or recognize that he shouldn't have been at her desk in the first place. But no; she allowed herself to be enchanted by a handsome man paying attention to her. She played right into his hands, and he took advantage of her, too, reading the contract to her and gently encouraging her to sign.

Thank God she hadn't! Thank God the Lord had been watching over her!

"I could have pressed you to sign, Minda, but I didn't. Do you want to know why?"

She tightened her arms across her chest and pressed her lips into a defiant line, refusing to answer him.

"I didn't push you," he said, "because you told me that you trusted me."

"Yes, I did," she said, angrily. "I *did* trust you. Thank you for rubbing my nose in my mistake!"

"But I didn't want it to be a mistake. And that was a shock to me. I *wanted* you to trust me. For the first time, I couldn't put my feelings aside and concentrate only on the deal. I can't explain it. But somehow I found myself involved in your life and going to church and meeting your tenants and caring about you. I don't know what happened," he said, sounding baffled by his own admission. "I found out how wrong I was about myself. I thought I was some kind of ruthless, big-shot businessman who knew everything. But then I came here and I ate pot roast and played baseball and . . . and it turns out I was just an arrogant jerk. I guess I'm saying that I enjoyed being with you. I was attracted to you. Against my better judgment, I wanted just to be with you."

For a fraction of a second, she almost bought it. He certainly could sound sincere when he wanted to. "Is this part of your act, Mark? Your plan to charm the widow didn't work, so now you're on to Plan B, The Great Confession?"

"Minda, honey, you're making this so hard," he said, softly.

That little endearment was her undoing. She felt her heart swell with the emotion of knowing that only a day ago she would have reveled in the sound of that word coming from his lips.

Honey. It was such a sweet word, tender and loving. How could he speak it so convincingly? How could he call her that, when the word was really nothing more to him than another tool to get what he wanted?

She turned her head away. She refused to give him the satisfaction of seeing her eyes shining with tears or knowing how badly he had hurt her. From habit, she used that old trick that she'd used after Dale died: blink several times, look up, swallow hard, take a deep breath. It worked again. But barely.

"Let me make it easy for you, Mark. Let's say—just for fun—that I succumb to your charm and sign that contract. What then? Were you planning to stay here in Denver or head back to New York?" She could tell by the look on his face that she'd stumped him. "You *were* going back to New York, weren't you?"

"I . . ." He cudgeled his brain to come up with the right words to say.

"I knew it. Once I signed the contract and you got what wanted, you were going to be on the next flight out." Her tone turned accusing. "So much for wanting to be with me. So much for getting involved in my life."

"I didn't think that far ahead. Minda, please try to understand."

"*You* didn't think that far ahead? Are you kidding, Mark? You don't put your socks on in the morning without a plan. Over and over you've told me how goal-driven you are, and now you expect me to believe you didn't think ahead to what would happen if I signed the contract?"

"I know it doesn't make sense. To be perfectly honest, nothing has made sense since the day I met you." How could he ever explain how much she had thrown him off his stride? "But I'm telling you the truth. I'm being as honest as I can be."

"You haven't been honest with me since the day you got here. It was all an act for you. Pretend to like the lonely widow and get her to sign away her property. I'm nothing but a sales commission to you."

"That's not true. Not now. Minda, you have to believe to me."

"No, it's your turn to believe me. You, Mark Cartier, will never get your hands on my building. I will not sell it to you or your company. Never. Do you understand me?"

She was surprised at how even and emotionless she sounded even though her future—the future she'd planned with Mark—had slipped through her fingers.

She struggled to keep the reactionary tears out of her eyes. She was on the verge of another crying jag. Her only chance was to get Mark out of her kitchen before she disgraced herself completely.

She pointed toward the kitchen door. "You're leaving now.

I told you last night that I didn't want to see you and I meant it."

"Minda, please listen—"

"Good-bye, Mark."

"I can't leave you like this."

"You have no choice. You have to leave. Now." She tightened her lips into a defensive line and kept her gaze focused on the soap dispenser at the kitchen sink.

He stood up, but his worried gaze didn't stray from her face. "After you've had some time to think about what I said, will you call me? Or maybe I could call you tomorrow?"

She couldn't help but hear the pleading note in his voice. *Good*, she thought. Let him beg her to talk to him. Let him beg her to sell the building for all the good it would do him. She'd *give* it away first.

She kept her eyes focused on the soap dispenser.

"I'm sorry, Minda. I'm more sorry than I can say."

In the next moment, he was gone.

Gone forever and good riddance. Only then did she let down her guard and allow the tears to flow once again.

21

Minda's words stung. They stung like a nettle that had gone straight into Mark's heart. Not because she'd misjudged him but because she'd spoken the truth. And because he'd hurt her. He'd never wanted to hurt her. It hadn't been part of his plan.

His stupid, arrogant plan had begun to unravel the moment he met Minda, but he'd refused to recognize it. Even as he was falling in love with her, he'd soldiered on, focused only on his meaningless goals and the promise of a big, fat commission check once she sold her building. Now he was in danger of losing both Minda and her building and he had no one to blame but himself. And his ego. And his misplaced drive for materialistic things.

It took every ounce of willpower he possessed to stay away from her for the rest of the day. Instinct told him to give her some space. Emotion told him to go to her bookstore, back her into her office and kiss her until she agreed to listen to him. But he didn't give in to emotion.

Lay low, he told himself, and give her a chance to calm

down. But that resolve didn't keep him from checking his phone throughout the day to see if he had a message from her. Or keep him from dialing her number several times himself, although he never completed the calls. Each time he dialed, he hung up, afraid of making the situation worse.

He couldn't remember the last time he'd felt so unsure of himself. For years he had cloaked himself in bravado and it always seemed to get him whatever he wanted in life. But now he felt like he was back in high school; like he was the different kid dressed in patched clothes. The kid who never had money to go to a movie or buy a lousy cheeseburger.

Doubt plagued him. By Saturday morning he was preparing himself for the worst. What if Minda wouldn't forgive him? What if she refused to talk to him again?

He felt his phone vibrate in his pocket and he grabbed at it, hoping against hope it was a message from Minda.

Paul's ID flashed on the screen.

Mark read Paul's text message twice. It was cryptic and unclear. He seemed to imply he could help Brady or Brady's mother. Maybe both. Mark sent a text message back, asking him to be at the baseball game that afternoon to talk more and meet Brady for himself.

The baseball game was the last fundraiser for the Orphan Train Riders reunion. Mark knew how important it was to Minda, how hard she'd worked to make the arrangements. Surely she wouldn't stay away from the game.

He felt a little flicker of hope spring to life. She had to be at the baseball game. Maybe then he'd have a chance to talk to her, to tell her how wrong he'd been. He'd beg her forgiveness for misjudging her and behaving like a jerk.

Lord, please make her listen.

He stopped, replaying the unaccustomed words again in his mind. It had been a long time since he'd last spoken to

God.

"Lord, please make her listen." This time, he said the prayer aloud. It still didn't sound right.

"Lord, please make her listen . . . if it's your will."

At one o'clock on Saturday, Mark knocked on Brady's apartment door.

"Ready to go?" he asked when he stepped inside and found Brady in his usual place on the sofa.

"I think so." Brady eyed the blue tee-shirt Mark was wearing with the words, *Eternal Joy Christian Church*, screen-printed across the front. "I like your shirt."

"Good, because I brought one for you." He held up a tee-shirt similar to his, but on the back, the name *Blythe* was printed across the shoulders. Beneath his name was printed a large "1." He tossed the shirt to Brady.

"Really? I can wear this?"

"Yes, but only if you're part of the team. I was thinking you could be bat boy today."

The light in Brady's eyes dimmed a little. "Oh."

"Something wrong?"

"I was thinking . . . maybe I should just hang around the apartment today."

"Are you saying you don't want to go to the game after all?"

"Oh, I want to go. I really do. It's just that sometimes I don't have much stamina. You know, like at the birthday party."

"No problem. You don't have to be the bat boy. You can just watch from the bleachers. And when you're ready to leave, just tell me, okay?"

"Okay." Brady still didn't make an attempt to get up off

the sofa.

Mark wondered if the whole idea of being physically weak was a matter of pride to Brady. "I was thinking," he said, casually, "it would probably be better if you didn't have to come right out and tell me when you're ready to leave the game. Why don't you just give me a signal of some kind?"

"A signal? Like what?"

"For example ... If you use the word, 'deposit' in a sentence, I'll know you're getting tired. And if you can work the term 'mortgage-backed securities' into the conversation, I'll know you want to go home immediately."

Brady laughed. "I'll do my best, but maybe we could come up with a signal that's a little simpler."

Mark's teasing smile softened. He took his baseball cap off and fit it on Brady's head. "Wear this. And when you take it off, I'll know you're ready to go home."

"Thanks. That's a lot easier."

"So, let's get to that game, okay?"

Once Brady got in the car, wearing his new shirt and Mark's ball cap, his energy level seemed to pick up. As Mark drove to the high school where the game was to be played, Brady watched the passing scenery, remarking on every landmark and noticing every detail.

"The leaves are starting to turn early this year," he announced. "Typically, they don't change color until October, but the nights have been pretty cold lately. In fact, we might get some snow tonight. The forecast said there's a chance of snow but for sure we'll have a cold rain. I hope it doesn't rain on the game. Do you think we'll have an early winter?"

Brady's happy chatter made Mark smile for the first time in two days. He looked over at Brady. His cheeks had some color to them and there was a spark of excitement in Brady's eyes.

The irony of it hit him. His own life was in a mess, but he was doing what he could to make Brady's life better.

Minda hated his guts but Brady looked at him as if he were some kind of hero.

"This is my school, you know," Brady announced later, as they pulled into the parking lot. "I used to go here, until I couldn't any more, you know what I mean?"

"I know exactly what you mean. But today, you're not here as a student. You're here as a member of a baseball team. Come on. Let's go size up the other team's players."

Mark didn't see Minda's car in the parking lot. The disappointment kicked him right in the gut.

She wasn't there. She intended to stay away. She was going to make good on her promise to never see him again.

For Brady's sake, Mark forced his lips into a smile as he led the way toward the ball field. There were quite a few people in the bleachers already and Coach Morgan had arranged for the concession stand to be opened, so there was a lot of activity, a lot of popcorn, and a lot of pent up anticipation from the spectators waiting for the game to begin.

Mark guided Brady toward the first row of bleacher seats where his brother Paul was in deep discussion with Pastor Walker.

"Brady, I think you already know Pastor Walker. And this guy is my brother, Paul."

Paul extended his hand. "Brady, it's nice to meet you. I've heard a lot about you."

"You have?"

"Yes. Mark told me you have a good instinct for business."

"Yeah, I watch the stock market pretty closely. And I'm pretty sure I want to go into real estate, just like Mark."

"Hmmm. I can see some deprogramming is called for.

Why don't you sit right here between Pastor Walker and me and let's see if we can't convince you to do the exact opposite of everything my brother told you."

Brady laughed and sat down, happily smiling at first Paul, then Pastor Walker.

"Remember the signal?" Mark touched his hand to his forehead and Brady nodded. Then Mark swiped his baseball glove at Paul's shoulder, saying, "Take good care of him," before he walked toward the field where Coach was already putting the team through warm-up exercises.

As he walked away, Mark heard Pastor Walker say, "You don't look so good, Brady. I'm not a doctor, but I'd say you have a serious nacho deficiency. We better get you to the concession stand right away."

Mark knew he'd left Brady in good hands. He joined the warm-up exercises until Coach blew a whistle, calling them to the dug-out. Mark's eyes searched the bleachers. There was still no sign of Minda.

Coach blew another long blast on his whistle, quieting the players and the spectators in the stands.

"Everyone! Can I have your attention? Pastor Walker would like to say a few words."

Pastor Walker stood up and faced the bleachers. "Welcome, everyone. Thank you for coming on this beautiful Saturday afternoon. We all know why we're here today: To raise funds to help pay the costs of the Orphan Train Riders reunion next month. We thank our friends from our sister church in Colorado Springs for coming here today to play baseball, glorify God, and help one of our brethren who happens to be very special to us. I'm happy to announce that this baseball game has already raised over five hundred dollars. On top of that, the good people who run the concession stand have agreed to donate fifty-percent of all food and drink sales to the reunion. So if you were planning to start a diet today, I hope you'll postpone it until tomorrow. And if each one of us visits the concession stand at least once, we'll be doing it for a good cause. Finally, I'm pleased to announce that an anonymous donor has pledged one-hundred dollars for every homerun scored during today's game."

Pastor's words were met by enthusiastic applause from the people in the bleachers.

"Now, will you bow your heads and join me in prayer? Let's ask God to bless these players and keep them safe as we do a little bit of the Lord's work today."

Standing with his team in the bright sunshine, Mark bowed his head. Silently, he joined his own prayer with Pastor's, asking for relief from the guilt he felt for hurting Minda. He knew he'd need God's help if he was to forget his own troubles and concentrate on playing his best for Coach's sake.

When Coach blew a long blast on his whistle, Mark took his position between second and third base. The spectators applauded as Pastor Walker threw out the first pitch. The game was underway.

Mark forced himself to concentrate on the batter. Despite his best intentions, his thoughts kept straying toward the bleachers now crowded with spectators.

He looked often at Brady, to satisfy himself that the boy was doing okay. And he kept looking for Minda but each time his eyes scanned the rows of spectators, he ended up disappointed.

She wasn't there. She was making good on her promise. She was staying away from the ball field so she wouldn't have to see him.

He frowned and turned his attention back to the game.

The innings dragged on and still no sign of Minda.

That hopefulness he'd felt earlier in the day began to wane. It was time to face reality. If Minda refused to see him again and she refused to sell her building, was there any point in staying? Perhaps he should leave and go back to New York. The thought depressed him. He didn't want to leave and he certainly didn't want to give up; but if Minda wanted time, he'd give it to her. He owed her that.

Coach's sharp whistle called the team to the dugout. While Mark waited for his turn to bat, he scanned the crowd again.

Still no Minda.

His heart felt like it weighed a ton, but he remained focused on the game. He had already made a mess of his relationship with Minda but he wasn't about to let Coach down.

He played well and he scored several runs that put his team comfortably ahead of the visiting team.

In the fifth inning, he was on the field and caught a fly ball to make the third out. From habit, he began jogging toward the dugout when his internal radar detected Minda's presence. His eyes scanned the bleachers. She wasn't sitting on the first row with Brady, Paul and Pastor Walker. He found her higher up in the stands, sitting with Tracy amid of group of people who were cheering for the church team from Colorado Springs.

She was there, watching the game. Watching him. He caught her looking at him. Startled, she quickly looked away, but for a fleeting moment, their eyes had met. He took that as a good sign. His spirits lifted and he forced himself to keep a straight face and not grin like a love-struck idiot.

"Hey, Mr. Cartier," Josh said, as soon as they got in the dugout. "I think your brother's waving at you."

Mark looked over at the bleachers. Paul waved casually at

him, then pointed to Brady.

Brady was no longer wearing the baseball cap.

Mark spoke to Coach where he stood sentry at the top of the dugout steps. "I've got to go, Coach. I'll miss my turn at bat but I promise to be back by the seventh inning."

He went over to the bleachers and crouched in front of Brady. "Let's get you home, buddy."

"I wish I could stay a little longer," he said, weakly. "This was a lot of fun. I can't wait to tell my mom. She should be home by the time we get there."

"Will she?" Mark's eyes lit with interest. "I'd like to meet your mother. So would Paul."

Paul immediately agreed. "I'd love to meet your mother, Brady. Do you mind if I come along?"

"Sure. That would be okay, I guess."

They said good-bye to Pastor Walker and headed toward the car. Mark threw one last look at Minda as he passed the upper row of bleachers. She was watching him. His eyes connected with hers and she didn't look away. A rush of hopeful emotion filled him. Hope that maybe she had forgiven him just a little.

"I'm glad to have a chance to meet your mother," Paul said as Mark drove them to Brady's apartment.

"Yeah? How come?"

"For a couple reasons." Paul turned slightly so he could look over his shoulder and see Brady in the back seat. "First, I want to compliment her on having such a fine young man for a son. But I also want to tell her about an organization I run."

"What kinda organization?"

"We help families in different ways. We arrange for housing and counseling and medical care. Whatever a family might need, we try to fulfill. I'd like to ask your mother if she'd be willing to let us help her. And you."

"I guess that's okay. But how could you help us?"

"Well, I was wondering if things might be a little easier for you if your mother didn't have to work so hard. Mark tells me she's gone a lot, working long hours at a restaurant. I bet when she gets home, she's pretty tired."

"Yeah, she is. She still takes care of me, though."

"What if," Paul said slowly, "I made arrangements so she didn't have to work. At all."

"Can you do that?"

"I'm pretty sure I can."

"You mean she could stay home with me?"

"Every day."

"That would be amazing! I'd really like that."

Mark pulled up to the curb in front of the McAllister Building. He let Paul and Brady out, with a promise to join them at Brady's apartment as soon as he parked the car.

A little while later he was climbing the stairs to the third floor apartments. In the hallway, he stopped at Brady's door; but instead of knocking, he succumbed to a whim and continued down the hall to Miss Whimple's apartment.

"What did you bring me?" she demanded, as soon as she saw him.

"I can see I've spoiled you." Smiling, he sat down in a chair next to hers. "Unfortunately, I brought nothing but myself today. Myself and my good-byes."

"Good-byes? Are you going somewhere?"

"I'm leaving town and I may not see you again for a while."

She narrowed her eyes as she scrutinized his expression. "What happened? Did you two have a fight?"

Leave it to Addy Whimple to go straight to the heart of the matter. He decided it wouldn't do any good to give her too many details and said, simply, "Yes."

"I see. That's too bad. I don't mind saying, I had pretty high hopes for you and Minda." She straightened as a sudden thought occurred to her. "Did you kiss her? If you haven't yet, you should. I know that if a handsome man kissed me, I'd think twice about throwing him away."

"Yes, I kissed her."

"Oh." She sounded genuinely surprised, then her eyes narrowed again. "Maybe you didn't kiss her *right*."

"I think I did. She seemed to enjoy it at the time."

"She'd be a fool not to. Anybody can see she's crazy for you. I wish you wouldn't give up."

"I'm not giving up. Let's just say, I'm taking a break. We each need time to figure things out."

She nodded. "That's probably for the best, but I expect to see you back here. Soon."

He smiled and leaned forward. He took her hand and held her fingers between the warmth of both his palms. "I'll be back. Soon. Until then, I'll miss visiting you."

She snorted, as if such sentiments were beneath her notice, but he could feel the pressure of her thin fingers closing slightly around his.

He let go of her hand. "I have to get back to the baseball game," he said, as he pulled his watch from his pocket and flicked it open to check the time. He snapped the cover closed as the chime began to play. "I told Coach I'd be back by the seventh inning and I—"

He stopped as Addy Whimple's fragile, claw-like fingers clutched at his wrist with surprising strength. Startled, his eyes flew to her face, alert to any sign that she was in some sort of physical discomfort. Her eyes were wide and her expression was frozen as she stared at his hand.

"Ma'am? Miss Whimple?" When she didn't answer, he felt his instincts go on high alert. "*Ma'am? Are you all right?*"

Her faded blue eyes traveled up to meet his. "Where'd you get that?" Her voice was strained and faint.

"Get what?"

"That watch."

Mystified, he looked down at the pocket watch in his hand. "I bought it at an auction in Chicago. Why?"

"I had a watch like that. It belonged to my father. It was supposed to go to my brother as soon as he was old enough to have it. But it was stolen."

Mark stared at her a long moment. Those instincts that were on high alert a moment ago suddenly switched to DefCon Five. Addy Whimple was staring at his watch like it was some sort of ghost from her past. Staring at it in the same way Coach Morgan had stared when he first saw it.

Impossible. Mark refused to believe there could be any connection. "*Where* was it stolen?"

"From the train. In Chicago."

"*What* train?" he asked, with deadly calm.

"The orphan train. I was just a girl. Just ten years old. I was on the train with my sisters and brother and when we were asleep, someone stole the watch."

"You were on . . ." Mark licked his suddenly dry lips. "You were on an orphan train? When?"

"1929. My mother put us on the train. Our papa had passed and we were hungry. She couldn't find work and she couldn't feed us. She told me to take care of them. She said I was responsible because I was the oldest. I did my best. God knows I did my best. But I was just a child myself. I couldn't keep us together. They took one sister, then the other, and then Albert. By the time the train arrived in Denver, I was alone." A mist of tears filled her eyes. "I never saw them again. And I've never forgiven myself."

Mark leaned back in the chair, feeling as if he'd just taken a sucker-punch to his stomach. He hadn't seen it coming. He stared at Addy Whimple. The words had come out of her mouth like a torrent, pent up for years with fear and regret and a host of other emotions he couldn't possibly understand. She looked back at him, her pale eyes moist with tears.

Logic told him the chances were next to impossible that his watch was the same watch stolen from Addy Whimple over eighty years before. Reason told him such a coincidence could never happen. It would take an utter miracle for this watch—*his* watch—to be the very same watch Addy Whimple carried on the train. The very same watch Coach Morgan remembered from his childhood. Because if it *were* the same watch, that would mean—

There was really only one way to find out. He stood up suddenly. "Ma'am, I need to take you somewhere. Will you come with me?"

"Where?"

"To a baseball game."

"Baseball!" She almost spat the word as she dabbed at her eyes with a corner of her blanket. "Why on earth would I—"

"There's someone I want you to meet."

"At a *baseball game*? I doubt that!" She sniffled and shook her head, defiantly. "No, thank you. I'll stay right here."

"I'm afraid you really don't have any choice in the matter. You can come willingly or I can carry you there. Which will it be?"

She locked defiant eyes with his determined gaze. After a moment she looked away. "Hand me that cane," she ordered. "Carry, indeed!"

22

Minda had been on the look-out for Mark's return from the moment he had left the game with Paul and Brady. Poor Brady looked exhausted and Mark kept a protective hand on the boy's shoulder as they walked toward the car.

She tucked her hands into the pockets of her hoodie. The weather was changing. The sunshine that had warmed the day earlier was now blocked by clouds. A slight wind had begun to blow, ruffling her hair.

She nudged Tracy with her elbow. "We should have brought coats."

"And gloves. Where do you think Mark went?"

"Maybe he and Paul took Brady home."

"In the middle of the game? You don't suppose there was something wrong, do you?"

"If there is, I'm sure he'll let us know." Or maybe he wouldn't, since Minda had made it clear to Mark she never wanted to talk to him again.

"I hope Mark gets back in time to play some more." Tracy looked at her mother, watching for her reaction. "He's a good player. He scored most of our team's goals."

"Runs," Minda corrected.

"Whatever. I was thinking, maybe we could invite him to have dinner with us after the game."

Minda forced her expression to remain calm. "I don't think so."

"Why? Because you guys had a fight?"

"How did you know?"

"I knew something was wrong on my birthday. When I came back after having pizza with Josh, I could see you were really upset and the next morning I could tell you'd been crying." She looked at Minda with an expression of understanding. "My eyes get puffy when I cry, too. I think it's, like, genetic or something."

"Could we not talk about this here?" Minda's voice was low and urgent. "Everyone around us is listening."

"Mom, I know you like him. Can't you and Mark just make up?"

Minda shot her daughter a fierce look. "Didn't I just say I don't want to talk about this?"

"Yeah, you did, but I'm eighteen now so I can do what I want."

"Fine. We'll talk about it later. But not here and not now. Okay?"

Tracy turned her attention back to the ball field.

Minda watched the players, too, but her thoughts kept straying back to Mark. She wondered where he was, what he was doing, and when he'd return to the game.

He appeared about thirty minutes later. Minda saw him from the back as he passed the bleachers and strode purposefully toward the field.

She sat up a little straighter, waiting expectantly for his eyes to stray her direction, as she'd seen them do all afternoon. But Mark didn't look for her at all. Instead, he walked to the baseball diamond and stood right in front of Coach, his lips only inches away from Coach's ear. Then, together, they left the field and headed toward the parking lot.

Minda frowned slightly. Something, she decided, must be wrong. Coach would never leave his players in the middle of a game unless there were some kind of emergency. She craned her neck to see if there was a commotion in the parking lot but the people seated on the bleacher rows behind her blocked her view.

She touched Tracy's knee. "I'll be back in a few minutes. Watch my purse."

Quickly, she climbed down from the bleachers and followed them. She was only a few yards away when she saw Mark open the passenger door of his rental car and extend a hand to someone inside.

She watched Addy Whimple emerge from the car and face Coach for what seemed like a long time. Then, to Minda's surprise, she saw Coach and Addy embrace.

Curious, she moved closer, watching and questioning. But her curiosity turned to concern when she saw Mark back away and lean against the front fender of the car, as if his legs could no longer support him.

Minda broke into a run and reached him in seconds. "What's wrong? What happened?" Uncertainty caused her voice to sound a little panicked.

Mark's hands were covering his face but at the sound of her voice, he looked up, surprised. "It's okay. Everything's all right."

But it wasn't all right. She could see telltale signs of tears on Mark's dark lashes and there was a flush to his face that told her his emotions were running high.

"What's going on?" she asked, worried. "Are you hurt?"

"I'm fine."

"What about Addy? Why is she here? And why is she hugging Coach?"

She made a move to approach Coach and Miss Whimple, but Mark grabbed her hand and held her fast. "No, don't go over there."

"Why? And why are you crying?"

He shook his head. "It's not every day that I see a miracle."

"Miracle? I don't understand. Please, tell me what's going on."

"It's not my news to tell. Be patient for just a few more minutes."

Minda's heart was pounding and there was an undercurrent of emotion in the air she couldn't deny. But there was also something comforting about Mark's strong hand holding hers. Unconsciously, she moved closer to him.

"Is everyone all right? Just tell me that everyone is all right!"

He wrapped his arm around her shoulders and gently pulled her against his chest.

"It's all good," he said softly against her hair. "Just give them a few more minutes."

Minda reveled in the feeling of his arms around her. That cool breeze she'd felt earlier was blowing harder now, but in Mark's arms she had all the warmth she needed. She clung to him even as she looked back over her shoulder to where Coach and Addy Whimple were facing each other. They were no longer embracing, but talking, smiling at each other, and wiping at their eyes.

Coach took a step back and tenderly took Addy Whimple's arm. As she leaned on her cane, he carefully guided her toward Mark and Minda. His face was streaked from tears he'd wiped away, but he was smiling.

"Minda, let me introduce you to . . . my sister."

For a moment, she wasn't sure she had heard right. "Your . . . your *sister?* Addy! Is that true?"

Miss Whimple started to speak but her voice came out instead as a choking sound. She put her hand up to cup the side of Mark's face. He dipped his head toward her, but instead of speaking, she tenderly kissed him on the cheek. Her tear-filled eyes met his. "Thank you."

He smiled fondly at her before he extended his hand toward Coach. "You must be Albert."

"I am." Coach clasped Mark's hand in a hearty shake. "I'm Albert Morgan. That's the name I've had since I was five years old, but it seems that my birth name was Albert Whimple."

He smiled down at Addy, but his smile quickly changed to concern when her body began to tremble. Coach and Mark both reached for her at the same time, steadying her.

"I think I need to sit down," Miss Whimple said in a weak voice. "These old legs don't hold me up for very long."

Mark took Miss Whimple's arm and with Coach's help, gently guided her back to the car. Mark settled her on the soft leather passenger's seat and stepped back so Coach could crouch beside her.

Bits of their conversation carried across the short distance to where Minda stood beside Mark.

"I never stopped searching . . ."

"All these years you lived so close . . ."

"There were four of us, you know. Anna and Amelia were just a little bit older than you . . ."

Watching them, Minda felt tears gathering in her own eyes. She'd never seen Addy Whimple so happy. "You were right," she said to Mark. "This really *is* a miracle. How did it happen?"

"You told me once that my watch meant more than I was willing to admit. It turns out you were right."

She looked at him. "Your watch?"

"After I took Brady home, I went to visit Miss Whimple and when it was time to go, I pulled out my watch. She recognized it right away. She heard the chime. The look on her face . . . It was the same look I saw on Coach's face when he reacted to the watch at baseball practice last week. I knew at that moment that they were brother and sister."

Minda looked over at the car. Miss Whimple was weeping softly and Coach was on one knee, trying his best to comfort her. "I think she's exhausted. This has been an emotional day for her."

"Will you help me take her home?"

She heard the softness in his voice. And the urgency. She knew that if she said, yes, she'd be agreeing to much more than simply settling Miss Whimple in her apartment.

Very well, Mark Cartier, she thought. If he wanted to go Round Two with her, she'd give him the chance. If he still thought he could charm her into selling her building, she'd show him just how immune she was to his plastic smile and persuasive words. She told herself she was strong enough to resist his touch and charm, even as she recalled how natural it had felt to feel his arms around her just a few minutes before. It left her aching for more.

Her brain told her to refuse to go with him, to hold on to her resolve and stay as far away from him as possible. But she couldn't ignore the emotions she'd witnessed when he'd first taken his hands away from his face. Then she'd seen the tenderness in his expression when he looked at Miss Whimple and realized that he really did have a good heart.

Maybe, she thought, he had told her the truth. Maybe he

had changed since he arrived in Denver. Or maybe it was just her own wishful thinking.

There was only one way to find out.

"I'll help. Give me two minutes to let Tracy know I'm leaving."

Minda ran back to the bleachers and climbed up to the row where Tracy was watching the game.

"Sorry, honey, but I have to leave."

"Is everything okay?"

"Yes, but something came up and I have to go to the apartment building. If I'm not back by the end of the game, do you think you can get a ride home?"

"Sure. I'll ask Josh to drive me home. To tell you the truth, I was going to ask him to hang out anyway."

Minda slung the straps of her tote bag over her shoulder. "Thanks, honey. I'll see you at dinner."

"I don't mind saying, I'm exhausted." Addy Whimple leaned heavily on her cane as she got out of the elevator and slowly headed down the hall to her apartment. "I'm not used to so much excitement in one day."

Mark put his hand at her elbow. "Will you be able to make it all the way?"

"I think so."

Minda went ahead of them to unlock the apartment door. Miss Whimple went straight to her favorite chair and sat down with a contented sigh. Her cheeks were pink from a combination of happiness, exertion and the cool afternoon air.

"And it looks like that storm we're expecting is coming through a little early. I'm already cold." She pointed toward the opposite wall. "The thermostat's over there."

Mark adjusted the temperature setting while Minda draped a blanket across her lap.

"Why don't I fix you some tea?" Minda suggested. "That should take the chill off."

"I'd like that, deary." She looked over at Mark. "And you. I want to talk to you." She took his hand as soon as he knelt down beside her. "Do you know how special you are, young man?"

"No." He shook his head, a little embarrassed.

"Don't argue with me. I'm an old woman, and I expect God to take me home any day now. I've already outlasted all my friends and most of my acquaintances. I always thought the next time I'd see my family would be at the pearly gates. But then the good Lord brought you to my life, and you brought me my family. You must have a very special relationship with God for Him to use you in that way."

Mark put his head down and ran his fingers through his hair. "You're giving me more credit than I deserve."

"No, I'm not. I'm giving God the credit. He's given you good looks, talent, wealth and success. And today He used you to reunite a long-lost brother and sister. What more does the Lord have to do for you to understand how much He favors you?"

"I haven't done anything to deserve His favor."

"That's the beauty of it, don't you think?"

He looked toward the kitchen to see if Minda was listening.

She was. Her hazel eyes were focused on his face and she seemed to be waiting for him to answer Miss Whimple. It was almost as if they were back to where they started; back to the wary, distrustful look in her eyes. Back to wondering what it would take to make her trust him. Again.

"Yes, He has given me more than I deserve."

Miss Whimple smiled, satisfied but a moment later, her expression changed. She wrinkled her nose. "There it is again."

"There's what?"

"The paint smell. Don't tell me you can't smell that."

Mark sat up a little straighter. He did smell something. But it wasn't paint.

It was gas. Natural gas. And it was quickly filling Miss Whimple's apartment.

Minda smelled the distinct odor of natural gas and immediately sensed danger. Her eyes flew to Mark's and they locked startled gazes for a fraction of a moment.

She reached over and turned off the stove at the same time Mark jumped up and turned the thermostat down. Then he opened both windows and pushed Miss Whimple's wheelchair toward Minda. "Get her out of here. All the way to the street. Stay there with her and don't come back in."

In the next instant he was out of the apartment, heading down the hallway, pounding on apartment doors as he went.

The door to Brady's apartment flew open and Paul poked his head out.

"Are you nuts? You're rousing the entire building."

Mark pulled his cell phone out and dialed 911. "There's a gas leak. We've got to get out. Everybody. Now."

Paul reacted immediately, hurrying Brady and his mother out of their apartment and toward the stairs; then he pulled his own cell phone out and began dialing his employees at Harmony House to marshal their help.

Within minutes, Minda wheeled Addy Whimple out onto the sidewalk.

A fire truck, sirens blaring, pulled up at the curb. Then

another. Within minutes, firefighters were everywhere. They were in the bookstore and apartment building, going into neighboring businesses and driving store employees and customers out into the street. At one point, she tried to follow the fire fighters back into her building, but a police officer stopped her.

More police officers arrived and pushed Minda, Addy and the growing crowd of spectators and displaced people down the street until they were a full city block away from the McAllister Building.

Brady and his mother joined her just as a light rain began to fall. Brady was still wearing Mark's baseball hat and carrying his precious computer tablet.

"We're going to wait at the coffee shop down the street," he said.

Minda nodded. "Good idea. You'll be out of the rain. Will you take Miss Whimple with you?'

"Aren't you coming with us?"

"I can't. Not yet. Not until I know everyone is safe. I'll come and get you as soon as they give the all clear."

Minda returned her attention to the building. She watched anxiously for someone to come out the door who could tell her what was going on. Her nerves were on end and it was all she could do to keep from pacing. The rain began to fall a little harder against her jeans and hoodie, but she didn't care. She couldn't relax until she saw Mark and he could tell her what was going on.

A few minutes later Paul came out on the sidewalk, still talking on his cell phone. She wanted to run to him and would have if not for the police officers. She had to settle for waving her hands high above her head to attract his attention.

"What have you heard? What's going on?" Her words

came out in a tumble of worry and confusion.

"They're doing one last sweep of the building to make certain no one is still inside."

"Did they say when we can go back in?"

"No, but it won't be for a while. These things take time."

Minda felt her heart sink a little. "Where's Mark?"

"He's still inside. He's helping the firefighters search the building to make sure everyone's out."

"He's not in any danger, is he?"

Paul smiled softly. "No. But he'd do it even if he were in danger. He's grown pretty attached to the people who live in your building, you know."

She looked down at her fingers nervously knotted together. "I know. That's what he told me, anyway."

"I think you have more evidence of it than just his word," Paul said, kindly. "I'm going down the street to the coffee shop to check on Brady and his mother."

"Addy Whimple is with them."

"I'll check on her, too. Will you be okay until I get back?"

"Yes," she said, even though she felt far from okay.

Why was it taking so long? she wondered.

Why wasn't Mark coming out to tell her the leak had been found and fixed?

And why wasn't he standing close beside her with his warm, comforting arms around her?

The thought startled her, but calmed her at the same time.

She had so many reasons to be angry with Mark, but she couldn't deny her attraction to him. She felt he had used her and she wanted desperately to see that fake, charming smile wiped off his face forever; yet at the same time, she cared for him. Against her better judgment, she cared for him. And she wanted him to be safe.

Those were the feelings of one human being for another,

she told herself. Those were simply the emotions of a good Christian woman, not the emotions of a woman in love.

Definitely, not a woman in love.

Her hazel eyes refocused on the front entrance of the apartment building. Staring hard, she willed him to appear.

She *prayed* for him to appear, safe and sound.

23

From the street corner Minda watched Pastor Walker come toward her with a hurried step. He was carrying one of the firefighter's raincoats. The freezing rain was falling steadily now. Soon it would turn to snow. The crowd of people who had gathered to watch the commotion had dissipated long ago in search of dry clothes and warm rooms indoors. But even as the onlookers left, Pastor Walker had arrived.

To Minda, he looked like a lifeline and she welcomed him with relief. "Pastor, what are you doing here?"

"Paul called me," he explained. "I came as soon as I could. Is everyone safe?"

Minda told him what she knew and listened as he expressed concern for the people who lived and worked in the McAllister Building; people he ministered to and knew and loved.

He draped the heavy coat around her shoulders and pulled it closed across her folded arms.

"Why don't we get you inside, Minda? Somewhere out of

the weather."

He sounded concerned but she shook her head. She refused to notice the cold rain that had soaked through her clothes and left her hair matted against her head. Right now, all she cared about was the safety of her tenants.

"No, thanks. That's my building. It's my responsibility."

"Everyone is safe, Minda. The last of your tenants were led out of the building almost an hour ago."

But Mark was still in there. Mark was still with the firefighters as they searched for the source of the gas leak in her building.

Her building. The building she was supposed to take care of. The building her tenants relied on. The building Mark warned her was crumbling.

Pastor Walker looked over to where Paul was standing a few feet away, ending a call on his cell phone. "Come over here a minute, Paul. Did you have any luck?"

"I think we've got it handled."

"Good work," Pastor said. "Paul has been working with his team at Harmony House and some of the other relief agencies in town to make sure everyone has a place to go tonight."

She looked up at him, stunned. "What do you mean? Are you saying they may not be able to go back to their apartments tonight?"

"There's a chance, so we're just making sure there's a plan in place. But let's not get too far ahead of ourselves. I'm sure the fire fighters will have accurate information for us soon."

As if on cue, Mark come out the front door of the building with the fire captain. They paused, deep in conversation, before they walked toward her.

Her wet fingers, numbed with cold, clutched the heavy raincoat a little tighter as she tried to read Mark's expression.

"Minda," he said, gravely, "this is Captain Anderson."

"Is everyone out?" she asked. "Is everyone okay?" .

"Yes, ma'am," the captain said. "Let me give you the current status. We turned off the gas line to the building. There's one confirmed gas leak on the third floor and we think we found another one on the sixth floor. There could be more."

"I don't understand," Minda said, desperately trying to make sense of the chief's words. "The building passed the last inspection."

"Well, for starters, it's an old building," the captain said. "It's over a hundred years old and it originally had gas lighting. I saw the big, overhead light fixtures in the bookstore and they looked like original fixtures. They were most likely gas lights that somebody converted to electric early in the last century. Same thing with the lights in the apartment hallways. Somewhere, one or more of the walled-up gas lines started leaking."

"But I never smelled any gas until today."

"Mr. Cartier tells me a tenant has been complaining of the smell at night. It's that time of year when nights get pretty cold here in Denver. It could be that the leaking pipe expanded just enough in the summer months to seal the leak, but now that the temperatures are falling below the freezing mark at night, the gas pipes contract and the leak opens up."

Minda nodded, trying to take it all in. "When can my tenants get back in to their apartments?"

"They can't, ma'am. The gas is shut off and that means there's no heat. With no heat, this building is uninhabitable. I'm afraid your tenants can't return until all the leaks are found and fixed."

Minda felt her mind begin to reel. She touched her fingers to her forehead and dragged a thin rope of wet hair from her eyes as she tried to make sense of the fire chief's words. "How long will it take you to fix it?"

"Fix it? Sorry, ma'am, but the fire department can't fix it for you. You'll have to hire a licensed plumber with expertise in fixing these old gas lines. And, based on my experience, those kinds of repairs take a long time and cost a lot of money. You'll have to rip out walls to find all the leaks. A building inspector won't sign off on the work unless you can prove you've traced every gas line to ensure there are no additional leaks."

She swallowed hard. "How much does that kind of work cost?"

"A building this size and this old? I'd say you're looking at a couple hundred thousand dollars. Maybe more."

She felt her heart sink to her toes. "But I don't have that kind of money. How can I fix my building and get my tenants back into their homes?"

"I'm afraid you'll have to work with the city building inspector on that. For the time being, the gas is turned off and we've aired the building out. We'll make arrangements for you and your tenants to go back in to collect only essentials you'll need for the next few days. We'll escort them in small groups and give them fifteen minutes to get what they need. Then we lock the doors and nobody goes in again until all the repairs are complete."

Minda stood there, listening to the freezing rain patter against the slick shell of her raincoat. A curious numbness settled over her.

Pastor Walker put his hand on her shoulder. "This is hard news to hear, but you'll get through it, Minda. You're strong and resourceful. And your brothers and sisters in Christ will help in any way we can."

"Yes, of course." Pastor Walker was right. Her friends at

Eternal Joy Christian Church would help as much as they could.

But he was also wrong. He was wrong about her. She wasn't as strong as he seemed to think. Thankfully, the freezing rain was beginning to pelt her face hard enough so anyone looking at her would think her red nose was the result of the cold rain instead of gathering tears. Let them all think she was strong for a little while longer. They'd know the truth soon enough; they'd see for themselves that she wasn't strong at all. In fact, she was pretty close to losing her composure altogether and showing all of them that she was nothing more than a big failure.

A failure at caring for the building that had meant so much to her husband. A failure at providing a safe and comfortable place for her tenants. Tenants who needed her. Tenants who trusted her. Instead of caring for them, she had ruined their lives. She had ruined her husband's legacy.

She'd ruined everything.

"My tenants—Where will they go?"

"Paul has already taken care of them," Mark said. "He's been on the phone non-stop with his contacts to arrange for places for everyone to stay tonight."

Minda looked at Paul. "Thank you."

"It's what I do," Paul said, kindly. "Remember, you and I have that in common. We both find homes for people and take care of their needs."

Paul's simple observation proved to be Minda's undoing. "But I haven't taken care of them," she said, in a small voice. She started to cry and didn't even try to hide it. "I almost killed them all."

"Hey, no one got hurt," Paul said, quickly. "As a matter of fact, Brady told me he thinks it will be cool to spend the night in a shelter. He thinks it's an adventure."

Minda sniffled and pulled herself together. "Brady always sees the bright side of any situation."

"I know. He's a good kid. That's why I invited Brady and his mother to spend the night at my house. I think they'll be more comfortable there. And tomorrow, I'll find a new place for them to live."

"Thank you, Paul." Minda reached for him and gave him a grateful hug. "And Miss Whimple? I don't want her sleeping in a shelter, either. I want her to come home with me."

"She's waiting for you down the street at the coffee shop with Brady and his mother."

Minda looked up at the fire captain. "I don't need anything out of the building, but I would like to get something for Addy Whimple."

Mark unzipped his hooded sweatshirt that was now soaked through with rain. He reached beneath his blue baseball shirt and pulled out Miss Whimple's Bible. "I grabbed this for her. Sorry it got a little wet. Is there anything else you think she needs?"

She shook her head. She knew Addy would only care about retrieving her Bible and no other possessions would matter to her. She took the Bible from Mark and held it close against her, protecting it from the rain under the firefighter's raincoat.

The strain of holding her emotions in check was starting to take its toll. She could either hold her emotions at bay or she could fight the teeth-chattering cold. She started to shiver. The cold and damp seemed to suddenly penetrate her clothes, her skin, her bones.

Mark reached over and took her cold, wet hand in his. "Come on."

"Where are we going?"

"We're getting you out of this weather, for starters. You

can sit at the coffee shop with Miss Whimple while I get the car."

"I don't need you to drive me home. I can take the bus."

"But Miss Whimple can't take the bus. For pity's sake, Minda, she's ninety-four years old and she's already exhausted. Frankly, you are, too." He put his arm around Paul's shoulder and gave him a brief hug. "You've got Brady and his mother? And everybody has a place to stay tonight?"

"We've got everyone covered."

"Then let's get out of this rain." Mark's grip on Minda's hand tightened. He refused to let go as he led her down the street toward the coffee shop.

Minda pushed the front door open and ran into the living room at full tilt.

Tracy was stretched out on the couch, reading a book. "Hey, Mom. *Mom?* What's wrong? Why are you soaking wet?"

Minda threw her tote bag into a corner and began shoving things out of the way so there was a clear path from the front door to the base of the staircase.

"There was a problem at the building and Miss Whimple is going to spend the night with us. I'll tell you all about it later, but will you help me now?"

"Sure. What do you want me to do?"

"Go upstairs and turn the bed down in the guest room. Quickly, please."

Tracy sprinted up the stairs just as Mark appeared in the doorway, carrying Addy Whimple in his arms high against his chest.

"Where would you like me to set her down?" he asked.

"Can you get her upstairs to the guest bedroom?"

"I think so." He headed for the staircase, easily carrying Miss Whimple's slight weight.

Addy looked over Mark's shoulder at Minda, who was climbing the stairs behind them.

"Notice how easily he carries me? Not even winded!" she said, through chattering teeth. "I like a man with muscles, don't you?"

Tracy was waiting for them in the hall. "Bring her in here."

Mark carried his willing passenger into the bedroom and tenderly deposited her on the bed. "She's freezing and her clothes are a little damp from the rain."

Miss Whimple reached out and clasped Minda's hand. "I could use that cup of hot tea now."

"Of course. I'll get it right away. Tracy, will you help settle Miss Whimple into bed?"

She led Mark out to the hallway and quietly pulled the bedroom door closed.

"Thank you for bringing us home."

"Will you be able to manage getting her up and down the stairs by yourself?"

"I think so."

"Minda . . ."

"I have to get some dry clothes for Addy." She hurried down the hall to her bedroom before he could say another word.

In her own room she retrieved clean, dry night clothes and a sturdy pair of wool socks. When she went back to the guest room Mark was gone. With Tracy's help, she got Miss Whimple changed and into bed.

"Are you warm enough?" Minda asked as she added an extra blanket on top of the quilted coverlet.

"Not yet. I don't mind telling you that rain was cold enough to chill my bones." She eyed Minda's wet clothes.

"You need to get warmed up yourself, deary."

"I'll change in a minute. First, I'm going to get you that tea you asked for."

"That would be nice."

Minda went out of the bedroom, softly closing the door behind her. In the kitchen, she found Mark waiting.

She ignored him but she could feel his gaze on her as she filled the tea kettle with water at the sink.

"What are you doing?" he asked.

"I'm making some tea for Addy."

"Now? Can't that wait until you get some dry clothes on?"

"No."

"Minda, you're soaked through to the bone. You need to get warm yourself before you do anything for anyone else."

"I'm fine."

She turned away from the stove to take cups down from the cupboard and found Mark blocking her way. Startled, she looked up and saw his blue eyes clouded with concern.

"I'm sorry."

"For what?"

"For what happened today."

"As far as I can tell, you had nothing to do with the gas leak. *Did* you?"

"You know I didn't."

"I only know what I read in that magazine. The article made you sound pretty ruthless. The article said you'd do anything necessary to close a deal."

"Not anything. I know I should have told you the truth about myself and my job and the reason I came here."

"I know why you came. You came to get your hands on my building using whatever means you had to."

"That's true. Well, it *was* true but only at first. That's why I came but it's not why I stayed."

She didn't want this particular conversation to go any further. She was too tired and too cold to keep her guard up for very much longer.

She forced herself to speak calmly. "Thank you for helping at the building this afternoon. And thank you for bringing Addy and me home."

"I really want to talk to you, Minda."

She raised a weak hand in defense. "Could we not do this now? I know we should talk again and I promise you, we will. But not now. I'm too cold and too tired; and after everything that's happened today, I'm a little overwhelmed."

"I understand. I'll give you some time but for now, will you let me apologize?"

"You already said you were sorry about the building."

"No. I want to apologize for not telling you who I was from the very beginning. For trying to trick you into selling your building. I underestimated you, and I'm sorry."

There it was. The apology she'd been waiting for. Hearing it gave her no satisfaction. As much as she hated to admit it, Mark hadn't really underestimated her at all. Instead, he'd played her perfectly and almost gotten away with it. It had taken him only two dinners and a few trips to church to make her fall head over heels in love with him. That's what was so hurtful. Until she met Mark, she never knew how lonely she was or how much she missed the simple pleasure of knowing a man loved her and was attracted to her.

The tea kettle on the stove began to whistle, saving her from having to give him an immediate response. With slow, measured movements, she poured the hot water into the cup and watched the boiling water saturate the tea bag.

"I really want to talk about this some other time."

"I'll come back tomorrow."

"No!" She didn't want him in her house again, especially

not in her kitchen. There were already too many uncomfortable memories of Mark in her home that she'd have to somehow banish from her mind. "I'll call you and we'll pick a time and place."

"Tomorrow?"

He was certainly persistent. "Maybe. I don't know. I can't think of anything right now except what happened this afternoon."

"Minda, your tenants are fine."

"But the McAllister Building isn't. I have to figure out how I'm going to get the money for the repairs that need to be done."

"I have it."

She blinked up at him. "You have what?"

"The money. I'll give you the money to make the repairs."

"Absolutely not." She was surprised that her voice sounded so calm. It was almost majestic.

"Minda, please let me help you."

"No, thank you. I'm already familiar with your brand of help."

"I know you don't have the money." He said the words as if he knew the exact balance of her checking account.

"It's none of your business how much money I have. And if it turns out that I don't happen to have hundreds of thousands of dollars just lying around, I'm sure I can get a loan."

She didn't know why she said that. She already suspected she could never qualify to borrow a two hundred pennies, let alone two hundred thousand dollars. Or more. Her balance sheet was a disaster with more liabilities than assets. Her debt to available credit ratio was as high as the stars in the Colorado sky. But she would never tell that to Mark Cartier.

His body language changed. Without even moving a

muscle, he seemed to get closer to her. His voice was low and intimate and pleading. "You keep trying to talk about money. I'm trying to tell you how much you mean to me."

He reached for her and she quickly picked up the mug of steaming tea.

"I have to get this to Addy."

She didn't wait for his answer. She left the kitchen and headed upstairs. When she was half-way up, she heard the front door close. At the landing, she looked out the window and saw Mark's car pulling away from the curb.

He was gone. He was probably headed straight to his hotel to pack his bags and be on the next plane to New York.

Good, she told herself, even though she didn't *feel* so good.

Tracy came out of the bedroom carrying Miss Whimple's clothes. "I'll take these down to the laundry room."

"Thank you, honey. And thank you for getting her settled. Is she doing okay?"

"Yes. Better than you, actually. Mom, don't take this the wrong way, but don't you think you ought to change or something? I mean, you can't be comfortable in those wet clothes."

"I'm not. And as soon as I deliver this cup of tea to Addy, I'm going to take a long, hot shower."

She knocked on the bedroom door and went in. Addy was sitting up in bed with her Bible on her lap. Minda placed the cup of tea within her reach on the nightstand.

"Is he gone?" Addy asked.

Minda pretended not to care. "Yes, he just left."

"Is he coming back?"

"No. He won't be back."

"Pity." Miss Whimple sipped her tea. "Seems a shame to waste all that time falling in love just to have it come to nothing."

"Who said I was falling in love?"

"I was talking about me."

Minda let out a surprised laugh. "*You* fell in love with Mark?"

"I'm not too old to appreciate a handsome man. Especially a man with a smile that can make your heart flutter and your knees go weak. Although at my age, that's not hard to do." She narrowed her eyes at Minda. "Can you honestly tell me you aren't a little bit in love with him?"

"Maybe I was a little bit. But it turns out that he only had eyes for my building. He wants to buy the McAllister building, Addy. That's the reason he came to Denver, to convince me to sell it. That's why he was nice to me and took me to dinner and went to church with me."

"I see. What about the other stuff?"

"What other stuff?"

"Bringing me flowers. Visiting me. Buying that thin, little computer thing for the boy down the hall. You think he did all that just to make you sell your building?"

"Probably." Minda didn't sound so certain. "I don't know. It's possible."

"And what about today? If he were as cold and calculating as you say, would the good Lord have used him to bring my brother and me together?"

"I don't know," she said again, defeated.

"Want to know what I think?"

"Probably not."

"I'll tell you anyway. For years you've been calm, sensible Minda, taking care of everybody but yourself. I never approved. I always said you deserved more in life than baby-sitting a building full of needy people and riding herd over your daughter. You've been so busy taking care of others, you never gave a thought to yourself. It's no wonder you haven't felt like a woman in seventeen years. It's no wonder that when a man finally pays a little bit of attention to you, you can't handle it."

Minda stared at her, shocked. "That's not true."

Addy thumped her palm against the Bible in her lap. "Do you know why this is so important to me?"

"Because it's the Word of God. Because you're a faithful Christian who reads—"

"Wrong!" Addy Whimple waved her hand impatiently. "This Bible is important to me because it's the only thing I have left of the people I loved." She opened the Bible and held it up so Minda could read the inscription:

To our darling Adelaide. May you walk in the ways of the Lord with this Good Book to guide you.
  With much love on your birthday,
  From Mama and Papa,
  Anna, Amelia and Baby Albert.

Addy put the Bible back down on her lap and lovingly pressed her palm against the page. "For eighty years, this is all I had to remind me that I was once loved and cherished, and that I had a family I loved in return. I resented being taken away from them. Over time, that resentment turned to anger and the anger changed to bitterness. I carried that bitterness with me all my life. I was mean, and I pushed people away who would have cared about me. Except for you. You wouldn't be pushed. Instead, you became a friend to me. The one bright spot in a miserable old woman's life. You've got a good heart, Minda. And God has brought you someone who loves you. Don't push him away. Don't end up alone and bitter with nothing to keep you warm but memories of someone who once loved you. Don't live your life wishing things had turned out differently."

Minda shook her head slowly. "It's not the same, Addy."

"Love is love, deary. And when we lose it, it changes who we are. I saw it happen when you lost your husband. And it'll happen again if you lose Mark."

"I'm still the same person I was before Mark ever showed up here."

"No you're not. I can see you hardening your heart against him already."

She hated it when Addy was right. "I don't know what to do."

"Talk to him. And listen with an open heart. Promise me you'll at least do that."

"I will. I promise. But right now, I'm going to take a hot shower then I'll bring you some dinner."

Miss Whimple settled back against the pillows. "Thank you, deary. I'd like that."

24

Minda's own dire prediction came true. No one was willing to lend her the money to repair the gas leaks at the McAllister Building. News of the building evacuation was plastered across the front page of the newspaper the next morning and it was the lead story on the local television news show. The entire town knew the seriousness of her situation.

At church on Sunday, Pastor Walker spoke of her plight to the congregation. They prayed together. They individually murmured sympathetic phrases to her. But no one offered to help her financially.

On Monday morning she called the bank that held her mortgage. The loan officer politely reminded her that if she had no tenants to pay rent and no store from which to sell books, she had no income to qualify for a loan.

The situation only grew worse from there. Minda called a contractor for an estimate to make the repairs. The amount he quoted was higher than what the fire chief had told her.

The second contractor she called quoted an amount that was higher still and estimated the repairs would take about three months to complete.

"This is a disaster!" Ellen said, when she heard the news.

"Shhh! I don't want Addy to hear." Minda got up from the kitchen table where she and Ellen were drinking coffee and peaked around the corner, into the living room.

Addy and Coach were sitting together on the sofa, oblivious to anyone but each other. Coach had arrived that morning with a scrapbook and several old photo albums. Together they were pouring over pictures of his childhood, taken after he was adopted.

Minda sat down again at the table across from Ellen.

"I know it's a disaster. That's why I need your help in coming up with ideas. I don't know where I'm going to get the money."

"Jim and I have some money in savings," Ellen said. "It's not much, but you're welcome to it."

"I appreciate that. But unless the balance of your savings account has five zeroes in it, it won't do much good. Thanks for offering, though."

"There must be something we can do," Ellen said, refusing to give up. "Hey, what about that contract?"

"What contract?"

"The contract Mark explained to you. From that company that wanted to buy the building."

"Are you suggesting I sell the building?"

"I sure am. Honey, it's no good to you now. Sell it and get what you can for it."

"I can't and we've already had this conversation."

"Why can't you sell it?" Ellen demanded. "With the money they offered, you can buy another building. You can buy five, if you want. But every day you hesitate, you're losing money. The loan guy at the bank was right. You have no income right now. None. Nada. What are you going to live on?"

"You don't understand." Minda hesitated, unwilling to tell her best friend the truth. The truth about how easily she'd been taken in by the very man Ellen had encouraged her to date.

"What is it I don't understand?"

Minda took a deep breath. "I found out that Mark works for the company that made that offer."

"I know."

Minda stared at her, certain she hadn't heard right. "What did you say?"

"I know what company Mark works for."

"How could you know that?"

"Easy. I did an Internet search on his name the first day I met him at church. I went right home and looked him up on the Internet and found out what he does for a living. You know, he's a pretty popular guy. I got over a hundred hits on him."

Minda glared at her. "When, exactly, where you planning to tell me?"

"Never. I admit I'm a busy-body but I'm not a meddler. There's a fine line. And you weren't having any trouble learning about Mark on your own. I saw no reason to jump in and spoil everything by telling you something that he was probably going to tell you himself."

"Well, he *didn't* tell me," Minda said, sharply. "I had to find out about him the hard way, thanks to you."

"He would have told you. He was quickly coming to a point where he had to make a choice: he could have you or he could have the building. He would have chosen you."

"So, now you're a busy-body *and* a fortune teller? Honestly, Ellen, how could you know that?"

"I guess I'm just a sucker for true love."

"True love? Is that what you call it?"

"Yes, I do. I knew from the moment I met him that he was nuts about you. You're the only person who doesn't see that Mark's in love with you."

Was he? He'd never said so. She'd never heard him say the word *love* out loud. He often looked at her with an emotion she thought was love. And he touched her and held her lovingly. And she thought she detected love in the way he kissed her. Definitely in the way he kissed her. But he never once said he loved her.

What had she expected? Just because she loved Mark didn't automatically mean he loved her back.

"Ellen Dailey, you're a hopeless romantic, you know that?" Minda forced a light tone to her voice. She picked up the coffee pot and replenished their mugs. "Before we get carried away, could we please get back to the subject at hand?"

"Okay, let's recap. You have to come up with an obscene amount of money to repair the building. So far, no one will give you the money. But let's say you manage to find a fairy godmother who magically gives you a couple hundred thousand dollars. Then what?"

"Then I make the repairs," Minda said, simply.

"Repairs the contractors said would take two to three months to finish. In the meantime, you have no income from the bookstore that's closed up because there's no heat. And you have no income from rents, because no one can live in your apartments. That means you have no money to live on. It also means you won't be able to make the mortgage payment on the McAllister Building when it comes due on the first of the month. If you miss a payment, you're in default on your loan, and that means the bank will start foreclosure proceedings. And because you have no income, you won't be able to stop the bank from taking possession of the building you just spent all your money repairing. Have I got it right so far?"

Yes, she had it right, but it was awfully hard to hear. "I never thought of it that way before."

Ellen gave her a sympathetic look. "I know. But we might as well put all the cards face up on the table."

"The picture doesn't look very pretty, does it?"

"I'm afraid not. Even if you do manage to get the money to make the repairs, you could still end up losing the building."

"There *has* to be some alternative."

"I can't think of one, can you?" Ellen asked, gently. "I know you don't want to sell the building, but it doesn't look to me like you have any choice."

Ellen was right. She had no choice. It was time to concede defeat.

"Okay. You win. I'll go see Mark."

"When?"

"As soon as I put my coat on. While I'm gone, will you stay here with Addy?"

"Sure. Anything else you want me to do?"

She nodded. "Pray."

"I'm here strictly on a business matter," Minda said, as she walked into Mark's hotel suite. "This isn't a social call in any way."

"I'm glad we got the ground rules straight." Mark closed the door and followed her into the living area of his suite. His tone was unemotional, but the look on his face was anything but. She saw the warmth radiating from his eyes when he looked at her, and it was all she could do to keep her voice even.

"I don't think I'll have to take more than a few minutes of your time."

"We can take as much time as you'd like, even if it's only for business reasons. What business would you like to talk about?"

Her first order of business was to ignore the tenderness in his voice. She set her tote bag on the table and pulled out the large envelope from Goble, Haines and Wyman.

"I came to talk about this."

His expression changed. "Okay."

She took a deep breath. "I want to accept the offer. I want to sell the building." Her mouth went dry as she spoke the words. The words she never imagined would ever come out of her mouth.

He held out his hand. Her own hand trembled as she passed the envelope to him.

"Let's sit down." He gestured toward the sofa.

She chose the chair instead.

He sat on the end of the sofa closest to her and removed the envelope contents. He fanned the papers out on the coffee table before her and stared at them for a long moment as if he were struggling for the right words to say.

"The thing about business deals is that they really should be negotiated. That way, both parties have input. Both parties stand a better chance of getting they want." He slid the pages of the contract in front of Minda and pushed the other pages away. "Unfortunately, this deal wasn't negotiated. In this deal, only the buyers get what they want."

She wasn't sure what was talking about, but she knew it didn't sound good. "What are you saying?"

"There's a clause in this offer that says the property has to be delivered in as-is condition. As-is means the building has to be in the same condition it was in at the time the offer was made. If the condition of the property changes in any way, the offer is void."

He pointed to a paragraph on page three of the contract but she didn't even bother to try to read it.

"Are you telling me your company doesn't want to buy the McAllister Building anymore?"

"No. They still want to buy it. But not for twelve million dollars. Not for one million dollars."

She almost hated to ask the question. "How much will they offer?"

He picked up a pen from the table and flipped the papers back to page one of the contract. He drew a line through the multi-million dollar amount printed in paragraph four and wrote a figure right above it. He pushed the paper in front of Minda.

The millions of dollars that Goble, Haines and Wyman had once offered her were gone with the stroke a pen, replaced by a dollar amount that wouldn't even cover the cost of the repairs.

She stared at the paper a long time. "I don't understand. This amount can't be right. What about the value of the retail space where the bookstore is? What about the apartment rents?"

"They're not interested in rental income."

"Are they going to pay the cost of fixing the gas leaks?"

"Repairs won't be necessary. Once they own the building, they'll tear it down."

There it was. The final death knell of the building her husband had loved and she had cherished for seventeen years.

She was going to lose her building and the money. She wouldn't be able to help any of her tenants. She wouldn't be able to keep her bookstore. The unfairness of it was devastating.

How did this happen? Three weeks ago her life had been

perfect. Three weeks ago she was helping people, raising her daughter, and content with her life. And then Mark had come along and showed her how empty her life had really been. He'd filled the emptiness with hope and love and the promise of a future with him. Then she'd discovered his treachery. He didn't love her after all. He'd only used her to get what he wanted, and it appeared he was going to win, thanks to a little bit of help from some obsolete gas pipes.

She focused her attention on her hands folded calmly in her lap.

"Do they really have to tear it down?"

"Yes." He didn't look at her, either. "It will be an empty lot by the new year."

"You make it sound like I don't have a choice."

"But you do." He leaned toward her. "You don't have to sell."

Desperately, she clutched at the hope he gave her. She was willing to consider any alternative. "How? What do you mean?"

"I can lend you the money to make the repairs."

But not that alternative. She stood up quickly, sending some of the papers scattering off the coffee table.

"No."

"Minda, let me help you."

"No! You don't really want to help me. This is just another one of your tricks to get the building."

"If you don't let me help, you'll *lose* the building."

"And if I lose it, it won't be to you."

"No one else will buy the building, Minda. The only value you have is in the land the building sits on."

"I'll sell the land," she said, with one last surge of defiance.

"When? You have no income. No money to live on. You can't make the bank payment that's due on the first of the month. Even if you found a buyer tomorrow, the sale can't be finalized fast enough to stop foreclosure procedures. You'll still lose the building."

"Threats, Mark? Sweet-talking the poor, lonely widow didn't work so now you're resorting to threats?"

"I'm not trying to threaten you, Minda. I'm trying to help."

"Don't bother. It was a mistake for me to come here. I should have known better." She scooped up her tote bag and headed for the door. She paused, her hand on the knob, and looked back.

She wanted to tell him how disappointed she was, how much he had hurt her.

"I'm sorry," he said, as if he could read her thoughts.

For a moment she almost gave in. She didn't, but a lot of the fight drained out of her at the sound of those two words.

Minda opened the door and left the hotel room, softly closing the door behind her.

Mark stood still in the quiet of the room. He picked up his smart phone and opened the text conversation he'd exchanged with his boss earlier that day; the same text conversation in which Robert Haines had dictated the new, hard-line, take-no-prisoners terms for buying the McAllister Building.

Marked tapped out a message. *New offer delivered.*

A few seconds later, he received a reply. *Signed?*

Not yet.

Extra bonus for you if she signs by midnight. Be on next flight to NY. See you in office tomorrow.

Mark pecked at the keys again. *No, you won't. I quit.*

Lord, please tell me what to do.

In the two days since she'd left Mark's hotel room, Minda

had repeated that prayer countless times. So far, she hadn't received an answer, but she had faith.

She'd exhausted all the options she could think of. Worrying about her tenants and the people who depended on her was taking a toll on her and she was having a hard time hiding her stress. Tracy noticed and demanded Minda tell her the details, from one adult to another. Minda gave her a summary of the situation, but she refused to talk about Mark's involvement.

Pastor Walker was also sympathetic and invited her to meet him at church to discuss options.

She drove to the meeting with a heavy heart, resigned to the fact that no other options existed.

She parked in the church lot and went into the office just as Pastor Walker was coming out.

"Hello, Minda."

"Are you leaving, Pastor? I thought we had a meeting."

"We do, but let's not talk in my office. It's too formal. I thought it would be nice to sit in the study." He took a few steps down the hallway and threw open the door. "Come on in."

She stepped inside the room and a flood of memories came back to her in a rush. Memories of Mark and the first time he'd held her hand. The first time she'd felt that spark of attraction for him. The first time she'd allowed herself to fantasize about his kisses.

She blocked the thoughts and stepped further into the room. Paul Cartier was sitting at the round table near the windows. He pushed a small stack of papers aside on the table and quickly stood up, smiling at her.

"I hope you don't mind that I ask Paul to join us." Pastor closed the door and ushered her toward the table with a sweep of his hand. "He was here sharing information about your tenants with me and I thought you'd like to hear."

"Of course! I'm so grateful for the help you gave everyone on Saturday. I don't know what I would have done if you hadn't been there."

"I just made some phone calls," Paul said, modestly. He sat down at the table beside Minda. "My team at the office did all the hard work. They're pretty good at working the phones and taking care of people in emergency situations. The good news is all your tenants have places to stay. Granted, some of them had to spend one or two nights in a hotel, but I'm happy to report that as of today, we've located housing for everyone."

"That is good news. In fact, it's the best news I've had in days."

Pastor Walker pointed to a computer tablet on the table in front of Paul. "Show Minda what you showed me. Wait till you see this, Minda."

Paul tapped the screen a few times and held the tablet up so Minda could see the display. "My team set up a database so we could track all your tenants. See? It lists each person's name, where they are currently housed, how to reach them by phone, the name of the agency that provided the housing . . . you get the idea."

"This is wonderful."

"Would you like me to email a copy to you? Then you'll have addresses and phone numbers for all your tenants and you can stay in touch with them."

She nodded. "Yes, please. I'd like that."

"Done. And I'll send you an updated list once we get the last of your tenants out of hotels and into housing."

"I don't know how to thank you, Paul. You've been so good to them. Ever since Saturday I've felt like I let them down. I'm very grateful you were there to make up for my failures."

Jenny Berlin

Pastor Walker looked at her with concern. "Minda, you're not a failure. You had no way of knowing about those leaks. No one ever reported a problem. No one who lived or worked in that building said they smelled natural gas."

"Addy Whimple smelled it."

Paul shook his head. "Yes, but she thought it was a paint smell. How could you know she was really complaining about something else?"

"I could have known, if I'd been paying attention. I should have been concentrating on my responsibilities. Instead, I was distracted by . . ." *Mark.* She'd been distracted by Mark, with his handsome face and movie star smile and dazzling blue eyes. She'd been distracted by a man who made her feel alive and happy just by looking at her. ". . . by *other things*," she finished lamely.

"I know you take your responsibilities seriously," Paul said. "So do I. Do you remember when we first met? I remarked that you and I were a lot alike, with the same mission of serving families in need."

"I remember."

"I also told you that I once tried to interest you in selling the McAllister building. Do you remember that?"

"Yes, I remember."

"At the time, I thought the McAllister Building was ideal for our ministry. I wanted Harmony House to buy the building and essentially run it in the same way you did, with families we serve living in the apartments. In fact, the only change I planned to make was to move Harmony House's offices into the retail space you use right now for your bookstore."

"Oh."

That's all she could think of to say. She had a thought—a glimmer of hope—that Paul was talking about the McAllister

Building for a good reason. Maybe even a spectacular reason. She clasped her hands together in her lap, and waited to hear what point Paul was making.

"I hope this isn't the wrong time to bring it up," he said, with a watchful eye to her reaction, "but Harmony House is still interested in buying the building."

Surprised, she took in a gulp of air in one deep whoosh.

"Don't say no yet!" Paul held up both hands as if he could halt her words. "I know how important your tenants are to you. The good news is that most of them qualify for assistance with Harmony House, as well. They can move right back into the same apartments they were living in as soon as we fix the gas leaks."

Minda felt her spirit deflate a little. She shook her head. "I can't fix the leaks. I don't have the money."

"Maybe I wasn't clear," Paul said. "My proposal is that you sell the building to Harmony House as-is. Harmony House will bear the cost of fixing the gas leaks as well as any other repairs that have to be done."

"As-is?" She'd heard that term before. Mark had used it when he explained his employer's latest offer to buy the building. As-is meant the value of the McAllister Building was as low as a snake in snowshoes. As-is meant whoever bought it would pay only pennies for the beautiful old place.

Paul nodded. "As-is. That just means you aren't expected to do any repairs or upgrades to the building before it's sold."

"I understand that. But it also means the building isn't as valuable."

Paul exchanged a look with Pastor Walker. From the stack of papers on the table he pulled a blank sheet off the top and wrote something on it. He passed the paper across the table to Minda.

"I think this is a fair offer."

Minda stared at the number he'd written on the paper. The number was nowhere near the original twelve-million dollars Mark's company had offered, but it had a dollar sign in front of it and several zeroes on the end.

With that kind of money she could afford to find a new location for her bookstore. With that money, she could continue to help some of her tenants, like Brady and Addy Whimple. She almost jumped out of her seat and hugged Paul.

She looked at the number again, and then looked at Paul. "Are you serious?"

"That's a fair offer, Minda," Pastor Walker said, sounding concerned. "Paul and I both think it's in line with market value. After considering the building's age and the work that has to be done, we hope you'll think it's fair, too."

"It's more than fair," she said, feeling hopeful for the first time in days. "I hadn't expected this at all and . . . Paul, are you *sure?*"

"I'm absolutely sure. Your building is ideal for Harmony House. I've always thought so."

"But it's far from perfect," she said, thinking she might as well lay all her cards on the table. "The plumbing pipes thump when someone runs hot water on the fourth floor. And the roof looks like a patchwork quilt of—"

"It's an old building," Paul said, cutting her off. "I'd expect there will be some work to be done."

"You don't understand. The heating system looks like . . ." What had Mark called it? ". . . a handyman's nightmare. And the electrical system is even worse."

"I know, Minda. We'll take care of it."

Minda felt his words were too good to be true. "And you'll allow my tenants to continue to live there?"

"Every one of them."

"And you won't raise their rent?"

"No. In fact, some of them might end up having their monthly rent reduced."

She could feel the moisture of grateful tears gathering in her eyes. She pressed her fingertips to her temples. "If everything you're saying is true, this will be the answer to all my prayers."

"Pastor Walker and I have been praying about it, too."

"What do you think, Minda?" Pastor asked. "Is it a fair offer?"

"It's more than fair. Thank you, Paul. You've made me so happy, I could kiss you!" she blurted.

Paul laughed. "Would you settle for a hug and a handshake?"

She put her hand in his and leaned forward to wrap her other arm around his shoulder. Seated at the table, it was an awkward hug at best, but heart-felt.

"Thank you, Paul," she said again. "I'm so grateful to you."

"It's my pleasure. And if you're ready, we can start the wheels turning now." Paul picked up another sheet of paper, scanned it quickly, and passed it to Minda. "This is a Letter of Intent. It's not a contract, it just means that you'll sell the McAllister Building to Harmony House for the agreed on price. Then you and I will work out the details of the deal in good faith. If it turns out we disagree on any elements of the sale, we agree to let Pastor Walker break the tie and we'll abide by whatever he decides."

Minda reached for Pastor Walker's pen. She read the page twice; then she set the paper down on the table and took a deep breath. Pen in hand, she began to sign her name.

"Don't sign!" Pastor Walker reached over and snatched the paper away. "Don't sign. Not yet. Not until you know everything."

"Pastor, don't!" Paul's warning was sharp.

"Sorry, Paul. I can't let her make this decision without knowing all the facts."

Startled, Minda looked from Pastor to Paul and back. "What facts? Is there something else I need to know?"

Pastor Walker nodded. "Yes, there is. You need to know where Harmony House got the money to make this offer to you." He pointed to the Letter of Intent lying on the table just out of her reach.

"What are you talking about? Doesn't Harmony House get money from donations?"

"You're absolutely right," Paul said. "The money came from *a donation*." He glared at Pastor Walker. "This was supposed to be a secret."

"It's your secret, not mine," Pastor said, unaffected. "As much as I think this deal will benefit everyone, I can't be a party to it if we don't tell Minda everything."

Paul leaned back in his chair and threw up his hands in a defeated gesture.

"Someone tell me what's going on." Minda could feel her anxiety level climbing again. Fresh worries careened around her head like bumper cars: worries about her tenants; worries about the repairs to the building; worries about how she'd get the money to live on. "Please tell me what you're talking about."

Paul shook his head and focused his gaze on the view outside the window.

It was up to Pastor Walker to tell her. "Harmony House got the money to buy the McAllister Building from Mark."

"Mark?" Her voice came out in a faint croak. "Where did Mark get the money?"

"Tell her, Paul," Pastor Walker commanded. "That's not part of the secret, is it?"

Paul shot Pastor Walker a look that promised future vengeance. "Mark's been saving for years to start his own business. Yesterday he donated all his savings to Harmony House. He gave us every penny he had."

"Are you telling me the truth?" she demanded in a voice of deadly calm.

"It's true."

"Partially true," Pastor Walker corrected. "Tell her the rest. Go on. You might as well."

Paul drew a deep breath. "He donated the money on one condition: that it be used to buy and renovate the McAllister Building. He even negotiated a new loan with the bank."

"I see." Minda carefully set the pen down on the table and folded her hands in her lap. She swallowed hard, blinked several times, took a deep breath. That old trick meant to keep her emotions under control worked. But this time, it wasn't emotions of loss and sorrow she was trying to control, but emotions of light and love. Mark was trying to save her building. He was trying to save her and what mattered most to her. And to do so, he'd given up what mattered most to him.

"Thank you for telling me."

Paul looked worried. "I hope what I just said doesn't change your mind about selling the building. Pastor was right; this is a fair offer and everyone will benefit."

"Yes, you're right, of course." She stood up, abruptly. "Will you excuse me, please?"

She moved toward the door without a hint of hurry, her emotions under control and a polite smile on her lips. But the reality was that she couldn't get out of Pastor's study fast enough. She practically ran across the parking lot to her car. She fitted her key in the ignition and allowed the feeling of hope to take root; hope that Mark loved her. She certainly loved him. God couldn't have brought a more perfect man into her life. From his perfect smile to his perfect voice to his truly good and gentle nature that he chose to reveal only for her. She loved him.

"Dear God, please make him be there," she prayed aloud. "Please make him be there!"

She drove straight to Mark's hotel and pulled up in front at the valet stand. Valet parking was an extravagance she never allowed, but this was an emergency.

The elevator ride to the sixteenth floor set her impatient nerves on edge so by the time she knocked on the door of Mark's hotel suite, her heart was pounding. The door opened.

"Minda!" Mark's expression change in rapid succession from surprise to pleasure then caution.

"May I talk to you? Please?"

He stepped back and ushered her into the living area.

She marched into the room with purpose, determined to say what she came to say and not lose her nerve. But the sight of a large, roller suitcase near the coffee table brought her up short. The pull handle of the suitcase was extended, ready for someone to wheel it out the door. Next to the suitcase was Mark's expensive leather briefcase, packed and zipped and ready to go.

She stared at them. "You're leaving?"

She felt him come to her side but she kept her gaze on the luggage, too stunned to look at him.

"I'm checking out of the hotel today." His rich, low voice was very close to her ear.

She looked up at him and blurted, "I know what you did."

His eyes widened momentarily. "You know *what*?"

"I know you gave Harmony House the money to buy the McAllister Building."

"How did you—? My brother was supposed to keep that confidential."

"He did. Pastor Walker told me." She could tell he was annoyed. He might even be angry. "Please don't blame him. He had his reasons."

Mark ran his hand through is hair. "Okay, now you know."

"That's right. I know everything. So you don't have to leave. You don't have to go back to New York right away. *Do you?*"

He followed her gaze to the suitcase. "I'm not going back to New York. I'm just checking out of this hotel room."

"And then where will you go?"

"I'm going to stay at Paul's house for a while. He took pity on my situation. Now that I'm unemployed, I can't afford to stay in a high-priced hotel suite like this one."

"You're unemployed?"

"I quit my job this morning."

"You gave all your money to Harmony House *and* you quit your job?"

"I decided it was time for a career change, although I hope I won't be unemployed for long. I suggested to Paul that he hire me to do some fundraising for Harmony House."

"What did he say?"

"He said he'd have to check my references first. Brothers!"

"But a charity like Harmony House won't be able to pay even a fraction of the amount you were earning before. *Why* did you quit? And why did you give up all your savings?"

"Are you sure you want to know?"

Her heartbeat quickened. "Yes."

"I tried to tell you the reason before, but you wouldn't listen."

She felt a big lump of emotion gathering in her throat that made it hard to breathe. "I'm listening now. I should have listened before and I'm sorry for that. "

"*You're* sorry? What on earth do you have to be sorry for?"

"For judging you. For making up my mind about you for all the wrong reasons. That's what I came here to tell you. At first I had no idea why you came into my life. I didn't trust you and I jumped to some wrong conclusions. But then I saw you change. I saw how gentle you were with Addy Whimple and how generous you were with Brady. You were so patient and understanding about Tracy, and the difference you made in Coach's life is nothing short of a miracle. I saw all of that and I ..." Her voice faltered. She looked down at the suitcase. "I changed my mind about you."

Coward. At the very moment she was supposed to tell Mark how she felt about him, she chickened out.

He shook his head. "You didn't misjudge me, Minda. You were right. I was focused on the wrong things. I thought money and possessions were all that mattered. And I was willing to justify my actions to get them."

"But you don't believe that now, do you?"

"No. Now I believe that the things I thought were priceless really had no value at all. You showed me that."

"I did?" she breathed.

"Yes, you did. You turned all my plans upside-down. *You* were the one who charmed *me*. And the more I tried to make you like me, the more I ended up liking you. And I liked the people you go to church with. *And* the people who live in your building. It was like some giant conspiracy that everyone was in on but me. Even my own brother."

"It sounds like you didn't stand a chance," she said, a hint of laughter in her voice.

"I was definitely out-numbered." He turned slightly so he was facing her, his lean body close to hers. "I've been a Christian all my life, Minda, but I haven't opened my heart to

God in years. I know there were times when He tried to speak to me but I wouldn't listen. I thought I knew best. Then I came here and you showed me what real treasures are. Not condos and clothes and cars, but home and family and living the life God planned for me. I think you're part of that plan."

There they were. The words she'd been waiting for. Mark had opened the door and she just had to step through it.

She looked up at him and flashed a dazzling smile. "I think so, too."

With a deep sigh, he pulled her into his arms and in the next instant, his lips were on hers.

His kiss had none of the tentative tenderness of their last kiss. This kiss was urgent and demanding before it softened into a slow, tantalizing pressure that she hoped would never end.

She wrapped her arms around his neck, dipping her fingertips into his hair and those wayward curls behind his ear that had tempted her before.

He lifted his head and looked down into her shining eyes. "I love you, Minda."

Minda looked away, suddenly unable to meet his gaze. The last time a man had told her he loved her was seventeen years ago. There was a time she thought she'd never hear those words again. She felt the pressure of gathering tears in her throat and behind her eyes. Out of habit, she summoned up her little trick to fight against them . . . then stopped. She didn't need to fight against her emotions. The emotions she was feeling now were honest and beautiful and real.

She looked up at him again and let the tears of joy fill her eyes. "I love you, too, Mark."

He smiled that lop-sided, natural smile that he reserved for her alone. But this time, she thought she detected a little bit of triumph in that smile. His arms tightened around her and he kissed her again.

Several moments later he raised his head with a reluctant groan. "Check out time is eleven o'clock. Let's get out of this hotel before they charge a poor man for another night."

"My car's downstairs."

"Will you follow me to the rental car office? I need to turn my rental in."

"Yes, and after that we need to go back to church. I have to sign that Letter of Intent."

"You mean you didn't sign it before you came here?"

"No. Once Pastor Walker told me what you'd done, I left. All I could think of was seeing you. I was afraid you were already on your way back to New York."

"Are you sure you want to sign that document? You'll be selling something that means a lot to you."

"The McAllister Building meant a lot to Dale. For a long time I confused the building with missing him. And I confused it with my personal ministry. Now I know that if I sell the building, I can still help people. I'll just do it in a different way and in a different place."

"Correction: *we'll* do it in a different way."

She couldn't argue with that. "You'll come with me to church, won't you? I'd like you to be there when I sign the Letter of Intent."

"Darling Minda, I wouldn't miss it for the world."

EPILOGUE

Two months later.

"S atisfied?" Mark asked, in a low voice.

Minda looked at the crowd of people gathered in Fellowship Hall and smiled happily. "*More* than satisfied. The Orphan Train Riders reunion is a wonderful success."

Mark took her hand and twined his fingers through hers. His gaze traveled over the large room. So many people had turned out for the reunion—many more than they ever expected—some from as far away as Ohio.

Most of the attendees were children or grandchildren of the original train riders but they came armed with information and stories to share. Tables and displays were set up around the perimeter of Fellowship Hall. Some of the people manning the tables presented guidance on how surviving train riders could research their birth families. Others displayed memorabilia from the agencies that ran the orphan trains.

Coach Morgan and Addy Whimple were sitting behind a table of their own, spread with the treasures from their pasts.

Coach brought his scrapbooks and photo albums, which he eagerly shared with people who stopped at the table. Addy had contributed a small box full of her own documents: her birth certificate, a yellowed train ticket printed with 'Denver' as the final destination, and the Bible that contained the precious inscriptions she'd once shown to Minda.

Most importantly, Addy displayed the worn remains of a sign she'd been forced to wear from a ribbon around her neck at every stop the orphan train made:

Name: Adelaide
Age: 10
Eyes: Blue
Hair: Blonde
Parents: English American
Can read and write.

"I used to hate this thing," she told Minda as she carefully placed the placard on the table top. "They made me wear it every time the train pulled into a station. They lined me up on the platform with the other children and people stared at us while they decided which one of us they'd take. I can tell you, they made me feel no better than the suitcase I was carrying. I don't know why I kept the wretched thing all these years. I suppose it's more of a reminder of what I overcame than where I came from."

Addy's stories of her experience on the orphan train attracted scores of people to her table. And later, when she and Coach recounted their story in one of the Sunday school rooms, the audience was standing-room only.

After their talk, several people crowded around Addy and Coach at the front of the room. One woman wondered if her mother, Anne, and Aunt Amelia, might be the long-lost sisters they'd been searching for.

At the back of the room, Mark slipped his arm around Minda's waist. "Wouldn't it be great if Miss Whimple and Coach found out today about their missing sisters?"

"I'm praying they do," Minda said. "But in the meantime, they've got each other, thanks to you."

He shook his head. "You know I can't take credit for that. The truth is, they found each other with the help of a little ol' pocket watch an angel told me to buy."

"Speaking of your watch, isn't it time for the presentation?"

Mark let go of her hand and took out his pocket watch. "It sure is. Will you help me get Coach and Miss Whimple back to Fellowship Hall?"

She gave him a quick kiss on the cheek. "I'll meet you there."

A little while later Mark climbed the steps to the stage and stood in front of the microphone. "May I have your attention please? Everyone, gather around for a special announcement."

He looked out over the crowd that packed the large room and was grateful. Grateful for the overwhelming turnout. Grateful for the loving people who helped make it all possible. He spotted Paul in the crowd, and Pastor Walker. At the refreshment table near the door to the kitchen, Tracy and Josh were casting looks of puppy-love at each other in between filling paper cups with punch.

And right in front of the stage, Minda stood beside Coach Morgan and Addy Whimple. Addy was in her wheel-chair looking a little tired but happier than he had ever seen her.

"I'll make this short," Mark said, into the microphone. He dangled his pocket watch from its chain held high above his head. "I think everyone here has heard the story of this watch. It once belonged to the Whimple family and God used it in a very special way to reunite Coach Morgan and Addy Whimple."

"Don't be so modest!" came a shout from the crowd.

Mark thought he recognized Pastor Walker's voice.

"Okay, I played a small part. God allowed me to hold the watch in trust until the time He was ready to reveal the watch to Coach and Miss Whimple."

"You're still being too modest!"

"Pastor Walker," Mark said, with a touch of exasperation, "you'll get your chance to talk to a room full of people on Sunday morning."

The crowd erupted in laughter and Mark felt himself relax a little.

"What you may not know," he continued, "is that this watch was an heirloom, meant to be passed from father to son. Coach Morgan was just five years old the last time he saw it in his older sister's hand. She was responsible for keeping the watch until he was old enough to have it. I made a promise to Coach that that if we found his sister, I'd give her the watch so she could fulfill her responsibility. That's what I'd like to do right now. It's my honor and privilege to return this watch to its rightful owner, Miss Adelaide Whimple."

The crowd applauded as Mark went down the steps to where Addy was sitting in her wheelchair. He crouched beside her and, cradling the watch in his hands, he presented it to her.

"Open it," she commanded in a voice barely above a whisper.

He did as she asked and the chime began to play. The applause died away, and the voices of the crowd gradually quieted until the only sound in the large, cavernous room was the soft chime of the hymn.

Addy let the notes play for a few moments, then she took the watch from Mark and gently closed the cover. Silently, she raised it to her lips and kissed it lightly. "That's for momma." She reached out and took Coach's hand and carefully placed the watch on his palm. "I think you're old enough to have this now. It belonged to our father who loved us very much. Take good care of it, brother."

Coach leaned over and kissed her on the cheek, a habit he had recently developed and didn't show any sign of tiring of in the near future.

The crowd erupted in applause and cheers. Then it seemed that everyone in the room wanted to personally wish Coach and Miss Whimple well. Minda and Mark stepped back and watched the well-wishers gather around them.

"I can't remember when I've ever been happier," Minda murmured.

"I can." Mark took her left hand and held it up so her diamond solitaire ring sparkled in the afternoon light. "When you said yes, that was my happiest moment."

He kissed her lightly on the lips and she melted easily into his embrace.

"Hey, you two!" Paul called out from a short distance away. He shouldered his way through the crowd of people to reach Mark and Minda. "Congratulations. You did a great job on this reunion. I was really moved by the people I met here today and the stories they told. I'm glad I came."

"I'm glad you're here, too," Minda said. "This is our only chance to say good-bye. We leave early tomorrow morning and we won't be back again for two weeks."

"Off to the far ends of the earth, huh? I hope you'll give my mother and father a hug for me."

"I will but I have to confess, I'm a little nervous about

meeting them. I hope they'll like me."

"You don't have to worry," Mark said. "I know they'll love you as much as I do. After all, you're part of the family business now."

"And I'll love them in return," Minda said, confidently. She looked down at her engagement ring, feeling contented and happy. The handsome, wonderful man standing beside her loved her and wanted to marry her; and he had reconnected with the faith of his younger years; reconnected in a way that had brought him one blessing after another.

He had gone to work for Harmony House where he became involved in the lives of the people served by that ministry. His knowledge of real estate and commercial buildings had come in handy, too, once Paul gave him responsibility for renovating the McAllister Building. Under Mark's direction, the repairs were made quickly and accurately, and he'd pushed through several long-overdue updates to the building's heating and electrical systems. All that was left was to pass the final city inspection and Minda's tenants would be able to move back into their apartments.

Paul smiled at her. "Just make sure you don't love our parents and that jungle they live in so much that you don't come back. We need you back here in two weeks. I've already scheduled the ribbon-cutting ceremony for the McAllister Building. The day after you two return is the day your tenants can start moving back into their apartments."

"That's the best news of all." Minda reached up on tip-toe to give Paul an affectionate kiss on the cheek.

"None of that," Mark growled. "If you're handing out kisses, I can help you find a more worthy recipient."

"I already know where to find one. Excuse us." She took Mark's hand and pulled him through the nearest door and down the hall to Pastor Walker's study.

"We can't go in here," Mark protested. "This is Pastor's study."

"Then we know we won't be interrupted." She shut the door and looked up at him with the light of love in her eyes. "This is a special place for me. It's the room I was in when I realized how much you loved me, even though you'd never told me so in words."

He drew her gently against his strong body. "A lot has changed since then."

"I like change."

"*You*? Since when?"

"Since the minute you walked into my life. Now, shut up and kiss me."

Mark Cartier, the man who once thought he could beguile Minda into doing whatever what he wanted, did the only thing he could do under the circumstance: He did exactly as he was told and kissed her.

The End

Learn More ...

Visit Jenny Berlin's website to learn more about the Orphan Trains. You can also listen to the hymn Mark's watch plays and read excerpts from Minda's gardening book, *Mrs. Plowright's 1908 Guide for the Genteel Lady Gardener.*

www.JennyBerlin.com

www.ingramcontent.com/pod-product-compliance
Lightning Source LLC
Chambersburg PA
CBHW072111250626
47159CB00007B/2403